Praise for GRAY MATTER:

"Not since *Red Dragon* has a more menacing serial killer roamed metropolitan St. Louis. Gripping and unique. A rip-roaring good read."
—John Lutz, author of *Single White Female*

"Shirley Kennett is a polished and poised addition to the ranks of contemporary mystery writers. You're going to enjoy her books."
—*Mystery Scene*

"Kennett has created a couple of likable sleuths in psychologist and computer whiz PJ Gray and old-fashioned cop Detective Leo Schultz. Their pursuit of a sociopathic killer will keep you turning the pages till the very end."
—Jean Hager, author of *The Fire Carrier*

"Kennett's devious creativity and bloodcurdling, realistic descriptive passages result in a terrifying and explosive thriller."
—*Booklist*

"If you're looking for a thrilling suspense novel, look no further than author Shirley Kennett."
—*Iowa City Press-Citizen*

THE MYSTERIES OF MARY ROBERTS RINEHART

GRAY MATTER

Shirley Kennett

Pinnacle Books
Kensington Publishing Corp.
http://www.pinnaclebooks.com

PINNACLE BOOKS are published by

Kensington Publishing Corp.
850 Third Avenue
New York, NY 10022

Pinnacle and the P logo Reg. U.S. Pat. & TM Off.

First Printing: May, 1997

10 9 8 7 6 5 4 3 2 1

Printed in the United States of America

To my husband Dennis, for his support,
encouragement, and love

CHAPTER

1

Dog stood at the stove, stirring the contents of an omelet pan. As he reached for the garlic salt on the counter, he savored a familiar aroma he hadn't enjoyed in years.

Too long, a voice groused in his mind. He thought it was Pa but he wasn't sure.

To the rest of the world, the schmucks, he had a real name. It was even a dignified name. But inside he was plain old Dog, as Ma and Pa had called him when they were mad, which was most of the time. He could practically hear Ma's shrill voice as he dutifully stirred, wearing boxer shorts and nothing else, in the kitchen of his suburban home.

The kitchen was small, with appliances, counter tops, and sink crowding a narrow aisle. It reminded Dog of the kitchen of a train where he had once worked, washing and chopping vegetables for the passengers, most of them elderly, who still traveled by train. He paused for a moment, remembering how their false teeth clicked as they ate, usually one per table, in the dining car. Most people wouldn't have noticed the tiny clicking noises above the steady rhythm of metal wheels on tracks, but he had always been fascinated with the mechanics of eating. Dog's memories and thought paths were sensory oriented. For a while his thoughts looped in remembered images, smells, tastes, sounds, and the feeling of an October night's air on his skin, the hair rising on his naked arms, legs, chest, and back.

It was a smell that brought him back to his own kitchen—a burning, acrid smell. He had neglected to stir while one memory triggered another, and the pan was smoking. Grumbling in disgust, he scraped the blackened sludge-like remains from the pan into the heavy-duty garbage disposal he had installed just last week. He turned on a fan, which seemed to circulate the smoke and smell without dissipating it. The kitchen windows were old and nearly painted shut. Usually, it was a struggle to raise them a few inches. He yanked hard at the window nearest him and it yielded to his annoyance, banging into the top of the frame hard enough to rattle the glass. The fan began to push the odor out.

He carefully washed the pan and, while the oil was heating again, sliced another portion of the soft, glistening mound on the cutting board.

Although he was a good cook, he hardly ever used the kitchen, preferring to eat almost all of his meals out. In fact, he had needed a special shopping trip to buy the omelet pan, a spatula, cooking oil, garlic salt, and paper plates. At least he had the same old mismatched stainless forks and spoons he'd had for years.

He glanced into the dining room, where a new electronic keyboard rested on the corner of the table. He was planning to try it out after dinner, because by then he would be able to play it masterfully. It wasn't quite the grand piano that his guest was used to, but it would have to do. There were, after all, practical considerations involved. His dining room, or for that matter any of the rooms of his small home, just couldn't accommodate a grand piano.

Guest, said a female voice in his head. Arleen, probably. *Is that what you're calling them these days?*

He tipped the omelet pan and the contents tumbled

onto a paper plate. He had always enjoyed music, ever since he listened to Ma's favorite radio station as a grubby toddler wearing a perpetual smear of syrup or chocolate or whatever on his face and a diaper that must have weighed a ton. Of course, classical piano was a far cry from the twangy country and western of his youth, but music was music, wasn't it?

There was, in his complex personality, a strong fragment which fought against chaos, which tidied up the disorderly situations Dog created. That was Pauley Mac, another childhood nickname. As he went into the dining room, Pauley Mac clucked at the mess Dog had left to clean up later in the kitchen.

The severed head of the pianist perched on his counter top, thoughtfully placed on a drain board angled into the side of the sink with the garbage disposal. The skull was neatly cracked open, vulnerable and horrible under the track lights, and the brain cavity was empty. At least the hammer and chisel he had used to open the skull had already been washed and put away.

When Dog finished eating, he switched on the keyboard and tentatively, then confidently, began stroking the black and white bars. His left arm was inexpertly bandaged with gauze, as telling as a virgin's stain on the bed sheets. The scratches hurt like hell, but he blocked out the pain. This was a time for the finer things, things of culture and class. Beautiful music played in his mind, and he was immensely satisfied with his guest's—now his own—talents.

A pounding on the door finally broke Dog's reverie. He opened the door, catching his neighbor Bill Weston with his arm raised to strike the door again.

"Oh, there you are. The wife and I were wondering if you could be so kind as to turn down that TV a notch. You see, Helen's not feeling well, and she's been trying to close her eyes and catch some Z's all afternoon."

He wondered whether Bill's line of sight allowed him to see into the kitchen. Hoping he had remembered to wash his hands and arms, and very aware of the leaky bandage on his left arm, he shifted slightly, although he wasn't tall enough to block Bill's view.

"Sure, Bill, I'd be happy to. You should have said something sooner. If it happens again, don't bother coming over—just pick up the phone. I'm in the book."

"Well, thanks much. I don't want to complain, you know, but the wife. . . . Say, with all that squawking we figured you were watching a horror movie. Which movie are you watching, anyway? I sure do like those slasher movies, but the wife, she prefers that supernatural stuff."

"Oh, it's just one of those old Bible stories. You know, lots of hell and damnation." With that, he managed to get the door closed.

The pianist made his first contribution to the internal chorus: *Squawking, indeed!*

Pauley Mac went back into the kitchen and shoved the window closed. It had been touch and go there for a minute. Dog did not like being interrupted. His animal ferocity could not cope with polite conversation, and fantasy images of tearing out Bill's throat reverberated in their shared mind.

As long as I'm already in the kitchen, Pauley Mac thought, *I might as well get started on the cleaning.*

CHAPTER

2

The rolling prairie, windmills, and bobbing oil drills had given way to cornfields and pastures as Penelope Jennifer Gray's old VW Rabbit convertible labored along I-70 west of Kansas City. Multi-headed sunflowers stood in the median of the highway, all facing the same direction, like inquisitive children clustered around a teacher. Hay, the summer's first cutting and nearly three weeks early, lay plumped in rows in the pastures, drying in the sun and waiting to be baled. The smells of clover and grass were everywhere, in the air she drew in deeply and in the tousled hair of the boy sitting next to her. The unseasonably hot afternoon sun had long since vaporized the sun block slathered on that morning, and the fried chicken she had eaten for lunch bobbed uneasily on a layer of grease somewhere in her midsection.

"When are we going to stop? You said an hour ago that we were going to put the top up. It's really, really hot!" Her twelve-year-old son, Thomas, had that slight whine in his voice which told her that self-destruction was imminent.

"OK, we'll take the next exit that has gas and eats. Geez, you're not going to melt!"

"Yeah, Mom, it's you I'm worried about. Witches melt, remember?"

Penny, whose few friends (even fewer since the divorce) called her PJ, smiled. She welcomed his attempt at humor, given the stiffness of their relationship recently. In fact, it was about the nicest thing he had said to her in some time. If Thomas was able to crack a joke under these circumstances, all was not lost. Providing, of course, that it *was* a joke.

She was on her way from Denver to St. Louis to start a job as a psychologist with the St. Louis Police Department's new unit, the Computerized Homicide Investigations Project, or CHIP. She knew that it was risky. There was a chance that the pilot project involving computerized simulations of crime scenes wouldn't prove itself out. Then she'd be a freshly-divorced parent without work in a new town. But she needed to get out of Denver, because Steven was there. Her ex-husband Steven married that girl half PJ's age the day after the divorce was final. PJ persisted in thinking of her as "that girl." Illogically, she felt that she would be continually running into Steven and that girl at the grocery store or restaurants, and she just couldn't stay in Denver. Moving was a good solution for her, but there was a complication. Thomas didn't want to move, didn't want to have his life disrupted, didn't want his parents divorced, didn't—period. Her relationship with him needed serious mending, as did both of their hearts.

So now she was fleeing from her lucrative position in marketing research, where she had used her unique combination of skills in psychology and computer science to help companies fine-tune new products even before the first customer plunked down the cash. She had piled a few belongings and her reluctant son into the Rabbit she'd owned forever and driven into the sunrise. It was Thursday afternoon, and she was looking forward to spending a long weekend in the comfortable mayhem of her sister's home in Kansas City before reporting in for work Monday morning in St. Louis.

At the next exit there was a convenience store that sold gas. While she scrubbed at the bug-splattered windshield and struggled with the convertible top, Thomas went inside to graze the snack aisle. He came out of the store with his hands full of sodas, chips, and cookies, and no change from the five dollars she had given him.

When it was her turn, she visited the bathroom first. Even though it was only May, the Kansas sunshine already seemed merciless, and sweat filmed her body. She splashed cold water on her face, letting some of it trickle down into her neckline and run between her breasts, feeling the cool tracks on her skin. She felt about blindly for the towel dispenser, which was empty. Sighing, she dried her face on the front of her T-shirt. In the store, she spotted some packages of cupcakes. She and Thomas shared the same birthday, and today was the big day: her fortieth and his twelfth. She decided that an impromptu party was just the thing to cheer them both up. Searching the shelves, she came up with a dusty box of birthday candles. On the counter next to the cash register was a bowl of matchbooks printed with the name of the store. PJ scooped one into the pocket of her shorts, hating to be perceived as a smoker but positive she didn't have any matches in the car.

When she paid, she found it disconcerting that the clerk's eyes didn't meet hers. Instead, his gaze seemed to roam sideways at about the level of her chest. On the way out, she looked down, certain that she must have some stain or food crumbs or worse on her front. She saw that her T-shirt had two wet spots, roughly hand-shaped, directly over her breasts. The soft bra she was wearing revealed her nipples, which had hardened from the cold water. She laughed out loud, but was pleased with the clerk's lustful attention. With her hair sprinkled with gray and twenty extra pounds rounding her figure, PJ didn't get too many surreptitious glances from twenty-one-year-old men. *At least,* she thought, *I still have one feature a man can stare at.*

She pulled the T-shirt away from her body so it didn't cling and climbed into the Rabbit.

"Close your eyes, son of mine. I have a surprise for you."

"Aw, Mom . . . "

"Just humor an old woman, please."

When his eyes were tightly closed, PJ removed the cupcakes from her bag and fumbled with the cellophane wrapper. The crinkling noise aroused her son's curiosity, and she saw his eyes open into slits. She marveled at the perfection of his black eyelashes, remembering her first glimpse of them as her newborn son nuzzled her breast in the birthing room.

"No peeking."

"Aw, Mom . . ."

"You know, you really should work on developing your vocabulary. You're not going to get far in the business world with a two-word repertoire." Her words brought a reluctant smile. She lit the candles, balancing the cupcakes on her knee.

"OK, open up. Happy birthday to us!"

Mother and son blew out the candles, and each ate a cupcake in trademark fashion: she pulled the chocolate icing off the top in a single sheet and savored it, then popped the entire bare cupcake into her mouth; he broke his in half and licked out the cream before eating the rest in deliberately small bites to make it last as long as possible.

It was a good thing they had that moment to remember, because the rest of the day went downhill from there. The heat and rushing wind set their nerves on edge. Long periods with no conversation gave them plenty of time to think about what had happened and what was happening. The breakup and divorce were fresh in both of their minds, and neither had the emotional distance needed to put their new lives in perspective. PJ thought that Thomas genuinely missed his father, and she, grudgingly, angrily, missed Steven too.

Detective Leo Schultz didn't have a private office. It irked him that after thirty-two years with the St. Louis Police

Department, he didn't have sixty square feet to call his own, with a door he could close when he needed to make a private phone call or just felt like scratching his butt or his balls, depending on what kind of day it had been. His desk was in a room with two other detectives and his immediate supervisor, Sergeant Leroy Twiller, all of them younger than he was. At age fifty-four, Schultz was the fossil of Homicide.

Hobbs over there probably hadn't even been born when I joined the Department, he snapped to himself.

Stuck at his current rank for many years and likely to remain there, he used to joke with his fellow officers about having reached his level of incompetence. There were no more jokes, at least not to his face. His most recent partner, a mere youth of thirty-five, was promoted three years ago. Since that time, his field assignments dried up, leaving him shuffling papers.

What had particularly irritated him was that a newly hired detective from Alabama had been using his desk yesterday while Schultz had a day off. The slob had spilled coffee on his desk pad and left Schultz's phone receiver smelling of some wimpy after-shave. Schultz had wiped the phone with a wad of dampened toilet paper, but the smell lingered, fueling his anger every time he lifted the receiver.

His phone rang, and Schultz picked it up with two fingers and held it a couple of inches from his ear.

"Schultz."

"Howard here. You had dinner yet? I got some sandwiches, good stuff. Come over to the office, we need to talk."

Schultz rarely got invited to Lieutenant Howard Wall's office, and when he did, it was to be chewed out about something. The lieutenant was Sergeant Twiller's boss, and Schultz generally didn't interact with him. But Wall sounded OK on the phone, almost congenial. Schultz figured that little piece Wall had on the side must be putting out regularly, since he was certain the lieutenant's home life didn't account for the good mood.

"Sit down, Schultz. Have a sandwich, ham or corned beef, your choice. Chips, too, those barbecued ones. Your favorite, right?"

This was not his usual interaction with Wall. Lowering himself into a chair, he reached out for the corned beef, unwrapped it, and dumped a pile of chips on the spread-out wrapper. Wall handed him a paper cup with a straw jauntily sticking out. For a minute or so, both men occupied themselves with the first bites of their sandwiches and a handful of chips, munching and swallowing almost in synch. Then Schultz sipped from the paper cup.

"Christ, Howard, when did you start drinking this diet crap?"

"Since my wife said my ass was getting so wide that my buttocks were total strangers to each other."

Schultz laughed and tossed another handful of chips into his mouth. He hated diet soda, but he took a big swallow. It seemed the expedient thing to do.

"So what's with the royal treatment? It's not like you buy me dinner every day."

"God, it amazes me to see those famous powers of detection at work." Wall leaned back in his chair, both hands grasping an overflowing ham sandwich. "Seriously, I've got a proposition for you."

This caught Schultz's attention. Howard released his chair, letting it fall down with a thump. He put down the sandwich and steepled his fingers, elbows resting on the desk. The gesture reminded Schultz of the childish rhyme about the church and the steeple. Mentally, he had Wall interlock his fingers and wiggle them—*Open the doors, see all the people.* From long association, Schultz knew that the man was trying to put a good face on something neutral, bad, or very bad.

"You've probably heard," Wall said, "about the homicide over on Euclid. Clint wrote up the scene. Take my word for it, it's going to be a juicy one."

"Yes."

"You've probably also heard about the Computerized Homicide Investigations Project, CHIP. There was a memo about it two, three months ago."

"CHIP. Yes. Sort of."

"The captain thinks that this homicide would be suitable for CHIP's first case."

"What does this have to do with me?" Schultz said.

"The project needs a detective to handle the field work. An experienced detective. You."

The sandwiches were forgotten. Schultz processed the statements, but his brain got stuck on "field work." After years of being relegated to desk jobs, he had almost given up the hope of getting an assignment like the one being dangled in front of him now. And if it sounded too good to be true . . .

"What's the catch?"

"I wouldn't exactly call it a catch, but the assignment does have special circumstances."

Schultz let his raised eyebrows speak for him.

"Your team leader will be a civilian employee of the Department, not a trained investigator."

Strike one.

"You will be expected to give the computer aspect of the project your full cooperation."

Strike two.

"Still with me? Your team leader is a female shrink whose previous job had something to do with testing shampoo."

Strike three. Batter out!

Schultz stood up without a word and turned toward the door. Then he remembered the intensity of field work, the gratification when justice was done, the good feeling of getting some creep off the streets. If he did a good job on this case, maybe he could drop the computer stuff and the shrink afterward and get back to straight investigative work. The lure was there. The lure was strong.

"How many of the other guys did you ask before you got around to me?" he asked Wall.

"All of them."

With his back to Wall, he smiled. At least the lieutenant was honest.

"What the hell. I'm your man."

By the time PJ pulled into her sister's driveway, she and Thomas were snapping at each other, and she was looking forward to dinner, a long, hot bath, and curling up with a good book, in whatever order she could manage. Her sister met her with the news that her new boss needed to talk to her right away. As Thomas unloaded their suitcases, unceremoniously dragging hers into the spare bedroom and his to the fold-out couch, she used the kitchen phone to give him a call.

"St. Louis Police Department. How may I direct your call?"

"Lieutenant Howard Wall, please."

A moment later, he was on the phone, sounding as if he had his mouth full of food.

"Dr. Gray, good to talk to you. I'm glad your sister's phone number was on your application. I figured you might stop there on your way to St. Louis. Hold on a sec." She heard the sound of papers being gathered up into a ball and tossed. "Oops, got to get a bigger wastebasket. Not as good a hoop man as I was in the old days." Apparently he had just finished eating dinner at his desk.

"What can I do for you, Lieutenant?"

"That's Howard, since we're going to be working together. May I call you Penelope?"

"I prefer PJ."

"Right. You're in KC, aren't you? That's about four hours away?"

"Yes, I just arrived at my sister's house, where I'll be

spending the weekend. My son's unloading the car, and I really should be helping him. What's this about?"

"Well, PJ, you might want to ask him to hold up on the unloading. I need you here tomorrow morning at the latest."

"What? Hold on a minute." She covered the mouthpiece.

"Mandy, could you take the kids into the living room? I'm having trouble hearing on the phone. I'll join you in a little bit." The noise receded like a train going off into the distance as PJ's sister Mandy herded her four children out of the kitchen.

"Now then," PJ said into the phone. "I thought I heard you say something about being in St. Louis by tomorrow?"

"There's been a murder. The captain thinks it would be the perfect kickoff for CHIP. We got a guy lined up for your teammate, name of Schultz. Detective Leo Schultz. He'll be doing most of the actual field work. In fact, he's getting started on the case using standard investigative procedures. It'll be up to you to bring the computer in on this."

PJ was silent for a moment, trying to compose a response. This was a major blow. She had really been looking forward to some time with Mandy, had planned to talk over the troubles she was having with Thomas and get her sister's down-to-earth advice. Even more disturbing was the fact that she had been led to believe that she would have several months to get CHIP up and running, and would be able to hire a couple of assistants. She decided on an approach that seemed reasonable to her.

"Howard, I really don't think I can make much of a contribution on such short notice. I only have my personally developed simulation software available, and even that might take me a week or so to bring up. There's a lot of customization to be done. Also, I thought I was going to have a couple of assistants, although I suppose I could get by with one to start." She thought it was a stroke of brilliance to toss in the carrot about having only one assistant rather than two. But the carrot was not picked up.

"You have an assistant. Schultz."

"I meant a computer analyst."

"Well, you have a point there. Nobody would mistake Schultz for a computer anything." He chuckled and made a slurping noise with a straw.

"I think it would be better to pass on this case. I'm looking at a six-month time frame, maybe four if CHIP gets two others besides me."

This time it was Wall's turn to be silent. After a long moment he sighed.

"Look, PJ, you're listening to what I'm saying but you're not hearing me." His voice on the phone was serious but managed to convey concern. "I know about your time frame. I know about your assistants. Shit, I'm the one who interviewed you, remember? I hate to drop this on you like this, but I don't have a choice. What I'm trying to tell you is that the captain's got a scorpion up his ass about this, and if you're not here and ready to roll by tomorrow morning, you don't have a job."

"I see." Her voice wavered. "Just a moment, please."

PJ put the phone in her lap. The stress and emotional pain of the last few months bore in on her, and this latest thing seemed too much to handle. For a little while she considered chucking the whole business and limping back to Denver. Or maybe running off to Timbuktu. When she thought she had recovered enough to keep her voice professional, she raised the phone from her lap.

"I'm hearing you now, Howard. Tell the captain I'll be there at eight AM sharp."

She and Thomas got wearily back in the car to drive to St. Louis. Thomas had not exploded as she had expected. He simply lugged the suitcases back out to the car.

PJ nervously gobbled a whole bag of jelly beans on the drive.

At ten PM, the lights of fast food places beckoned, and PJ pulled into a motel right off I-70 in St. Charles, across the Missouri River from St. Louis, or at least from St. Louis County. Close enough. After checking into a basic room, she and Thomas devoured burgers and fries, then went back for a second helping and a milkshake for PJ.

Throughout it all, Thomas hadn't said much. She knew he was disappointed to leave Aunt Mandy's, but the only complaint he voiced was that the pillows in their non-smoking room smelled of cigarette smoke. He showered and dropped into bed. In a couple of minutes he was asleep, and she heard his soft breathing. Listening to it relaxed her. She used to sneak into his room at night just to watch his face in the glow of his man-in-the-moon night light and to listen to his breathing. It amazed her then, and still did, that she had known him so intimately, that he had grown within her body, eaten what she ate, and circulated the oxygen her lungs provided in his own red cells. She felt an almost mystical link to her son. Her whole body ached with love and with the fear that she had done something—taken him away from his father—that had hurt Thomas deeply. From her vantage point in the midst of her own emotional needs and imbalance, she couldn't see how she could repair their relationship. And it didn't look as though there was going to be any time to work on it right away. Other adult concerns intervened, such as getting herself established in a new city and earning money to pay for cupcakes and milkshakes—little things like that.

After showering, she sat on the edge of the bed, her hair wrapped in a towel. She dialed Wall's home phone number, to check in and to get some facts about the case so that she wouldn't be the only one in the dark tomorrow morning.

She learned that a thirty-five-year-old white male named George Burton, occupation pianist, had been found dead in his Central West End apartment. The body was decapitated by a sharp instrument such as a meat cleaver, and the head was not in the apartment. The skin of his back was carved (probably before death, according to the medical examiner's report) into a kind of bas-relief portrait of a dog. A passable three-dimensional effect was achieved by stripping the skin away to make the low portions. The victim was tied straddling a chair backwards, presumably so that the killer could carve the bas-relief on his back. Blood was found on the chair and carpet, along with a puzzling set of four indentations in the carpet. The indentations were positioned as though the killer had pulled up a chair to sit next to the victim, but none of the chairs in the apartment matched the pattern of indentations.

Long after the call, she lay awake worrying whether she had done the right thing for herself and for Thomas, replaying hurtful scenes between herself and her ex-husband Steven, and mulling over the basic facts of the murder that Wall had given her on the phone. She had a good imagination, and she was awake most of the night.

CHAPTER

3

A hot shower followed by an icy rinse raised PJ's spirits in the morning. Her clothes, hung in the bathroom the night before, also benefited from the steamy environment. Now instead of being completely mashed and wrinkled from the suitcase, they merely looked like she had worn them for a hard twelve-hour workday. As if to make up for their appearance, she spent extra time with her hair and even dabbed on lipstick. As she closed her makeup case, she noticed in the mirror that the chestnut hair that rested easily on her shoulders had already curled up in spite of her efforts to curl it under. There were lines at the corners of her gray eyes—*smile crinkles, surely, not that nasty kind*—and more than a few gray hairs mixed with the chestnut.

Thomas, under strict orders not to leave the motel room, was marshaling his supplies for the day: magazines, books, snacks, and the TV remote control. In spite of the current difficulties in their relationship, she trusted him when he promised that he would stay in the room. As soon as she could get a chance, she would look for a place to live, probably a rental home, and get him registered in school. If she was lucky and found a place right away, he could finish out the last three weeks or so before summer vacation. She blew him a kiss, which evoked a typical twelve-year-old's response of revulsion, and drove to work.

It was a good thing that she had gotten an early start. The volume of traffic took her by surprise. She spent a good twenty minutes just crossing over the Missouri River from St. Charles into St. Louis County, listening to a morning talk show on the radio, inching forward in traffic on I-70, then the Innerbelt I-170, and finally Highway 40. She bit her lip nervously while driving, and there was nothing left of her lipstick by the time she pulled into the crowded lot at the Headquarters building on Clark Avenue downtown.

PJ had never been in a police station, even a neighborhood district office. Before her divorce, she would have been comfortable in a new situation. She had a professional poise and confidence which radiated to others and buoyed them through difficult situations. She was, after all, a trained psychologist and a pioneer in the use of computers in simulation studies. She had published several articles in prestigious journals, presented papers at conferences, and participated in seminars. But when your husband suddenly decides he loves another woman, it does something to your confidence. She knew that she had enough inner strength to pull through eventually, but her self-esteem was still struggling with the blow, and some days were better than others. She tried to put her doubts aside and concentrate on meeting her CHIP teammate, Detective Leo Schultz.

The two of them pressed into PJ's tiny office as Wall, standing in the doorway, brought PJ up-to-date. The office was a former utility room which PJ suspected was still being used as one until about ten minutes before her arrival. The wooden desk was scarred with knife marks and marred with cigarette burns. Her swivel chair was green vinyl—thankfully no rips—and the metal arms were burnished by years of contact with elbows and palms. The ceiling fixture was a fluorescent rectangle which hummed and occasionally blinked, like a person with an unpredictable nervous tic. She couldn't help comparing her new office to the one she had occupied in Denver: sleek, spacious, and sunlit.

PJ was not a tall woman. She was just short enough that retrieving items from the top shelves of kitchen cabinets was a problem. Many times she had simply knocked an item off with a long-handled spoon and caught it before it hit the floor. When she sat in her chair, trying to establish that important first impression as a confident professional, she first tilted back so far that she thought she was going to go over, and then, righting herself, discovered that her feet dangled three inches off the floor.

The room was airless, had rusty circles on the linoleum floor, and smelled of old wet mops. Since there was no heat or air conditioning vent, the only way to get air circulation was to open the door, which subjected the occupants to the noise and bustle of the men's room directly across the hall.

PJ shut out the disconcerting surroundings and listened attentively as Wall gave the details, some of which she already knew from their phone conversation. On the wall directly in front of her was a blackboard, mounted hastily and crookedly, which had two photographs taped to it. One showed a smiling mid-thirties man, handsome and dressed in evening wear, standing in front of an audience, arms spread wide to scoop in their appreciative applause. The other was a graphic shot of a headless corpse, tied upright in a chair and pitifully unable to shield its fatal disfigurement from the camera. The pictures showed the same man, before and after the handiwork of a person who could only be loosely classified as human. She pulled her eyes from the photos, but her gaze kept wandering back whenever it lacked discipline.

Her mind raced with ideas for computer simulation, not only of the crime scene itself but a re-enactment of the crime. She wondered how her teammate would take to high-tech detective work.

Leo Schultz was, she estimated, in his mid-fifties and

clearly an indifferent dresser. He was a large man, tall and thick through the waist, whose ill-fitting clothes suggested that he had put on weight. The cramped office seemed intolerably filled with his presence. His arms and legs, which at one time had been hard and muscular, were now rounded, plumped like hot dogs that swelled when they cooked. The ceiling light reflected from a bald spot on the crown of his head. The reflection seemed brighter than the actual radiance accounted for, as if the bald spot drew in light rays from a disproportionate volume of space and bounced them back. Most of his hair was clipped short and hugged his head, except for a few long grayish-brown strands which he combed over the thinning area at the front. Even though he was thirty or forty pounds too heavy, his face was long and thin, with cheeks that used to be firm but now sagged a little, and a prominent nose that towered above the rest of the landscape. His skin was wrinkled, with lines drawn like a road map around his eyes and mouth. He had either spent a lot of time in the sun or he was a heavy smoker; either could account for those wrinkles. PJ took a deep breath, but couldn't detect any smoke odor. His eyes were deep brown, what could be an attractive and warm feature, but on him seemed misplaced, as though a puppy's eyes had somehow gotten on the face of a rhino. He sat tipped back in a ridiculously small folding chair, sullenly doodling in a notebook during the briefing. It seemed clear to PJ that Schultz was unhappy, but she was unable to tell whether it was because of her, the pilot computer project, or a generally negative approach to life.

Probably all three, she thought.

"I'll leave you two to get acquainted," Wall said. He closed the office door and left, abruptly cutting off the noise from the bathroom and the hallway traffic.

She almost chuckled at Schultz's reaction to that. He lowered his chair and his face took on a trapped look which he concealed almost immediately, but not quickly enough for a psychologist to miss it. PJ deliberately let the silence stretch out in the stuffy room. She wanted Schultz to make the opening gambit.

Two full minutes later, she acknowledged that he had won round one. Apparently the detective was no stranger to awkward silences.

"Well," she said pleasantly, "would you rather I call you Leo or Schultz or Detective?"

"My friends call me Schultz. But let's keep this strictly professional. You can call me Leo."

My, my, she thought.

"Look, lady, let's get a few things straight right from the start. I took this assignment so I could get back out on the street where I belong. If that means I have to work with a shrink and a glorified adding machine, then that's what I'll do, see? But there's working with and there's working *with,* if you get my meaning."

"Yes, I certainly . . ."

"And while we're talking ground rules, let me make it clear that you're going to leave all the detective work to me. That's me, *Detective* Leo. There's a reason I've got that title and you don't. You keep your pretty little nose buried in that computer and we'll get along just fine."

"Are you done? Could I possibly get in a word now?"

Schultz settled back magnanimously. "Yeah, go ahead."

PJ gathered what dignity she could while sitting in a chair with her feet off the floor, like a child sitting at the teacher's desk. Well, it was her desk, however humble and worn. Besides, she had dealt with hostility and sexism before, and her favorite response was to squelch it unmercifully.

"Detective, you may have noticed when we were introduced that I was *Doctor* Gray, not just plain old Penelope. There's a reason I have that title and you don't. The reason is that I'm a highly trained professional in my own field and I've been hired to head CHIP. That is why we are meeting in my *office,* not at your *desk.* Make no mistake about who's in charge here." She tapped her chest with her finger.

"I . . ."

"One moment, Detective, I'm not finished. Ordinarily, I would prefer us to work companionably as teammates. We can be more productive that way. But I can see that's going to be a problem here. So I put it to you: work on CHIP on my terms, or get the hell off the project. Today. Now."

"Christ, lady, don't get your ass in an uproar."

"My name isn't *lady,* and the condition of my posterior is far too personal to be of concern to you. My friends call me PJ, but you can call me Penelope. Or just plain Boss."

Schultz wasn't down for the count. He leaned forward and put his elbows on her desk. "You ever arrest a perp and get your ribs knocked in? You ever sit in an interrogation room with a creep who'd just as soon slit your throat as eat? You ever walk into a dark alley and get that tingle in your spine waiting for the knife?"

PJ folded her hands on the desk. "No."

"My point exactly."

"Have you ever," PJ responded, "tried to talk a guy down from a PCP high and gotten your nose broken for your effort? Have you ever had a woman slit her wrists in the bathroom in your office? Have you ever held a dead baby in your arms who was battered to death by a man under your care?"

Schultz pursed his lips. "No."

"Well, I have, Detective. I may not be an expert in investigative techniques and I may have done marketing studies for consumer products and I may have been born with a vagina rather than a penis, but I have done all those things." PJ felt her breath coming faster and took a deep breath to calm herself. "In addition, I happen to know a little something about the criminal mind."

"Shit, can't we come to some agreement here? I think we got one of those storms in a teapot going here."

"That's tempest in a teacup." They sat for a moment, glaring at each other. This time Schultz broke the silence.

"Maybe we can start this over. It seems to me we've both got a lot on the line here, but let's not forget what our jobs are. We're talking about catching some creep that sliced up a man and chopped off his head. We're talking about putting that creep in jail and sending the key to Mars."

"I'm ready to focus on that task as soon as you are." It wasn't much of a peace offering, but his hadn't been much of one either.

"Well then," Schultz said. It was as close to a concession as Schultz was going to get, and PJ realized that. She decided it was time to be gracious.

"Well then, we need to set some priorities," she said. "I'll take a look at the computer equipment later in the day, but right now we need some more facts. We need to visit the scene of the crime." Too late, PJ realized how trite that sounded.

"Yeah, Doc, that's usually a good start for an investigation."

PJ sighed. "Come on, Leo, knock it off. I know I set myself up for that one. What I meant was that I need a lot of data about the victim's apartment. Measurements. Furniture. Everything."

"Why?"

"In order to recreate the apartment, and the murder within the apartment, on the computer."

"You lost me there, but I'll rustle up a tape measure."

"Eager to please, eh?"

Schultz grinned a grin that sparked an uneasy feeling in PJ. If she had met a stranger in a bar and he had grinned at her like that, she would have beaten a path to the exit.

"Always, Doc, always."

When he left, PJ was suddenly overwhelmed with the whole situation: the divorce; her son's emotions; the new job; her tiny, smelly office; the graphic details of the murder; her confrontation with Leo; the photos on her wall; the prospect of visiting the murder scene; even her wrinkled clothes. Tears brimming in her eyes, she fled her office. In a stall in the ladies' room, which stank of smoke in spite of the sign pasted on the door which said "Do not smoke in this bathroom!!!," PJ Gray, polished professional woman, psychologist, and computer expert, took stock of her first morning on the job. It had one bright spot—she felt she had held her own with Leo—but on the whole was not an auspicious beginning.

CHAPTER

4

When Schultz left PJ's office, he stopped at the water fountain across the hall alongside the door of the men's room. He looked around and noticed that the hall was acceptably uncrowded. He took a small pill box from his pocket, shook out four ibuprofen tablets, and tossed them back with a swallow of water. Then he went back to his desk, operating on automatic. He was angry, but it would have to keep for a few minutes. He needed to make a phone call to request a car assignment.

"Vehicles."

"Doris, that you?"

"Doris retired about three months ago. This is Casey," a polite voice responded. "What can I do for you?"

"Doris retired? Christ, she wasn't that old. Did she get sick or something?"

"As far as I know, she simply left after thirty-five years of service. Doris insisted on no fuss, so there wasn't even a party. She and her husband are traveling around out West in a motor home."

"Christ."

"Can I help you?"

"Yeah, sure, I need a vehicle. Name's Leo Schultz, detective in Homicide. Authorized by Lieutenant Howard Wall."

"Unmarked? Any particular requirements?"

Schultz knew what she was asking. Some assignments required a flashy car, but Homicide generally got the compacts with vinyl seats. Schultz hated vinyl seats. He got a heat rash in his crotch and on the back of his thighs whenever he sat on them, particularly if the car didn't have airconditioning.

Abruptly he realized that Casey's voice sounded very pleasant, even when conducting Department business. He formed an image in his mind. Casey was about twenty-five years old, long blond hair in one of those heavy braids down her back, sleek legs, compliant breasts that would comfortably fill his large hands . . . Schultz hadn't slept with his wife in a long time, three or four years at least. Their relationship just didn't include sex anymore. You wouldn't have sex with a roommate, particularly an unpleasant one, and that's how Julia seemed to think of him. Schultz, like other cops, knew more than he ever wanted to about the hazards of sex with a stranger. He preferred fantasy, and Casey was shaping up nicely.

"Detective? Any requirements?" He heard her tapping a computer keyboard, and the spell was broken. Temporarily at least—there was always tonight, after Julia had gone to bed.

"Nothing ritzy. Air conditioned, cloth seats, no loud colors. Automatic transmission."

"I'll see what I can do. When do you need the car?"

"Now. I'll be going down to the garage in about ten minutes."

"I see. Well, I'll do my best." Schultz heard more clicking. "There, I've got one for you. Ask for license number MBF 181."

"Thanks. Say, you new to the Department?"

"Why yes, I've only been here a few weeks. Just got my master's degree in Sociology, but I couldn't get a job in my field, at least not yet." Her voice dropped to a breathy level. "Don't tell my boss, but I've got a line on a job in Aspen. Can you believe it? It would be a dream come true.

I could ski all winter and hike all summer. When I wasn't working, of course." Casey laughed, a soft tinkling sound that made her seem like a teenager.

Schultz smiled and tossed another log on the fantasy fire. Then he got out of the conversation before she could ask him if he was new to the Department too.

After the pleasant diversion of his phone call, he stopped by Sergeant Twiller's desk to let him know he had accepted the new assignment and would be working on CHIP. As he expected, Twiller already knew about it. Schultz headed to Wall's office, his anger returning. He tapped on the door and stepped in without waiting for an answer. It was his old, confident style, fueled by an issue he needed to take up with the lieutenant.

"I've got to get something straight with you. I . . . " It dawned on Schultz that Wall was on the phone. The man gestured for him to sit down, and took a couple of minutes to wrap up his conversation, dropping the receiver emphatically into its cradle.

"You get a line on that hot item in Vehicles?" Wall said. It wasn't the opening Schultz was expecting, and for a moment the fantasy that was cooking away on the back burner swept over him. How did this man know?

Wall snickered. "I can tell by the look on your face that you've talked to Racy Casey. Been over to Vehicles yet? You've got to take a number out in the hall, the traffic's so bad over there."

"Christ, Howard, do you ever get any business done in this office? Any police business, that is? Besides, I'm a happily married man."

"Yeah, and I'm running for president next year. Anything that happens in this Department is police business, and she's the biggest thing that's happened in this Department in ages. Biggest being the operative word there."

The two men sat in companionable silence for a moment.

"I hate to prick your balloon," Schultz said, accenting

prick, "but could we get serious here?" Somehow his anger had drifted away.

"Yeah, yeah, I know what you want to talk about. You don't like working for a woman."

Schultz sat back in his chair. *Was that it? Was that the whole problem?*

"Bullshit. I'm as modern as the next guy," Schultz said. *Depending, of course, on who the next guy is.* "I just naturally assumed I was going to be in charge, that's all."

Howard did the thing with his fingers again, elbows on the desk, fingers making the steeple. "Schultz, let's not try to fool anybody. You're as modern as a Neanderthal. PJ Gray—Doctor Gray—is the head of CHIP. You've known that since the first time I mentioned it to you. That's what she was hired for, and that's the way the captain wants it. That's the way I want it. If you want off the merry-go-round, now's the time to speak up."

Thoughts raced through Schultz's head. He briefly considered how nice it was to get out from under Sergeant Twiller's thumb. He had never gotten along with the man. He wondered how wide a berth he could give both the doc and the computer without Wall coming down on him, and decided he would play it by ear.

"I guess I'm still your man."

"There's no guessing involved here," Wall said.

"All right, damn it. Just tell me I don't have to use that fucking computer myself."

"That's it?" Schultz said. "That's MBF 181?"

"Yup." The garage attendant wasn't very talkative. He was accustomed to disbelief.

Schultz gazed at his assigned vehicle. It was a Pacer, a blast from the past, and it was red. Well, sort of red. It had faded to an indescribable shade of orange. He opened the driver's door and checked the dash.

"Shit, no air!" At least it had cloth seats. He slid in and noticed that it was a stick shift.

One out of four requests isn't bad. Nice to know things haven't changed while I've been warming a chair.

"I suppose this is the only one available," Schultz said. He tried his winning smile on the attendant, the one he had practiced in the mirror and determined to be his least frightening. His telephone charm hadn't worked on Casey, but Schultz was, despite the weight of experience to the contrary, an optimist when it came to his ability to be winsome.

"Yup."

He made a show of fastening his seat belt and then turned over the ignition. He rolled down the driver's window, which stuck halfway down. The attendant hovered at the window.

"What?" Schultz said irritably.

"I gotta warn ya—keep a good hand on the wheel. She's been rolled and knocked out of whack. She tends to drift a little, even on the straightaways. You know, kind of walk sideways like a crab."

"A crab. Yeah, well, ain't that fitting. Thanks for the warning." As he pulled away, he unfastened his seat belt. He never wore one, even though that was probably against Department regulations.

PJ was waiting on the steps when Schultz pulled up. There was something a little disconcerting about her, like a bowl of Jell-O that's been dropped. You can scoop it all back into the bowl, but it will never look the same. Schultz, who thought he was good at reading people, saw vulnerability in her face that was quickly masked when she realized he was looking at her.

So the bitch isn't cast iron all the way through, he thought. *Just three-quarters.*

On the drive, Schultz got the feeling the car was going to walk up on the sidewalk while he was steering straight ahead. He tried to relax about it; it wasn't going to go away anytime soon. He asked PJ why the crime scene sketch made by Clint wasn't good enough for her purposes. It seemed that she wanted details that weren't included, such as the style and colors of the furnishings, wallpaper, paintings, and even the accessories on the coffee table. When Clint drew up a scene, he measured accurately but recorded things generically, like "sofa" or "stove." PJ said that the more realistic she could make her simulations, the more useful they would be. Schultz had an opinion about how useful anything done on the computer would be, but this seemed like an easy way to placate the woman.

Burton's apartment wasn't far from Headquarters. It took less than ten minutes to get there. He had lived on the second floor over a coffee shop. There was an alley right next to the building that led to a couple of parking spaces in the rear, and stairs up to a private entrance. At the base of the stairs, Schultz let PJ go first with a wave of his hand. He wasn't being chivalrous. He didn't want PJ to notice the way he climbed the stairs. He had arthritis, something that he was trying to conceal. If the lieutenant knew something like that was slowing him down, he probably wouldn't have offered Schultz the field assignment. If he wanted to get away from that desk, he couldn't let anyone know about it. Some days were a lot worse than others, and, much to Schultz's disgust, this was one of the bad days. The ibuprofen he had taken earlier hadn't done much good. His left knee didn't have the normal range of motion, so he couldn't bend it enough to alternate feet while climbing the stairs. He had to bend his right knee, put his right foot up onto the next stair, and then, clinging to the railing, pull his stiff left leg up. That meant he had to go up one step at a time with a little pause on each step, like a toddler just learning to negotiate stairs. He hurried as well as he could manage to keep close behind PJ so that she wouldn't turn around at the top and have to wait for him.

The alley and stairs were clean, and there was even a

planter full of flowers right outside the apartment door. The flowers were beginning to wilt. Schultz's wife Julia had always been interested in container gardening, and so Schultz knew that containers like that needed to be watered practically every day during hot weather. There wasn't enough soil to hold a lot of water. The sight of the wilted flowers made him sad, as if it represented his own relationship with Julia. There just wasn't enough soil left in the marriage to hold water.

Schultz exchanged small talk with the officer at the door while he and PJ pulled on the gloves which Schultz had brought along in his pocket. The gloves were as much for their own protection as to safeguard evidence. Whenever blood was present, investigators wore gloves to protect themselves from blood-borne diseases like AIDS. The scene was still sealed and guarded, undoubtedly irritating the owner, who would want to get in there and clean up. Something about a bloody murder scene made people want to clean it up as soon as possible, to deny that anything happened. Schultz wondered what it would be like if human bodies were left where they fell, like the bodies of animals killed in the road.

We'd be stepping over them on the sidewalks, and most houses would have a room that nobody else could use for a while. A good long while.

"Remember, Doc," he said to PJ as he lifted the crime scene tape for her to duck under and swung open the door, "don't touch anything. The ETU, Evidence Technician Unit, has already worked the place, but you never know what will turn out to be important. Also, there will probably be a smell, but it should be mild."

"You don't have to treat me like a simpleton. I can handle this."

Schultz got the distinct impression that she was reassuring herself, not him. She stepped into the room just ahead of him. He waited for the predictable response, and he got it. She stepped back quickly, bumping into him, and ducked back under the tape into the relatively fresh air of the alley.

"Come on back in when you're ready. No hurry." He stepped further in and flicked on the lights. He took a deep breath and blew it out his lips noisily. By his standards, this was a clean site. The smells of death and blood and fear were in the room, and he knew all of them and all the combinations of them, but there was no overriding smell of decomposition. The body had been discovered only twelve hours after death when the cleaning woman let herself in with her key Thursday morning. The air conditioning had been turned all the way down on the dial to fifty-five degrees, presumably by the killer. The unit had been laboring against the unseasonably hot May weather, and had kept the place at about sixty-two. So it was practically like the body had been in a cooler. The air conditioner had been turned off by the evidence techs, though, so that they could check the filter on the blower for hairs and fibers that weren't indigenous to Burton's apartment. The stale uncirculated air was heavy with the scent of blood beginning to rot rather than simply dry. But that was nothing compared to some of the scenes Schultz had handled. There had been a couple even he couldn't stomach: floaters, whose fat had turned to soap and whose stench could stab his gut and empty his stomach even years afterward.

The living room itself was a pleasant surprise. It was high-ceilinged, modern, full of recessed lights and spare furniture, and full of interesting angles. Even Schultz, who was devoid of a decorating sense, was aware that considerable thought had gone into creating a highly personalized space. A gleaming grand piano was prominent, as were art objects displayed tastefully on pedestals and bookcases. On a marble top table which was angled to fit a corner stood a beautiful glass vase holding a dozen red rosebuds. Some of the buds had opened while others tightly concealed their inner mysteries. Schultz made a note to check for flower deliveries in the past couple of days. The flowers were fresh enough that the delivery could have been the same day as the murder.

The blue-gray carpet was plush and very responsive underfoot, like walking in thick, healthy grass. For a moment Schultz shut down his external senses and imagined wiggling his bare toes in it, and it would be cool and damp, with the scent of fresh clippings and the sun flashing on the creek behind the house and birdsong rippling, landing lightly on his ears . . .

Schultz grew up on a small family farm in rural Missouri. His boyhood was practically the stuff of dreams, free, linked only to nature and the rhythms of the seasons. Two sisters and his parents had died in the fire that destroyed their home, started when lightning struck the old oak in the front, the one that was hollowed out with a beehive in it. A burning branch had landed on the roof of the house, and the turn-of-the-century frame building had gone up in flames like the huge bonfire that Old Man Keeney started every Halloween. Leo and his brother George, ages nine and six and the time, went to live with their Aunt Lydia in St. Louis. She was a city woman through and through, the kind who would get upset if the boys brought in a jar of fireflies or a pocketful of frogs. The joys of his early life in the country gradually slipped away from Leo, but someplace inside that little boy still ran barefoot.

By the time Schultz refocused on the surroundings, he had gotten past the smell. It was something he knew from experience, that after three or four minutes of exposure, the effect diminished. His olfactory sense would be overloaded and would screen out the odor. If you kept going in and out to get fresh air, then your nose would suffer anew each time. It was the same principle as going into a house with pets. The dog or litter box odor might be obvious to the newcomer, but the residents simply—and truthfully—couldn't smell it.

It was a trick of the trade he wasn't ready to share with PJ. She hadn't earned it yet.

Schultz also kept a change of clothing back at HQ, and he usually washed his hair after a scene visit by lathering his head with the watery pink stuff that passed for soap in the men's room, rinsing with cold water, and drying with paper towels. Newcomers didn't realize that they brought the smells with them, on their hair and clothing.

To the right of the door was a sofa and a couple of chairs, what interior design magazines would call a "conversational grouping," and it contained the only sign of struggle: an overturned end table. Blood stained the carpet a few feet from the sofa, and among the stains was a kitchen chair. Small circles of the stained carpet had been excised by technicians. Schultz knew from the photographs that the victim's headless body had been found tied to that chair. George Burton had spent his last moments alive sitting backward in a chair, his legs spread wide to straddle the chair back, his arms tied at the wrists and secured tightly to the ladder back wooden chair. His ankles were also tied, apparently to provide a steadier work surface. The work surface was the skin of the victim's back. Schultz remembered the close-ups of the murderer's knife work. Segments of skin had been stripped away on the victim's left shoulder in a patch about eight inches square. Within the square, some segments were left intact, forming a pattern best seen from about four feet away. The pattern was the head of a dog, done in bas-relief so skillfully detailed that it was unmistakably a mutt.

Schultz stood for a moment, trying to imagine what it would feel like to be tied in a chair with your skin flayed open, inhaling the prospect of death along with the smell of your own blood with each painful breath. He imagined that Burton wondered what form death would take, and he hoped that the man never saw the stroke coming: his head was lopped off.

Just then PJ stepped in, her professional demeanor back

in place like a mask. He had been perversely pleased by her reaction to the smell. It seemed to him a justification that civilian employees of the Department had no place horning in on his investigative work. He conveniently forgot that there had been a time more than a quarter of a century ago when he reacted in an even worse way, when Schultz the rookie cop had clamped his lips together long enough to get out of that alley, and then thrown up on the front seat of his squad car and Detective Ralph Owens. Owens rolled his eyes skyward and enriched Schultz's already formidable vocabulary, but took it well, considering.

PJ paced around the living room for a few moments, then her eyes riveted on the stains and the chair. Schultz wondered if she would succumb to the urge to get some fresh air, but she stuck it out. He also wondered what would happen the first time she got to the scene before the body was removed. She said that she had seen the results of suicide, but suicide was merely a tragedy. Murder left behind a residue of hate or madness or both.

"Where are those copies of the detailed sketch?" she asked. Her voice was surprisingly under control.

"Right here in the folder. Are we going to use them as a basis for what you need?"

"Yes. We can mark right on them the type of data I want to collect."

She began to circle the room, making comments which he jotted on the sketch. She also used a tape recorder. Occasionally, she asked him to measure a distance which was not already marked on the diagram. When they reached the area of the sofa, he cautioned her to avoid the indentations in the carpet. He didn't want them scuffed up and lost.

"Is there a piece of furniture missing? Did the techs take something?" she asked.

"Now, that's the sixty-four thousand dollar question. Something heavy made those dents," Schultz said, bending over to peer at them, "and the pattern doesn't match anything here."

"So the killer brought a folding lawn chair? And maybe a picnic lunch?"

Schultz glared at her.

"That was a joke, Detective," she said sarcastically.

"Actually, you could be right, for all I know. We don't know what a wacko who carves up living skin like that considers important."

At the mention of the mutilation, she turned quickly away. It seemed that her composure had a time limit; the longer she had to maintain it, the more slippery it got.

"I think I can finish up in here. I've got a good idea what you're looking for now. Why don't you start on the kitchen?" Schultz surprised himself. If he didn't know better, he might think he was getting considerate.

PJ went into the kitchen gratefully. She was trying hard to be professional about the whole thing, but the plain truth was that she was upset. When she set foot in that living room, her objectivity went on vacation.

Being in the kitchen was much better. There was a door between it and the living room, and she swung it shut, then wondered if she was supposed to have touched the door, even with her gloved finger. She figured that Leo would give her hell for it regardless.

One of the first things PJ noticed about the kitchen was that it was not as orderly as the living room. It looked as though the room was off limits to the cleaning woman. There were familiar smells in the room, although it took her a few minutes to realize it as her nose flushed out one set of smells and registered another: kitty litter and canned cat food. Dishes with something dried on them, egg, she thought, were stacked in the sink. The countertop was cluttered with objects such as notes, coins, a wallet, and a watch, as though the owner emptied his pockets and dumped the contents on the nearest flat surface. Twist ties, plastic bags, a bunch of bananas in a cheap basket, already spotted and well on their way to becoming compost, and the requisite food processor rounded out the picture. A plain wooden table was shoved up against one wall, with ladder back chairs crowded around the three open sides. She knew where the fourth chair was, and that refreshed her memory of the scene in the living room.

Underneath the table was a jumble of boxes which took up the whole space. It would be impossible to pull up a chair and get your knees under the table. Not that you would want to, because the top of the table was piled high with boxes too. Apparently Burton ate out a lot or ate standing up. The kitchen was not large, and the appliances were old workhorses, avocado-colored and plainly showing their years of use. PJ realized that Burton undoubtedly kept the door closed when—or if—he ever had company. He would entertain guests out in the airy living room and hope that no one would offer to help in the kitchen.

Only a rough sketch had been made of the kitchen, so PJ set to work making notes and dictating her impressions. She had already formed an idea that the murderer might have obtained whatever it was he used to cut off the victim's head right here in the kitchen. Since no fingerprints other than Burton's and the cleaning woman's had been found in the apartment, there was no way to tell which rooms the killer had entered. Leo had interviewed the cleaning woman last night, Thursday night, while PJ was driving to St. Louis. The cleaning woman had an evening job as a server with a catering company. She had been working at a party Wednesday night between seven PM and midnight. The murder occurred around nine PM.

He could have stood right here, she thought. *The killer could have noticed that there was no knife block on the countertop and wondered which drawer they were in. Why did I automatically assume it was a he?*

She eased some of the drawers open. The drawer next

to the sink stuck a little, and she tugged harder. When it finally slipped open, she gasped. Inside she saw an assortment of butcher knives, paring knives, and an ominous looking old-fashioned meat cleaver. Looking closely, she noticed a dark smear on the edge of the cleaver. She made a note to ask Leo if the kitchen implements had already been considered when looking for the murder weapon. Then she thought that might be too obvious and that she would just further entrench Leo's opinion of her as an incompetent teammate, and even worse, an incompetent boss, if she mentioned it. She knew she had a lot to prove to him, and wondered why it should matter so much to her.

She went over to the table and turned one of the chairs around. She intended to sit down—*what the hell. Leo's already got me for touching the door*—and use her lap to hold the sketch. The chair leg brushed against one of the boxes under the table, knocking it over. She had assumed the boxes were full of something, but apparently they were empty and precariously balanced. Something gray and furry zipped from the overturned box into another one.

PJ did what most people would do. She yelped.

A moment later the door swung open hard enough to bang the doorknob into the wall. Leo rushed in and came up to her, his belly swaying a second after the rest of him stopped.

"What?" he said, his voice a bit too loud for the confined area.

"It's nothing," PJ said. The tips of her ears were hot, and she was glad that her hair covered them. "I knocked over a box and something ran out, a rat maybe. I just got spooked."

"Oh, yeah, it was probably the cat. Burton had a cat, and I suppose it's still in the apartment. Animal Control should have been here by now. They'll probably come by this afternoon."

PJ digested this, her ears returning to normal. "What will happen to it?"

"How the hell should I know? Whatever it is they do to strays, I guess. Burton's got a sister, but she's allergic. Can't get within thirty feet of a cat, she says. Anyway, he wasn't supposed to have a cat here. Landlord doesn't like pets, tries to keep them out."

PJ decided this was as good a time as any to ask about the kitchen knives. Leo couldn't possibly think any worse of her than after she yelped like that at an ordinary cat.

"Detective, I noticed a whole drawer full of cutlery in the kitchen, serious looking stuff like butcher knives and a meat cleaver. Have you considered those?"

"As what?"

She thought he was deliberately provoking her. "One of them could be the murder weapon, of course," she answered testily. "Let me show you the cleaver."

"Let's take a look. But I should tell you that in most cases of premeditated murder, the creep brings the murder weapon in with him and takes it out with him. Crimes of passion, impulse killings, that's where the kitchen knife or gun from the bedroom comes in," Schultz said. "It seems to me we're talking premeditated here. With an impulse killing, if there's mutilation, it's fast and furious. Whatever you might think of this guy's artistic ability, there's no question that the skin carving took some time to do. Also, there's nothing to indicate that the killer went into the kitchen."

"What about the chair where the victim was seated? It matches these chairs at the kitchen table, and there are only three of them left in here. Usually there would be a set of four. That seems pretty conclusive to me. The killer came in here to get a chair and while he was here, he saw the drawer full of knives." She noticed that Schultz automatically assumed a male killer, too.

"No go, Doc. The chair is close but it's not a match. The scrollwork on the ladder back is different. It looks like Burton may have replaced a chair that broke with a similar one. Don't blame you for missing that little detail, though—that blood in there is mighty distracting, it being the first time for you. The chair might have been anywhere in the apartment. In fact, there was a pile of clothes on the bathroom floor which looked like it could have been dumped off a chair."

PJ held her ground. She opened the drawer and pointed out the cleaver with the dark smudge.

"Well, it looks like it could be blood," Schultz said, "but it could also be a dozen other things. The search of the surrounding area, including the trash, didn't turn up a weapon, though. Just the usual: dead animals and some stuff that the guy from the Medical Examiner's office said was a human placenta. I'll get a tech to come back out and bag up all the stuff in that drawer. Could be this creep decided to hide the murder weapon in plain sight." Leo went back out to the living room.

Feeling a little smug, PJ sat down in the chair. In the back of her mind she had been wondering about the cat. She had a fair idea what would happen after Animal Control came, and it wasn't good. Her ex-husband Steven had also been allergic to cats, like Burton's sister, and so she, a cat person from birth and probably before, had been catless for years. It hadn't occurred to her until this moment that being free of Steven, the first time she had actually thought of it as "free," she could get a cat. She decided on the spot that she would do so, and that she wanted Burton's cat, which she hadn't even seen yet except as a frightened gray blur.

She pulled off her right glove and put out her hand toward the box into which the cat had disappeared. "Here, kitty, kitty," she said, using her most sincere you-can-trust-me-I'm-kind-to-cats voice. "Nice kitty."

A tentative meow came from the box. After another minute of coaxing, the cat came out and sniffed her fingers. She sat still and let herself be examined. The cat was young, no more than six or eight months old, and beautifully marked, sleek and healthy. She—PJ was somehow certain the cat was a she, it was something in the way she walked—was gray tiger-striped on top. About midway down each leg, the stripes stopped and there was a band of solid orange. The cat's belly and paws were pure white, and there was a white tip on the end of her tail, which was now waving like a little flag of truce. Her eyes were the color of honey with the sun shining through it and her whiskers were long and elegant.

It wasn't until the cat jumped up into her lap that PJ noticed that the fur around the cat's rear was smelly, damp from being licked by the cat, and stained brown. A quick examination confirmed both that she was correct about the cat's sex and that the cat had soiled itself. The licks she had aimed in that direction weren't doing a good job of cleaning up. Her front paws looked a little odd, too, kind of dirty around the feathery edges which reminded PJ of a snowshoe hare's feet. PJ had once had a cat which crapped on himself every time he got into a fight, and had to be bathed before he could be let back into the house. This cat must have been very frightened, and PJ closed her eyes as something dawned on her.

The cat was probably in the apartment at the same time as the murderer.

Just then, Leo came back in. The cat snuggled deeper into the crook of her arm, burying its face.

"I see you found the cat," he said.

"Yes, and I'm taking it home." She raised her chin defiantly.

"Hey, Doc, everybody's got a soft spot. You don't have to act so defensive."

"Is that so, Leo? Where's yours, exactly?"

There was a strange croaking sound, and she realized Leo was laughing. "I think I had one," he said, "but thank goodness it healed over."

She smiled. Maybe this was going to work out after all.

CHAPTER

5

"I want to talk to the investigator who's handling the murder of that piano player," Pauley Mac said. He was in his bedroom, perched on the edge of the bed, using the old black rotary phone he'd brought with him from Florida. "I have some information about the case."

"One moment, please," said the 911 operator. "I'll transfer you to Homicide. Stay on the line."

You bet, bitchy, said Dog to himself. *Bitchy, witchy, slit and tit, let's do it doggie-style. I'm just the Dog to do it.*

Pauley Mac rolled his eyes up in exasperation and sent Dog back to his corner. Not that he usually stayed there.

"Homicide."

"I told the operator I want to talk to the officer who's working on the piano player's murder investigation. I may have important information. Can you tell me who that is?"

"Just a minute, let me check. Looks like it's Schultz, Detective Leo Schultz."

"Why, I think I know him," said Pauley Mac. "He that skinny guy with long black hair?"

"Not this Leo Schultz. He's about six feet tall, heavy, and hasn't got much thatch on the roof, if you catch my meaning." The clerk chuckled at her own joke. "He's signed out to field investigation right now. I'm sure someone else can help you. Let me transfer you."

*You can help me, slut. Help me fuck you. Slick chick, lick
dick. I'd like to get a sniff of your ass . . .*

"Thanks, that sounds like just what I need," Pauley Mac
said, ignoring the voice in his head. He waited until he was
put on hold and then hung up.

It had been so easy to find out who was working on the
Burton murder. It was a little game he played. When Dog
was in his killing cycle, he used another aspect of his personality, Pauley Mac, to keep track of things by sidling in
close to the investigation. In the past he had been a janitor at a police station and a morgue attendant.

The killing cycle had been in a dormant phase for a
couple of years, but something had triggered in Pauley
Mac the deadly stirrings, the inner imperative to kill again.
The voices of those killed during his previous cycles
echoed and argued in his mind. Pauley Mac believed that
he acquired the special knowledge of the deceased by consuming the victim's brain.

When he was a child, his abusive parents told him over
and over that he didn't have the brains of a dog. One day
he decided to prove them wrong. With a child's reasoning,
he killed a neighbor's dog, cracked its skull with a rock,
and ate its brain. After that, he responded to his parents'
beatings and tirades by growling. As a teenager, Pauley
Mac killed them and others, until the killing urge diminished. Years would pass, blank times of his life, during
which he held menial jobs (no-brainers, he would chuckle)
and sometimes bought himself some female company.
Then he would get the urge again, the desire to fill the void
inside where love should have been. If he could just do this
thing or have that thing, life would somehow be better. So
he killed in cycles, and each cycle had a theme and was
marked by some ritual which was important to him at the
time. The theme of the last cycle was sports, and as far as
he was concerned, he was now a well-rounded athlete, even
though he still got out of breath when he took the basement stairs two at a time. The new theme was fine arts, and

since Pauley Mac had recently taken up whittling, the ritual was carving his self-portrait into his victim's skin. His first carefully chosen victim was a pianist from the St. Louis Symphony Orchestra, because Ma always thought playing the piano was a fine thing to do.

Pauley Mac checked the phone book, but as he suspected, there were several listings which could be the man he wanted. Or it could be none of them, if Schultz had an unlisted number. This did not faze him at all; it simply meant that his search would have to get more personal. He selected some clothes that made him fade away and become practically invisible in public. Jeans, not too tight, not too baggy, worn-looking but not tattered, and a clean blue work shirt with a name tag over the pocket: Mike, your basic blue collar worker on his lunch break.

Dog usually went around nude at home, so Pauley Mac had to be careful to make sure clothes were in place before Dog went out. Sometimes Pauley Mac slipped up, and Dog made it out the front door naked. Pauley Mac remembered one time in particular that Dog had opened the door on Halloween night and sent a group of trick-or-treaters squealing down the block. Looking back on it, they both thought it was funny.

Pauley Mac drove over to Euclid Boulevard and parked a couple of blocks away from Burton's apartment. He got out and walked to the coffee shop, where he took a small table near the window and ordered coffee and a grilled cheese sandwich, no pickles. He didn't know whether Detective Schultz was in the apartment now or not, and couldn't risk walking to the rear of the building to check. But he felt confident that sooner or later, he would catch a glimpse of his man in this area.

He had been there about an hour and was on his third cup of coffee when Schultz came into the coffee shop. He knew at a glance it was the man he was looking for, but he was surprised to see that the detective was accompanied by a woman. A good-looking one, even though she was older than he usually liked, he thought as he ruthlessly squelched Dog's baser comments. She was curved where a woman should be curved, and solid-looking. He liked a woman with enough padding that her hip bones didn't jut out. He thought that if you could see a woman's ribs, she was just too insubstantial to use for sex, at least the kind of sex he liked. Dog growled in assent, and a thrill traveled up and down Pauley Mac's spine like an elevator.

Maybe we can slide it in, Dog said. *Hot slot, wet pet, juicy Lucy.*

Pauley Mac watched as Schultz ordered a cup of coffee to go and the woman ordered a large Coke. He noticed that they paid separately, which meant that there was no connection between them, romance, sex, or even close friendship, at least not yet. The woman must be a cop too, and they had probably just begun working together. They left, and within a couple of minutes a car came out from the alley and turned onto Euclid. He couldn't make out the driver, but the good-looking woman was sitting in the front passenger seat holding a large box on her lap which blocked his view of the driver. The car was faded red, a model he didn't recognize, but he caught the license number. He got up to leave, using the bathroom first. He let Dog have a little fun in there, spraying and smearing the walls, since he wasn't planning to come back to the coffee shop.

CHAPTER

6

"Open up, it's Mom," PJ said as she knocked on the motel room door. She had tried her key, but Thomas had the security chain fastened. She was glad he was so sensible. He opened the door right away. As she reached to give him a hug and a kiss, he pulled away slightly and shoved a potato chip in his mouth. That certainly cut out the prospect of a kiss.

"Mom," he said, talking around the chip, "don't do that mushy stuff. We've talked about that before."

"I didn't think it was too much to ask for my son to greet me with a hug after I've had such a rough day," she said irritably.

"You think you've had a rough day! I ran out of soda three hours ago."

A glance at his face told PJ that he was serious. Irritation grew into anger. "You listen to me, young man . . ."

She knew that annoyed Thomas big time, and she really shouldn't have done it. Thomas turned his back on her, mumbling something which she barely caught but which she thought came from her A list of banned words. There was an A list, a B list, and a C list. Using a C word cost Thomas a dime, a B word cost a quarter, and an A word cost a dollar.

"That will be one dollar, please," she said icily. The mumbling continued.

"Two dollars. Care to go for your whole allowance?"

She could tell by the stiffness in his back that they weren't making much progress on rebuilding their relationship. He went to his luggage, dug into a pile of underwear, and came up with two wrinkled dollars. He held them out to her, mouth set, not meeting her eyes. She took them, then thought for a moment and handed one back.

"We'll split it. I may have been a little short-tempered there."

"Yeah, you could say that." The dollar disappeared into his pocket.

"So how's the cat?" she said, grateful to change the subject. Schultz had driven her by the motel and she had smuggled the box containing the cat into the room earlier today. She wasn't sure if the motel allowed pets and she hadn't decided yet if she was going to own up to acquiring a cat. She could probably salve her conscience with the thought that she hadn't owned a cat when she checked in, so she hadn't really lied then.

"It's still in the bathroom. It made some noise and then it shut up. Do you have any idea what that animal's rear smells like? What do we need with a cat, anyway?"

"It's a she, and that's your dad's prejudice showing. I happen to love cats."

"Well, I don't, and it's going to be a nuisance. It'll get fur on my black T-shirt. Whew!" he said, sniffing in her direction. "Speaking of smells, you smell weird."

PJ sighed. She could hardly wait to wash her hair. She had thought it was psychological, that smell of blood floating around her face all afternoon.

"Let's give her a try, OK? Maybe you'll like having a cat around. She can be a wonderful companion," PJ said, just a little too brightly.

"Yeah, and so is a twenty-dollar bill, but it doesn't put fur on my clothes and barf on the rug."

"Did she?" PJ said, suddenly concerned. "Barf on the rug?"

"No, but it will eventually. What's in the bag, anyway?" He had noticed a small plastic bag that PJ had brought home.

"Cat food. We'll talk about it again, but now I don't have time to argue. We're keeping that cat, and I've just decided to let you come up with a name for her," she said. At least it felt good to be in control about something. "I have an appointment with the real estate woman in an hour, and I need to shower first. Are you sure you won't come with me?"

"Nah. I told you I don't want to look at houses. I don't even want to be here."

His face was so sad that PJ wanted to reach out and cuddle him. "I know, Thomas," she said softly. "I wish things hadn't turned out this way, but they did, and now we've got to make the best of it."

"If you hadn't been so wrapped up in your work and paid more attention to Dad, maybe he wouldn't have hopped into bed with Carla."

She recoiled, wondering how the two of them were ever going to get back on neutral ground, much less be a loving family again.

"That hurt," she said. "You have no right to say that. You don't know the whole story, and anyway, it's none of your business. I'm the adult, remember, and you're the child. What goes—went—on between your father and me is our business." She was striking out, and her voice had a strident tone, but she didn't care. Thomas turned away again, and this time she let him go.

In the bathroom, she stripped off her clothes and let them fall in a pile on the floor. The cat came out of the box, where she had evidently been sleeping, and kneaded the pile. Then she looked up at PJ and meowed plaintively.

"I know, little one, it hasn't been a fun day for you either." She dumped a package of Tender Vittles on the floor and refilled the cup of water she had left for the cat earlier in the day. She ran the shower as hot as she could stand it and stood with her face turned up to the water, letting the smells and the stress run down the drain.

It had been a busy afternoon. She had gotten a tour of the computer facility, found that her equipment was still in its original boxes in a corner of the room, and carried them back to her office. No one had volunteered to help, and she couldn't find a rolling cart, so she had to make several trips. Then it had taken a while to unpack everything, stacking the manuals under her desk where she wouldn't have to see them again and could use them to prop her feet up. It seemed odd to her that the Department had laid its hands on a Silicon Graphics workstation costing tens of thousands of dollars but there wasn't a single spare multiple plug outlet with a surge protector to be found in the building. She shrugged and went out to buy one at Radio Shack. While she was there, she picked up some diskettes, another thing she had found was in short supply. She didn't want to make a fuss about these out-of-pocket expenses on her first day, but her pockets weren't very deep. If she couldn't get supplies in a timely manner, she would have to make an issue of it with Howard. She could use a computer desk in her office, too, although she might have to suspend it from the ceiling to fit it in. The monitor took up a good part of her desk, and the keyboard was too high to be comfortable. It shouldn't be at desk height. The brains of the computer sat on the floor next to the desk in a tower cabinet. She hadn't unpacked the laser printer yet, and didn't have any idea where she was going to put it. By the time she got the workstation booted up, it was after five o'clock. She had rushed out, only to get stuck in traffic again.

After staying under the hot shower until the bathroom was satisfyingly steamy, she toweled dry and dressed quickly. She said good-bye to her sulking son and promised to bring him a take-out meal. She made it to the real estate woman's office in a remarkable fifty minutes after walking through the door of her motel room.

An hour and a half later she was on her way back to the room. She spotted a pizza place that was right next to a grocery store. She ordered a pizza to go, then picked up a few things in the grocery store while waiting for the pizza to be prepared. It had been time well spent with the real estate agent. The woman had told her that just that morning a house had come up for rent that was something special. The home was located on Magnolia Avenue in South St. Louis, close to PJ's work so that she would not have to commute like she did today. There was easy access via Hampton Avenue to I-44 or Highway 40, or she could make her way into downtown by staying off the traffic-clogged highways and sticking to the city streets.

The first thing she had noticed when she stepped inside the door was that the home didn't stink of stale cigarette smoke. That gave the place a leg up right away. It was a brick story-and-a-half, with wood floors, stained glass windows flanking the fireplace, a modern kitchen, and two huge bedrooms upstairs. Each bedroom had a little door inside the closet leading to an attic space under the eaves. The rooms were light and large, the yard was small, private, and edged with old-fashioned perennials, and there were two—count them, two—bathrooms, one upstairs and one down. The upstairs bathtub stood on tiger claws grasping marble spheres, and PJ claimed that one for herself instantly. Thomas could run up and down the steps whenever he needed to use the bathroom. Maybe he would burn off some of his antagonism.

PJ had signed the papers right then, leaning on the kitchen counter. Her heart was as light as it had been in the last several months, which was odd considering that just hours ago she had been to her very first murder scene.

The grocery store had yielded essentials such as root beer, cookies, more cat food, pet dishes, a litter pan, litter, an inadequate-looking scoop, and a cat shampoo that promised silky, shining fur. The pizza smelled great in the

car, and it was all PJ could do not to lift the lid of the box
and grab a piece.

When Thomas opened the door, she held out a can of
root beer as a wordless apology. The can was snatched
away and the top was popped before she could even say
hello.

"Neat! My favorite kind. Thanks, Mom. Hey, what's
that smell?"

"Pizza."

His eyes widened and he smacked his lips comically. PJ
burst out laughing. It felt very good to smile at her son.

After pizza and cookies, they both sat around moaning
melodramatically and holding their stomachs until prac-
ticality intervened. Thomas went to the car to bring up the
rest of the supplies, and PJ screwed up her courage and
went to the front desk. She had decided not to hide the
presence of the cat, since they were going to have to stay
in the motel for about a week. She was pleasantly surprised that all she had to do was pay a fifty dollar damage
deposit.

She couldn't put it off any longer. The cat had to be
bathed. She went into the bathroom and locked the door.
Then she rummaged in her cosmetic bag until she came up
with a little-used nail clipper. She had decided to clip the
cat's nails first, to lessen the damage to her hands and
arms when she plopped the feline into a sinkful of warm
water. She closed the lid on the toilet and sat down. The
cat jumped into her lap as soon as there was a lap. She
pushed her over on one side, took a front paw in her hand,
and gently squeezed to expose the claws. The cat didn't
protest; apparently this was familiar territory. Then she noticed the dark material which filled the grooves on the un-
derside of the claws. It looked as if the cat had been digging in dark red, almost black, clay. PJ remembered that
earlier in the day, the fur around the cat's front paws had

looked dirty. That was gone now; evidently, licking did accomplish something. With sudden clarity she knew what the substance under the claws was. It was blood. This cat had not only been terrified by the killer's intrusion into Burton's apartment, it had apparently fought tooth and nail, or rather tooth and claw, for its own life and that of its owner. At least there had been one success.

PJ shivered with the knowledge that she was most likely holding a witness to the murder on her lap.

It was definitely important enough to call Schultz at home. The phone was answered by a female voice. There was a loud background noise. A TV was playing a sitcom, and the phone must have been very close to it.

"Good evening. This is Penny . . . er, Dr. Gray. I work with Leo Schultz. May I speak to him, please?"

"Yeah, hold on. He's taking a crap. I'll get him." The voice sounded as if interrupting Schultz from this personal function would be a source of satisfaction. Several minutes passed. PJ couldn't quite make out what the TV program was, but judging by the escalating laughter, it must have been reaching its predictable comedic climax.

"Schultz. Just a minute." The receiver was muffled, but she heard him yell anyway. "Julia, turn that fucking thing down! I couldn't hear a goddamned freight train in here, for Christ's sake!" The background sound level dropped marginally.

"Sorry about that. Wife's a little hard of hearing, or maybe she just likes to make me think she is. That way, I might say things around her I might not otherwise."

"Leo, this is PJ. I'm sorry to bother you at home."

"No problem."

"Remember that cat I found at Burton's place today? I was getting ready to clip her claws when I found something dark stuck under them. I think it's blood. I think it's the killer's blood."

"How do you know it didn't scratch Burton himself or some guest of his?"

"Because of the way she held still and purred when I was going to clip her claws."

"Say again?"

"The cat is very gentle. She had been kindly treated by Burton, or she wouldn't just lie quietly and let me squeeze her claws to clip them. I don't think she would scratch anyone unless her life depended on it."

There was a pause as Schultz digested this. She knew he was trying to decide how much credence to place in her story. PJ smelled the used pizza box, and she asked Thomas if he would please take it out and find a trash can someplace else. She didn't want to wake up to that smell.

"OK, Doc, we'll roll with it. I'll have a tech come over and get a sample, if I can roust someone at this time of the night. Or do you think we need a vet? But you know it wouldn't hold up in court anyway because there's been a lousy chain of custody. That sample should have been taken before the cat left the apartment."

"I didn't know about it until now. And no, I don't think a vet is needed."

"Also, that cleaver with the smudge on it turned out to be a dead end. It was blood, all right, but it was chicken's blood. Nice try, though."

As they waited for the technician to show up, Thomas drifted off and flicked on the TV. After a few minutes of channel surfing, he settled down with a science fiction movie, definitely grade B judging by the glimpses PJ got. PJ checked the telephone to make sure it had modular connections, then brought out her PowerBook, a laptop computer. She connected the internal modem to the phone line and dialed into an intentionally obscure bulletin board for hard-core VR—Virtual Reality—enthusiasts.

She skipped lightly over unsecured online conversations just like Thomas surfed cable stations, relaxing as she settled into an old routine. Nothing that she saw bore the ID she was looking for, but she was certain that he would be monitoring, if not actively participating, at this time of night. Finally, she selected a heated discussion on the merits of molecular wire technology, and joined the round-robin commentary. After a few appropriate responses, she entered a phrase with agreed-upon code words.

Planetary alignment Mercury/Jupiter. RSVP secure PVT1.

Other participants, realizing she was requesting a secured conversation, deftly wove her out of the exchange, but not without flaming her for using them as a vehicle. She chuckled as her screen lit up with an animated hand giving her the finger. Then she switched to the path which had been designated *PVT1,* entered her password, and waited. After about five minutes, words appeared on her screen.

Merlin here. What's the buzz, Keypunch?

It was the same greeting she had been getting for the past twenty years, and it fit like a comfortable old bathrobe. She had met Merlin during her college years, at a time when online communication was an arcane field, a computer backwater treaded by techies with no dates on Saturday night. She suspected then (and still did) that Merlin was one of the professors from her computer science courses. They had fit together like two halves of a friendship necklace, the kind preteen girls wore with the heart broken in two with a jagged edge. Merlin had been a mentor, and more, a good friend, for half of PJ's life. Their relationship was conducted entirely by computer communication, an easier task now in the days of bulletin boards and public online services.

When PJ first studied computer science, programs were entered into mainframe or minicomputers using punched cards. Students wrote their programs on green and white coding sheets, then keypunched them on noisy machines with unwieldy keyboards that punched combinations of holes into sturdy cards. The cards were fed into a special reader and digested by the computer. Students carried around large boxes of the cards, eyeing each other's productivity and ogling at the complexity of another's program based on the size of the card deck. PJ's flying fingers, trained on her father's manual typewriter, were the envy of her fellows, and she acquired the nickname of Keypunch Kid. She was so accurate that she never bothered to verify her work. Verification was done by typing the contents of each card twice. The keypuncher was rewarded with a satisfying "kerCHUNCK" sound as the machine matched the two versions, pronounced them exactly the same, and punched a small extra rectangle in the upper right corner of the card. Her card decks didn't bear the telltale verification notch, but they worked anyway. Then microcomputers came along with their onscreen programming and editing, and keypunch machines faded away, a chapter of computer history which rarely evoked fond memories.

But the nickname stuck.

For a moment PJ closed her eyes and let comfort seep in. She used mental imaging, a quick method of relaxation that Merlin had suggested years ago: *picture your forehead smooth and wrinkle-free, and tension melts away.*

With her forehead wrinkle-free for the first time since she woke up this morning, she began to type.

Nice to hear from you. Don't you have anything better to do than check keywords waiting for me to show up?

Merlin's response was immediate, and the conversation was off and running.

You know that's background monitoring. I wasn't holding my breath. But I did think you'd be on tonight. Isn't this your first week of work on your new job?

My new job wasn't supposed to start until next week, but you're right. Today was the first day, and I feel like I've been hit with a wrecker ball.

All of PJ's frustrations came rushing back, and she tried to fend them off.

There, there. Tell Merlin all about it.

Don't patronize me, you old fart. I've had enough games for one day.

Sorry. You can cry on my cyber-shoulder if you want to.

Everything I try to do seems so hard, it's like walking in molasses just to get dressed and face the day. I miss Steven, and then the next minute I hate the bastard. He's really screwed up my life, but it's still my life, and I have to make the best of it. And then there's Thomas. He can be such a little prick sometimes, and he knows just how to get under my skin. My job pays a lot less and Steven's salary is gone, my boss is a rubber-stamp for the captain, and my group that I'm supposed to be forming only has one guy in it and he's a male chauvinist pig. Tomorrow the pig gets a couple of people assigned to help him out with the field work, trainees or something, he calls them lowlifes. What help do I get? Nada.

Is that all?

No. I was supposed to have a few months to get the project going. Instead I've gotten assigned a horrible murder case on my first day. I had to go to the victim's apartment and I almost lost my breakfast in front of the pig.

PJ's screen went blank. A moment later, a large violin filled the screen. The bow scraped across the strings and sad squeaky music emanated from the PowerBook's speakers. PJ chuckled. Merlin rarely let her get away with self-pity, and it seemed that this was not one of the times.

Whoa, there, Keypunch. Sounds like you need some fatherly advice from old Merlin. Not that you'll listen.

1. Of course being a divorced mom is difficult. But remember this: it's a very rare divorce where there isn't blame on both sides. And yours was as common as a dandelion.

2. Thomas has a lot of the same pressures that you do, translated into a twelve-year-old's world. Plus the simple curse of being twelve years old. Why don't you try being the adult in the relationship and let him be the child?

3. Money is the curse of the proletariat. Or was it the salvation?

4. Ditto for bosses.

5. Male chauvinist pigs make good bacon and you're an

*old pro with the butcher's ax. If all else fails, put a curse
on 'im.*

*6. You have my sympathy on the last point. I never could
stand the smell of blood.*

7. The word for the day is "curse."

By the time PJ finished reading the list, she was laughing out loud. Thomas looked up from his movie, but she
shook her head in his direction and he resubmerged. A
conversation with Merlin always went like this, with his
wonderful combination of sympathy, humor, and a bucket
of cold water in the face, in just the right proportions. He
loved making numbered lists, and she hardly ever got out
of a conversation without one.

Thanks. I feel better already. I think.

*Always glad to beat someone about the head and shoul-
ders. Now then, down to business. How's business?*

*I suppose you mean my actual work. That could be the
bright spot in this whole mess. I really feel like I could make
a contribution. You know, do something in the public interest.*

Well, la-de-da!

*Don't be such a cynic. If I can do my part to make the
world a little safer, that's something. Maybe a lot better
something than working with consumer studies.*

I always knew you were a knightess in shining armor.

*You're just jealous. You've never done a worthwhile thing
in your life.*

Yes I have. I met you.

That made PJ pause. Merlin rarely expressed himself so
openly.

*You're sweet to say so. But I have another motive for talk-
ing with you tonight besides airing my gripes.*

*The truth comes out at last. You only want my body, not
my mind.*

*Quiet, you exasperating phantom of cyberspace! Besides,
you should be so lucky. What I really want is a connection.*

*I want to know who in this town is working with VR and
would maybe, if I beg really hard, lend me an HMD.*

*I take it your new employer doesn't provide niceties like
Head-Mounted Displays.*

*Let's just say I went out today and bought my own surge
protector and box of diskettes. I doubt that money for an
HMD is suddenly going to appear in my budget.*

*I think you've assessed the situation accurately. Let's see,
I think there's a group at Wash U. I'll poke around and let
you know.*

That was just what PJ wanted to hear. Washington University
would be a great place to make contacts in her new
community. Merlin seemed to know someone, or someone
who knew someone, just about everyplace. She wondered
how many others like herself were strung out across the
world, orbiting Merlin like the numerous satellites of
Jupiter. Merlin always seemed available to her. It had never
occurred to her before that he might be carrying on conversations
with others, that someone from Tallahassee or
Spokane might be sharing a triumph or commiserating
about a failure tonight.

For the first time, it occurred to PJ that Merlin might
be a computer program, not a real person.

As soon as the idea blossomed in her head, she rejected
it. Merlin was far too sophisticated, warm, and just plain
human to be a collection of coded routines.

Thanks, Merlin. Goodnight.

Anything for you, Keypunch. Sleep well.

As PJ was signing off from the session, there was a
knock at the door. She folded the PowerBook shut and
glanced at the bathroom door. The door was ajar; one of
them had accidentally left it open. She let the technician
in, and then knelt down to fetch the cat out from under
her bed.

CHAPTER

7

In the morning, PJ registered Thomas for school, using the address of the rental house to establish residency in the St. Louis City school district. Both of them had been up late the night before. The evidence technician hadn't arrived until nearly midnight to take a sample of the blood from under the cat's claws, and then there was the ordeal of bathing the smelly creature. Thomas went through the whole morning routine without saying a word. She knew why. He was not eager to go to school when summer vacation started in a little over two weeks. He did not want to be thrust into a situation where everyone else had established friends and routines and he was an outsider, only to break up for summer a short time later.

She knew that Thomas thought she had absolutely no understanding of the difficulty he faced. That wasn't true, but of course there was no use telling a twelve-year-old that she had once been that age, and that her self-esteem had risen and fallen according to the whims of her peers, that she had endured her share of tearful rushes to her room, slammed doors, and crushed feelings, and thoughts that she was the only one in the world who ever got a zit.

She was hoping that he would be able to break into the social structure and form at least one friendship that would have a chance to develop over the summer. Then when school started in the fall, he would have a connection—he wouldn't be the odd guy out. So, wondering if she was doing the right thing, she left a message for Schultz that she would be in a little late, and then dragged Thomas to registration. Much to his dismay, the school secretary offered to have him start that very day. As he was led away, he shot her a black look that could have withered a sturdy oak. As her former confident married self, it wouldn't have bothered her. As a newly-divorced single parent, she found herself questioning all of her parenting decisions.

When she finally got to work, lugging in a large box, it felt as though it should be quitting time. She dropped the box off in her office and went looking for Schultz. Unable to find him, she touched base with her boss Howard Wall, and immediately regretted it. She had a brief but intense conversation in his office. He was under pressure to show something, anything, from the CHIP project, and he was perfectly willing to pass along the pressure. He was like a hydraulic pipeline that narrowed and propelled its noncompressible contents faster and faster. Those further down the pipeline got blasted. Well, there was someone down the pipeline from PJ, and he wasn't there to defend himself. On the way back to her office, she left a cryptic note on Schultz's desk: See me ASAP.

She surveyed her office with a critical eye. The box, which was the same one she had used to take the cat home from Burton's apartment, was full of her personal office items. Her first tasks were to straighten the place up and install the fan and halogen desk lamp she had brought with her. Flipping the chair over, she adjusted the seat down to a more comfortable height. Then she turned off the humming fluorescent overhead light and closed the door, blocking out most of the traffic and bathroom noise. Immediately the room felt better. The fan was a cheerful white with blue plastic blades, very quiet while running, and powerful enough to keep the air in the tiny office in constant motion. She tilted it up toward the ceiling so that it wouldn't disturb papers on her desk. Not that there were any papers currently on her desk, but she felt that situation would change rapidly. The lamp cast a wide circle of bright light over the desktop, and she angled it away from the monitor so there wouldn't be any glare. For a moment she simply basked in the breeze, her feet resting comfortably on the floor, and studied the shadows around the edge of the room. Then she emptied the rest of the box, setting out a picture of Thomas, a Mickey Mouse clock, and a pencil cup containing her prized Space Pen she had bought at the Smithsonian Air and Space Museum. Tomorrow, if she had time, she would bring in some prints for the walls. PJ had a collection of wildlife prints, mostly big cats. Most of them would overwhelm this office, but she could think of two or three that might work. Then maybe she could paint the walls some weekend, surely they wouldn't mind.

Suddenly the door flew open hard enough to smash the doorknob into the wall. Schultz filled the doorway. There was a momentary look of confusion on his face, quickly replaced by a sheepish grin.

"Didn't your mama ever teach you to knock?" PJ said.

"Sorry. Nobody ever closed this door before. I didn't think you were inside. It gets God awful hot with the door closed." Realizing he was rambling, Schultz closed his mouth. Then he took in the improvements. "Say, this place looks better already. I could get jealous."

Schultz didn't look like a man who had gotten an intimidating note from the boss. In fact, PJ thought he looked downright buoyant, like a hangman with a new rope. She decided to act neutral. "Sit down, Leo. What can I do for you?"

Schultz gave her an exaggerated leer. "Any number of things, Doc."

"Really, Detective, you are in a strange and ornery mood today."

"Strange and horny might be more like it, Doc, but the more you're around me, you'll find that's not unusual."

She gestured at a chair and he lowered himself into it. She noticed that he seemed to flex his knees with care as he sat down.

"I guess you're wondering about my note," she said, channeling the conversation back to the subject she had in mind. She was trying to figure out how to tell Schultz that she wanted him to do a lot of what she considered gruntwork while she sat in her office preparing a demo for Wall.

"Note? Did you leave something at my desk? I came here straight from the crapper. Washed my hands, first, though. You should feel honored. I don't always do that, especially if I'm heading for the lieutenant's office."

PJ let her annoyance show. Somehow her conversations with Schultz never went as planned. "Anything new on the case?" she asked.

"Turns out that stuff under the cat's claws was the bonafide shit. You mind that kind of language, you let me know, OK? I can be real genteel when I need to, just got to work at it, that's all. Anyway, it was human blood, and it didn't belong to Burton. The creep didn't leave any fingerprints, but he left something even better. Considerate bastard, just handed me the knife to cut his balls off with."

"I assume you're referring to DNA matching. Aren't you forgetting a few things?"

"Such as?"

"You have to have a suspect before you can match the DNA to the sample from the cat's claws. The last I heard, a comprehensive DNA database like the FBI's fingerprint file didn't exist yet, so there's nothing to search through. Secondly, I thought you were the one who was skeptical about whether the blood belongs to the murderer. Even if it turns out to be from the murderer, how could you ever prove that the cat scratched the suspect during the murder and not out on the street someplace?"

Schultz waved his hand dismissively.

"You have a suspect?" PJ said.

"Nope."

"Then why are you so cheerful this morning?"

"Gut instinct, Doc. Instinct says we're going to get this guy, and now we've got something to nail his ass with when we catch up to him."

PJ sighed. Schultz was assuming that the cat scratched the killer while he was in Burton's apartment. Personally she thought that was highly probable, just about a certainty, but there was room for doubt. Not only that, Schultz himself had pointed out that the chain of custody for the blood sample was compromised. The cat had been taken from the scene and the evidence that it was carrying under its claws had left police custody. Objectively, they both knew that made the blood sample legally worthless. But she understood Schultz's desire to view it as solid evidence: it was a link to the killer, a blood trail, and Schultz was a bloodhound baying at the scent.

It was time to let the bloodhound off the leash.

She thought she knew just how to approach the situation. She tried to put some silkiness into her voice, but found herself out of practice.

"I'd like to get your input on something," she said. "I'm trying to decide what would be the best use of my time on this investigation. I could come with you while you do indepth interviews with Burton's friends and neighbors. My psychology training would add some insights. On the other hand, the computer aspect of CHIP should be up and running as soon as possible, since this is a pilot program. That means I should stay in my office and work on the computer for the next, oh, three or four days. Do you think you could handle the field interviews by yourself?"

PJ was surprised to see a flash of anger on Schultz's face.

"Doc, I'm not as dumb as you think I am, or even as dumb as I look," he said. "I know who's boss here because Wall whipped my ass about it. I don't need any fine speech or shrink mumbo-jumbo, and I don't want to be patronized. We're going to work together, we've got to talk straight to each other. Don't give me any of this phony 'get my input' crap."

PJ folded her hands on her desk. She realized that she had been deliberately manipulative. It wasn't like her. Her morning with Thomas had been stressful, then Wall had pounced. The temptation to spread her bad attitude around had been irresistible, and Schultz was paying the price. There was only one thing to do: apologize.

"Yes, you're right. I'm sorry. It won't happen again."

"All right then, where do we go from here?"

"In plain English, Howard is bugging me for a dog and pony show on the computer by Friday. The only way I can have anything is for you to carry the entire field investigation by yourself until then."

Schultz grinned. PJ thought he looked a little like a maniacal elf when he did that. It must have been the way his cheeks rounded up and reddened.

"Now that I can understand," he said. "You just plant your butt here and tap your keys or flap your floppies or whatever it is that you do, and I'll go track down who saw what at Burton's place. Suits me just fine. Besides, I've got help coming on board, two officers who are studying for their exams to make detective. That looks like it's going to be it: the two of us and the two of them. I guess Lieutenant Wall figures the computer means we can put fewer warm bodies on this job, and less experienced ones, too."

"I know about that. Howard told me this morning, in between making it clear that I won't get any computer analysts anytime soon, and that I'd better have something to show by Friday all by my lonesome. I'll be able to help out more as soon as I make some progress on this computer stuff. I'm not abandoning you."

"Yeah, yeah. I'm a big boy. You don't have to aim my dick so I can piss."

"How . . . colorful. I can assure you, Detective, that if I were to aim a man's dick, it wouldn't be so that he could urinate."

"Why, Doc," Schultz said with a feigned look of shock on his face, "I didn't know you cared."

Schultz left the office feeling good. Without any maneuvering on his part, it looked like he was going to get exactly what he wanted. The shrink and the computer were going their way, and he was going his. He had been rehearsing various scenarios leading to that end, and now it was dumped in his lap, at least for the rest of the week. With any luck, that could be all the time he needed.

When Schultz held the report of the blood analysis in his hands, he had a feeling he couldn't explain—wouldn't even try—to anyone else. It was as though a thin shining thread ran from his hands out into the darkness, a shimmering cord that connected him to the killer. He would feel his way along the thread and at the other end he would confront a monster. He had gotten the same feeling once before, the only other time in his life he had worked a series of murders. That time, it had been a psychopath who burned the sex organs from young boys with a welding torch before crucifying them. Schultz had been on the case from the beginning, and he was there when the creep was hauled off and when the judge banged the gavel after reading the death sentence.

The other end of this thread was indistinct, fuzzy, almost as if it had multiple terminations. Could it be a group of wackos at work? Schultz shuddered. One thing he knew was that this killer would take more victims, and soon. He wondered how many more graphic photos would be taped to the blackboard in PJ's office before he worked his way to the end of the thread.

Crime studies showed that serial killers tended to kill in batches, usually of three victims, then mysteriously disappear, only to surface weeks or months or years later in a new locality. Then again, the patterns were loose, and whenever law enforcement officers tried to predict behavior, the results were inconclusive. These killers were people who by their very nature didn't fit the mold, who couldn't be grouped with the rest of humanity. The ones who were caught were usually caught because of an arrogant mistake. There was no telling how many acted out their fantasies for a lifetime and went to their own graves leaving behind a secret cache of victims far more ponderous than Jacob Marley's ghostly chains.

Schultz had other reasons for feeling good. When he got home last night around eight PM he found a note from his wife saying that her weekly card group had changed from Wednesday to Tuesday nights, so she wouldn't be home until after midnight and could he please take out the trash before he went to bed. He went out and got himself a hot meatball sandwich for dinner, with a bag of BBQ chips and a two-liter bottle of regular Coke replete with sugar and caffeine. He ate in the kitchen while reading the paper—a luxury, since Julia didn't like him to read at the table. He carefully bagged all the trash and took it out to the curb for pickup. Then Schultz took a long, hot shower, propped himself up on the bed with pillows, and mentally summoned Casey, the woman with the breathy voice from Vehicles. She was beautiful, adventurous, and remarkably sensitive to the time and attention needed to bring a man in his fifties to orgasm three times.

On top of all that, his arthritis wasn't bothering him much today.

He tucked a notebook and a pen in his shirt pocket. Whistling, he hit the road in his orange Pacer, one hand dealing with the idiosyncrasies of the stick shift and the other tightly gripping the steering wheel as the car crabbed down the street.

CHAPTER

8

Pauley Mac waited patiently in the dark in his 1991 red Dodge pickup. It was something at which he excelled, this waiting business. Dog could never have put up with it. In fact, the last time Dog had waited in the pickup, he had tested his teeth on the steering wheel. A disgusted Pauley Mac had covered it with one of those leather sheaths that laced up.

The truck was parked in an alley which gave Pauley Mac a view of the stage entrance of Powell Symphony Hall. Inside there was a performance going on, a ballet Pauley Mac did not know the name of and did not care about. The focus of his attention was the guest performer, a man named Ilya Vanitzky, whose picture he had seen in the paper. He was handsome, blonde, lithe, and skilled in an area of the arts yet untapped by Pauley Mac. The last item was the one that interested him. Pauley Mac was not concerned with the appearance of his victims, their charm or lack of, or their sex. He was on a shopping trip to acquire a set of skills, and their packaging was inconsequential to him as the labels on soup cans.

The newspaper article said that Vanitzky was known worldwide for his aerial abilities, leaps of uncommon height and grace. Pauley Mac considered it a stroke of luck that Vanitzky's performance schedule brought him to St. Louis during this particular killing cycle. He pictured himself sailing through the air, cartoonishly suspended at the top of a leap, given a special dispensation by the force of gravity.

My son, the human Mexican jumping bean, Pa said derisively in Pauley Mac's head. *Couldn't do jack-shit as a real man, wants to be some kind of faggot toe-twiddling dancer.*

Dog growled, and Pauley Mac complacently stepped aside as Dog put Pa back in his place, hounding him and snapping until Pa retreated.

Pauley Mac wanted to try something just a little different, something audacious, this time. He had gone to Powell Symphony Hall a couple of days ago, with his janitor uniform and props—a mop and a rolling bucket filled with dirty suds. He knew he was invisible dressed that way; busy performers rushing this way and that to rehearsals just didn't notice him, or anyone who looked like him. It was nothing personal. It never was.

He had been searching for a special place, a place where Dog could do his self-portrait quietly but within the ambiance of Powell Symphony Hall, which was as grand a place as he had ever seen. Eventually he found it, as he knew he would: a deserted dressing room at the end of a hallway. The door was unlocked, and inside there was a marvelous old style makeup table, with a mirror bordered on three sides by bare round light bulbs. He cleaned the mirror and wiped each of the bulbs before flipping the switch. Only a couple of the bulbs were burned out; the rest gave a marvelous light, just right for detail work. There was only one problem. Vanitzky would have to remain unconscious throughout. The walls seemed thin, and Pauley Mac did not want to risk any screams being heard in the more populated areas of the Hall. Dog wouldn't be able to fully enjoy the carving process.

A small price to pay, in a life full of terrible accommodations.

Getting Vanitzky into the empty dressing room was a puzzle Pauley Mac worked on for a couple of days. For the last two nights, he observed Vanitzky leaving by the very same stage door he now watched from the dark cave of the pickup's interior. Each time, the performer was met by a tall black-haired woman about twenty-five years old, who clung possessively to his arm and guided him to her car parked in a nearby lot. The two went back to his hotel, undoubtedly for more than a drink and small talk, and she left about two hours later.

Finally he settled on a plan. When the woman walked to the door, he would sneak up behind her, knock her out, and remove some article of her clothing, probably her underpants. Then he would meet Vanitzky at the door, make up some story that his woman had a pleasant surprise for him, wave the underpants close enough so that Vanitzky could pick up her juice smell, and tell him that he should wait in a certain out-of-the-way room for her.

You wouldn't want to miss this, no sir, he would say. *The door's unlocked, and inside you'll see a mirror, and in the mirror—well, that's part of the surprise.*

Headlights in the alley behind him brought him out of his fantasy. It could be a police car, and Pauley Mac had to be careful. He had all of his things with him tonight, all of the special things he needed to improve himself, resting on the passenger seat next to him. It wouldn't be good to be stopped by the police, especially hanging around in an alley where he had no plausible reason to be. He started the pickup and rolled slowly ahead. A sudden inspiration hit, and he rolled down the window and aimed the White Castle bag that contained the remnants of his dinner in the direction of an open Dumpster. The cops, if it was a cop car behind him, would think that he was just a night worker on the way to his janitor job or wherever who had been having a bite to eat before starting work. An uncharacteristically lucky toss, the bag hit the lid of the Dumpster and bounced in. Pauley Mac stuck his arm out the window and raised two fingers for the two-point shot. One of his victims—he really did prefer the term guest—

in a previous cycle was a college basketball player named Leonard Wolper.

Thanks, Lennie, you really came through for me that time, he thought.

There was no response. Lennie was kind of a sulker; in fact, he hadn't said a word since joining the assembly of voices in Pauley Mac's head.

Rolling up his window, Pauley Mac kept right on going out of the alley and made a right turn on Grand Avenue. The car behind him, which he could see clearly now under the street lights, was a police car. It turned left. Pauley Mac was acutely aware of the pickup's license plates, which spelled out BADDOG. It had been a delicious joke but an unconscionable moment of weakness when he got those plates. He hoped that the cops didn't make the tenuous connection between his license plates and the dog carving on the body of the pianist. He needed freedom of movement, and he didn't want to get rid of the pickup. As he drove home, he mulled over the idea of stealing a plate. But he had other things on his mind, more important things. It would be too dangerous to go back to the alley now and wait for the woman to come to the stage door. If he was caught in the alley again, the cops would remember that the pickup had been there earlier, and he couldn't very well get out of it by throwing another fast food bag.

This was already Friday evening. Tomorrow night was Vanitzky's last performance in St. Louis. If Pauley Mac wanted those dazzling leaps for his own, and he did, then it had to be tomorrow night.

Or tonight, at Vanitzky's hotel. Pauley Mac smiled. Time for Plan B. He only had to wait a couple of hours until the woman, with Vanitzky's come sliding down her thighs, left the hotel. He knew a lot of ways of getting into a hotel room. He had once been a room service waiter, studying hotel guests as he delivered covered trays. He would later imagine them feasting, gulping down the hot entrees in the privacy of their rooms, eating in the uninhibited manner of people who knew they weren't being watched, wiping their greasy hands and lips on the pristine napkins he folded into decorative shapes that only he could appreciate.

He flipped on the radio, and let Dog howl along with Elvis.

CHAPTER

9

P J took a bite of a doughnut and slurped some coffee that she had reheated in the microwave down the hall. It was too hot, and she knew right away that she had burned the tip of her tongue. It was late Friday evening, and tomorrow was going to be a busy day. She and Thomas were moving into the house she had rented. In one whirlwind shopping trip last night, she had purchased an entire houseful of modest furniture. She had brought very little with her from Denver: personal items, clothing, office things that were important to her like the Mickey Mouse clock, her computer, her collection of wildlife prints, and the odd assortment of prized possessions of a twelve-year-old. Her ex-husband Steven and his floozy Carla were living in her ex-house and sitting on her ex-furniture and having sex in her ex-bed, probably on her ex-favorite sheets. But that was in the past, she reminded herself. It had been her choice to leave Denver abruptly.

Thank goodness for MasterCard. Rather than deplete her cash which she was keeping for emergencies, she had charged the furniture. Some adjustment was necessary now that she was going to have to get by on one income, and a reduced one at that. But she took comfort in the fact that millions of single parents had walked that path before her, and they had found the inner resources to make things work out.

Her tongue still tingling from the hot coffee, she gazed in frustration at the computer screen. It was nearly eight PM. She had phoned Thomas at the motel hours ago and told him that she would be late. He had, miraculously, wanted to invite a friend over for the evening, a boy named Winston he had met at school. PJ hadn't met Winston yet, but she had given her approval, keeping her fingers crossed that the kid wouldn't turn out to be a junior terrorist or a smoker or something. Thomas had said that Winston liked computers and cats, so he couldn't be all bad.

She knew that Thomas still resented the move to St. Louis. He had not fit as seamlessly into school life as she had hoped, so the prospect of a friend for him was a bright spot. She hadn't been able to get beyond his antagonism in more than a superficial way, although she admitted to herself that she hadn't really been trying too hard this week. The time just didn't seem right for either of them to make any breakthroughs in their difficult relationship. PJ felt that once she demonstrated her worth at work, she would have the emotional energy to deal with Thomas. It had become important to her to prove to Wall and Schultz that hiring her was a good decision.

After the initial excitement of discovering the blood under the cat's claws, she seemed to be running in place. It was painfully obvious that Schultz was not just ignoring her, but doing it gleefully. After putting in long hours in her tiny office, she made some progress profiling the killer and developing a sketchy VR for the crime scene. But her playbacks still seemed crude and jerky due to their hasty development, and didn't seem to be shedding any light on the investigation.

With parental thoughts buzzing around in the back of her mind, she tried to focus on the simulation she was putting together. The demonstration for Wall had gone well this afternoon, at least from his viewpoint. He was amazed because he had never seen VR techniques applied to crime scene analysis before, so anything would have looked good to him. But PJ knew the potential of what she was doing, and she knew how far she was from realizing it. For several years she had been interested in computerized simulations as an extension of her work in marketing research. She had developed, in her free time, an advanced program which allowed her to define a world by scanning in photos or drawings. The computer would then extrapolate the two-dimensional input into three-dimensional representations, first in black and white wire-frame mode, and then in solid form, with colors and realistic shading. It was her own personally-developed software which she brought with her to this new job, and which had left Wall practically speechless, an accomplishment she cherished.

Regardless of how convincing she could make the three-dimensional effect, it was still on a flat screen, and she couldn't really get *into* the virtual world that way. She needed a crucial piece of hardware for the next step, a piece that the Department didn't have. It wasn't likely to be made available in the forseeable future, either. She needed a Head-Mounted Display—HMD—to really take the user inside this virtual world.

PJ was the type who hated to go home until she got to a natural stopping point in her work. She had been plugging away all evening, trying to resolve what she felt should be a simple issue. How did the indentations in the carpet in the murdered man's apartment relate to the murder? She popped the rest of the doughnut—a double mouthful—in her mouth, and almost simultaneously heard a soft knocking on her door. She hastily swallowed, using the hot coffee to wash down the soggy lump. "Come in," she said, licking icing from her fingers. "The door's open."

It was Schultz, and he looked for all the world like a downtrodden peasant from fifteenth-century Europe. All he needed to complete the picture was a change of clothes and a bow slung over his back. His ebullience and semi-camaraderie of three days ago had leached away. She was about to remark on his appearance when she remembered that a Schultz who wasn't gleeful was a Schultz who had made no progress.

The killer could be closing in on his next victim right now, tonight. PJ could practically feel the killer's breath hot on her neck, and she knew that Schultz felt it too. Her work was more than an intellectual exercise.

"Sit down, Detective, and I'll put on a fresh pot of coffee. You look like you could use some."

Schultz sat down heavily and stretched his legs out in front of him. PJ went through the mechanics of measuring and pouring, letting him get settled. Out of the corner of her eye she saw him pop two or three small pills into his mouth and swallow them dry. As the warm, reassuring smell of coffee began to fill the office, she sat down and faced him.

"Nobody saw anything," he said. "Nobody heard anything. Everybody must have had their heads up their asses not only during the murder but for two days before and after."

"Nothing turned up in the interviews?"

"Is there an echo in here?" He accepted a cup of coffee and sipped it noisily. "We talked to all the other tenants in Burton's building and a few on either side. Dave and Anita make a good team. I sent them around together. Dave's not real high wattage, if you get my meaning. I can't picture him as anything but a patrol officer, a good solid cop who knows his job and does it day in and day out. Anita, though, she'll make a good detective, in ten, twenty years. God, they're young. Anita looks like a little elf who should be helping Santa out at the North Pole."

PJ saw some animation in his face as he talked about his assistants.

"Anyway," he continued, "no suspicious freaks hanging around, no unusual noises, nobody seen entering or leaving the apartment. Got any more doughnuts?" He was rummaging around in the bag on PJ's desk as he asked the question, and was rewarded with a chocolate long john.

"Christ, Doc, you've got lousy taste in doughnuts. Nothing beats those sugared jellies."

"I'll have to remember that the next time I buy doughnuts for you. After all, I did pick these out for myself," PJ said. "Burton's apartment faces the rear of the building and the steps lead up from the alley. Are you surprised that no one witnessed anything?"

"Shit no. I'd be surprised if any of those tenants witnessed their own turds."

"Well, there you are."

"There I am and there you are, too, Doc. Or did you forget you're running this show? Speaking of shows, how'd the dog and pony one go?"

"It went great. In fact, if you have a few minutes, I'd like to give you the same demo Howard got."

"Yeah, I got some time. I just came in to look over the photos again, see if I missed anything. Besides, the sooner I go home, the sooner my wife can put my balls in the vise she keeps on the night stand. Then my shit-for-brains son can come along and tighten the screw."

PJ didn't know whether she was expected to laugh or not. Wall had not briefed her on Schultz's home life. Presumably they would learn things about each other the more they worked together. For the moment, she assumed his home life left something to be desired.

Well, so does mine. We've got a little something in common, Detective.

She cleared her throat and turned to the computer.

She closed the simulation she had been working on and made selections to start over, using manual intervention again. She had been using manual mode all evening, so that she could examine the shapes of the furniture in the apartment. She had been trying to rotate an item or combine two or more items to make the pattern of indentations in the carpet.

Schultz seemed to be daydreaming, so she swiveled the monitor more in his direction and tapped it with her fingernail. He had a terrific ability to tune out when computers were involved, an ability she wished she had to apply to other things, such as her son's favorite CD.

"Let me give you a little background first," she said. He focused on her with a dutiful but glazed look on his face. "Really, Detective, someone of your intelligence should be able to follow this easily." She was rewarded with a scowl, but he did seem more alert.

"Virtual Reality refers to a customized environment created within a computer's memory. It could be the interior of a starship, Alice's Wonderland, or a murder scene. There are two ways to experience it. You can simply watch the world on the computer screen, where all the people are three inches high and you're seeing them as an outside observer. Or you can enter the world using an HMD. A Head-Mounted Display, or headset, is worn like a helmet. Inside are two small computer screens which project images to each eye separately so that the mind interprets three-dimensional vision. Remember those old View-Masters that kids use?"

Schultz nodded. "My son had one of those a long time ago. Kept breaking the little picture wheels."

"Same idea. You see only the world that the computer puts right in your face, and it looks real. Advanced HMD's have motion sensors. As you turn your head, the view the computer gives you changes accordingly. So you can look around. You can also move in any direction, using a joystick to control direction and speed. Sophisticated systems replace the joystick with a glove that detects finger and hand movement and translates it into movement through the virtual world, and also allows you to manipulate virtual objects. In the future there might be entire body suits or special treadmills so you can simply walk in the direction you want to go."

PJ gestured at the computer setup in front of her. "We don't have an HMD to use, although my software can handle it. I'd like to get my hands on one, but for now all we can do is observe the two-dimensional Virtual Reality, or VR. I'll step through this in manual, so we can follow it closely. There is an automated mode, where the computer tries to put together all the known parameters in a smooth run-through, making logical extrapolations. Unlike most Virtual Reality simulations, mine has a smidgen of artificial intelligence. More than a smidgen, actually."

She pointed at the screen. "Here's the outside of the door. There wasn't any sign of forced entry, so we have to assume that Burton opened the door voluntarily." The large screen showed a 3D view of the porch and the stairs leading up from the alley. A male figure dressed in jeans and a work shirt began to climb the stairs. He wasn't a stick figure or a flat paper doll type, but a rounded, shaded miniature person. Even though he was only three inches high, you could practically reach out and pinch his arm and expect him to say ouch. PJ was justifiably proud of the people who inhabited her virtual worlds. The man on the screen was carrying a long, thin package. He moved in a generally lifelike fashion, but was a little jerky moving up the stairs. His legs left blurs of motion on the screen, and his arms pumped out of cadence with his legs. PJ winced.

That should be fixed by now, she thought.

Then she glanced at Schultz. His eyes were open wide, and he was staring fixedly at the screen.

"What is this?" he said. "Some kind of video game?"

She should have found his comment exasperating, but somehow it did not bother her. It was too sincere. She paused the simulation, and the figure halted, one foot raised to climb the next stair. "No, it's a representation of the crime scene and the sequence of events that happened there. It also gives us a chance to look at things from different perspectives and try out different ways the crime could have happened."

"Who's that guy on the stairs?"

"He's the killer, a composite figure I call Genman, for generic man. I've also got a Genfem and a Genkid. In this case, I entered some parameters about the suspect based on a psychological profile I'm working up. Until we have more to go on, the killer is male, white, thirty-plus years old, slim, height about five-nine, average features, the blend-into-the-crowd type."

Schultz shrugged. PJ restarted the action. Genman knocked on the door. A voice behind the door asked who it was, and Genman responded that he had flowers to deliver. As the door began to open, PJ stole another look at Schultz. He was nodding slightly; evidently he agreed with her theory that the killer got inside the apartment by claiming to be a delivery man from a florist. The red rosebuds that were in Burton's apartment had not been delivered by any local florist. PJ believed that they were left behind by the killer, even arranged using gloved fingers in a vase that belonged to Burton, to taunt the police.

When the door opened, Genman pushed his way into the room, shoving Burton back into the area just to the right of the door, where there was a sofa and a couple of chairs. There were a couple more glitches in the simulation during which the figures swayed in lazy arcs. The long thin box Genman had been carrying was carelessly tossed on the floor, spilling red rose buds onto the plush blue-gray carpet. PJ heard Schultz grunt as he noticed that the Burton figure actually looked like Burton.

"What the hell? That guy . . ."

"Yes, he looks like the victim. I scanned a photo into the computer and superimposed it on another Genman. Once I do that, the customized Genman is fully operational with Burton's features—eyes open and close, lips move, and so on. Not that it's perfect. Sometimes it looks a little like one of those dubbed Japanese monster movies. I can do the same kind of thing with the furniture, scanning in the shots of the apartment so that the sofa really is Burton's sofa rather than an approximation generated from the information we recorded. But I haven't had time yet."

On the screen, an eerily lifelike Burton stumbled back

over an end table, knocking it over and himself to the floor. While he was down, Genman stood over him, drew a small pry bar from his waistband, and struck him on the head. Burton closed his eyes—rather melodramatically, PJ thought, making a note to herself to review the routine that controlled movement of the facial features—and slipped into unconsciousness. Since the victim's head was not recovered, PJ postulated that the killer got control of the situation by a blow to the head. Burton was a substantial man, and wouldn't have been easy to tie up while he was struggling.

Then the computer simulation followed his movement into the kitchen, switching rooms so that the kitchen was now displayed in 3D. Genman paused, inexplicably with his head on backward for a few seconds, and looked around the kitchen while donning gloves, the thin latex kind used in thousands of medical offices. Schultz had told her that the killer had been smart enough—or lucky enough—to choose gloves that weren't too thin. Most people didn't realize that fingerprints could actually be left through ultra thin gloves if the wearer had well-defined ridges on the tips of his fingers.

In the kitchen, Genman encountered the cat, which was sitting on the countertop. As he approached, the cat flattened itself, skipping the arched-back bluff posture and going directly to a fearful, all-out defense. Genman veered toward the cat, which struck out viciously with its front paws as soon as he was close enough. A bloody gash appeared on Genman's arm, and the cat took advantage of the distraction to disappear in the boxes under the kitchen table. Genman snatched up the kitchen towel—missing from the apartment—and wrapped it around his forearm.

Schultz scowled as Genman, now with his head facing properly forward, picked up a kitchen chair and carried it back into the living room. Then he returned to the kitchen and rooted through the drawers, coming up with a heavy cleaver and a paring knife that glittered on the screen as he held it up. PJ knew that Schultz was scowling because he didn't agree with her reasoning that the killer obtained the weapons from Burton's kitchen.

Back in the living room, the killer placed the chair a few feet from the sofa, dragged Burton into it, and secured Burton's arms and legs with two lengths of clothesline, the old-fashioned white rope kind, from his pockets. At that point, PJ halted the simulation.

"I've been trying to figure out what happened next. I have a strong feeling that those indentations in the carpet are important, but I just can't figure out the how or why of it."

Schultz looked thoughtful. She expected some sort of compliment, but it wasn't forthcoming.

"Doc, I'm trying and trying, but I just can't see how this cartoon stuff is going to help us get that creep off the street. It's not telling me anything I didn't know already. And it is telling me a few things I think are wrong."

PJ recognized his reference to the killer getting the weapons from the kitchen. She sighed. "I think it's valuable. Howard thinks it's valuable, and so does the captain, or I wouldn't be sitting here. You just don't have an open mind about it."

She met his gaze. There was more than defiance there, more than a bad mood, more than aching joints. There was something she never expected to see in Schultz's eyes: fear of the unknown. It dawned on her suddenly that his attitude was a cover-up for an insecurity about technological advances. All around him, police work was moving into areas that he had no experience with and that younger members of the Department took to like kittens to yarn.

He's worried about being left behind. He's worried about being seen as a dinosaur. Maybe he's right to be worried.

She closed her eyes for a moment. "Detective, I know this approach must seem strange to you. I assure you that the kind of work you do is not just valuable but essential. Maybe no one's ever told you that straight out. What we're trying to do here is develop a tool to help you and others like you, not replace you."

She saw a flicker of reassurance in his eyes, but it died immediately.

"That would be like replacing Sherlock Holmes with a toaster," he said. "Not that I figure I'm in the same league as old Sherlock, but then again, that computer can't make breakfast either."

"Actually it could, by controlling . . . Never mind. Detective, don't you have something else to do? Or at least somewhere else to go?"

"Yeah, I do. You're the one who asked me if I had a few minutes. I'll be at my desk," he said, pointedly looking around at her office, "going over some photos of the scene. Give me a holler if you need anything." He rose, leaning on the desk and favoring his left knee. He paused in the doorway and turned for a parting remark.

"Speaking of somewhere else to go, Doc, don't you have a home life?"

PJ pointed grimly at the door, like the Ghost of Christmas Yet to Come, and Schultz ambled through.

Life in the Department was routinely unusual, an oxymoron that people in Schultz's line of work would nod at and accept, and he had weathered stranger happenings. In spite of his bluster about the computer, he had been amazed at what he had seen, not that he would let on to Doc. It made him feel excited about the future of police work and sad that he was not really going to be a part of that future—he was winding down to retirement, betrayed both by his arthritic knees and an accumulation of the poison that society had been injecting into his veins for decades.

But here he was, doing field work again, sensing that shining thread that led out into the darkness to the mind and heart of the killer, to a man who was not really human even though he certainly wasn't unique in the human experience.

Maybe the old man wasn't ready for the scrap heap yet.

Schultz sighed and lowered himself into his chair, which squealed in protest under his weight like a skittish horse. His knees ached, and he opened the second desk drawer on the left and took out an unmarked brown pill bottle. After checking to see if anyone was watching—*stupid shit, nobody's around down here but me and Doc, and that's because neither of us have the sense to go home*—he nestled four ibuprofen tablets in his large palm and swallowed them with coffee.

It wasn't unusual for Schultz to be in the building at this time, when the night shift alternately dozed and worked in frantic bursts of activity. He and Julia had lost the intimacy of their earlier married life. They lived together now as a practical arrangement, although sometimes even that seemed precarious to Schultz. His twenty-five-year-old son, Rick, seemed to have no career prospects other than petty thievery.

Schultz would never openly acknowledge the loneliness he felt to PJ or anyone else, or the secret dream he had that there should be something more to life, even for a man in his mid-fifties who had seen more pain than anyone should.

This case had high personal stakes for Schultz, not only because he wanted to bring the killer to justice, but because he wanted to prove that he could still do field work. He sensed, behind PJ's defensive posture, that the stakes were high for her also—she had a great deal to prove about herself and to herself. He understood and respected that.

But he didn't plan to make it easy.

He removed a large brown envelope from his desk drawer and laid out the contents across his desk. It was a copy of the file set of photos of Burton's apartment and its depressing contents, including Burton himself. He went over them in detail, trying to reconstruct the murder, trying to inch his way down the thread. After fifteen minutes or so, the ibuprofen started working on his knees and he felt more relaxed. He crossed his arms on his desk, lowered his head, and slept.

A hand on his shoulder woke him. It was PJ, and she was clearly excited about something. Glancing at the clock on the wall, he saw that it was only nine-fifteen, less than an hour after he had left her.

He went with her back to her office. She flitted down the hall while he plodded along behind. The office still smelled of coffee and doughnuts, and the cone of light from her desk lamp drew him away from the edges of the room, which were gloomy and ill-defined. Once again she swiveled the computer screen so that it faced in his direction.

"Remember I said that my software had an automatic mode that was boosted by AI?"

"Say that again, Doc, and pretend you're talking to a human being this time, OK?"

The comment rolled right off her. "All right. When you were in here earlier, I was using the manual mode to step through the virtual crime scene. I mentioned that there is also an auto mode, which directs the computer to fill in unknown events—to use its imagination, I guess you could say. I was getting ready to go home, and I decided to try a quick auto run to test out some changes I made in the facial expression routine. The results were interesting. I want you to see this. Don't say a word. Just watch."

Schultz obediently nodded. She made a couple of selections rapidly from the drop-down menus. Once again, the screen showed a 3D view of the porch and the stairs. Genman climbed the stairs, carrying the box containing the flowers, and knocked on the door. Burton asked who it was, and Genman gave his spiel about delivering flowers. The door opened and Genman forced his way in, spilling the flowers onto the floor. Burton stumbled back and fell. Genman hit him on the head with the pry bar, then stood over the prone man and pulled on latex gloves. It was all the same as it had been before. Schultz was about to say so when PJ hushed him and pointed back to the screen.

Instead of going into the kitchen, Genman left the apartment. He went back down to the alley and opened the passenger door of a stylized car which was not recognizable as any particular model. He removed a large gray case about as tall as his arm was long. It looked substantial, but he had no difficulty carrying it back up the stairs, so it must have been either empty or simply lighter than it looked. Once back in the apartment, he locked the door and went into the kitchen. The display followed him there, into the room piled with cardboard boxes. He encountered the cat, wrapped his bloodied arm in the kitchen towel, and picked up one of the kitchen chairs.

Back in the living room, the killer placed the chair a few feet from the sofa, dragged Burton to it, hefted him with difficulty, and sat him up with his legs straddling the back of the chair. He secured Burton's arms and legs with two lengths of clothesline from his pockets. Then Genman positioned the gray case next to the chair and unlatched the lid. He took out a rolled vinyl case tied with string and a large item wrapped in brown paper. He put the large package down on the floor and removed the paper. A gleaming, wicked-looking cleaver was revealed, the kind that you might find in a Japanese steak house. He sat down on the large carrying case, putting himself at the right height to work on Burton's back. Then he put the rolled vinyl case on his lap and took from it a small cutting tool. At that point, PJ reached for the mouse. She double-clicked on the vinyl case. The motion halted and a description appeared in the upper left corner, along with an enlarged view of the open case.

It was a set of sculptor's tools, with straight and curved blades of varying lengths and thicknesses, some for crude stone work and some for exacting detail.

PJ clicked again, and Genman resumed his grim business. He carved rapidly on Burton's back, his arm moving in a blur.

"This isn't real time," she said, speaking almost in a whisper. "The computer analyzed the detail of the carving and indicated that it took about an hour and a half. I requested a hundred-to-one speedup on this part of the simulation, so it will take about fifty-four seconds."

Genman changed tools repeatedly in a cartoon-like speeded up way, and blood dripped rapidly on the carpet. Somewhere along the line Burton had regained consciousness, and occasionally he moved, arching his back in pain and throwing back his head. His soft moans were silenced with a click of the mouse as PJ muted the sound. Schultz was surprised to find himself relieved that he could no longer hear the man's agony. Although his logical mind knew that this was only a simulation, he was caught up in what he was seeing, and thought of the representation on the screen as Burton. After all, it had Burton's face. He was acutely uncomfortable watching the events on the screen, even though the movements were speeded up a hundred times, which made them look jerky and artificial.

It was a long fifty-four seconds.

Genman's hands slowed and returned to normal speed. He stood and admired his work. From within the large case, he drew a small thirty-five millimeter camera and took several pictures, starting a dozen feet away and ending with a close-up of the carving.

PJ spoke, startling Schultz. "Serial killers often take souvenirs or photos or both of their crimes. That's part of the psychological profile I entered."

Genman put the camera back and took out a black plastic trash bag and set it on the floor. He picked up the cleaver.

Schultz fought the urge to turn his eyes away from the screen. His heartbeat thudded in his ears and he tasted bile at the back of his throat. The hairs on his arms rose as he watched the three-inch figures on the screen perform their deadly duet.

Burton was conscious. He knew what was coming, and he struggled with the ropes as only those who smelled death in the air around them could.

Genman stood up, grasped Burton's hair, and stretched his neck. With a smooth, practiced swing, he severed the head. The body convulsed, tied in the chair, as Genman held the head over the already blood-soaked carpet to let it drain. When the blood flow diminished, which was surprisingly soon, Genman maneuvered the head into the bag and sealed it.

The tools were meticulously cleaned with white towels and then placed into the large carrying case along with the red-stained towels, the kitchen towel which had stanched the flow of blood from the wound given by the cat, and the head. Genman latched the case and carried it over to the apartment door. The view momentarily left Genman and zoomed in on the carpet, showing the four indentations. The killer's weight had pressed the rubber feet of the carrying case into the pile.

Genman noticed the flowers on the floor. In the kitchen he opened cabinets until he found a cut glass vase. He filled it with water and took it back into the living room, where he arranged the red rosebuds artlessly and stood the vase on a marble-top table.

The case was heavier on the way out. Genman toted it down the stairs with both hands and put it back into the passenger seat of the car. The screen went black.

Schultz breathed out noisily. His face was hot, and he was certain he looked flushed. "That's some story you've got there."

"Yes. It affected me, too," she said simply. Schultz glanced at her. He could tell that was an understatement. The tightness of the skin around her eyes and mouth made her true feelings apparent.

"Can you show me that carrying case again? I'd like to see it close up."

"Sure." PJ ran the simulation back a short way, until the case was on the screen. She double-clicked on it. The enlarged view showed first the outside and then the inside, padded with gray foam shaped in a bumpy pattern. The text indicated that it was a hard-shell case used to carry photographic equipment or large slide projectors, the kind that have a built-in screen for presentations.

Schultz stood and found that his legs were shaking. "I don't know about you, Doc, but I've got to get away from this place for awhile. Let this whole thing sink in. See what comes of it after a night's sleep." He met her eyes, and saw that excitement had replaced the sadness of a few moments ago. It was a feeling he knew well: the excitement of the chase.

"Come on, Leo. That was the most dramatic thing you've ever seen. Don't I get a few words of encouragement, or even some faint praise?"

"Let's not rush it. There are some good ideas there, but don't underestimate good old-fashioned detective work."

"And you're just the good old-fashioned detective to do it."

"Damn straight."

"Well, that part about the night's sleep sounds good to me," PJ said. "I'm famished, though. Can I take you to dinner first, before we split up? Kind of celebrate?"

"I'm not sure what we'd be celebrating, and no dame takes this married man out to dinner."

"Tell you what. You know this city a lot better than I do. You choose the place, and I'll pay."

"We split the bill," Schultz said, already halfway out the door, "and I'm not sure I know the kind of places where shrinks congregate. Especially brainy female shrinks."

"Why, Leo, I didn't know you cared."

He ducked his head back into the office to scowl at her, but she was on the phone with her son.

"Tuck yourself in," she said in a soft voice, "and I'll give you a kiss on the cheek when I get home. Miss you."

The scowl slid off his face like syrup sliding off a stack of pancakes, and he was stabbed by a longing for close family ties, intimacy, or just a sincere "miss you" on the phone. He put his hands in his pockets and hurried off down the hallway, leaving her to catch up with him.

CHAPTER

10

They ended up at Millie's Diner, an unpretentious place with chrome-legged stools, glass sugar dispensers with shiny tops, the kind with little flaps that always dumped out too much sugar, and black-and-white checkerboard linoleum. PJ wasn't exactly sure what the difference was between linoleum and vinyl flooring, but she was certain that the floor of Millie's Diner was linoleum. It had just begun to rain outside, and flashes of lightning stopped the rain drops in midair and froze the wetness in rivulets as it ran down the large windows. The rivulets formed a pattern on the window that reminded PJ of the veins and arteries in the Visible Man she had put together as a child. She had been fascinated with the plastic man, with his hands spread as if in supplication and his see-through abdomen that opened so that the organs could be removed and studied, and the tantalizing but undetailed bulge of his groin.

There were a few customers at scattered tables, but no one at the counter. PJ would have preferred one of the tables near the windows, but Schultz headed directly for the counter and she trailed along like a baby duck following Mama.

"Hey, babe," Schultz said to the woman behind the counter, "saunter over here and take our order, willya? A guy could starve to death in here."

The woman shot him an icy stare and returned her attention to her order pad. Apparently it contained something fascinating, because it was a full five minutes before she approached them. PJ passed the time listening to her stomach rumbling and flipping open the flap on the sugar dispenser with her fingernail and letting it fall.

Tink.

"Yeah, what'll it be, you old coot? And where'd you get this looker? She don't seem like your style. Too classy." In a theatrical aside to PJ, she said, "Say, Dearie, you sure you want to sit next to this guy? I always got to wipe the stool with disinfectant after he leaves. The floor, sometimes, too."

By now PJ had caught on that this was familiar territory for both of them. No response was really expected of her. She settled down to enjoy the exchange.

Tink.

"This place could use some class, and I'm not just talking about the food. This is Doctor Penelope Jennifer Gray," he said, rolling out the syllables of her name so that they impressed even her. He looked directly at PJ. "This, in case it isn't obvious, is Millie, the owner of this so-called eating establishment."

"Pleased to meet you," PJ said.

Tink.

"I'll have a double burger," Schultz said, "and don't give me one of those paper-thin slices of tomato this time. Christ, you must get a hundred slices out of one tomato. And a decent-sized serving of fries, which means more than I can count on one hand." As Schultz spoke, Millie poured him a cup of coffee.

"Yessir, Your Majesty Sir, this time I'll only get fifty slices out of the tomato. Got a rotten one I been saving for you anyway." Millie looked expectantly at PJ.

"May I see the menu, please?" PJ asked.

Millie shot a triumphant look at Schultz. "There, you see, that's class. You should take notes."

Schultz wasn't the least bit fazed. "Double burger. When you can spare the time."

After PJ looked over the menu, she ordered a double burger, an order of fries, and a chocolate milkshake. Schultz nodded approvingly. They talked about the weather until the food arrived. It came on heavy white china plates and was adorned with Millie's trademark, a toothpick holding a tiny flag aloft over the bun. In spite of Schultz's degrading remarks, her burger was delicious, if a little greasy. There was a veritable mountain of fries, and the slice of tomato was about three-quarters of an inch thick.

"So, Detective," PJ said as she twirled a fry in ketchup, "what do you think of CHIP now?"

"Same thing that I thought yesterday and the day before. Video games are no substitute for honest police work."

PJ decided to ignore the jab about video games. "You mean that what you just saw in my office didn't give you any ideas? Didn't help the investigation?"

"We saw one scenario. There are others."

"You are a stubborn ass."

"And proud of it. Just ask Millie."

"You seemed more enthusiastic back in the office. In fact, I seem to recall that you were genuinely affected."

"I get affected by porno movies too, but that doesn't help solve murder cases."

Exasperated, PJ paused for a moment. She ran her tongue over the roof of her mouth, feeling the coating of grease.

"How would you like to play the part of the killer?" she said. "Be right in the action?"

"I don't get any thrills offing people, Doc."

"That's not what I meant. I mean that the next step for the simulation would be to put you in the world and let you move around like the killer did, seeing what he saw."

"I have only two words to say about that: video game."

"If you're so dead set against using computers on this case, why did you get involved?" PJ said. "Why did Howard put you on CHIP?"

"You want a truthful answer to that?"

"Of course. I think I have a right to know."

Schultz paused. "Well, I guess you'd find out anyway. I took this assignment because it looked like the only way I could get back into field work. I'm not cut out to be a desk jockey, and that's what I've been for the past ten years."

"Oh? What happened then? Step on the boss's toes?"

Schultz grunted. "Don't be fooled by Lieutenant Wall's sweet face. He's got balls of steel, and toes, too." Schultz slurped his coffee noisily. PJ could hear the quiet hum of other conversations around the diner but no distinct words. A gust of wind blew rain against the window. Millie walked by to deliver a gigantic slice of apple pie to a customer. Schultz waved at her, pointed at the pie and held up two fingers. When he continued, his voice was steady and low. "I got a black mark against me when my partner got killed back then. No formal charges, nothing like that, but the Department's a weird place. Not like out in society where you're supposed to be innocent until proven guilty. The guys just closed ranks, and all of a sudden I was on the outside of the circle looking in."

"How did your partner get killed?"

"Christ, Doc, you want it all at once, don't you."

"I'm a psychologist. I'm accustomed to hearing everything in a one hour session. Doesn't foster patience."

"Vince and I had this creep nailed for burglary, had an informant who saw him peddling the hot stuff from the back of his pickup and bragging how he was going to rob himself enough to open a warehouse. Anyway, we went to his apartment. We had this guy figured for a lamb, thought he would get spooked and try to run out the back when the cops knocked on his door. So I sent Vince to the front door and I went around back myself. Vince was just a kid.

He was twenty-eight. Hell, my son's almost that old now. I went up the fire escape. That's when I made my second mistake for the day."

"What was the first one?"

"I didn't check this creep out enough. Turns out pushing hot VCR's was just a sideline for him. He was a dealer, had a stash in his place worth maybe five hundred thousand."

"He wasn't a lamb, then?"

"No. My second mistake was when I poked my head up to the window to see what was going on. There was a frosted window that was open three, four inches, and I figured it was the bathroom. I don't know what I was thinking, maybe that I could get in quietly from the back. I took a quick look and ducked back down. I saw the creep in the bathroom, his back to me. I saw his face in the mirror. He was shaving. I didn't think he saw me because he acted real cool. Didn't jerk his head around, didn't even look sideways. Cool. How was I supposed to know he was in the bathroom? I didn't know what else to do, so I tried a second look. That's when I knew he had seen me."

The two slices of pie arrived, and Schultz stopped talking while Millie refilled his coffee cup. PJ inhaled the apple pie scent, closed her eyes, and let the memories flow: floured hands, spiral peels of apples, open jars of spices, crimping the edges of the crust together with her fingers as her mother guided her eager hands. She brought a forkful to her mouth.

"Good pie," she mumbled to Millie around the mouthful.

"Thanks, Dearie," Millie responded. She directed her cutting gaze at Schultz, who sat with eyes downcast. "Class."

"So what happened?" PJ asked after Millie left.

"When I took a second look, he was gone. That's when I knew I had spooked him toward Vince. Not to me, like it should have been, but to Vince. I went in through the bathroom window. I heard the shotgun blasts, two of them. Vince took it in the chest and in the face. Never had a chance. I took the creep down, shot him right through the heart while he stood looking down at Vince." He paused, raised his eyes. PJ saw a hint of fire in them. A cold fire.

"Self-defense, of course," he said.

"Of course."

"After that, nobody was anxious to be my partner. Big surprise there. I did some desk work while Internal Affairs checked me out for use of deadly force without cause. They couldn't make anything stick, but by then I was an outsider. Never was able to get back in. Worked a few cases solo, but just couldn't seem to get the fire lit again."

PJ nodded. As a psychologist, she knew there were many variations of job burnout, and those who worked in law enforcement experienced the whole range.

"When Howard talked to me about this assignment, I got so excited I nearly crapped in my pants. Seems like the fire was still there after all. But I have to tell you, I intended to have as little to do with you and the computer as possible. After a week, I still feel that way, at least about the computer."

"I guess I should be flattered I'm not lumped in with the computer."

"Now it's your turn on the hot seat. What brought you here to St. Louis? How'd you ever get involved in police work? You know, you're not exactly the typical grist for the Department mill."

"Detective, I know this is going to seem like I'm trying to evade your questions, but I really need to get back to my hotel now. I'm tired, and I want to see my son. We can talk again some other time."

"Yeah, isn't that typical shrink talk. I spill my guts and

you button up. At least give me the Reader's Digest version, OK? And no bullshit."

PJ laughed. "You mean condensed? All right, in one hundred words or less, and no bullshit. I moved here to get away from my ex-husband. We just got divorced. He was fooling around with another woman young enough to be his daughter. I took this job primarily because I wanted to use the VR software I developed. Now that I'm here, I feel like I might be able to do something worthwhile, help people, fight crime, that sort of thing. I have a son who probably blames me for breaking up his happy family. I can sense your dedication, but I find you infuriating at times, and it's all I can do not to pick up the computer and bop you over the head with it."

"Fair enough. But I still expect the full story sometime." Schultz was rummaging in his pockets. He came up with some folded bills, and motioned Millie over to the counter. PJ and Schultz paid separately. PJ left a dollar tip tucked under her pie plate. Schultz left a quarter, explaining that he didn't want Millie to think he liked the food. Or the service, for that matter.

"It's nearly midnight," he said as they prepared to dash through the rain to their cars. "I'll see you back to the hotel."

"Oh, you don't have to do that. It's out of your way."

"Don't give me any sass, Doc. I'll follow you. When you get to the parking lot, stay in your locked car until I get there. We'll walk in together."

PJ thought his suggestion was very strange. She was sure the hotel was in a nice area. But if he wanted to play Mr. Protector, she had no objections.

He opened the door. She thought he was opening it for her, and she moved forward. Instead, she almost collided with him as he pushed his bulk through ahead of her and took off at a fast walk. She heard his voice drifting back through the rain.

"You just wouldn't believe some of the things that go on in hotels these days."

Pauley Mac tapped on the hotel suite door. "Room service."

There was a pause. Pauley Mac was certain that Ilya Vanitzky was checking him out through the peephole in the door. He smiled, confident that his bearing, his outfit, and the tray he was carrying would pass inspection. After all, he had done this before, though with different intentions.

"I didn't order anything."

Aware of the peephole, Pauley Mac made a show of checking an order ticket. "This is room 468, right? An order was placed fifteen minutes ago. Chocolate covered strawberries."

"Was the person who ordered named Katrina?"

"Don't know. Tall woman, mid-twenties, dark hair. Paid cash. Could I bring these in now, sir?"

"Yes, of course. One moment, please." There was a certain sensual warmth in the voice, in spite of the neutral content. Perhaps Katrina was more than a two-night stand.

The door opened to reveal a handsome man in a bathrobe, hair wet from the shower. "Put them on the table."

Pauley Mac strode confidently into the room. He expected Vanitzky to follow him over to the table, letting the door close, but he didn't. He simply stood there, dripping, with the door open to the hallway.

"Could I get you to sign this ticket," Pauley Mac said, "to show that the delivery was made?"

That did it. Vanitzky let go of the door, which closed automatically, and came over to the table. As he obediently bent to sign, Pauley Mac struck him on the back of the head with the paperweight he had concealed in his pocket.

He had used the paperweight before, and was quite fond of it. It was a pewter statue of a horned toad, squat and substantial, with thick, pointed projections down the spine. It had belonged to Pa, and heaven only knows what he used to do with it. Pa certainly wasn't talking.

Pauley Mac's internal chorus chattered like housewives at a coffee klatch. Some voices, darkly emotional ones, urged him on. Others screamed at him to stop, that what he was doing was wrong, and that there was still time to walk away from it—walk away from everything, stop the killings, go somewhere and start over. But the dark voices, with Dog to shore them up, won out every time. Pauley Mac wondered what would happen if he invited in a guest who was as strong-willed as Dog.

No way, good lay, fat chance, bitches dance, came Dog's throaty sing-song, slicing through the babble. *Cut butt, slice nice, slide glide.* Now that the first blow had been struck and the outcome of tonight's work was a certainty, a wild animal excitement took hold of him. Pauley Mac felt the hot flush and stiffening between his legs, and Dog moved his hips, thrusting them into the air. He yanked open the zipper on his black slacks and stroked his erection frantically. Pauley Mac was barely able to propel himself into the bathroom and grab a washcloth to avoid spilling his come on Vanitzky's prone form. He stuffed the sticky cloth into his pocket along with the pewter toad.

From the other pocket, he pulled surgeon's gloves and put them on. Taking the key, which was one of those plastic cards with a combination punched into it, from the top of the television, he went down a back stairwell and out to his pickup. The storm that had been threatening earlier was in full swing, with lightning splitting the sky and rain driving hard, finding its way down the back of his neck as he dashed to the truck. On the way back he got even wetter because he couldn't go at a full run. He carried a large black case, a cube about twenty inches on a side, back up to the suite. It was almost midnight, and the halls were deserted.

Schultz pulled into the hotel parking lot right next to PJ's Rabbit. He thought the cars made a good pair, his reddish-orange Pacer and her Rabbit convertible in blue which had faded practically to gray. The door on the driver's side of the Rabbit flew open and PJ ran for the lobby. Cursing under his breath, he took off after her. The ache in his knees was back, and his left leg was too stiff to make good time. She beat him to the lobby.

"What's the idea?" he said, trying to catch his breath. "I told you to wait in the car."

"I can take care of myself. I shouldn't even have let you come."

"Yeah, well, creeps wait in parking lots for good-looking dames like you. How'd you like some jerk to grab you by the throat and have your skirt up over your head before you get a chance to scream?"

PJ looked defiant. "I'm not wearing a skirt," she said. "I only did that on my first day to impress everyone. Basically, I hate skirts."

"Oh. Well, tear your slacks off, then."

"Shut up. People are staring." There was a man at the front desk looking in their direction.

"Say, Julio," Schultz said familiarly, "how's it going?"

"OK, man, keeping out of trouble. How you doing?"

"Same. What're you doing out here in the sticks?"

"Safer for my family, man. I got two daughters."

Schultz nodded and gave PJ a slight push toward the elevators. "That guy used to be a security guard in an office building downtown. I knew he had gotten a job as a night clerk in a hotel, but I didn't know it was out here in St. Charles."

He pressed the button and rocked back on his heels. "Good guy. Probably got a gun under the counter."

"Is it just hotels that bother you, Schultz, or are you planning to follow me home every night when I move into a house? Which, by the way, is supposed to happen in about," she looked at her watch, "seven hours from now."

"I guess I have a thing about hotels."

They were in front of her room. "As long as you're here," PJ said, "why don't you come in for a minute and get dry? We'll have to talk quietly because Thomas will be asleep, though. I have some soda and ice."

"Is it diet soda?"

"No."

"I'm game."

Inside, she went over and kissed Thomas on the cheek. He was sprawled sideways across the bed, and shifted under her light kiss. She pulled the covers up as best as she could, considering that he was lying sideways. Then she headed for the bathroom.

"I'm going to get out of these wet clothes. Here's a towel."

A towel came flying in his direction. He caught it and dried his hair, musing that a washcloth would have been sufficient for that. Then he folded the towel onto the seat of the only chair in the room and sat down heavily. A cat jumped up into his lap, and he rested a hand on its sleek body. He had always liked cats, as much as he liked any animals, which wasn't much. After a couple of minutes he sensed that he was being watched. He looked over at the boy's bed and saw that Thomas was sitting bolt upright in bed, staring at him.

The boy was sturdily built, with a large bone structure that would support substantial muscular development when puberty struck, but now seemed to jut out at odd angles. His hair was thick and black, and he wore it in a blunt cut with a weight line at mid-ear. His eyebrows and eyelashes were black and luxurious also, in contrast to the rest of his face, which seemed cheated by comparison: thin lips, angular cheeks, chin, and nose. The light in the room was just bright enough to show his deep aquamarine eyes. Schultz tried to remember if he had even seen eyes that particular shade, and came up blank.

"Who the fuck are you?" Thomas said.

The bathroom door opened and PJ stood there in a long white bathrobe.

"That will be one dollar," she said, with a touch of amusement in her voice.

Thomas wasn't amused. "What's going on here, Mom? What's this guy doing in our room in the middle of the night? And what are you doing in your robe while he's here?"

PJ almost burst out laughing. "Really, Thomas, it's not what you think. At least I don't think so. What exactly are you thinking?"

Schultz didn't know whether to open his mouth or not, so he sat and watched the events unfold.

Her son's anger flared because PJ seemed to think the situation was funny. His face was red and contorted. "What I'm thinking," he said, "is that you hopped into bed with the first man you found. Boy, it didn't take you long. We've only been in town a week!"

PJ stood flabbergasted.

"Maybe Dad didn't spoil things after all. Maybe it was all your fault," Thomas continued. He was practically yelling with pent-up anger. "Maybe you're going to walk out on me now, too, with your new lover. Dad told me that you were a lying bitch. I told him he was all wrong, but now I'm not so sure!"

PJ still stood with her mouth open, unable to respond to her son's outburst.

Schultz stood up, dumping the cat on the floor.

"That's enough, son," he said. "There's nothing going on here except simple hospitality. I work with your mother at the St. Louis Police Department, and she invited me in for a soda. Anything else is in your dirty mind. Now, I think you'd better apologize and get back to bed before I haul you out of here and explain to you how to talk courteously to grownups."

Dog hummed tunelessly and mindlessly as he sat on the black case putting the finishing touches on a new portrait. It was always the same thing that he hummed: the "Star-Spangled Banner." Pa had been a baseball fan.

He had been tempted once to taste some of the scraps of skin and flesh he carved away, but that seemed unnecessary, and overly Dog-like. No need to go for the appetizer when the main course was so . . . available.

Vanitzky had stopped screaming about an hour ago, and his head was lolled forward against the back of the chair. He was conscious but lost in an internal world where there were no painful strokes and no blood running down the curve of his back, first a few trickles, then a small river.

Satisfied with his carving, Dog stood up and flipped the latches of the case he had been sitting on. He pulled out an instant camera and took several pictures of his efforts. The flashes were harsh against the subdued color scheme of the suite. He put them into the case while they were still gray and undeveloped, with no hint of the horror they had captured. It was always fun to see how they came out when he got back home.

He removed from the case a machete, an old one with a worn and nicked wooden handle. The blade itself had a couple of notches in it, but had been carefully sharpened with a whetstone he kept wrapped in a piece of blue flannel. Ma had told him it was a little piece of his birthing blanket, the one she had wrapped him in herself after she squatted, pushed him out her sex tunnel, and caught him. Carrying the machete in his right hand, he walked in front of Vanitzky and slapped his face lightly.

Dog always liked to see the look in their eyes as he held the head steady by the hair and swung the machete.

After waiting patiently for the blood to drain, he

dropped the head into a plastic bag, the great big kind with a zipper on top used for freezing cakes and pies. Pauley Mac had discovered them when he worked in a train kitchen, and he always kept a supply. Then he sealed the zipper, put that bag inside another, and sealed it also. Finally, he nestled the heavy bundle in the foam cutout inside the black case.

The next hour or so was spent cleaning up. There was a rough wiping with a hand towel from the bathroom. Then he stripped and carefully packed his bloody clothes in more plastic bags. He wiped himself with baby wipes (the travel pack, so handy), and dressed in fresh clothing from the black case. Then all of the used items were carefully stowed in the case, which was latched and locked. He looked around for an unusual item, anything which would attract the attention of the police, leaving them puzzling over the significance of it. It was something he did at every scene, like arranging the roses in the pianist's apartment. Nothing jumped out at him, so he decided to leave the tray with the chocolate covered strawberries which he had used to get into the room. He wiped it carefully with a clean washcloth until it gleamed and he was certain that no prints remained. He helped himself to a couple of the strawberries as a reward for his effort. Finally it was time for the inspection, to make sure that the place was clean of anything to connect him to the scene. For the first time, he glanced into the bedroom of the two-room suite.

The mussed bed sent unmistakable signals. Dog wanted to go over and roll in the sheets, but Pauley Mac ruled against it. After all, Dog had already had his fun today; now it was Pauley Mac's job to make sure the place was clean.

There was a video camera on a tripod, pointed at the bed. Pauley Mac could see from the doorway that the camera wasn't recording. There was no little red light. He didn't have a video camera himself, but he knew how they worked. He liked to clown around in front of them in stores. It always amazed him when he saw himself on camera or even in the mirror that there was only one reflection. It seemed to him that there should be thirty or so, jumbled on top of each other, with his own identity a pale outline underneath them all, like multiple exposures on film.

It didn't take much imagination to figure out that Vanitzky had videotaped his sexual encounter with Katrina. Pauley Mac revised his opinion of the relationship; it was probably a pay-for-play situation after all. He considered winding back the tape and watching it, but he didn't want to enter the bedroom. That was one less place Pauley Mac had to worry about being clean. Besides, he wasn't sure how to connect the video camera to the television for playback. There was no VCR in the room.

Reluctantly, Pauley Mac turned his back on the tempting scene. He picked up the large case, now considerably heavier than when he had brought it into the room, and moved it over to the door. He noticed the indentations left by the case in the plush carpeting next to the chair containing Vanitzky's beheaded body, and carefully scuffed them out with his shoes. Suddenly he remembered that the pianist's apartment had been carpeted, and most likely he had left behind a similar set of indentations.

Always said he had the house habits of a pig, that boy, Ma interjected. *Always leavin' his mark on them floors, be it a puddle of piss or dog shit on his shoes. Could always tell when little Pauley Mac done walk through a room.*

It could have been funny, but coming from Ma it wasn't.

Other voices in his head berated him for his carelessness. There was a distinct undercurrent of satisfaction from those who wished that he would be caught. He quieted them all; there was still work to be done.

At the door, he removed his gloves and pushed them into his pocket with quick, nervous movements. It wouldn't do to be seen in the halls wearing gloves like that. He turned the doorknob using the washcloth he had used to polish the strawberry tray, put the case out in the hall, and closed the door, again with the washcloth, which disappeared into his pocket on top of the gloves. Soon he was outside, satisfied that no one had seen him. The pickup with the BADDOG license plates headed home. There was just time for a snack before bedtime.

CHAPTER

11

When the phone rang, PJ sat up groggily. Her feet seemed pinned down, and she remembered the cat sleeping on the bed, curled next to her feet. She let a couple more rings go by as she swung her legs over the edge of the bed, disturbing—what was the name Thomas and his friend Winston had come up with? Megabite, with an *i*, not a *y*, that was it. Clever name. She realized she was rambling mentally, shook her head, and looked at the clock radio on the night stand. Four-fifteen. She had been asleep less than three hours.

Thomas, who was also awakened by the phone, stumbled into the corner of her bed on his way to the bathroom. She was reluctant to answer. Since phones were invented, people have feared that jarring ring in the middle of the night. It was always bad news, except when it was a wrong number and then you couldn't get back to sleep anyway, lying there with heart pounding, breathing shallow and fast. As a psychologist whose patients sometimes looked inward at this time of night and saw only despair blacker than the night outside, she had particularly dreaded night calls. She reached for the phone.

"Hello."

"Sorry to wake you, Doc. I wanted to wait until morning but the lieutenant thought you should be notified right away."

It was Schultz. His words and the tone of voice in which they were delivered made her alert instantly.

"I'm listening."

Schultz sighed. "There's been another murder, same MO. A ballet dancer, whatever you call a male ballerina. In a hotel on Lindell Boulevard. Call came in through 911."

The hairs on PJ's arms rose, and her breath stopped in her throat. Something Schultz had said about hotels, about strange things happening in hotels. She glanced at the bathroom door behind which her precious, confused, and infuriating son was tending to his private functions. She heard a reassuring splash of water in the sink.

"Still there, Doc?"

"Yes, I'm sorry, go on."

"Man named Ilya Vanitzky. His girlfriend Katrina Rolls was with him in his hotel room until nearly midnight, doesn't know exactly when she left. She came back at three-forty-five because she forgot her insulin kit. She's diabetic, needs a shot first thing in the morning. She lost her spare kit a week ago and hadn't replaced it. Seems she's constantly misplacing the stuff. Her shrink told her she does it to be self-destructive because she hates herself deep down. Anyway, she opened the door with the key Vanitzky had given her. She was surprised that he didn't have the safety chain fastened. He always made a point of it. She was more surprised when she turned on the lights."

PJ's imagination filled in the scene Katrina saw. The toilet flushed, and Thomas came out and sat on the edge of her bed. She found his presence comforting.

"I suppose I need to come to the hotel," she said.

"Well, you are the leader of the pack, Doc," he said. "Sometimes the crown ain't too comfortable, if you get my meaning."

"Yes, Detective, I certainly do. And sometimes the tail end of the dog is just that: the tail end. It doesn't always get to wag the dog."

Schultz chuckled, a kind of gurgling noise that sounded like a garbage disposal fed a heavy meal. "I'll have to remember that one, Doc. I might get a chance to use it sometime."

He gave her directions to the hotel, and she hung up the phone. She thought that her son looked beautiful, simply because he was alive and sitting on her bed with his young face so serious and his mussed hair standing straight up.

"I need to leave for a while."

"I figured that." His voice sounded contrite, but there was still a touch of defiance in it that no one but herself would have been able to pick up. Last night—no, just a few hours ago—he had sullenly apologized for his outburst and lay down with his back to her, cutting off any further discussion. Now she had to leave him with his anger and hurt, knowing that she would have to deal with his feelings, and her own, soon.

"You'll have to go over to the house by yourself," she said. Today was Saturday, the big moving day when they were supposed to get settled in the rental house she had found. "I'll make arrangements with the hotel desk on my way out. They'll have a taxi waiting for you about eight. The furniture's coming at nine. I'll leave the house keys and some cash on the dresser. Get room service for breakfast. You might as well try to get some more sleep now."

Thomas stood up.

"I'm sorry about this," PJ said. "I know I should be there. It's a big thing, moving into our first house with just the two of us."

"Three. There's Megabite."

"I thought you didn't like cats."

"She's OK."

"Can you handle this?"

"Yeah, Mom, I can handle it," he said. He started to walk away, then turned back and came up to her as she was sitting on the bed. He kissed her lightly on the forehead. "See you later."

She wanted to throw her arms around him and pull him close, tousle his hair, and breathe in his little boy smell that hadn't caught up with the changing, angular body that was launching itself into puberty.

Instead, she blew him a kiss as he snuggled back under the covers. He didn't even see it, let alone reach up and catch it the way he used to when he was little.

Schultz met her outside the room.

"Can you handle this?" he asked bluntly.

She had questioned her son with the same words, but in a gentle fashion. She could see that Schultz was not in a gentle mood.

"Yes, I can handle it," she said testily. "I don't know what you think of me, Detective, but I'm not some fragile peach blossom who faints at the sight of blood."

Schultz shrugged and opened the door. PJ was aware of a blur of activity as several people moved around the room. She paused for a moment, and Schultz grabbed her arm and pushed. The smell was there, iron-rich and fresh, but she was expecting it. She took a deep breath and willed herself to show no reaction. She looked around with interest. What had at first seemed a blur now seemed more like a complicated dance.

"Here. I'll hold your clipboard while you put these on," Schultz said, holding out a pair of latex gloves.

While she was obediently putting on the gloves, a couple of technicians who had been standing in the center of the room with their backs toward her moved apart and went to opposite sides of the room. She was left with a clear view of Vanitzky's body.

It was much worse than the photographs of the previous murder scene. The body sagged in the chair, bloody and violated. She found herself staring at the stump left behind where his head was lopped off, unable to force her eyes away from the unnatural, incomplete shape. An image of biting a round Tootsie Roll Pop, pulling it off the stick, and crunching it to get to the chewy stuff inside, the way she used to do when she was a child, surfaced in her mind. She pushed it aside before it could sicken her. Instead, she thought of the woman who discovered the body, Katrina something, and what she must have felt when she opened the door. Only a short time before, Katrina had received this man's tenderness or simply his lust. In either case there was a bond between them, now severed as sharply as Vanitzky's neck.

PJ became aware of a pain in her chest and discovered that she hadn't taken a breath in a while. Struggling to keep her emotions and her stomach under control, she made a wide circle around the chair and its sad burden. She ended up in the suite's bedroom. The first thing she noticed was a camcorder on a tripod, aimed at the bed. The implication was clear. She heard Schultz's voice, low and intimate, as if he were whispering in her ear.

"Check it out, Doc. The guy liked to get it on camera when he was getting it on. Probably thought he was God's gift to women, too. He had a great body—from the neck down, at least."

In the middle of mayhem, PJ blushed. She had remembered that her ex-husband, Steven, once recorded the two of them in bed by putting a camcorder on the dresser. To cover her embarrassment, she cleared her throat and spoke up.

"Have you considered what might be on that tape? What if the killer was the lover?"

"You mean Vanitzky was bisexual? Involved with both Katrina and some man?"

"Well, yes, if we're still on the assumption that the murderer is male."

"Could be, but I think all we'll see on that tape is lovely Katrina and the dear departed going at it."

"Nevertheless, I'd like to view that tape as soon as possible."

"So would I, Doc, but we've probably got different reasons. I could use a cheap carnal thrill about now."

PJ's mouth curled down in a frown. Was nothing sacred to this man? "I'll sketch the bedroom. You can work on the other room."

"Suits me. The view's better, anyway."

"What do you mean?"

"From the window in this room all you can see are air conditioners. The other room has a view of Forest Park. I always liked the park at sunrise."

It was nearly eight in the morning by the time PJ got to her office at HQ. Schultz was off somewhere arranging to view the videotape. PJ put some coffee on to brew and slumped into her chair. She called her hotel to make sure that the taxi would be waiting for Thomas, and found out that he had left early, a half-hour ago. There was no phone service at the house yet, so she was out of touch with him. She sipped her coffee, thinking that she had been out of touch with him for some time. Wrapped in her own blanket of anger and misery, she had not had the emotional stamina to help anyone else. As she thought about it now, she felt that she was improving, regaining her sense of purpose.

How about that? she thought. *Murder cures the post-divorce blues. As long as it's someone else's murder. Geez, now I'm thinking like Schultz.*

Schultz came in and helped himself to a cup of coffee. "Come on," he said. "It's time to go watch lover-boy in action."

She followed him to a room filled with audio and video equipment. Lieutenant Howard Wall was inside, sitting with his chair tipped back and his feet propped up on a worn green table which looked like it had served in World War II.

"This is Louie," Schultz said, nodding at a man in a wheelchair. "He does all our audio/video work."

"Hello, Louie. You too, Howard," PJ said.

"Let's see what we got. Crank it up, Louie," said Howard.

Louie waited until PJ and Schultz found seats, then he started the playback on a large monitor that rested precariously on the other end of the green table, opposite Howard's feet.

It was a good video production. The lighting was just right, the camera was positioned to capture the most action. Apparently Vanitzky had some practice at this. PJ was embarrassed at first, sitting with three men watching such an intimate encounter. But there were no vulgar remarks, in spite of the way Schultz had behaved back in the hotel suite.

Vanitzky was a considerate lover, tender and gentle.

When it was over, Katrina sat on the edge of the bed pulling on her clothes. They conversed playfully and set up a date for the next evening. PJ could see the insulin kit, in a small blue zippered bag, lying on the night stand as Katrina kissed her lover good-bye. Shortly after she left the room, the sound of a running shower came from beyond the camera's range. The camera remained focused on the bed; no one had thought to turn it off.

There was the sound of knocking on the door. Howard pulled his feet off the table, dropping his chair with a thump. They all leaned forward. There was a mumbled conversation.

"I can boost that later," Louie said.

There was silence. Ten minutes went by as the camera showed nothing but the bed, tangled sheets, and pillow still bearing the outline of Katrina's head as she pressed herself against it when she came. There were other noises off-camera, a door closing, other ones that couldn't be identified immediately. More silence. The minutes crept by. Then there was a scream.

The killer had started his carving.

Everyone in the room could feel the knife high up between their shoulder blades, slicing a hot streak of pain. PJ rose from her chair in agitation, then sat back down. After a couple of minutes, Howard spoke.

"God Almighty, couldn't anyone hear that?"

"Nope," Schultz answered. "The hotel prides itself on quiet rooms. There's a lot of sound-deadening stuff in the walls, ceilings, and floors. Now if you happened to be walking in the hall outside, you might hear something through the door."

Soon after the screaming subsided. A little bit of the tension left the room. At least for the moment, Vanitzky was beyond pain.

"Come on," Schultz urged. "Walk into the bedroom. Go take a piss or something." They were all hoping that the murderer would come within camera range.

A strange sound, almost like buzzing or static, came on. Howard gestured to Louie to raise the volume, and they strained to hear.

"Shit," said Schultz. "Shit. I know what that is." Three faces turned in his direction.

"The bastard's humming. The fucker's slicing the life out of somebody and he's humming the 'Star-Spangled Banner.'"

CHAPTER

12

P J and Schultz went to Millie's for breakfast. PJ was eager to leave. She wanted to drive over to her new home and check on Thomas and the furniture. She also wanted to distance herself from what she had just seen and heard. Images floated through her mind, Vanitzky and Katrina embracing, the bloodstains on the carpet underneath the chair, the arc of the cleaver in her simulation. She needed rest, and she needed to be with her son. But Schultz's request to join him for breakfast seemed compelling.

There weren't many customers. PJ surmised that the diner crowd ate early, and it was almost nine o'clock. It surprised her that Millie was not behind the counter, but then she felt silly for being surprised. The diner was open from five in the morning until midnight seven days a week; it was too much to expect that Millie would be there during all of the open hours. She ordered hot tea and a bagel with peanut butter. Schultz, who did not banter back and forth with the waitress named Kelly, ordered a full breakfast of coffee, juice, sausage, eggs over easy, hash browns, and extra toast. For a moment PJ amused herself picturing the cholesterol mounting an assault on Schultz's arteries. When she glanced at him, she saw that he was tossing back what looked like a small handful of pills, which he swallowed with orange juice.

She had noticed that he moved slowly, almost grudgingly, in the morning, moving his arms, legs, and fingers in small arcs and conservative motions. He favored his left leg when he got up to use the bathroom. She put the facts together—gulping pills, probably ibuprofen, morning stiffness—and decided that he had arthritis. PJ's father suffered from rheumatoid arthritis, the kind that twisted his hands and made them nearly useless by the time he was forty. He was the editor of the *Newton Daily News,* published since 1902 in the small southeastern Iowa town of Newton, where PJ grew up. She remembered wrapping her father's hands in steamy towels every morning, a small comfort offered by a loving daughter and accepted graciously, even when it made him late for work. When he couldn't use a typewriter anymore, PJ typed his articles for him, and patiently handled the big red marker for him, awaiting his directions when he edited copy, which he did at the kitchen table every evening. Dad had died when PJ was away at college, but Mom still lived in a big, white two-story with a wrap-around porch on the edge of town, which is to say about two minutes from downtown Newton.

"How's your arthritis this morning?" she asked.

Schultz stared at her, his face unreadable. "What makes you think I have arthritis, Doc?"

PJ was not so tired that she couldn't recognize a defensive reaction. It was time to tread softly.

"My dad had pain in his hands, later in his knees. He used to climb stairs one step at a time, kind of dragging one leg behind him, not bending it."

"What's that got to do with me?"

Getting nowhere, PJ decided to drop it. It really wasn't her business, anyway. She had simply been concerned.

"Not a thing, Detective. Not a thing." She pressed her teabag against the side of the cup with her spoon. She picked up the sugar dispenser. First the little flap stuck, then it suddenly let loose a torrent of sugar into her tea. She sighed.

The smell of Schultz's breakfast was heavy in her nostrils. She had been amazed when she studied the physiology of smell to discover that what the sense organs were responding to was airborne molecules of the substance being smelled. When she smelled sausage, it was because actual sausage molecules had floated into her nose, dissolved in her nasal mucous, and been detected by olfactory receptors. Then her brain interpreted, from experience, that those particular molecules made up the smell of sausage. That led her to thoughts of what was in her nose when she smelled unpleasant things: a rotting animal, feces, blood. Blood on a carpet.

"Did you notice," she said as Schultz filled his mouth with a huge forkful of eggs backed by half a sausage link, "that there were no indentations in the carpet?"

"I was wondering if you'd catch that," he said. "Kelly, who's in the kitchen this morning? These are the best damned eggs I've ever gotten here, and you can tell that to Millie when she hauls her ass in here."

Kelly came over and leaned on her elbows in front of Schultz. Her uniform, unlike Millie's, was unbuttoned at the top. PJ could tell that Schultz got a good view, and that he was enjoying it. The waitress patted his hand lightly and then straightened up; evidently even a steady customer was entitled to only a few seconds of titillation.

"Thanks for the compliment," she said. "We don't get many here. People treat us like we was invisible and got no feelings. The cook's a new guy, quiet type, don't even know his name yet, Petey, somethin' like that. But he's good. Handles them orders when things are really hoppin' in here and don't bat an eye. Works right through his break, too. But I'll tell you one thing," she lowered her voice conspiratorially, "the guy hums all the fuckin' time he's workin'. 'Bout to drive me crazy." She made a small circle with her towel on the counter, as if considering how far to take the confidence. "There's another thing too, and I'll tell you 'cause you're regular and all. But don't you go tellin' Millie. I don't want no trouble."

"I won't." Schultz winked at PJ. She was certain that Kelly saw it, but the woman continued anyway.

"One time when I was pickin' up an order, I felt somethin' creepy, like I was bein' watched. I turned around, and there he was lookin' at me like I don't have no clothes on. Reminded me of a big ol' hungry dog lookin' at a steak on the other side of a tall fence. He don't say a thing, just hums, so I go on 'bout my business. My guess is the guy just ain't gettin' it regular, if you know what I mean. Maybe new in town." A customer at a table waved at Kelly and pointed at his coffee cup. "Yeah, yeah, I'll be right there."

When she was gone, Schultz put down his fork. "Odd that she should mention humming."

"I noticed," said PJ. "I've been thinking about that, from a psychological point of view. Sometimes humming is just a nervous habit that people pick up, like drumming their fingers or biting their nails. It's an example of a stress reaction, when people are repeatedly caught between the fight and flight responses. They can't lash out directly at what's causing the stress, and they can't get away from it either. The body is prepared for physical confrontation, but the mind says no. The physical response leaks out, so to speak, and the person bites his nails or develops a twitch or pops his knuckles. Or hums. That's probably what's happening with the cook. Maybe he hates his job, thinks he could do better, but is trapped for some reason."

"Aren't we all," said Schultz, as he mopped up egg yolk with a piece of toast. PJ averted her eyes. Although she herself ate eggs occasionally, they were always thoroughly cooked. She thought of runny egg yolks as liquid chicks.

"So the cook probably has a mild stress disorder. But there is a more serious aspect. Some mentally ill people hum as a disassociative technique. It occupies their senses, like white noise, in order to block out an underlying chaos.

Incessant humming, or a variation such as whistling or thumb-twiddling, is also seen in people with dementia, like Alzheimer's patients, who are trying to cope with a slippery mental organization."

"You saying our creep's senile?"

PJ smiled. "No. I do think, though, that he might be humming to distance himself from what he's doing, or from what some part of him is doing, during the killing. He could be a multiple personality, although that is more common with women."

"Could the killer be a woman?" Schultz said. "We've checked out Katrina thoroughly. She has a solid alibi for the time of the Burton killing, but can't prove her whereabouts after she left the hotel the first time."

"I don't think that fits the profile, but anything's possible."

Schultz paused for a moment. The cook had come through the swinging door from the kitchen with a mop and pail. The sound of classical music drifted out to the counter while the door was open, then was abruptly cut off.

"Could be this place is getting too high class for me," Schultz said. "That didn't sound like the stuff Millie usually plays. Next we'll have cloth napkins and candles on the tables and more forks than we know what to do with. Hey, cook," Schultz said, gesturing at the man wielding the mop, "good eggs."

The cook turned and gave him a thumbs-up, then went back to his mopping. He was, for the moment at least, not humming, although his lips were pressed together as though he was having difficulty keeping the humming inside.

Schultz and PJ got refills of their coffee and tea. Schultz wanted to go over the computer simulation in detail, as if he needed to hear it from PJ, as well as see it on the screen. So she talked him through it, then told him she was anxious to get going. She paid her bill, left a dollar tip, and headed out. She turned at the door to tell Schultz that she wasn't going to be in the office the rest of the day or Sunday either, and saw a curious tableau.

Kelly had retreated to the far end of the diner for a modicum of privacy and was pushing up on her considerable bosom with one hand and adjusting her bra strap with the other. Schultz was hunched at the counter, sipping his coffee and gazing ahead, mind busy behind blank eyes. She had seen him in that posture before. The cook, who was now mopping the table area out of Schultz's sight, was staring fixedly at him. PJ idly wondered if the cook was bisexual, then briefly considered how Schultz would be as a sex partner.

It was not an appetizing thought.

Strangely reluctant to disturb the scene with the information about her whereabouts, she left quietly. Schultz knew she was moving into her new home this weekend, so she decided to let the great detective figure out the obvious.

CHAPTER

13

Pauley Mac settled into the rhythm with the mop, pushing in circles, rinsing, squeezing. He was convincing at it, just as he was convincing as a cook in a diner. *A man of many talents,* a cultured voice said caustically in his mind. He almost laughed out loud. That piano player, Burton, had a great sense of humor.

He stayed close enough to the counter to hear the detective and the woman talking. It was odd to hear people talking about him as if he wasn't there. As he had been maneuvering his pail through the door of the kitchen, he had heard Doctor Gray say that the killer could have multiple personalities. Pauley Mac had read about multiple personalities, but he didn't think that he fit the description. After all, there were no blackouts or lost time when one personality suppressed the others. Pauley Mac and Dog knew about each other and cooperated, more or less, in the business of animating the body they shared with each other and about thirty other guests.

He wondered what Schultz would do if he knew he was in the same room with the killer. He wondered what the bitch would do. Schultz would probably stand up, pull a gun from underneath that jacket that couldn't possibly button over his gut, and splash Pauley Mac's multitalented brain onto the freshly-mopped floor. Dog and Pauley Mac both savored that image for a minute or two.

When the conversation drifted back into his awareness, he thought that he had missed something, something important that had to do with computers. Then he concentrated on what they were saying.

The bitch was talking about the murder of George Burton as if she had been there all along.

They knew about the floral delivery man ploy.

They knew about the carrying case. They knew that he sat on the carrying case while working.

They knew about the cat scratching him—Dog growled—and they had a blood sample. His blood, intimate and incriminating, gotten from underneath the cat's claws.

They knew about his set of tools, but probably not that he had murdered that storekeeper and then taken them. He used whittler's knives, not stone cutting tools.

They knew about his machete—though they thought it was a kitchen cleaver—but probably not that he had licked Ma's and Pa's blood from it.

They knew about plastic bags and how they kept the blood from dripping, making sure he didn't leave a trail down the hallway. But they thought that he would use an ordinary garbage bag. How crude.

But they were close, so close.

How was this possible? How?

It must have to do with the computer that was mentioned at the beginning of the conversation, although Pauley Mac didn't know exactly how. He had been in Radio Shack and played a game on a computer, two little figures punching and kicking. He couldn't imagine Shithouse Schultz getting anything useful out of a computer. It had to be the bitch.

Pauley Mac checked her out carefully from head to foot while swishing his mop in circles. No doubt about it—she had that hard, smart look that he associated with white coats and needles and pills in little paper cups.

Suddenly she stood up to leave. He wanted to follow her, but his shift wasn't over until after lunch. It had taken some maneuvering on his part to get this job, and he didn't want to irritate Millie in his first week.

After finding out that Schultz came to the diner frequently, he followed one of the cooks home. The cook was a man who couldn't have been more than sixty years old but who could pass for eighty. He lived in a musty apartment building. Pauley Mac disdained concealment and followed him brazenly up the stairs, pulling on rubber gloves as he climbed. The landing smelled like piss. Dog wanted to stop and sniff, but Pauley Mac kept moving, a few steps behind the old man. When he opened his apartment door, Pauley Mac shoved him in and came in behind him, slamming the door.

The man was terrified. The smell of his fear was nearly as strong as the smell of the last meal prepared in the apartment: canned hash. Pauley Mac calmed him down by speaking reasonably, saying that he wanted the cook's job at the diner, and offering him fifty dollars if he would quit immediately, no questions asked. With Pauley Mac waving a fifty dollar bill in his face, the man called Millie and told her that he was leaving town suddenly to tend to a sick relative, sorry about the short notice, just got the news, he had no choice, didn't know when he would be back, if at all.

When he got off the phone, Pauley Mac pocketed the fifty and twisted the old man's neck like he used to do to the chickens when he was a boy. That had been his job ever since he got enough strength in his arms.

He figured that the old man didn't have any talents that were useful, so there was no reason to take his head. All the old man could do was cook greasy eggs and burgers, and Pauley Mac could already do that. The cook's death was a practical matter, a means to an end. He had considered not killing him, just scaring him out of town, maybe breaking an arm or a couple of fingers. But if the old coot went to the police, there would be trouble at the diner, questions at the very least.

He dug the car keys out of the man's pocket, went outside, and pulled his rusty Buick into the alley around the back of the apartment building. Then came the risky part. He brought the body down the rear stairs, hefted over his shoulder in a fireman's carry. The old man was as light as if he really had been a chicken, and Pauley Mac, though lean, was tough and wiry. He put the body in the passenger seat, propping it up by fastening the shoulder belt and leaning the head against a greasy toss pillow he fetched from the couch in the man's apartment. It looked as though the passenger was simply taking a nap, except that his head rolled unnaturally whenever the car turned a corner.

He drove south out of St. Louis, parallel to the Mississippi River on I-55. On a deserted stretch of two-lane blacktop near Crystal City that followed the high, rocky bluffs, he stopped the car in the driving lane—there was no shoulder—and shoved the cook's body into place behind the steering wheel. He pushed the Buick and watched as it rolled downhill to an exposed turn with no guardrail.

Pauley Mac walked a couple miles back to the four-lane highway, peeled off his gloves, stuck out his thumb, and caught a ride with a trucker who had a delivery in the west county area. He got out at the St. Charles Rock Road exit of I-270, thanked the driver, and walked several miles to his house. When he got home, he had a blister on the heel of his left foot.

The next morning he showed up at the diner just as Millie was taping the "Cook Wanted" sign in the window. His job interview consisted of fixing Millie breakfast. A few minutes later he was tying an apron around his narrow waist as Millie's newest employee.

Pauley Mac watched the bitch's hips swing as she walked toward the door. He considered rushing over to her, slitting her loose trousers and tight underpants with a knife, and bending her over a table, pressing her face into a customer's plate of eggs and bacon while porking her from the rear.

He'd almost certainly lose his job if he did that.

Resigned that he would have to track her down later, he turned his gaze back to Schultz, mopping all the while. The bitch might be the one with the fancy computer, but the man whose buttocks sagged over the stool was the trained policeman. If she kept whispering juicy tidbits—*tidbits, tit bites, tit bites, boob lubes,* Dog playfully intoned—into Schultz's ear, he just might put the pieces together. That wouldn't do at all. Pauley Mac had plans, exciting plans, for the future.

While browsing through a magazine at a supermarket checkout line, Pauley Mac had come across an article entitled "Childhood Innocence." In a flash of prescience, he knew that he was looking at the theme for his next killing cycle, be it months or years from now. He had tried it on for size by walking past a preschool when the children were playing outside in the yard. Dog had little interest in chubby little girls with hairless slits and tiny dots on their chests where tits would grow or soft little boys with thighs like drumsticks and toy pricks dangling between their legs like those little hot dogs people serve as appetizers. But Pauley Mac wasn't concerned about appearances. He wanted abstracts like playfulness or belief in Santa Claus and the Easter Bunny, things that had not been a part of his own childhood.

The morning of Pauley Mac's tenth birthday should have been full of childish promise, a day of wishes fulfilled, family warmth, cake, and candles. Instead, it was one of the mornings that he dreaded, the kind that seemed to be happening more frequently. Pa was between jobs and had been up late with his friend Joe, sitting on the broken down porch, sharing cheap whiskey, and tossing empty bottles into the bedraggled weeds that passed for a front yard.

Ma had been in a foul mood all evening, ranting about Pa's drinking the devil's blood and cuffing Pauley Mac's head whenever he got within arm's reach. She had gone to bed early and was snoring when Pauley Mac crawled into bed next to her. She woke slightly, and cuddled against his back. He could feel her breasts pressing against him. He thought of them as balloons filled with some putrid substance that would poison him if she pressed against him hard enough, or when she squeezed and kneaded them with her hands. He lay stiffly, eyes open, hoping against hope that Pa would fall asleep on the porch.

Not this time. Pauley Mac finally fell into a restless sleep. When he woke at dawn he felt his father's weight against him in the bed, like a log that would roll on him and crush the life from him, and he would be squished flat like that toad he had smashed with a rock.

He had shared their bed as long as he could remember. When he tried to slink off and sleep somewhere else in the house, he was beaten and reviled until, cowed, he returned. Many times they were tired and rose groggily in the morning, and he would fix himself breakfast from whatever kind of food was in the house and escape to school, or, during the summer, into the woods. But not this morning, a morning that should have been full of promise, of birthday giggles, of cake and candles.

Pa turned to face him, a crude expectation in his eyes and his rotten breath in Pauley Mac's face. Shaking with fear and resignation and disgust, Pauley Mac knew that after he was done pleasuring Pa, Ma would expect her turn.

There was never any tenderness, not even when Pa shuddered and spurted, or when Ma twisted in the sheets. Instead, they cursed him as though he were to blame for their acts, as though all of the evil in that house flowed from him. He was worthless, he was dirt, he would never amount to anything. He would never have any of the finer things in life, and he had somehow kept them from having them, too. Nothing he could do was good enough. He didn't even have the brains of a dog. Of a mouse. Of a worm.

Pauley Mac nursed his bruises and his cracked ribs, his cuts and his black eyes. He looked at his parents with terrible hate and with equally terrible longing, wishing that he could do something to earn their approval, so that they would love him in return. Or, at least, stop beating and cursing him. He knew that something vital was missing from his life, but he didn't know the extent of the darkness inside himself.

That day, his tenth birthday, after he cleaned himself as well as he could with a cold dirty washcloth and dressed, he skipped school and went out and got himself the brains of a dog. He cracked open the skull of Old Bert, the neighbor's ancient hound, with Pa's machete. Then he scooped the warm soft tissue out with both hands, ate it raw in the woods, gagged, threw up, and ate some more.

It didn't work. Even though he now had the brains of a dog, had literally made them part of his body, still his parents didn't love him. He despaired, and lay trembling in the bed between them.

When he was twelve, he thought perhaps he simply wasn't lovable, so he killed a boy who was popular at school and devoured some of his brain, choking down the torn, bloody pieces, willing himself not to vomit them back out. Then he tossed the body, with its head attached but half empty, in front of a train. It was splattered so badly, no one suspected that part of the brain was missing.

When he was sixteen, he dropped out of school. He came to believe that Ma and Pa needed to be closer to him in order to love him. A lot closer. So he killed them both while they slept in the bed with the sheets stained with come and juice. He told the sheriff that a man had broken in, murdered his parents, beaten him, and stolen the cash Ma kept in the lard bucket in the kitchen. The sheriff had his suspicions, but he also knew pretty well how Pauley

Mac had been treated, so he simply told Pauley Mac to move on out of the county and preferably out of Tennessee altogether.

Schultz was gone from the diner. Pauley Mac finished out his shift mechanically and drove home in his pickup truck. He was depressed, and he blamed it on the bitch. It was Saturday afternoon. He didn't work tomorrow, so he could spend the next day and a half in the cocoon of his home. He went into the dining room and played the electronic keyboard for a time, closing his eyes and letting his fingers wander over the smooth keys as beautiful music played in his mind. His depression lifted, and he spun and launched himself into the air, first from the bed and then from a kitchen chair, trying out his newly-acquired dancing ability.

He was not aware until hours later that he had twisted his ankle. When he did notice it, he couldn't decide whether to apply ice or heat to the injury. He knew that when the twisted ankle first happened, the application of an ice pack would reduce swelling. Later, heat would relieve the pain. But where was the dividing line, he wondered. An hour? Three hours? Since he didn't know exactly when the injury occurred—surely it hadn't happened while he was dancing, since he was supremely graceful—he settled for applying heat. He wrapped his right ankle in towels dipped in boiling water and minimally cooled. Wincing at the heat and discomfort, he plopped heavily into a chair. The heat eased his pain and he slept, head lolled to the side, jaw hanging open.

The rest of the weekend slid by quickly. The cook's death was a minor article on page twelve of the Sunday *Post-Dispatch*. Another one of those unexplained one-car accidents, no hint of foul play. Monday Pauley Mac was at the diner promptly at five in the morning, his ankle almost back to normal, just hurting a little when he put his weight on it a certain way. The bitch doctor came by about eight o'clock and bought a couple of rolls to take to the office. Pauley Mac couldn't hang around her, though, because Millie happened to be in this morning. He stayed in the kitchen, a model employee.

Schultz didn't show at all. No matter. Pauley Mac knew what his own next actions would be. After lunch, he went home and took a nap. Then he showered and ate an indifferent meal. At five PM, he was waiting, parked on a side street near the building where the bitch worked. She came out about a half-hour later, and he followed her home. She was easy. She didn't even check the mirror.

The next afternoon, after his morning shift at the diner, he put on a pair of blue coveralls and drove over to the bitch's house, where she lived with a son who was just about the age Pauley Mac was when he killed his first human. He wondered what it was like for the boy growing up with a head doctor for a mother. Probably about the same as growing up with Ma and Pa.

Why, thankee, son, that be right sweet of ya, ya worthless turd, Pa replied.

He walked around into the back yard with a clipboard, just your friendly gas meter reader at work. It was tidy, with stepping stones leading to a round perennial garden surrounding a bird bath. The recent rain storm had filled the bird bath, and the perennials were up and growing. It was lovely now, but at the height of summer it would be spectacular. Pauley Mac remembered the time he had planted a few beans outside the back door of his house, scraping the poor soil with a bent spoon, watering the little trough he had made. When the bean plants were a couple of inches high, Pa had spotted them. He knew in an instant that they were important to Pauley Mac, so he stomped them to the ground and pissed on them for good measure.

Boy, you misrememberin' that. I done stepped on them plants accidental-like.

"Shut up, Pa," Pauley Mac said as he picked the lock on the back door. It wasn't as easy with gloves on as without, but he knew they were necessary. Inside it was cool and dark. Window shades were drawn on the kitchen windows. It looked and felt safe, and he had the urge to sit quietly for awhile, so he did. He dropped into a kitchen chair and closed his eyes. There were so few places of refuge for a man who carried the echoes of thirty or so murders in his head. Not that he regretted them or felt guilty. If he felt anything at all, it was that he was entitled to their skills, their lives. But it was like trying to cover yourself with a blanket that was too small. There was always a little piece of you sticking out, a foot, an elbow, hanging out in the cold nothingness.

He opened his eyes and inspected the kitchen. There was little clutter. A new toaster, still in its box, occupied a prime piece of counter space. Next to the stove sat a small microwave oven with the label proclaiming all of its features still stuck on the front glass. A single coffee cup stood on a drain board next to the sink. A dinette table and four swivel chairs, one of which he was sitting in, stood under a window. Pauley Mac rose and moved quickly through the kitchen. The lethargy had passed. He had his sense of purpose back. He knew what he was looking for, and it wasn't in this room.

The only exit from the kitchen besides the door to the back yard led to a short hallway, only eight feet long or so. Other doors opened from the hallway into the living room, dining room, bathroom, and a multi-purpose room which could have been a guest room or study. The dining room was empty, but the living room had inexpensive-looking new furniture in it. He checked each room carefully, spotting what he was searching for in the study. But he didn't enter right away; he wanted to spend more time in the house. The front door was in the living room, with no entry foyer. Immediately to the right of the front door was a staircase.

Sitting on the stairs was a cat, staring at him.

He had seen that cat before, and it had shed his blood. Dog felt the hairs on his arms and back rising, and a tension in his throat. He growled, low and menacing. At the sound, the cat spun away and ran up the stairs. Before Pauley Mac could interfere, Dog gave chase, taking the stairs two at a time. The cat disappeared into the bedroom on the right just as he lunged, barely missing the tail, which was fuzzed up several times its normal size.

Pauley Mac put a stop to the chase, because he had a reason for coming that wasn't four-footed and furry. He wanted to frighten the bitch, let her know she was vulnerable, and give her a message that she should not use the computer again. He wanted to transform this safe haven into one of anxious checking of door locks, nervous starts at any unusual sound. He looked around upstairs. There were two bedrooms and a bath. Both bedrooms had the same kind of inexpensive new furniture he had seen downstairs. He wondered why everything was new.

He could not get much of a feeling of the type of person she was. Pauley Mac always liked to study people, although sometimes the only opportunity he really had was the look in their eyes when he drew back his machete. He knew he was different from others, or rather that others were different from him. He wondered what it would be like to fall asleep with only your own thoughts inside your head, rather than the babble of voices—voices like pinballs bouncing around inside his skull, careening from ear to ear, spinning down into that place just behind his eye sockets.

He went back downstairs and into the study. There was a folding card table in the center of the room, and on top of it rested a computer. He picked up the chair and smashed the computer, pounding repeatedly until he was sure it was unusable. In the kitchen, he opened the refrigerator. There wasn't much inside, a few cans of soda, a package of lunch meat, but evidently someone liked ketchup, because there were two bottles, one opened and one unopened. He took the opened bottle and poured out a large pool of thick red sauce on the kitchen table. He dipped in a gloved finger and wrote the letters *"YUR RONG"* on the wall next to the table, coming back to load up his finger numerous times. One of his voices, a schoolteacher, chided him for his spelling, but he was used to that. Sometimes he wished he could get rid of Henry Wu. He should have been more selective.

Pauley Mac could read well, well enough to make sense of news magazines, which put him ahead of millions of other Americans. He had attended school, anything to get out of the house. He had dragged himself in when he was sick, so sick that he should have been in a bed with blankets piled high and his mother bringing him steaming soup.

But of course there wasn't much chance of that happening.

He had even gone on holidays, hoping that Ma and Pa didn't find out that he spent the day in the woods. But whenever he had tried to express himself in writing when he was a child, when he brought home carefully lettered paragraphs about pets or summer vacation, he was severely put down for it. Ma didn't read, and neither did Pa. They simply didn't realize what a banquet the written word presented to their son, because they didn't partake of it themselves. They didn't object much when he learned to read in school, but Ma found it threatening that he could take a blank piece of paper and make marks on it that she couldn't decipher, and she made sure he knew about it. So Pauley Mac ended up with a strange dichotomy: he could read, but sweated and trembled whenever he had to write something, and what he produced was childish. He knew it was an emotional block of some kind, but he couldn't break through it, especially not with Ma around him twenty-four hours a day.

Pauley Mac appraised his message, and was pleased that

the ketchup seemed to add a threatening tone. He wanted to deliver a clear message for the bitch to back off, not to use her computer anymore, that she was headed in the wrong direction. And he especially wanted to frighten her, to let her know that he could enter her private space whenever he wanted and do whatever he wanted. That gave him another thought, another way to heighten his message. He went to the sink and rinsed the ketchup off his gloved fingers, then opened drawers until he found where the utensils were kept. It was a pitiful assortment. There was only one knife, an all-purpose one with a blade about eight inches long and a worn handle. He looked with disdain at the dull, nicked cutting edge.

Telling Dog to be quiet, he took the knife in his hand and moved toward the staircase.

"Here, kitty, kitty . . ."

CHAPTER

14

PJ left work early to pick Thomas up at school. Since the incident with Schultz in the hotel room, Thomas had been alternately subdued and angry. But he had coped amazingly well with the move, and even had his friend Winston over yesterday. The two of them had gone into the study to use PJ's computer directly after dinner, closing the door. When Thomas came out for some snacks a couple of hours later, she had gotten a glimpse into the room. What she saw cheered her. Thomas and Winston were using a multimedia encyclopedia, and the screen was filled with colorful dinosaurs. Papers were scattered about, and it looked as if the boys were working on their homework together. Megabite was on top of the monitor, which PJ knew was warm and a coveted nap spot for the cat, with her front paws loosely dangling over the edge. Then Winston activated the dinosaur scene, and a triceratops began fending off a tyrannosaurus rex. Megabite pawed tentatively at the moving figures, a predator finding something in common with the two behemoths twisting and lunging on the screen.

Nonsense. Just a cat responding to motion, to creatures she saw as gray and about the size of mice.

The next time she saw Thomas was when he came out and asked if she could drive Winston home. On the way back, after dropping the boy off, she tried to question

Thomas about his new friend. All she learned was that Winston lived with his dad, that his mom was in a treatment center someplace, and that Winston was generally thought of as a nerd because he was smart, not athletic, and liked computers.

She could understand why her son had approached this boy. Thomas was an outsider, the new boy in class. Rather than try to push his way into the social circles that existed there, he had circled the outside like a predator—*there's that word again*—eyeing a herd of antelope, looking for the easy target. It wasn't an ideal situation, because she felt that Thomas might just be using Winston. But at least they both got some companionship out of it, someone their own age to bum around with. If Winston was as smart as Thomas said he was, then he certainly was able to see right through the sudden friendship. And who knows, maybe the boys would become good friends in spite of their beginnings.

That was yesterday. Today Thomas had been angry, barely speaking to her, barely able to keep his voice civil, his words stinging like sleet driven by a vengeful wind. The ride home from school was silent and tense.

PJ pulled into her driveway, a gravel one almost entirely given over to grass, with two narrow wheel paths still defined. Driveways were an oddity in her neighborhood. Most people had to park on the street. The city lots were too narrow for an attached garage. The occupants of those few homes which had detached garages in the rear were considered uppity, and generally it was a self-fulfilling prophecy. The most common sight in the neighborhood, though, was a statue of the Virgin Mary next to the front steps. Most were modestly surrounded with a well-tended flower bed, with bricks set on a slant for edging. A few went so far as to have spotlights set into the lawn, so that Mary was on duty twenty-four hours a day.

Around the back, PJ's driveway ballooned out into a rough circle, again mostly taken over with grass. She turned the car around and left it pointing back out toward the street. She and Thomas got out at the same time, but she paused to admire the lilies-of-the-valley that were blooming at the base of the birdbath.

"Mom, the door's open. And you're the one who's always telling me to lock up."

She turned around, but before she could respond, Thomas had shoved the door open and gone into the kitchen.

"Holy shit!" he yelled.

PJ dropped her purse and ran for the doorway. Inside she saw Thomas standing still, staring at the wall. There were letters on the wall, large and crudely drawn, in something red, terribly red, that had dripped down the walls like bloody tears. For some reason she couldn't make out what the letters spelled, but the implication was clear: someone had been in her home, some sick person had violated her clean white walls.

"Megabite! Where's Megabite?" Thomas said, his voice cracking. He suddenly took off toward the stairs, and PJ was too far away to grab him.

"Stop!" PJ ordered in her most commanding, professional voice. It worked. Thomas halted on the third step. "Turn around and come back here immediately. We're going outside to call the police. Whoever did this might still be in the house."

"Now what?" he said, as they stood in the back yard, staring at the house like it had just fallen there from outer space.

PJ tried to compose herself. She was the adult here. "We'll both go next door and call from Mrs. Brodsky's house. Then you'll stay there until after the police check the house."

"Like hell I will."

"Thomas!" Her voice was harsh. She softened it, reached out to touch his hand. "Just go along, OK? Just let me deal with this. Don't make things harder than they are."

She walked next door. The yards weren't fenced, so she simply cut across to Mrs. Brodsky's back door and knocked. She knew the old woman was slow getting to the door, so she counted to fifty before knocking again. This time she only got to twenty before the door opened.

"Why, hello, Penelope," Mrs. Brodsky began. Then she took in PJ's face. "Whatever is wrong, dear? You look like you've seen a ghost."

"Mrs. Brodsky, could I please use your phone? My house has been broken into, and I need . . . I need . . ."

"Come in. You too, Thomas. I'll phone for you. It's ever so easy, now that all you have to do is dial 911." She ushered them into her kitchen, hands gently guiding, touching PJ's shoulder, the top of Thomas's head. PJ let herself be led and coddled, just for a few minutes. Then, after Mrs. Brodsky had placed the call, she dialed Schultz's number at work. He picked up after the first ring.

"Schultz."

"Leo, this is PJ. Somebody broke into my house and wrote things on the wall," she blurted.

"You didn't go in, did you?"

"Just right inside the kitchen. Then Thomas and I went next door. The neighbor called 911."

"Good. Stay there. I'll be right over."

"Leo? Are you still there?"

"Yeah. What?"

"I'm worried about my cat."

"Stay put. Let the uniforms go in the house. You hear me?"

It seemed like only moments until two blue-and-white patrol cars pulled up at the curb, but it had been long enough for Mrs. Brodsky to thrust a cup of hot tea in her hands.

She heard the woman offer to fix Thomas some hot Oval-
tine, heard him decline in a polite but strained voice.

Soon afterward, Schultz's bulk occupied the center of
the kitchen. Mrs. Brodsky orbited, offering tea, but was
chased from the room by a glare from Schultz. Thomas
wandered outside, under strict orders not to leave Mrs.
Brodsky's yard.

"OK, tell," Schultz said.

"I left early to pick up Thomas from school. Well, you
know that. When we got home, the back door was open.
Thomas went inside before I could stop him. On the wall
of the kitchen, there's some writing, big drippy red letters.
I don't know what they spell. Thomas started to go upstairs to look for Megabite. That's our cat. I stopped him,
and we both came over here to Mrs. Brodsky's."

"The boy shouldn't have gone inside," Schultz said
gruffly. "Could've taken a bellyful of shot or a knife in the
throat."

"You don't have to tell me that," PJ flared.

"All right, take it easy," Schultz said.

"That writing—it's red. Do you think maybe," PJ swallowed and lowered her voice, although she and Schultz
were the only ones in the room, "it's cat's blood?"

"I hope not. I'm going over to talk to the uniforms,
make sure the house is empty. You stay here."

"No, I want to come."

Schultz sighed. "Suit yourself. You will, anyway."

They walked over to the house and Schultz consulted
with the two patrolmen who had remained outside. As he
was talking with them, the other two came out the back
door.

"Nobody there," one of them said. "Writing on the
kitchen wall, some smashed equipment in one of the other
rooms downstairs."

Schultz nodded and headed for the door. PJ quickly
caught up with him, and found that Thomas was right at
her elbow.

Schultz stepped inside and stood, gazing at the two-foot-high letters, now almost obscured by the watery tracks the liquid made running down the wall. Then, to PJ's horror, he walked over, stuck his finger in the red stuff and sucked it noisily into his mouth.

"Ketchup," he said. "You really ought to get that thick kind that doesn't drip."

It was decided to have an Evidence Technician Unit come out to photograph the wall and dust for fingerprints in the kitchen and study, especially around the smashed computer. Schultz didn't think that the break-in was associated with the investigation of the murders, but he decided not to take that chance. The ETU came and went, doing their jobs quickly and professionally.

"So you think some neighborhood punk broke in here?" PJ asked.

"Some semi-literate punk who just got the urge to trash someplace."

"And that's your considered professional opinion?"

"Yeah."

"Well, I don't think much of it. Why . . . "

"Mom," Thomas interrupted, "can I look for Megabite now that the ETU's gone?"

"Of course. I'll help you," she answered before Schultz could get a word in. "Let's try the bedrooms. I think she would have been too scared to stay down here."

They went upstairs and separated. She was on her knees looking under a dresser when she heard Thomas.

"Mom, I found her!"

A moment later: "Yuck! She's got crap all over her rear end."

She grabbed a towel from the bathroom on her way into Thomas's room. He was sitting on the bed, cradling the young cat, oblivious now to the mess and smell. She sat down next to him and wrapped the cat in the bath towel, holding it on her lap. Megabite purred softly and began kneading the terry cloth with her paws, pulling up little picks in the material.

Relief settled in, and PJ felt her shoulders sag. Her mouth was dry, and she swallowed a couple of times. She hadn't realized how much she had come to care for this cat in just a few days. Now a rush of memories came: how the cat greeted her when she got home, a delicate scratchy-tongued lick on the cheek in the middle of the night, the tooth marks in the corner of a magazine that had been knocked off the counter during a midnight frolic. Thomas was obviously attached, too.

"Where was she?"

"I looked in the closet, and I noticed that I had left the little door to the attic open," he said. Each upstairs closet had a door in the back, about four feet high, to access the storage space under the eaves. "She came right out when I called her. Oh, Mom, she's OK." His eyes filled with tears and he leaned against her shoulder, suddenly twelve, suddenly frightened. "Something awful could have happened," he said, so low that she could barely hear. "I saw that red stuff on the walls . . . "

"Don't think about that anymore, sweetie," she said, hugging him. "I was worried about the same thing. But Megabite's just fine." She stroked the cat's head, and Megabite responded by bumping up under PJ's hand. "A little smelly, though."

He drew back a little, the expression on his face cycling between relief and worry. "Yeah. I'll help with the bath this time."

She pulled her son in and rested her cheek on the top of his head. "I'm so glad we're all OK. Something like this can be pretty scary." It was an invitation for him to talk, but he didn't, so she continued. "At least now I'll have an excuse to get a new desktop computer. That other one was a real dinosaur." A thought occurred to her, and she pulled herself away. "Here. You hold Megabite. I need to go back downstairs to talk to Leo."

PJ stopped in her own bedroom to check the contents of the closet before going downstairs.

"Sit down, Doc," he said. He sat heavily in one of the swivel chairs, the one that faced the vandalized wall, leaving PJ to sit with her back to the wall. She noticed small things like that.

"We found the cat, upstairs in the attic."

Schultz nodded, his face unreadable.

"Leo, I'm worried. What if Thomas and I had been home?"

"Then the vandal wouldn't have come in. Creeps like that like to leave their mark behind and get out, they don't like an audience while they're trashing a place."

"So you still think it was a vandal? Not related to the investigation?"

Schultz pursed his lips and blew air out noisily. "To tell you the truth, I'm puzzled. I can't see a clear relationship to the case, but I can't rule it out either."

"It looks to me like someone came in here specifically to smash the computer. That means he knew I had a computer in the first place. He didn't know about the laptop, though—it's still up in the bedroom closet, untouched."

Schultz didn't respond. He was staring at the writing on the wall.

"Another thing. I have this hunch about the cat. She acted exactly the same as she did when she was in Burton's apartment. She got so frightened that she soiled herself, and then hid until the whole thing was over."

"So? Cats do that kind of stuff all the time."

"No, they don't. Not this cat, anyway. Something really bad scared her, something that she remembered, poor thing. I think the same person was in my house." She paused, struck by what she had said. "I think the killer was here, right here in this room."

"You're wrong," Schultz interrupted.

"How do you know that?" PJ said. "I know it's only a hunch, but I think it's . . . "

"No, no, not you. That's what the letters say: *you're wrong,* spelled Y-U-R-R-O-N-G."

"Oh. Wrong about what?"

"I'm getting a bad feeling about this. When you combine the message with the bashed-up computer, it seems like somebody's trying to tell you that you're on the wrong track with the computer simulation."

"That seems plausible."

"Well, that means somebody—the killer—knows that computers are involved in the investigation. Knows that you're working on the case. That hasn't been given out to the media yet, I'm sure of that. So how would the killer know?"

"Are you thinking that the killer could be someone in the Department?"

"Christ, I hope not. But cops have flipped out before."

"What if it's Howard? He knows everything we've been doing."

Schultz snorted. "Not a chance. I know for a fact that he upchucks at the sight of a little gore. Got a weak stomach, never got used to it in all his years on the force. Maybe you haven't noticed his absence from both of the crime scenes, but I have. It's common knowledge."

"Maybe that's just a cover."

"You wouldn't say that if you'd ever been on the receiving end of his lunch."

"No." PJ laughed nervously. "No, I suppose I wouldn't. Who else, then?"

"Don't know. I'll look into it, though. But the whole thing could be unrelated to the killings. Could be the creep is a neighborhood punk who did this on a dare and is out there laughing at us now. You know, rattle the new person who just moved in. Kind of like the 90's version of toilet papering a house. Come to think of it, has your son hooked up with anybody strange?"

"I don't think it's unrelated."

"Because of the cat?"

"Because of the cat." PJ folded her arms across her chest. She was sticking to her hunch.

"As far as I'm concerned the jury's still out. I've seen too much random weirdness to dismiss the punk explanation out of hand." Schultz met her eyes and held them. "How's Thomas? And how are you doing?"

The whole episode had taken an emotional toll on PJ. She hugged her own arms tightly and shivered.

"Thomas seems to be taking this in stride. As for me, I don't know what to think. I'm scared. I feel violated, and I'm mad, too—that somebody could come in here and do this and get away with it."

"That's normal. That's what the creep who did this wanted you to feel, whether it was the killer or a neighborhood jerk with too much time on his hands. I do have a couple of suggestions, though," Schultz said.

"Yes?"

"Get the boy out of the house. School will be out for the summer soon, and then he'll be home all day by himself. Send him to live at a relative's house. Send him to camp. At the very least get somebody to stay with him. Then get yourself a car phone, one of those little portable cellular phones. The Department will pick up the tab. Call it safety equipment, or you can bury the expense someplace."

"I'll think about it."

He stood, bracing his right hand on the table and levering himself to his feet. She stood also, and for a moment it seemed like he was going to approach her, perhaps put an arm around her shoulder.

The moment passed.

"You got any rags handy?" he said. "I can get this wall cleaned up in no time."

PJ rummaged under the sink, coming up with a handful of dish towels and some spray cleaner. She was comforted by Schultz's solid presence as he swiped at the wall.

In a few minutes, the letters were gone, although there were a few stained areas which PJ was already planning to paint over.

"You and your son get some rest," Schultz said. "I'm going back to HQ to do the paperwork on this break-in. I'll see you tomorrow. Breakfast OK?"

"Sure," PJ said. "The diner, I suppose?"

He headed for the door and looked back over his shoulder.

"Take care, Doc."

When the door closed behind him, she went to fasten the lock. "Why, Detective," she said softly to herself, "I didn't know you cared."

Upstairs, PJ found Thomas still in the same position: sitting on the edge of the bed with the cat wrapped in a towel on his lap. He stood up when she came into the room, carrying the feline bundle in the crook of his arm.

"Let's take her to the kitchen sink," he said. "I've had about enough of this smell."

Thomas didn't say anything about the absence of the ketchup letters, although she caught him stealing glances at the wall. They worked smoothly together, and Megabite, indignant but clean, soon left the kitchen to methodically lick herself dry. PJ fixed grilled cheese sandwiches, and they sat at the table to eat dinner. Thomas pointedly did not put ketchup on his sandwich as he normally would have. Megabite, with face, paws, and tail mostly dry, back and belly still damp, came back in long enough to graciously accept a few bites of bread and cheese.

Thomas seemed too calm, too put together. PJ knew she certainly didn't feel that way.

"Thomas, I've been thinking about what happened. Maybe it would be a good idea for you to go away for awhile, until this investigation is over."

"You think it was connected to your work? Are you in any danger?"

She smiled. "It's sweet of you to ask. No, I'm not," she

said firmly. "Detective Schultz has things well in hand at work. But he thinks that you shouldn't be home by yourself once school lets out. And I agree with him."

"Where would I go?"

"To your dad's house, of course."

"No," Thomas said. "No way. I don't want to go back there. I'm just getting settled here. Don't ask me to do that, Mom." His voice was plaintive.

"It would just be for a little while. I'd feel better knowing you were safe."

"I'm OK here. I just got a new friend. I really like Winston. The worst thing is I couldn't take Megabite with me. You know how Dad is about cats."

In spite of the circumstances, it was gratifying to hear Thomas talking about Steven that way. Until just a short time ago, it seemed that Thomas and her ex-husband were on one side together, she on the other.

"All right. We'll drop it for now," she said. "But I want to talk about this again when school lets out next week. And I want you to stay in the after-school program every day until I get there to pick you up."

"Sure thing."

Thomas helped clean up the computer mess, putting everything in bags for the trash. Nothing was salvageable. They went upstairs to read for awhile before bedtime. The grilled cheese smell lingered in the house, and PJ could still smell it when she brushed her teeth.

Thomas held it all in until he was actually in bed, forehead kissed and blankets snugged around his neck. Then he broke down, letting all the fear and hurt and frustration spill out, not only about the break-in, but about everything that had happened since before the divorce. PJ listened to the jumbled outpouring, held him and rocked him, murmured that everything was going to be all right, her own cheeks wet with tears.

They were beginning to heal, and to help each other to do so.

CHAPTER

15

Over coffee, toast, and dry scrambled eggs, a toothpick flag pinning her wheat toast to the plate, Schultz told PJ that he was beginning to think that the killings might be sexually motivated, a gay sex triangle gone wildly astray and torn apart by jealousy. She discounted his theory on the basis that neither of the victim's genitals were mutilated, a hallmark of sex murders.

"There was mutilation, just not at the right spot. Maybe the freak had bad aim." She glared at him, but he continued, unperturbed. "Or poor eyesight."

"There's also the fact," she said around a mouthful of toast, "that Burton and Vanitzky didn't seem to know each other and didn't seem to have any friends in common."

"That's not a fact. That's a supposition based on what we know now. There could be a third person."

"Vanitzky's female lover says no way he was bisexual."

"Come on, Doc. You should know better than that. After all, you can't tell by looking, can you?" He gave her an exaggerated wink, and was rewarded with raised eyebrows.

"Besides," he continued, "there's that video tape. Vanitzky's bed warmer said he'd done that before, taped them together. Was the guy just an egotist? Was he maybe selling those tapes, or sharing them with somebody else?"

"You're missing the obvious," PJ said. "He would tape one lovemaking session, then watch it the next time. Like foreplay."

"Oh, is that what your ex-husband would do?"

Evidently her momentary embarrassment when she saw the video camera hadn't gone unnoticed. PJ sat for a moment, pushing egg around with her fork, hearing the metal-on-metal clatter from the kitchen, and noticing that the stainless steel fork had a deeply-carved rose pattern on the end.

"Detective, keep your bloodhound nose out of my personal life," she said in an even voice, "and I'll keep my psychology training out of yours."

"Touchy, touchy. He wouldn't still have any of those tapes, would he?"

Schultz was grinning like the Cheshire Cat. PJ figured that silence was the best response; no use getting drawn in further. She ate some more of her eggs, took a leisurely drink from her coffee cup. Letting her gaze wander around the room, she noticed the cook putting a couple of plates on the section of countertop that served as a pass-through from the kitchen. Their eyes met briefly. His were brown like the mudpies she made as a child, and with about the same amount of emotion. It was as though he was looking inward, unfocused. She found herself hoping he hadn't overheard her conversation with Schultz. She was embarrassed enough already without additional people getting in on it.

"There's something I've been meaning to ask you," she said, changing the subject. "Have you researched other cases similar to this? For example, doesn't the FBI"—she saw Schultz wince when she said FBI—"keep records on violent crimes?"

"I checked that out early, maybe a day or two into this assignment. There's nothing that matches the skin carvings of dogs, but there are a number of unsolved cases in which the body was found decapitated. The only thing in the St.

Louis area dates from the 1950's, so it's probably not our lad."

"Were any of the decapitated corpses mutilated?"

"Yes, some of them. You really don't want to hear the details over breakfast, do you?"

"No, I guess not. But are there patterns?"

Schultz sat back heavily. "Hard to say. Other than the obvious lack of a head, there's no long-term consistency. There might be a pattern, a particular mutilation or way of killing, that connects two or three. Then there might be a gap of months or even years, then another two or three that are similar. But the first set seems unrelated to the second set. There's nothing to link them positively to the same person. But I can't help thinking about how well prepared the murderer was. That carrying case has in it everything he needed, from carving tools to plastic bags. That requires either a great deal of foresight or . . . "

"Or a lot of practice. Are you thinking that our man is not new to the killing game?"

"Yes. Perhaps he worked the bugs out of his technique on less challenging victims: animals, kids, maybe people close to him, relatives or friends. Now he's graduated to less vulnerable targets."

They were both silent for a moment, thinking about Burton and Vanitzky.

"There's been an FBI agent sniffing around," Schultz said, "a guy named Ted Walmacher. I'll ask for his help on that. It should be right up his alley, since he loves correlating things. You can tell by the coordinated outfits he wears."

"I thought all FBI agents wore dark suits and trench coats."

"You haven't met Ted."

"Hmmm . . . "

"Is that a professional 'hmmm,' Doctor Gray?"

"Pretty good, isn't it? There's a whole course in saying 'hmmm' that we psychologists have to take, and I got an

A," she said. "Serial killers usually maintain the same method of killing, as a kind of ritual. The method is based on something important to them, something that they are fixated on but might be hard for an outsider to fathom. I've never heard of a serial killer changing the method substantially."

"What if the method is more connected to the decapitation?" Schultz asked. "The rest is secondary, just window-dressing. Then there would be a consistent pattern."

"That's true. Or we could be dealing with a killer who is capable of breaking out of a ritual and creating a new one. That would be a new wrinkle in serial killing."

"There's nothing new under the sun, Doc. No matter how crazy a guy is, no matter how clever he thinks he is in coming up with exotic ways to kill somebody, you can bet it's been done before. The human race has had thousands of years of practice."

PJ's morning at her desk was uneventful. Schultz didn't want to talk about the break-in at her home the previous day. He said he was letting it ferment, whatever that meant. He and his assistants went off to have a conference in the lunchroom, a dismal place with no windows and a bank of vending machines along one wall. When the phone rang, she welcomed the interruption.

"Doctor Gray? Doctor Michael Wolf here. I believe we have a mutual friend. Goes by the name of Merlin."

"Merlin. Yes." PJ chided herself for her uninspired response.

"I'm working with a group at Washington University School of Engineering. My specialty is biomedical engineering."

PJ was wondering what this had to do with her, and why Merlin had put this man in touch with her. Doctor Wolf's voice was confident, deep, and warm. Maybe after their last online chat, Merlin thought she needed calming down.

"I've been trying to develop VR simulations of surgeries as a training aide for medical students. You know, let them wave their scalpels at a VR abdomen before they try it out on the real thing. Better than cadavers, who don't bleed realistically or suddenly stop breathing. Could also be used with one surgeon who's an expert at some new procedure teaching another surgeon halfway across the country, networked together, and working in the same VR surgical suite."

Now she understood why this man was talking to her.

Thank you, Merlin!

"It sounds fascinating, Doctor Wolf. Um, did Merlin happen to mention . . ."

"Call me Mike. Whenever I hear Doctor Wolf, I think somebody's talking to my father. Yes, he did mention that you were doing some research in criminology, and that you'd like to get your hands on an HMD."

Research in criminology?

"Well, yes, I would. I've got the rest of the hardware, and some software I've developed over the past five years or so. But I'm on a limited budget"—she wondered if she should have said grant—"here, so I was hoping to borrow a headset. Temporarily, of course."

"It so happens I've got two. I won't need the other one until the second half of my project, which is probably four or five months away. At least. Could be a year. That's when I'll be ready to have a shared VR with a surgeon on either end of the line. And get this—I've got the gloves, too, so that surgeons or med students can pick things up and use them in the VR."

PJ knew that he was referring to a specialized input device, a pair of gloves that the user wore which had sensors embedded in the fabric. The sensors fed information to the computer about how the wearer was moving his hands. It was like wearing a joystick. You could curl your virtual fingers around a virtual scalpel, pick it up, and use it on a virtual patient. It was more than she had hoped for. "Doctor . . . Mike. When could we get together on this?"

She heard a chuckle. "Merlin said you were a fast mover. How about today? Lunch?"

"Sounds terrific."

"There's a great pizza place right across Millbrook Boulevard from the campus. It's called Giorgio's. I can walk there from my office. Can you make it, say, at twelve-thirty?"

PJ got directions and hung up. She was elated, and caught herself wondering what Mike looked like. His voice had been very pleasant, and, she had to admit to herself, downright sexy. It amazed her that she noticed. Since she and Steven separated, her sex life had not just been on the back burner, but off the stove entirely. When Steven dumped her for a woman whose body would look at home on a centerfold photo, PJ's self-esteem took a major blow. That she was able to notice and respond to the undercurrent in Mike's voice was, she figured, a good sign. She was suddenly conscious of a feeling of warmth low in her abdomen. Her vaginal muscles contracted, squeezing a phantom penis, and the warmth traveled quickly up to her navel and down to her knees, as though a hot white light had flashed across her midsection.

Checking her watch, she discovered that she had about fifteen minutes before she had to leave. She grabbed her purse and headed down the hallway to the ladies' room.

The full length mirror was not overly cruel to her. The twenty extra pounds she had been carrying around since the divorce certainly hadn't disappeared, though. This morning she had selected pleated trousers, a lightweight wool blend with enough substance so that it didn't cling to the fullness of her hips or thighs. The trousers were forest green, and she had paired them with a short-sleeve silk blouse in an ivory shade that went well with the green. The blouse was full cut and draped smoothly from a round neckline. It was tucked into the trousers, and her waistline was still well-defined and supple. The extra weight seemed to collect at her hips, thighs, and, she noted critically when she checked her profile, her backside. Around her neck was a slim gold chain that held a heart-shaped locket. Inside were two pictures of her son; one of them was a recent replacement for a picture of Steven. Her shoulder-length chestnut hair framed her face attractively. The gray hairs mixed in gave an honest impression of maturity that was echoed by the tiny wrinkles at the corners of her eyes and mouth. Her skin had a fresh appearance, still tight over her well-defined cheekbones and at her throat. She had worn no makeup today. Her gray eyes were clear, so light they were almost colorless, but lively and intelligent.

She opened her purse, opted for a swipe with a deep red lipstick, then blotted most of it away so that her lips had a subtle red tint. She powdered her nose even though it wasn't shiny.

Oh, geez, look at me. I'm acting like a teenager. He's probably married. Or gay. Or ninety years old. Or all of the above.

Giorgio's was nondescript on the outside, but the inside was full of character. There were starving artist-type oil paintings covering almost every inch of wall space, and red and white checkered tablecloths atop round tables. Heavy red drapes were drawn over the windows, making the place dim and cool compared to the dazzling sunshine of early summer outside. Candles in crystal holders shaped like snowballs adorned every table, and most of the tables were occupied. She told the hostess that she was meeting Doctor Wolf, and was led to his table.

As she approached, she was aware of his eyes reflecting the candlelight. Then, as her eyes adjusted to the low light level, she became aware that something else was reflecting the candlelight. He was bald, his head as smooth as an egg.

"Go ahead," he said in that warm voice, now with a touch of amusement. "Get a good look. Everybody does."

"I'm sorry," PJ stammered. "I didn't mean to stare. It's

just so unexpected. But certainly not unattractive." He didn't rise to shake her hand, so she took a seat and looked him over appraisingly. He sat still for it. It was hard to guess his age. When she had first seen him, the baldness automatically made her think he was sixty or over. A closer look at the vitality of his face revised her estimate down to the early forties. She couldn't tell his height exactly, since he was sitting down, but he seemed about average height. His face was angular, with well-defined cheekbones and chin. His nose was large and sharp. Absurdly she thought of slicing cheese on it. His eyebrows were shaggy and full, as if to make up for the lack of hair northward. His eyes and eyebrows were indeterminate in color in the low light, but she had the impression they were the deep, threatening gray of a summer thunderhead. His chest and arms were muscular, but not overly developed. He was wearing a white T-shirt with a gaudy toucan and the words "Save the Rainforests" on the front. There was a softness at his waist, a slight bulge that tattled of cream sauces or candy bars. PJ thought that he used to exercise regularly but spent more time at his computer lately than in his jogging shoes. Thinking of the view of her own profile in the mirror, she admitted to herself that she was perversely pleased that his body wasn't perfect, that it showed signs of wear and age, stress and indulgence, like her own.

She wondered if he liked slightly short women with ample posteriors and a little gray in their hair.

A waitress came and brought menus and goblets of ice water. PJ opened her menu flat on the table and stared at it even though it was really too dim to make out the items. She was giving him his chance to check her out. She was well aware that his eyes were roaming her downturned face and her upper body. The low warm feeling she had felt earlier seemed about to recur, and her nipples hardened in anticipation. She raised the menu to cover her chest. The silk blouse did not offer a lot of concealment.

"So," she said, "what's good here?"

They ended up with house salads topped with red onion slices, black olives, chunks of mozzarella, and buttery croutons heavily flavored with sage. Mike ordered bread sticks, which came surrounded by a cloud of garlic aroma, and virgin olive oil with freshly ground pepper floated on top to dip them into. Individual pizzas arrived next, each in the iron skillets in which they were baked. The conversation was light, mostly about interesting places to visit in St. Louis. Mike had lived in the city all his life, had been born in Barnes Hospital across from Forest Park, grown up in the Central West End, and attended Washington University for his undergraduate and graduate degrees. Although he was well-traveled, he always came home to roost. Then she gave him the basics of her life, about growing up in a small town in Iowa, wanting to become a psychologist to help people, of her fascination with computers as a tool for investigating the mind.

"Divorced?" he asked.

"Yes."

"Me too." And that was that.

Halfway through her pizza, PJ dropped a forkful of food, and hot chunks of tomato rolled down her silk blouse, leaving an oily trail and ending up in her lap. At the beginning of the meal, she would have been horrified to make such a blunder. By that time, though, they both simply laughed about it. Mike swiped an extra cloth napkin from an unoccupied table and she did the best she could with it. He even offered to help, but given the location of the stains—between her breasts and in the crotch of her pants—she just raised her eyebrows and kept wiping.

They were comfortable together.

When PJ got back to her office, she was in a good mood, and it wasn't entirely due to the wine she had at lunch. On her desk was a large duffel bag containing the headset that Mike had lent her. She had seen the bag on the floor next to his chair in the restaurant, a lumpy shape in the dim light, and wondered why he had brought his laundry along. Later, when he was putting the bag into the trunk of her car, she told him that, and they both had a good laugh about it.

Just as PJ reached to unzip the bag, the phone rang.

"Damn!" She considered not picking up, decided that was unprofessional.

"CHIP team, Gray speaking," she said into the receiver.

"Hello. I'm trying to reach Mr. Schultz, Leo Schultz."

Figures.

The voice was low, female, and slightly nervous.

"Just a moment, I'll transfer you."

"Wait, wait. Are you working on the Ballet Butcher case?"

PJ was aware that the media had connected the two killings. Some details, such as the absence of the victims' heads from the scene and the skin carvings, had miraculously been kept from the public. So far, at least. But journalists had picked up on the theme of murder in the artistic realm—musician, dancer. Who's next?

"Yes, I am."

There was a hesitation on the other end. Finally the voice blurted, "I hate to ask this, because I know I'd hate to get asked myself, but are you the secretary or something?"

"No," PJ said, letting some irritation leak through.

"A cop, then?"

"Not exactly. I'm a civilian employee. There's a special task force," *more like a task farce, for all the results we're getting,* she thought, "assigned to the investigation. I'm the head of the task force."

"Great. I'd rather talk to a woman anyway. The clerk in Homicide gave me Schultz's name but your phone number."

"May I help you with something?" PJ looked longingly at the duffel bag on her desk.

"Yes. I believe I have some information about the case. I think I've seen the killer."

PJ tensed. "What makes you think that?"

"An experience I had last night. Listen, I really want to talk to you in person about it. Can I come in and see you?"

"Now?" PJ blurted. "I mean," she backpedaled, "couldn't you give me some details on the phone? Then I could have Detective Schultz contact you. He's in charge of all the field work."

If you weren't before, Leo, you are now.

"I really need to talk to someone. I'm kind of spooked."

PJ detected an urgent tone in the voice, almost desperation. Her psychology training kicked in. "OK, we'll talk. I'll get Schultz and we can all talk about it together. How's that? Can you be here in half an hour?"

"I can be there in about five minutes. I'm on Market Street, across from City Hall, at a pay phone. Leave Schultz out of it, OK? I don't connect well with men."

"Oh, I see."

Yes, I do indeed.

PJ had of course encountered lesbians socially and professionally, both as patients and colleagues, but they always seemed to set her on edge. She worried about silly things, like what if something she said was misinterpreted. A female patient once asked her for a date after a particularly intense series of sessions. PJ was totally unwilling to compromise the therapist-patient relationship. On those grounds, she gently declined. But she was reluctant to examine her own feelings closely. What if the request had come outside of therapy? What would she have done? She pictured Mike's face, and felt the warm flush of attraction.

Nope, she thought, *the pull just isn't there.* Then she became aware of the pause in the conversation, and hoped the woman hadn't noticed it.

"Ask for me at the front desk. I'm Doctor Penelope Gray. You'll have to get a pass. I don't believe I got your name?"

"Sheila Armor. Like a suit of armor."

PJ hung up the phone and immediately dialed Schultz's extension. No answer. She didn't know anything about interrogating witnesses. Was she supposed to tape record everything? Take notes? Be hard and cynical or soft and understanding?

She was on her own, just as she was when she was in a closed room with a patient. She would have to handle it, and she knew that she would, somehow.

OK, so you wanted to do something in the public interest. Well, here comes the public.

PJ hurriedly put the duffel bag in the corner of her office. She started fresh coffee brewing and got out a pad of yellow lined paper and a pen. The coffee had just started to drip through when there was a firm knock at her door.

"Door's open," she said. She made sure her face was composed.

Sheila Armor didn't so much enter a room as capture it. She was tall, lithe, and vibrant. Reddish-blond hair cascaded in luxurious waves to her neatly rounded bottom. Her complexion was fair and clear enough to be used in the "after" photo in an acne medication ad. Her eyes were a startling green and her mouth was as delicate as a cherub's. She was nearly six feet tall, and most of that height was wrapped in a length of sheer material, wound many times around her body in a complex fashion, leaving her shoulders and ankles bare. The muscles of her bare arms were well-defined, and she had the body tone of a weight lifter combined with the suppleness of a dancer. The overall impression was almost too much for the tiny office to contain.

PJ stood to shake hands, conscious of her own five-foot-three height and the extra flesh padding her trousers. Sheila's grip was as firm as her muscular arms implied, and it lingered as the woman appraised PJ's face. Finally, she released PJ's hand and sank into a chair. Despite the fabric wrapping her body, she managed to cross her legs neatly at the knees, a feat PJ would have thought impossible. PJ noticed that she was wearing open sandals, and that her toenails were painted in a rainbow of colors.

PJ said the first thing that came to mind. "I'll bet you created quite a sensation out front."

Sheila's laugh was genuine. "Generally I bring someone along to scrape the men's jaws off the floor after I've gone past," she said. "God, I'm glad you answered the phone. I feel so much better now that I'm here. I probably sounded like an idiot on the phone."

"Well . . ."

"At least I know I can relax here. You look kind of formidable, but that stain on your blouse gives you away. Salsa? Marinara?"

"Pizza," PJ responded.

"Now I know I'm in good hands."

PJ liked this woman. There was none of the awkwardness she had experienced before in direct conversation with lesbians. She was convinced now that any problem she may have had in the past was in her own head, not intrinsic to the relationship. She grinned inwardly. What on Earth had she been worried about just a few minutes ago?

"Would you like some coffee?" she said.

"Please. Black. Are you a medical doctor?"

"No. Psychologist." PJ poured, and the two regarded each other over steaming cups.

"Thanks. I live on caffeine during the day. I usually don't eat anything until six or seven in the evening." Sheila patted her trim tummy.

PJ started to say something about food and lost causes, but Sheila kept right on talking.

"You don't know who I am, do you?"

"I . . ."

"That's OK. I'm probably not a hot topic in scientific circles. I'm an artist." She shook her head; reddish waves threatened to tumble into her coffee cup. "A good one. Humble I am not."

"Most artists aren't."

"We are an obnoxious lot, aren't we? I just finished a one-woman show at a gallery in Clayton. I've got another one in Paris in a couple of months. Had to hold back some pieces from the current show for the next one, which really burned the little prick who runs the gallery. Serves him right. Tried to stick his greasy paws on my ass. Say, is that sexual harassment or something?"

"Could be." PJ was smiling. She was swept along on the irrepressible tide that was Sheila Armor, and she was enjoying herself. Briefly she wondered how Schultz would get along with this woman. She doubted that they could stand to be in the same room together.

"Well, anyway, I've been reading about the Ballet Butcher, the guy who whacked that marvelous pianist Burton and that ballet soloist, what's-his-name. I've heard Burton play—what a shame he's gone. The dancer I never saw. Can't tolerate looking at guys in tights."

"What exactly is your involvement with the case?" PJ thought that sounded very cop-like. Schultz would approve.

"Yesterday I saw the killer. I'm sure of it. He was following me."

A little alarm went off in PJ's head. Delusions, persecution, paranoia . . .

"Do you want to talk about it?" It was a textbook opening. Sheila gave her an odd look.

"Of course. Why else would I be here?"

PJ nodded and sat back in her chair. "I'm all ears."

"Last night about midnight I walked home from my lover's townhouse. She only lives a few blocks away, but we decided not to live together yet because . . ." Sheila got a far-off look for a moment. "Oh, that's beside the point. Anyway, I was walking home alone. Then I felt—don't laugh, now—an evil presence behind me on the sidewalk."

PJ searched Sheila's face. The woman was biting her lip, waiting to see if PJ was going to believe her.

"Now you know the other reason why I didn't want to talk to a man," Sheila said. "I can just imagine telling a male cop that."

"You might be surprised." PJ didn't elaborate. She was thinking of Schultz. There was a depth to him that she had not explored, would not be permitted to explore. When he got that look on his face, staring off, seeing nothing but inner scenarios, she felt that something mystical was going on in him. She sensed that he was trying to reach out and connect himself to the killer, not physically, but psychically. Not that she would dream of broaching the subject with him.

"I turned around to look," Sheila continued, "which was probably not the brightest thing I've ever done. I saw a shadowy figure, definitely a man, about thirty feet or so behind me. He seemed startled that I had turned around. Then he started acting drunk, you know, staggering around on the sidewalk. He lurched over to a fire hydrant, unzipped, and pissed on it."

PJ said nothing. She didn't want to break Sheila's concentration. Sheila took a sip of her coffee, and PJ noticed that her hand trembled slightly.

"I know he wasn't drunk. He only started acting that way when he knew I had seen him."

"OK, so somebody might or might not have been following you. What makes you think it was the killer?"

"Because I'm an artist. You might not be aware of it, but in the art scene I'm hot. I've been in the newspapers, on talk shows. There was a lot of publicity from the gallery. He wasn't just following some juicy piece of tail down the street. He was following me, specifically." She leaned forward earnestly. "Don't you get it? Musician, dancer, artist. I'm going to be his next victim."

Even though she knew that Sheila was waiting anxiously for her reaction, PJ took the time to weigh the woman's credibility. The scale didn't tip either way.

"What did the man look like?"

Sheila sighed. "I knew we'd get around to that. I don't have much to offer. It was dark, he wasn't standing under a street light. Average height, lean build, wearing a T-shirt and jeans. I didn't see his face because he was wearing a baseball cap, and the bill of the cap hid his face."

"Anything else at all? Color of the cap?"

Sheila shook her head.

"What happened after that?"

"He kind of grunted while he was pissing, a strange sound, maybe more like a growl. Before he finished, I turned around and ran home. As far as I know, he didn't follow."

"Why didn't you call the police right then, when you got home?"

"I don't know. I was really spooked. When I get scared, I can't talk about it right away. My throat closes up. It took me all this time to work up the nerve to make that phone call."

PJ began making notes on her pad while everything was fresh in her mind. Sheila sat in silence as PJ's pen scratched across the paper. Finally, PJ put the pen down and looked up.

"What're you going to do?" Sheila asked. She nervously outlined her lips with one delicate finger tip.

In that moment, the scales tipped for PJ: this brash woman had revealed a hidden vulnerability at considerable cost to herself. Why would she do it if it was meaningless? There had to be something there.

Sheila had said that she felt an evil presence. In PJ's work, she was supposed to be nonjudgmental. Actions were adaptive or nonadaptive, destructive or constructive. But not evil, because that implied a moral judgment. Yet as soon as Sheila had said it, PJ knew that she thought of the killer that way, too. An evil let loose on the world, and she had to play her part in stopping it.

"The first thing I'm going to do is talk to my partner about this." *Amazing how that word* partner *rolls off the tongue*. "Then I'm going to get a protective watch started. Right away. Tonight." PJ hoped she wasn't blowing smoke; this woman was hanging on her every word.

"I want you to go home and stay there," PJ said. "Can you take a few days off work?"

"My studio is in my home. Once I get there I won't have to go out."

"What's your address and phone number?"

PJ took down the information, and Sheila stood up to leave. At the door, she pivoted. "You get this guy," she said, with a low feline ferocity in her voice. "He's evil. I know he's evil."

And she was gone.

CHAPTER

16

Schultz was sitting at his desk, trying to ignore the conversation Barnesworth was having at the next desk over. Early on, just as a game, he decided to count the number of times Barnesworth used the word "fuck" on the phone. He lost count after five minutes and sixty-three times. He was trying to block out the distractions and let his thoughts and feelings about the killer come into that quiet place inside his head, the place where connections were made, where intuition lived. Now that he had a couple of assistants, he had sent them back over territory he had already covered to get their take on things. He was going over their written reports, absorbing their impressions, and seeing how they fit with his own. Just as the background sounds were beginning to fade, he saw PJ coming into the room. Sure enough, she made a beeline for his desk.

"Oh, there you are," she said.

"Shrinks say the damnedest things." He was annoyed at the interruption, and she wasn't going to get off easy. Besides, he had little patience with those who stated the obvious.

She did a mock recoil, a comic expression on her face and her arms raised to ward off continued criticism. He felt his mood lighten. A little.

"I tried to call you earlier. You must have been away from your desk," she said.

"Is that what they call taking a piss these days?"

She sighed. "I can see you're in a rotten mood. I'd come back later, but I really need to talk with you about a visitor I just had."

"The Terminex guy finally get around to your office? He was in here yesterday."

This time all he got was silence and a glare.

"You really ought to work on that sense of humor, Doc. Don't they say humor is food for the soul?"

"That's good for the soul, not food. The state of my soul is my business, not yours."

"This is starting to sound like your first day on the job. I thought we'd come a long way since then."

"You just don't know when to drop it, do you? Could you please come to my office?" She glanced at Barnesworth, still cursing on the phone. "It's quieter there."

"Hey, Barnesworth, you hear that? Doc says shut up."

Barnesworth covered the receiver with his hand. "Go fuck yourself, Schultz."

Schultz shrugged. "Pleasant guy," he said to PJ, in a voice loud enough for everyone in the room to hear. "Good attitude. Must come from jacking off in the stall in the men's room every morning." That got him a rude gesture from Barnesworth. "Yeah, everybody knows what you're doing in there, you prick."

PJ grabbed Schultz's arm, pulled him out of the room, and propelled him down the hall.

"Shithead," he tossed back in Barnesworth's direction.

The rest of the short trip down the hall passed in sullen silence. PJ took her seat behind her desk as Schultz sat down heavily in one of the two folding chairs she was still using. He wondered if she knew that her requisition for actual chairs would never make it past Wall's desk. He picked up a rubber band and fired it at the ceiling. It rebounded and landed in PJ's hair, but she was unaware of it.

"Hostility," she said.

"Yeah. Ain't it wonderful?"

She was trying to keep a straight face, but her eyes were twinkling. "It does have its uses. I'd have to agree with you about Barnesworth. He's an asshole."

"A true B & P," Schultz nodded happily.

"What's that? Or do I even want to know?"

"Brown and puckered."

"Now that we've settled that, can we get some business done?"

"Sure. What's up, Doc?"

PJ groaned in mock exasperation. "A woman came to see me right after lunch. Her name was Sheila Armor. She's an artist. Have you ever heard of her?"

"Nope."

"I hadn't either. But she said that she's big news in the art world. Last night she was followed on the street by a man she thinks is our killer."

"I had one a couple days ago who thought the Ballet Butcher lived in the apartment downstairs because the jerk had weird taste in music."

Schultz watched PJ's face fall like a chocolate mousse that's just had the oven door slammed.

"I assume you're not taking these reports seriously," she said.

"That's not exactly true. You just have to be selective. For instance, the old lady who turned in the guy downstairs because he played loud music might have been well-intentioned, but she was dead wrong."

"How do you know that?"

"It's hard to explain. Experience. Street sense. What separates you and me."

"There's that hostility again, Detective. The woman who was here seemed very credible to me."

Schultz backed off. "Give me the particulars. Facts. Impressions."

"Well," PJ hesitated, "first of all, she's a lesbian. But that's got nothing to do with it."

"Then why are you telling me that first thing?"

"Because you told me to give you impressions, and that's what I noticed first. In fact, I knew that before I even saw her."

"Doc, you're rambling. Take a deep breath and start at the beginning."

"All right. When I got back from lunch I got a phone call from a woman. She asked for you. I was about to transfer her when she asked, practically pleaded, to talk to me instead. Because I'm a woman." PJ seemed to be waiting for some smart remark, so Schultz didn't oblige. He liked to keep 'em guessing.

"She came in to talk. Last night she was walking home alone—"

"Time?"

"Nearly midnight. From her lover's townhouse. She sensed someone behind her and turned around."

"Stupid shit."

"Yes, she felt that way also. There was a man there, and as soon as he was seen he began to act drunk. Pissed in the street."

"Maybe he wasn't acting. Maybe he was just doing what drunks do."

"But when she first saw him, he seemed startled, and not drunk at all."

Schultz leaped ahead. "So she thinks it's the Ballet Butcher stalking his next victim: an artist."

"Exactly," PJ said, nodding. "She ran home and was too scared to talk about it last night, just blocked it out until today."

"What did the freak look like?"

"She didn't get a good look. Too dark." PJ checked her notes. "Average height, lean build, wearing a T-shirt, jeans, and a baseball cap."

"What team?"

"She didn't . . . Detective, are you making a joke of this?"

Schultz plastered a "Who, me?" look on his face.

"Look, Doc," he said, "let's take a look at what we've got here. A woman walks alone late at night, maybe a little nervous, a high-strung artist type. A drunk ambles down the same piece of sidewalk, answers a call of nature. She gets spooked, high-tails it home, drops into bed in a tizzy. Reads the newspapers, sees an article about a guy offing people in the arts. Puts one and one together and gets three."

"If you had been here, you would have seen that there was more to it than that."

"Why wasn't I here? Doesn't this fall in the area of field work? She didn't come in here to play games on your computer."

"I told you, she didn't want to talk to a man."

"What, I got balls, makes me insensitive?"

"In this case, yes."

"OK," he said, waving his hand dismissively, "you wore me down. Did you get the broad's address? I'll stop by and have a talk with her. Maybe I'll send Anita. At least she's got tits."

PJ hesitated, tapping her pencil on the desk.

"Out with it, Doc. Reticence isn't your style."

"I promised her a protective watch."

That shut Schultz up for a full minute.

"You planning on parking your ass in a car doing surveillance?"

"I would think that falls in your area."

The look he gave PJ should have withered her on the spot, but she took it pretty well.

"All right, here's the deal," he said. "I'll try to get tonight covered. Notice I said *try.* I'll do it myself, or get Anita or Dave. Tomorrow you go to Lieutenant Wall and explain to him you want a surveillance team assigned to you. Based on your finely-honed detective skills."

"Fair enough. I understand your resentment."

"Bullshit shrink-talk."

"What do you want me to say?" PJ flared. "That I'm so glad we see eye-to-eye on this?"

"Are we done here? I've got some actual police work to do at my desk."

"I've had about enough of this, Detective." She stood up, agitated, and put both hands on the desk. The rubber band in her hair slid off, momentarily distracting her as it landed on the desktop. "Are we going to work together or not? I need a decision right now."

Schultz abruptly stood up and faced her. She drew herself up to her full height, which came to about the middle of his chest. There were a lot of things he could have said, but he knew only one thing mattered.

"I want to catch this bastard. I want to hang him up by his thumbs and cut his balls off. That clear enough for you? Yes, damn it, we're working together."

She slammed her fist down on the table. Her voice was low and hot, like a tomcat answering a challenge.

"Then let's catch the bastard, before he kills again."

Schultz stopped in the men's room on his way back to his desk. He splashed some cold water on his face and dried with paper towels. There was a rage in him today, and it came from his lack of progress in the investigation. He knew he had tossed some of that rage in PJ's direction, but what the hell. She was a big girl. She could handle it.

He could almost hear the seconds ticking away, knowing that another murder would come soon. How exactly he knew that, he couldn't say. The golden thread that bound him to the killer, that would eventually connect them heart to heart and mind to mind, was growing stronger, taking shape and extending out into the darkness. But not fast enough.

At his desk he tried once again to find that place inside where thoughts came and went and left behind shadows of truth. The "Star-Spangled Banner" that the killer was humming in the video tape from Vanitzky's place kept popping into his head, and along with it something that PJ had mentioned: the man following Sheila Armor was wearing a baseball cap.

He was reluctant to admit it, but that slim prospect was about the only thing he had going at the moment. Although still skeptical, he decided that surveillance wouldn't do any harm. Schultz debated calling Anita or Dave, remembered that Dave had a birthday party for his daughter tonight, and that Anita was deep into a summer flu but was trying not to show it. He decided to take tonight himself and approach the lieutenant about personnel tomorrow. He would get over to Armor's apartment about seven PM, when it was still daylight. The first murder had occurred around nine PM, the second about one AM. Obviously, the killer did his nasty work in the dark.

At about five-thirty, Schultz was clearing his desk to leave when his phone rang.

"Schultz."

"Yo, Schultz. This is Cortman, Narcotics."

"Yeah?"

"Thought you might appreciate knowing about a bust we made this afternoon. Thought you should hear it from a friend, you know?"

"What is it?" Schultz was tense. He thought he already knew what the man was going to say.

"Your son, Rick. He was picked up for selling marijuana outside a junior high."

"Christ. No shit?"

"No shit. He was observed making a couple of sales before he was collared. You could maybe talk to the arresting officer. That's Ricardo, Jesus Ricardo. Know him?"

"Yeah. Tall dude, lots of gold rings, knife scar on his left cheek."

"That's the guy. Since this is a first drug-related arrest . . . well, you could talk to Ricardo, see if you and he and the DA's office can work something out."

"Yeah. Maybe I will. Thanks for letting me know."

Schultz hung up the phone and sat, staring at his desk calendar which was still showing April. His thoughts were disjointed. The boy's birth, Julia crying out, Schultz whisked into the waiting room, pacing and sweating. Three candles on a birthday cake. Rick's first bicycle ride. A young teenager, going around with bandages on his face to make others think he had nicked himself shaving. His driver's license, first night out on his own in the family car. Then the troubling times: suspended for vandalism at school, brought home drunk a few times by understanding fellow cops. Mood changes, shoplifting once, quarrels over staying out late. Rick giving them the news that he was dropping out of college, couldn't hack it. Moving back in, sleeping late, jobless. Moving in with a friend after a big argument with Schultz.

Lazy. Insolent.

He and Julia were at opposite poles on how to deal with Rick, had been for many years. But Schultz deferred to her, left the decisions to her because he was out of the house so much, by necessity in the early years, by choice later on.

Now his son, a cop's son, had chosen to embarrass good old Dad by selling drugs to twelve-year-olds.

He wasn't in any hurry to spring Rick from the grasp of the Department. He knew he could, if he wanted to. He could collect some favors. But first, he was going to go home and talk to Julia about it. Really talk, for a change. He wasn't going to let her defend the boy and then clam up, refusing to discuss it.

He was going to shove this in her face, by God.

Angry and deeply ashamed, Schultz left to confront his wife at home and later, he figured, his son in jail. He was going to get a late start on his surveillance at the Armor place, but his blood was up, and it was such a long shot anyway.

CHAPTER

17

Pauley Mac wearily lugged the case into his kitchen. Before opening it, he tended to other problems. His arms and face were scratched, and bruises were beginning to show there and elsewhere. He washed and dried carefully, and applied some antibiotic cream. He decided against bandages, figuring that would look a bit melodramatic.

The case contained the head of Sheila Armor, an artist, and she had fought ferociously. He had gotten into her apartment by imitating the special knock that her female lover used. He knew that the lover sometimes came by around seven PM, so that's when he timed his visit. Pauley Mac had found out that the lover, an executive at a marketing firm, wouldn't be over this evening. She was cheating on Sheila with a secretary from the firm. He had seen the two of them, dressed for excitement and heading out for the evening, and was certain, from prior observation, that they would come back to the executive's townhouse to spend the night.

Pauley Mac didn't have a disguise this time. He was counting on surprise to get him inside the door, and he was clutching the pewter toad he used to knock his guests unconscious. When she answered the door, it was obvious that she had been working. She was wearing only a man's T-shirt which must have been a tall size, because it skimmed her thighs, and she was a tall woman. The T-shirt had originally been white, but it was covered with streaks of paint, some of them still wet. She carried a brush in her right hand, loaded with bright blue paint.

She must have had some self-defense training. She was quick and strong, and several inches taller than Pauley Mac. He got inside the door, but when he swung the pewter toad, she blocked his arm. The toad and the paint brush went flying across the room, and both were left empty-handed. There was a scuffle. He slipped on the polished wood floor of her living room, and he thought that she was going to get the better of him. He scrambled to his feet. It was pure luck that Pauley Mac landed a punch to her jaw, forcing her to tumble backward and hit her head against a steam radiator.

The pain of his first knife stroke on her back brought her abruptly back to consciousness, but by then she was securely tied.

When he was packed up and ready to leave her apartment, he looked around for the special item to leave for the police. He hadn't brought any props with him this time, like the roses or the chocolate-covered strawberries. He wandered around the apartment, trying to get an idea. He ended up in the large room that served as her studio. On an easel was an unfinished painting of a woman and her daughter enjoying a picnic in a park. The young girl's arm was outstretched and her face was lit with delight as she pointed out the beautiful sunset to her mother. The sun, clouds, and sky were incomplete, with only a few brush strokes to suggest the shapes. Pauley Mac smiled. With his gloved hand, he picked up one of the brushes which were lying in disarray on a nearby table, and went back into the living room. He dipped the brush in the woman's blood on the floor, where it was seeping in between the wooden planks, and returned to the canvas. He drew in a childish-looking half-circle sun on the horizon, with straight lines sticking out of it to represent the rays of sunshine. He wondered how long it would take the police to notice that the sunset on her latest—and last—painting was not done by Armor but rather *of* her.

At home, he debated not using her brain because he felt that she would be one of the hostile guests, the destructive voices in his mind that urged him to make mistakes. But it would be such a waste. He really did want to learn to paint, and he liked this artist's style. He had read about her show in the *Riverfront Times*. He had showered and shaved carefully, put on some nice clothes—his only really nice outfit—and gone to the gallery in Clayton. Her work appealed to him. She did mostly landscapes, in a vibrant style that practically leapt off the canvas.

This was one of his riskiest adventures, because the woman actually saw him the day before when he was following her home. Pauley Mac was scared when he was seen, but Dog had the perfect solution, one that came naturally, pissing on that fire hydrant so that she would think he was just a drunk. Typical of Dog, anyway.

By the time he cleaned up the kitchen, stomach comfortably full, it was nearly midnight. He studied the instant photos he had taken in Armor's apartment, and was pleased with his work. Digging the photo album out from the bottom of his underwear drawer, he slid the photos into plastic sleeves. He couldn't resist paging through the rest of the album, regretting for the hundredth or thousandth time that he hadn't had an instant camera during the earlier part of his self-improvement program. Looking at the photos gave him an erection, but he had things left to do, so he let it subside.

Pauley Mac opened the freezer door atop his refrigerator and studied the contents critically. With the two other heads already inside, there simply wasn't room for a third unless he threw out some ice cream. His favorite flavor, too: chocolate chip cookie dough. Dog would have thrown it out, but Pauley Mac wouldn't stand for it.

When he was younger, he used to preserve the heads, having studied the method of the Jivaro Indians of Ecuador. After a while it got to be awkward lugging the lot of them around in a suitcase. Even shrunken heads take up room when they accumulate. To make things even more unpleasant, some of the guests reproached him in his mind whenever they caught a glimpse of their own heads.

Besides, Dog liked to travel light.

One afternoon, when he lived in Illinois, he rented a boat from a marina and dumped them all in Lake Michigan. He thought of it as a spring cleaning effort.

He decided to save the two that were already frozen and get rid of the fresh one from tonight, primarily because of the long hair attached to it, which meant it would take up more than its fair share of room in the freezer. He might have to look into buying a stand-alone freezer. When he started his next cycle, Childhood Innocence, he would need more storage room. *Although,* he mused, *using children could be a space-saver.*

He bundled the woman's head in burlap and drove to Busch Wildlife Area, a reserve in St. Charles County with a lot of fishing ponds. He selected one of the gravel turnoffs that led to a numbered pond. It was overcast that night, so there was no moonlight to help him out. He had to use a flashlight when he shut off the headlights and got out of the truck. Pauley Mac weighted the bundle with rocks and tossed it into the pond. He had done this before, in other parks in other states. He imagined that fish or snapping turtles pulled the burlap open and ate the flesh. The previous skulls were never recovered; perhaps they settled into the muck at the bottom of the pond.

An image came to him of an aquarium that had been in his fifth grade classroom. It had one of those plastic miniature human skulls on the bottom with an air hose tucked inside so that air bubbled out of the eye sockets. One memory triggered another, and he sat in his pickup for a time, with the window rolled down, remembering, listening to the night sounds and the voices in his head.

He thought he heard a whisper from Sheila Armor. It wasn't pleasant: *I'll get you, you cocksucker.*

Perhaps he had made a mistake with her after all.

CHAPTER

18

"**W**hat's the matter," said Millie, "fries not greasy enough for you?" She looked with uncharacteristic concern at Schultz's plate. He had taken a couple of bites of his burger and left the fries untouched after dousing them with ketchup.

Schultz pulled himself back to the present. "Nah, they're OK. I just got a lot on my mind, that's all."

"Anything I can do?" she said. Schultz was surprised to hear that from Millie. He raised his troubled eyes to hers.

"I mean," she said, "you being a paying customer and all. Not that you're a decent tipper."

A smile began to work at the corners of his mouth, then gave up.

"Yes, there is something you can do," he said as she looked at him expectantly. "I need change to use the phone." He shoved a dollar bill at her.

Wordlessly she broke the bill at the cash register and handed him an assortment of dimes and quarters. He left his customary quarter tip and went to the pay phone near the bathrooms. He dialed Sheila Armor's number to introduce himself and let her know that he'd be outside watching the rest of the night. It was almost ten PM.

Her answering machine picked up on the fourth ring.

Hello. I'm home now, but I'm working, so I won't come to the phone. Don't bother leaving a message, just call me later.

Chris, if it's you, we're on for tennis tomorrow at seven,
usual court. Don't be late this time. Bye.

He left a message anyway.

He drove to her address, which was on Northwood off
Skinker, and parked the car across the street, a couple of
doors down. Then he walked around the building to check
for rear exits. Armor lived in a three-story apartment
building. Around the back there were two fire escapes, one
on each end of the building, which led to an alley. The alley
ended at Armor's building. It served the apartment building next door, and dead-ended there, too. There was a narrow passage to the street. The whole arrangement was
designed for trash pickup, so that a truck could pull between the buildings and empty the Dumpsters around
back. From where Schultz was sitting, he could see the
front door and the alley exit onto the street. It wasn't
ideal—there should be somebody around back to be dou-
bly sure—but it would have to do for tonight.

Her apartment number was 2-A. That should put her on
the second floor, left-hand corner. She had three windows
facing the street and two more on the side of the building.
All of them had shades tightly pulled down. Evidently, she
liked privacy. Some light leaked out around two of the
shades.

He had a large thermos of black coffee to help him stay
awake, and a bag of nacho chips he had picked up when
he put some gas in the Pacer. He stretched out his aching
legs as much as he could in the driver's seat, set up a pattern for his eyes to roam, and let his thoughts drift. They
homed in immediately on what had just happened at home.

Schultz's life had been turned upside-down.

On his way home from the office, he had decided that
he was going to be firm with both Julia and his son Rick.
It was time to let Rick face the consequences of his behavior and, if necessary, serve his time. He wasn't going to
rescue the boy—the man, after all, at twenty-five—and if

his wife didn't like it, she could pack her bags and move out.

Much to his amazement, she did just that.

It happened so swiftly that it hadn't really sunk in yet. He was still numb, with a little blossom of heartache starting to open somewhere inside. All that night, as he chugged down coffee, shoved handfuls of chips into his mouth, and watched Armor's apartment, he wondered where he had gone wrong.

No one entered or left the building after he arrived. He knew that there were a lot of elderly residents in the area, and they generally didn't go out after dark or have company late at night. Around midnight, one of the lights in Armor's windows went off. The other went off an hour later. Apparently she was tucked in for the night.

Dawn sneaked up on him. He needed to go to the bathroom. He was out of coffee, out of chips, out of excuses in his marriage, and apparently out of Julia's life. Later, he checked his watch. Tenants were starting to come out of the building, a few on their way to work, some just out to walk the dog. It was past seven-thirty. Hadn't Armor's phone message said that she had a tennis date at seven? He sat up abruptly, banging his knee on the steering wheel. She should have left practically an hour ago.

He got out, brushed the crumbs off his clothes, stretched his stiff legs, and felt his left knee pop painfully. He entered the building and knocked on the door of 2-A. No answer. He went downstairs, found the superintendent, flashed his badge, and pulled him away from breakfast to open the door.

Schultz was the first one in. He saw that Armor was home, but in no condition to answer the door. He stepped back out quickly, but not before the smell of blood, coppery and abundant, had filled his nostrils.

He used the super's phone to call in the homicide and waited for the blue-and-whites and the ETU to arrive. He was certain no one had gone in the front door, and equally certain, because of the layout in the back with the blind alley that butted up against other buildings, that no one had gone up the fire escape. His mind caught and held a single thought: he had held a vigil for a woman who was almost certainly dead even before he arrived, a woman who was killed while he, the professional detective, the protector of the public, was home arguing with his wife.

The technicians had been in the apartment almost an hour before Schultz worked up the nerve to call PJ. In the meantime he had determined that the reassuring lights he had seen from his car going off in two different rooms were lamps controlled by plug-in timers. He had been taken in, lulled, by something that probably wouldn't have deterred a second-rate burglar.

He didn't meet PJ's accusing gaze when she arrived. This time she couldn't stay in the room while the body was still there. He helped her out and left her sitting on the stairs while he went mechanically through the scene analysis.

That afternoon, in the middle of relating the last twenty-four hours' events to an incredulous Lieutenant Wall, he hit bottom. He got up, held up both hands in a warding gesture, and left the room. He sat in the stall with the only working toilet in the men's room, ignoring increasingly urgent requests to finish up.

PJ found out from Barnesworth where Schultz was and barged into the men's room without knocking. A patrolman about to unzip in front of a urinal thought better of it and left. She pounded on the closed stall door.

"Come out of there, you worm! If I have to, I'll crawl under the door so I can hear your excuses face-to-face. And you know I'll do it, too!"

All the fight had leached out of Schultz. He opened the stall door.

"That's better," PJ said icily. "I'd like to know why a

woman who sat in my office and told me she was in danger is now dead. How could you mess up so monumentally?"

"I fucked up," he said sullenly, "and Armor paid for it. I'm sorry."

"That just fine, Detective. You're sorry. A woman is dead, and that's all you've got to say?"

"What else can I say?"

"You can start by telling me exactly what happened."

The door opened, and Lieutenant Wall stuck his head in. "Schultz . . . " he said.

"Not now!" PJ practically shouted. "Go away!"

Wall obediently vanished.

"Come on, let's go back to my office," she said. "This is no place to talk. It stinks in here."

She shoved Schultz angrily. Then, without thinking, she drew her hand back and slapped him across the face.

He took the blow without reacting, then led the way across the hall. She slammed her office door when they were both inside.

"I've got to congratulate you, Detective. I've never slapped anyone before. You're the first one to get under my skin enough."

"I deserved it, Doc. If it'll make you feel any better, you can do it again."

PJ dropped into her chair and threw one leg over the burnished arm. "Damn it, Schultz, tell me what happened."

"I didn't promise I'd make it over there. I was skeptical, but I decided to go myself. I wish to God I could go back and make that decision over, send Dave or Anita. I just wasn't on top of things. Some family problems came up after work yesterday. Not that that's an excuse, but I was late getting over to Armor's place. She was offed before I even got there. I spent the night guarding her corpse. Shit!"

PJ composed herself. Her professional concern asserted itself in spite of her anger and grief. "What sort of family problems?"

"Nothing that should have interfered with my work."

PJ waited him out.

"My son Rick got arrested yesterday. Pushing drugs. Julia wanted me to fix things and spring him. I said no, let the jerk swing in the breeze. We had a big fight about it. She left."

"You separated from your wife?"

"That's what I said, didn't I? She's gone. Split. Thirty years down the tubes, and the only thing I've got to show for it is a son in the slammer."

PJ felt again the emotional heat of her own discovery of Steven's infidelity, his leaving, their divorce, his marriage to Carla.

"I'm sorry to hear that," she said, and meant it.

"Yeah, well, I feel rotten about what happened. My home life shouldn't screw up my work. Lieutenant Wall certainly knows that, and he hasn't exactly been reluctant this morning to tell me about it. Christ, my voice was on her answering machine. I look like an idiot."

"You're human, aren't you?" she said softly, her anger starting to fade. She hadn't forgiven him for his costly lapse, but at least she understood it. She had made blunders before in her professional life. There was that time when she hadn't taken a suicide threat seriously, turned off her pager, and gone out for an anniversary celebration with Steven. Her judgment had been dead wrong, and she knew what it was like to live with that.

She was about to reach out and pat his hand, but he sensed it and pulled away.

"Don't get mushy, Doc. Or is that just professional technique?"

"A little of both, I think. I'm not sorry I slapped you, though."

Schultz nodded. He finally raised his eyes to meet hers, and they held the connection, a very human connection, sharing their grief.

"Sometimes things happen that shove everything else in

your life aside," she said quietly. "I call it the steamroller effect."

"I don't buy that, Doc. The Armor woman should be alive today."

PJ put aside her recriminations, because she wanted, now more than ever, to solve this case. The stakes had just gone sky-high. "Do you still want to catch the killer and hang him up by his thumbs and cut his balls off?"

"That's a damn silly question. Of course I do."

"Then I've got some news about the case," PJ said. "You've been so busy sitting in the toilet that you haven't heard the latest. There's been a break."

Schultz didn't react.

"Snap out of it, Detective! I need your skills now. I need your experience to get that killer off the street."

"Maybe what you need is somebody else. Somebody competent."

There. It was out, PJ thought to herself.

"I've already spoken to Lieutenant Wall," she said. "I made it clear that I wanted you to stay on this case. On the CHIP team." She didn't mention that Wall had pressured her to accept a replacement, and that she had threatened to leave if he pulled Schultz out.

"What the hell for?"

PJ hesitated. That was a good question. Would it be better to work with someone else? Where was her relationship with Schultz going? Did she still trust him? She studied his face and held his challenging gaze. She knew from her own experience with the patient who committed suicide that he would be living with his mistake for a long time. She decided that she probably would never forgive him for letting Armor's life slip through his fingers, but that she could trust him not to do anything like that again. As soon as it was made, the decision settled in and got comfortable.

"Because I don't want to break in a new person," she said. "I'm tired of explaining what virtual reality is."

"I guess I can understand that," Schultz said. His face

softened a little, but his eyes were hard with resolve. He cleared his throat. "Did you say something about a break in the case?"

"Yes. Sheila's head," she said with a catch in her voice, "has been recovered. From a fishing pond in"—she glanced down at the notes on her desk—"Busch Wildlife Area. The story I got was that the pond had become shallow, nearly filled with silt. There was a lot of runoff during the spring rains from a parking lot that was being built nearby. So the pond was closed to fishing and scheduled for restoration. The dredging crew made the discovery at seven-thirty this morning. It's already been matched to Sheila's dental records."

"So it was found while I was still sitting there in my fucking orange car with my thumb up my ass." He shook his head. "Why would the killer toss the head in a shallow pond?"

"The pond was posted for restoration, but the sign was small. I guess he missed it in the dark."

"Maybe he's beginning to screw up. They all do."

"That's not what my research shows. I've been digging into the literature on serial killers. It's my impression that the majority are never caught. They're careful, compulsively so. The ones who make mistakes are the ones who have something driving them to it, making them sloppy. A deeply-buried wish to get caught, to be stopped. The true sociopaths, the ones who have no conscience, no remorse, believe they can kill with impunity, and a lot of the time they get away with it."

"Not this creep," said Schultz, shaking his head. "I don't give a flying fuck about whether he's remorseful or not. He's not getting away. He's got a little devil sitting on his shoulder, whispering in his ear and getting him to make mistakes. That little devil is me. After all, I'm a real pro at screwing up, myself."

"You may not be far wrong, Detective," PJ said. There was something there, something in what he said. A piece of the puzzle, but where did it fit? Then she noticed the crestfallen look on Schultz's face, and realized that he thought she was agreeing with his self-criticism about being a pro at screwing up. "Not about messing up. Something else . . ."

"Was there anything distinctive about the condition of the head?" Schultz said.

His question pulled her mind back into a painful track. "Yes, there was. The skull was cracked open and the brain cavity was empty."

"Christ," he said, shaking his head again. "Any chance the little fishies did it?"

"Not in that amount of time. It was submerged for maybe only eight to ten hours. Not with the way the bones of the skull were cut. The medical examiner doesn't want to be pinned down just yet, but she thinks it was a chisel."

PJ noticed that she had a terrible headache. The desk lamp was angled toward her. She imagined its light stabbing into her eyes, racing over her optic nerve to her brain, casting shadows on its undulating surface. She reached out and tilted the shade away.

"So the freak took the head with him, cut open the skull, took out the brain, and disposed of the shell."

"The meat of the walnut," PJ said softly.

"You saying this guy ate the brain?" Schultz rose and began pacing. Evidently he couldn't take the concept sitting down.

"Maybe, maybe not. From the remains, there's no way we can tell exactly what he did with the brain, only that he removed it for some reason. Personally, I think there's a good chance we're dealing with anthropophagy. An excellent chance."

"English, Doc. In English."

"Cannibalism."

"Christ. This is new territory for me," Schultz said.

"Consider it an opportunity for professional growth."

CHAPTER

19

At lunch Schultz eyed his food with suspicion, as though Millie had plopped a slab of raw human brain on his plate rather than the grilled cheese with bacon he had ordered. He was still having difficulty taking in what PJ had told him. His own theory to account for the missing heads had been that the killer was taking grisly souvenirs. The new information put a different spin on things.

He waved at Millie, pointed at his coffee cup.

PJ was sitting at the counter next to him. She had a large bowl of salad in front of her, but she had barely picked at it. Schultz speculated that PJ was the only customer since Millie opened her doors who had ever ordered the Chef's Special Three-Greens Salad. It came with sliced hard-boiled egg on top. Millie's trademark flag toothpick, jammed into the white of the egg, presided over the bowl. Schultz wondered what Millie would do if she ever ran out of them.

"So, Doc, what's your take?"

"I just don't have one yet, Leo. I've got a lot of bits and pieces flying around in my head."

He decided that being called by his first name wasn't so bad after all. Millie came over and filled his coffee cup, and he realized that he was falling down on the job in more than one way. He hadn't needled her since planting his butt on the stool.

"I don't think much of your new painting," he said to Millie, pointing to a framed work on the wall behind the counter. "Hire yourself an interior decorator? Or did some bum off the street sell you that piece of crap?"

"Smartass," Millie said. "Dearie, I just don't know why you hang out with this guy. No class."

PJ bobbed her head affirmatively and impaled a piece of egg yolk with her fork.

"It so happens my new cook painted that," Millie said. "Brought it in, said he did it in an art class he was taking at night, and asked if he could put it up. First time I've seen the guy smile. I'm supposed to say no?" She looked at it, tilted her head, said, "Yeah, I guess I shoulda said no."

It was an amateurish watercolor. Millie said it was supposed to represent a crowded baseball stadium, but Schultz couldn't make out anything but blobs of bright colors.

Schultz glanced up, saw the cook watching him from the kitchen pass-through. His eyes looked hot, as though he was feverish, but his face was pale, bland, expressionless. "Hey, cook," Schultz said good-naturedly, "stick to fixing eggs. You got a knack for it. Leave the artwork to the artists."

PJ reached over and tapped his arm. "That was rude. Don't make fun of his efforts. Maybe it's important to him."

Schultz decided maybe he had been a little harsh. "Well, just remember," he said to the cook, "practice makes perfect."

The cook grinned at him, a grin that would have been at home on a jack-o'-lantern, complete with the candle flame lighting the eyes from the scraped and violated interior.

"Guy's always taking classes," Millie said, lowering her voice in a confidential manner. "I think he's lonely, got nothing else to do at night, if you get my meaning. Last week, it was dancing class. He was whirling around in the kitchen, broke a stack of dishes and a couple of mugs. I couldn't bring myself to take it out of his salary, though. Apologized all over the place, swept up all the pieces, like a little kid who broke the cookie jar."

Millie went off to wait on another customer, and Schultz and PJ resumed their conversation.

"So if the freak's a cannibal, how come he hasn't taken a couple of bites out of an arm or a leg? Or gotten himself a piece of ass, literally?"

"I don't know. I've been puzzling over that, myself," she said. "It has to be a ritual of some kind, maybe a human sacrifice kind of thing, like the Aztecs cutting out hearts while they were still beating. Maybe I can do some scenarios on the computer."

"That doesn't fit with the carving of a dog. The guy's worshipping dogs?"

"Maybe the dog is a servant to carry the message to the gods. Who knows? We may be going off the deep end here."

"If you're looking for a rational explanation, you're not going to find one," Schultz said. "That's the nature of this beast. Did you hear that the blood under Armor's fingernails looks like a good match for the sample we got from your cat's claws?"

PJ's face lit up. "No, I hadn't heard that. Where did you get it?"

"Wall told me, collared me right before we left for lunch. That's what he was coming into the men's room to tell me when you ordered him out." Schultz chuckled. "Tucked tail and ran."

"Why wasn't he looking for me?"

"I hate to be the one to break this to you, Doc, but you're an outsider. You work for the Department, but you're not a cop." He saw the indignation flare up in PJ's eyes. "Don't get me wrong, you've got some good ideas. But you haven't been through the shit that the rest of us have. You haven't paid your dues."

PJ struggled visibly with her response, apparently considering and discarding several ways to react.

"You're right," she said. "In this field, I haven't. But I think that my feelings about catching the killer, about stopping what he's doing, are every bit as strong as yours. In your case," she looked at him searchingly, "I think that you would step between him and his victim, physically put yourself on the line to save others. I think you've probably done it before. Whether I could do that, I don't know. I've never been faced with it."

"And I hope you never will be. I've killed before," he said, "and I might get myself into a situation where I'll have to kill again. Cops know about that, we live with that thought every day, although it's not at the front of our minds. But let me tell you something. No matter how justified it seems, no matter how right it is that the creep get blown away, it diminishes a person somehow." Schultz met and held her concerned eyes. "It feels like leaving a piece of yourself behind. A piece of your humanity. You lose too many of those pieces and God knows what you become."

They sat together in silence. The next time Schultz glanced at PJ, she seemed lost in thought.

"What's the going rate for a shrink's thoughts?" he said. "Must be a lot more than a penny."

She laughed lightly and genuinely. He knew in that moment that she trusted him, in spite of what he had done, regardless of the fact that a friend of hers—that's what Armor was, even though the two women had just met— lay on a slab in the morgue. He wasn't sure how he had earned that trust, but he knew for certain he was going to do everything possible not to lose it. Forgiveness was another story. He wasn't asking for it, and he wasn't expecting it.

"I'm just daydreaming," she said. "Some things that you said—well, I don't actually have anything yet."

Schultz knew that look. He had seen it on his own face

in his bathroom mirror a number of times. She was onto something, but the pieces weren't fitting together yet.

As Pauley Mac lowered a basket of fries into the bubbling grease, his hands shook with anger even though his face was blank as a notepad. A cannibal! How could they think such a thing? He had been tempted—Dog was tempted—to savor the meat, not just the one organ to be consumed for a higher purpose. But he had resisted! And now to be accused of something so savage, so base. Of course they didn't understand.

He wasn't happy with the news about the blood he had left behind under the woman's fingernails. He should have taken the fingers with him. But that problem paled next to the insult about being a cannibal.

The bitch was to blame. She was the source of his problems, she was the one who insulted him. He decided to leave her another warning. If that didn't work, he would have to kill her, even though that would be risky. The detective wouldn't like that, he was sweet on her, probably slipping it in, gripping those solid hips with his cop's hands, thrusting and grunting. No one was watching him, so Pauley Mac let Dog put one hand under the greasy apron he was wearing and stroke the bulge at his groin while the other hand was busy flipping burgers.

Hasty taste, thigh pie, piece of tail, go to jail.

CHAPTER

20

After lunch, Schultz went back to his office and resolutely phoned Ted Walmacher at the St. Louis office of the FBI. He was kept on hold by a haughty secretary for ten minutes. He used the time to walk to the men's room, get a handful of damp towels, and carefully wipe the telephone receiver. It smelled like after-shave lotion again. That schmuck from Alabama who called himself a detective must have sneaked in and used Schultz's desk again.

"Walmacher here."

"Schultz, working the decapitations. I'd like to come over and talk to you about those unsolved cases you researched."

"You didn't think much of them at the time. What changed your mind?"

"My boss changed my mind. Doc thinks our man's got a string of corpses behind him."

"At least somebody over there's got some sense."

"Yeah, and we're all hanging on her every word, too."

"No need to get snotty. Can you make it at, say . . . three o'clock? I'm having lunch with the mayor's secretary. It's my chance to catch up on the local dirt."

"Christ. Better take along a shovel. Make that a front loader. Sure, three's fine."

* * *

Ted Walmacher rose from his high-backed leather swivel chair, and stood behind his desk, an expanse of oak that looked like it had cost the lives of a small forest. Schultz thought about his own battered metal desk and squeaky vinyl chair.

Feds.

"Nice to see you again, Schultz. Coffee?"

"None for me, thanks. Let's just get on with it, OK?"

Ted sighed. "You know it doesn't have to be like this, Detective. We're on the same side, after all."

Personally, Schultz thought it was more of a Little Red Riding Hood/Wolf relationship.

My, what big teeth you have, Grandma.

Schultz sat for a moment, taking in Ted's appearance. He seemed little changed from the last time they had worked together more than ten years ago. He had been over forty then, so he must be at least fifty years old now. He was tall and solidly built, the kind of man you might want to have at your back in a tough situation. But the impression was spoiled by a round, almost babylike face which rode his shoulders like a balloon, bobbing frequently and for no apparent reason. The face was unlined, his cheeks were pink and round, and his lips belonged on a pouty nightclub singer—a female one. He was blond and blue-eyed, which added to the babyish appearance of his face. He wore a gray pin-striped suit with a pink shirt, red and gray striped tie, and a red vest. His clothes fit well and didn't look off-the-rack.

Ted pointed to three thick stacks of folders on his desk, probably at least sixty of them altogether. "How far back do you want to go?"

"Back to the beginning, of course," Schultz said. Obvious questions were a pet peeve of his.

"Well, you said that you're working on the assumption

that your killer is in his mid-to-late-thirties. That means we should start at least thirty years back."

"Thirty? I would have thought maybe twenty."

"Nah. Some of those guys make their first kill in grade school. Nine, ten years old."

"Christ. Kids that age are supposed to be spray-painting sidewalks or something, not killing people."

Ted shuffled through the folders, setting aside a few older ones. "Looks like 1967 is our first case that falls in the right range. April, 1967, Spokane, Washington. Headless corpse floating in a river. Identified as May Brinkwood, a prostitute. Apparent cause of death was strangulation. Little hard to tell, I guess."

"I think our man is into some sort of ritual that involves leaving his mark elsewhere on the body. We can probably rule out any cases that don't have some form of mutilation."

"OK," said Ted. "I'm easy. Let's sift those out and see what's left."

He pushed one of the stacks toward Schultz. They worked silently for a quarter of an hour. They were left with about thirty folders.

"Sure you don't want any coffee?" Ted said.

"Yeah, I'll take a cup," Schultz said. "Looks like I'm going to be here awhile."

Schultz put the notebook and pen he had brought on Ted's desk. He flipped open the first folder while Ted busied himself with the coffeepot on a table in the corner.

"September, 1976, Fallsburg, Tennessee," he read aloud to Ted. "Couple murdered, found headless in their home. Donald Lee and Cathy Sue Macmillan. Multiple stab wounds were the cause of death, and they were decapitated afterward. Sheriff's report indicates robbery as the apparent motive, probably by a transient. 'Course that motive doesn't explain the fact that the victims were stabbed numerous times, especially in the area of the heart, and that their heads were never found."

"A very angry robber, presumably."

"Another aspect to it is that Donald Lee and Cathy Sue were not exactly the finest examples of the local citizenry. Both alcoholic, known to be violent, prior arrests for assault and prostitution, respectively."

"Sounds like they could have had a lot of enemies," Ted said. "The Sheriff might be protecting somebody local."

"My thoughts exactly." Schultz opened the next two folders and spread them out on the desk next to the Macmillan file. "Moving on: November, 1976, Nashville, Tennessee, and a month later, same town. First victim Arleen Witcomb, second Henry Wu, both teachers in the public schools. Multiple stab wounds, this time in a circular pattern around the heart, then decapitation. Local law enforcement made a big deal of both of them being teachers, and I imagine other teachers in the community were pretty spooked. But nothing else happened."

"Sounds to me like the killer moved out of Fallsburg but didn't get very far."

"Could be." Schultz's eyes landed on a couple of lines in the Fallsburg sheriff's report and stuck there. A chill went through him, and it wasn't from the graphic photos in the folder.

"Says here Donald Lee and Cathy Sue had a son who was sixteen years old at the time they were killed. Boy left town afterward."

Ted nodded, with his back to Schultz. "Yeah, Paul Edward Macmillan. I remember him from the file. I've been through all of these cases, most of them a number of times. Anyway, the sheriff investigated him and he was cleared. He left town supposedly to go live with friends of the family in Atlanta."

"Wonder if he ever made it there, or just got as far as Nashville?"

"That might bear looking into. The sheriff down there, what's his name, Youngman, I think, might know about that. I imagine he's retired by now, since he was over fifty at the time of the murders. Could be dead already."

Schultz sipped his coffee, which was hot and strong enough to get up out of the cup and walk across the desk. "Good coffee," he said with enthusiasm. "Most people don't brew it nearly strong enough."

The two sat for a moment, eyeing each other over the rims of their cups, Ted's head bobbing silently in between drinks. Schultz was starting to feel better about the whole afternoon.

They split the stack, each taking half of the cases to review, then switching so that both men got a look at all the cases.

In order to function, Schultz had to counter the overload of pain that practically dripped from the folders. It was a sickening compilation of gruesome killings and imaginative mutilations. There were groups of three or four murders with a similar technique, then a gap of up to two years. The locations were all over the map: Tennessee, Florida, Virginia, Illinois, Arizona, Minnesota, Louisiana, and Pennsylvania. The victims showed a lot of variety: by sex, age, occupation, race, even social class. The only thing they all had in common was decapitation following the mutilation.

"Do you really think all these murders could have been committed by the same guy?" Ted asked.

"I talked with Doc about that. She said that psychos tend to stay with one MO because they're fixated on reliving some aspect of their past. But she admitted there's the possibility that somebody could break the pattern . . . " Schultz stopped, suddenly putting together something else he and Doc had talked about.

"Yes? Pattern?" Ted said.

"Oh, sorry. I was just thinking about something else that came up during that same discussion. I said that the decapitations themselves might be the ritualistic pattern, and everything else is incidental, almost whimsical, depending on what's going on in his life at the time. Then there would be consistency over all the murders."

"Whimsical?"

"Well, a poor choice of words. If you consider the different types of mutilation." Schultz tapped his pen thoughtfully. "There is a strong suggestion of patterns running through all of them. Bones broken symmetrically. Burns arranged in lines. Slices of skin removed from both arms and both legs. Disembowelments with intestines arranged in loops. Stab wounds in a circle around the heart. Fingernails and toenails removed in a matching pattern. Acid painted on the symmetrical parts of the body. And the latest, carving the skin to form a recognizable pattern, a picture of a dog."

"Sounds to me like the guy is trying to put some structure in his own mixed-up life."

"I'll leave that kind of speculation to Doc," Schultz said. "I'd like to leave my own pattern on him: a bullet to the heart and another one smack between his eyes."

Ted chuckled. "Yeah, I know what you mean." The two men sat companionably, Schultz at ease with the FBI agent for the first time.

Schultz took copious notes. He was planning to request copies of the files, but it would take some time; hundreds of photos and pieces of paper were involved. It might be a couple of days before he could get the entire set, and something was pushing him, telling him he didn't have that much time to spend. In fact, he was suddenly eager to leave. An idea had taken shape in his mind, and it had the same sharp-edged quality to it as previous hunches, the ones that had panned out.

Schultz wanted to talk to the sheriff who handled the case in Fallsburg, Tennessee. He wanted to talk about two headless corpses and a sixteen-year-old boy who fled from the terrible memory of his parents' murder.

Or fled from the scene of his own bloody handiwork.

He wanted to find out what type of person this boy

Paul E. Macmillan was, and hear first hand about the investigation.

He wanted to go back to the beginning.

By the time Schultz had made his exit from the FBI office, phoned both PJ and Wall to let them know what he was doing, tossed a change of clothes, a travel alarm, and his toothbrush into a canvas tote bag with cute kittens on the outside, and grabbed a quick bite of dinner, it was almost seven PM. Logically he should have made plans, gotten a good night's sleep, and left in the morning. But logic had little to do with it when he realized that the tenuous thread between himself and the killer was really beginning to take shape. It had begun when he held the Macmillan case folder in his hands.

A sense of connection.

A typed name on the page that had riveted his attention.

Schultz headed south from St. Louis on I-55 in his Pacer, automatically and continually correcting the pull to the right that the car had. He picked up a map and some nacho chips, cookies, and soda at a gas station in Cape Girardeau. On the open highway he found that the Pacer really didn't shudder too badly unless he pushed it over eighty. He made it to Memphis before midnight, and picked up State Road 57 just east of town. According to the map, the road paralleled the state line between Tennessee and Mississippi, just five miles into Tennessee. Another hour passed before he got to Fallsburg, and he pulled in at the first motel he found. The place was called the Restaway, and it had a dozen tiny little cabins. There was a car parked in front of one of them. The owner was grumpy when he finally answered Schultz's persistent pressing on the buzzer, and he tacked on an extra five bucks to the room rate.

Schultz carried his tote bag into the small but surprisingly clean room. He set his alarm clock, stretched out on the well-used mattress, closed his eyes, and slept.

Six hours later, the strident alarm jolted him awake. It seemed as though he had just gotten into bed a moment before. He sat up and swung his legs over the side of the bed before he could reconsider it. His knees were locked up, especially his left one, and he walked stiff-legged into the bathroom. A hot shower cleared his mind and limbered up his legs. The bath towels were so skimpy it took two of them to get him reasonably dry. He wondered if a couple staying at the Restaway would argue over who got to take a shower first.

He had paid in advance, but he went back to the motel office to turn in his key and ask directions to the sheriff's office. Fallsburg was the county seat, with a population of about eighteen thousand. He ate a full breakfast at a place that reminded him strongly of Millie's Diner, except that it was run by a tough looking man with tattoos covering just about every inch of his formidable arms. Schultz was certain that there were never any arguments over the bill.

Seeing the town in the daylight, he realized that it must be economically depressed. There were liquor and pawn shops everywhere. The downtown section was centered on the County Court Building and City Hall which faced each other across a narrow rectangle of park land. Stretching out on either side were a couple of blocks of brick two-stories with offices for attorneys, bail bondsmen, and title companies. Most of the buildings were a little shabby looking, with decrepit awnings, cracked glass held in place with silver duct tape, or crumbling chimneys. Past the office area, there was a shopping district, with the usual hardware store, department store with window displays that hadn't been changed in years, a few clothing and shoe stores, and a small theater with a genuine marquee showing a movie that had played months ago in larger cities. The ceramics shop had a "Going Out of Business" banner in the window.

The sheriff's office was directly across the street from the courthouse. It was located in a squat cement building that looked out of place, as though it had been dropped in by military helicopter as a forward command post. It did have off-street parking, which saved Schultz from having to feed the parking meters that lined the downtown streets. The only spot that was left was marked "Official Parking Only." He pulled in and rooted in the glove box for the sign that identified the car as an official police vehicle of the St. Louis Police Department. He placed it on the wind-shield, only half expecting it to be taken seriously. The Pacer didn't have an official look to it.

The office was actually pleasant inside, with a furnished reception area and paintings by local artists displayed on the walls, each with a discreet price tag in the corner. Judg-ing by the dust on the frames, they weren't hot sellers. He stepped up to the window, showed his ID, and asked to talk to Sheriff Youngman. He was told that Al Youngman had retired ten years ago. The current sheriff, a man named Treacher, was out on a call. He ended up at the desk of a deputy, a middle-aged woman named Rita Wellston who was both professional and courteous, a combination that was hard to find. He explained his reason for coming from St. Louis, and asked to see the file on the Macmillan killings.

"What year was that again?" she said.

"1976."

"OK, that would be down in the archives."

The archives turned out to be a locked room in the base-ment. Inside were cardboard boxes containing file folders, each labeled with the year. It didn't take long to locate sev-eral boxes with 1976 written on them. Murder cases were in red folders, and there were only two out of all the boxes for that year. One was for the Macmillans and the other was for a man who shot his estranged wife.

Deputy Rita, as she liked to be called, obligingly dupli-cated the Macmillan file while Schultz waited. There wasn't much to it. Other than the photos and written descriptions of the crime scene, there were only a few pages of reports of interviews.

It looked like the sheriff had given up pretty easily.

Over coffee in the small lunchroom, Schultz grilled Rita on her knowledge of the case, which was practically nil. She hadn't been a deputy at the time, hadn't even moved to Fallsburg until she got divorced twelve years ago. Sheriff Youngman had mentioned it to her when she first hired on because it was an unsolved case which the office was theoretically still working on. She doubted that Bob Treacher, the current sheriff, knew any more about it than she did. She said she would let Bob know that Schultz was in town, in case he did have any information for him.

"The person you need to see is Al Youngman," she said. "I'm not sure how thrilled he'd be to talk about the case, because it kind of rankled him that he didn't solve it and close it for good. Maybe he'd be eager to hear about your interest, or any light you can shed on it. Or maybe he doesn't want to be reminded. He lives out on Harvest Road, right past the big orchard. Got a little place, ten acres, runs a couple of cows and some chickens. He had a heart attack a couple of years ago, but it doesn't seem to have slowed him down much."

"I'll try not to get him too excited," Schultz said. He got directions, thanked Rita, and collected the copies she had made for him.

On his way out of the building, he noticed that none of the paintings had sold this morning.

The orchard on Harvest Road was impressive. Acres and acres of fruit trees were well tended in neat rows. Schultz wasn't exactly sure, but he thought he saw peach, cherry, and apple trees as he cruised slowly by the orchard's long road frontage. Al Youngman's property adjoined the orchard land. Schultz passed it before realizing that the fruit trees lining the driveway were not just more rows of the orchard. He backed up—Harvest Road didn't exactly carry a lot of traffic—and pulled into the driveway.

Before he was halfway to the house, a black German shepherd ran out from around back. It stopped directly in front of him and held its ground, barking and showing serious teeth. He inched the car forward, but the dog didn't budge.

A man came into view carrying a mesh basket full of something green. The man was short, maybe five-six, but had a compact strength and an easy grace to his walk. His still-mostly-red hair was shot with silver, and the bare arms that sprouted from his T-shirt looked like they were accustomed to outdoor work, and up to the job. His body was lean and flat where it was supposed to be flat. Schultz knew that Youngman was in his seventies, yet he appeared twenty years younger. Heart attack or not, Schultz found himself wishing that he would look that good at seventy-five.

The man's face showed friendliness overlaid with healthy caution. He stopped about fifteen feet from the car, right behind the dog.

"That's enough, Oscar," he said. The dog stopped his barking and sat down, but his ears remained on alert. The man spoke bluntly to Schultz. "Who are you?"

Schultz leaned out the window. "I'm Detective Leo Schultz from the St. Louis Police Department. I'm looking for the former sheriff, Al Youngman."

"Let's see some ID," he said.

Schultz hung his ID out the window. The man squinted at it, then walked up closer and took the leather wallet from Schultz and held it up close. "Can't see to read without my glasses," he explained, and then handed it back.

Schultz could see that the mesh basket was full of freshly-harvested green onions, with dirt still clinging to the roots. The pungent early summer smell brought back his own childhood memories: he and his brother George working in the garden, pulling onions, pelting each other with dirt clods.

"What's your business with Youngman?"

"I want to talk to him about the Macmillan murders back in 1976. I think there could be a connection to a couple of recent murders in St. Louis."

The man sighed. "Lord, the bad stuff never stops, does it? Pull on up. I'll get cleaned up inside. I've got some lemonade made. I was ready for a break anyway." He turned to the dog. "Oscar, go lay down." The big black dog immediately trotted over to the shade of a large oak tree on the front lawn. He lowered himself to the grass and put his head down on his outstretched front paws, still watching Schultz and the car.

Schultz pulled up closer to the house and got out under Oscar's watchful eyes. He went up on the front porch and sat down on a wicker chair with a flowered cushion on the seat. The porch furniture didn't look like something Al Youngman would pick out himself. A few minutes later, the man came out the front door carrying a tray with two tall glasses of ice and a pitcher of lemonade. He set the tray on a small table, poured, and handed Schultz a glass. Then he pulled a wicker rocker up close to Schultz's chair, leaving the table and the pitcher between them.

Schultz touched the lemonade to his lips and felt them puckering in anticipation of full contact. He took a big swallow. It was strong and barely sweetened. When it hit his stomach, it promptly dissolved the contents. It was great.

"Hope the lemonade's OK with you. I don't like it very sweet," Youngman said. "Marge and I used to fight about it all the time. The day she died, nearly three years ago now, she fixed a pitcher and must have put three cups of sugar in it. I told her she'd have to drink it all, and darn if she didn't do just that."

"It's perfect," Schultz said. He was thinking that the way things looked, he wasn't going to be spending his old age sipping lemonade in wicker chairs, bickering with Julia about how much sugar to use. Loneliness stretched out in front of him like a bleak highway, flat and deserted to the horizon. He squelched the thought and yanked himself back to business.

"I understand that you were the sheriff in 1976, when the Macmillans were killed. I got some basic information from the FBI files on unsolved violent crimes, and I also visited the office in town and got a look at the case folder. But I wanted to dig deeper, get some impressions from the person on the scene. That would be you."

Youngman nodded. "You mentioned a possible connection to other murders. Could you tell me about that first?"

Schultz briefly described what he was up against in the St. Louis cases, and the similarities that had led him to Fallsburg, Tennessee. Youngman nodded and sipped his lemonade as Schultz talked. The older man paused during the descriptions of the state of the victims' bodies and stared off into space, as though he was somewhere else, seeing things that were burned into his memory. After Schultz finished, Youngman was quiet for a time, composing his thoughts.

"Donald Lee and Cathy Sue," he said. "What a piece of work they were. Piece of shit, actually." He poured himself another glass of lemonade. "Moved here about 1970 or 1971 from Kentucky or Arkansas, never did know exactly. Donald Lee got himself a job at Clinger's place, a manufacturing plant that makes concrete culvert pipes, drainage systems, that kind of stuff. Still does, in fact. It's on the southeast edge of town. You probably haven't been by there."

Schultz shook his head.

"At that time old Jeb Clinger was having financial troubles. Sometimes he couldn't meet a payroll. The plant didn't attract solid family men who needed a steady income. The dregs of the county worked there. Clinger's son Jack has done a much better job with the plant, turned it into a good place to work. At the time, though, it was a rough place, and Donald Lee fit right in."

"A violent man?"

"A drunk, and violent whether he was soused or not. Wife was the same. I broke up fights at their place a number of times. Sometimes they went at each other with knives. Could never figure out which one to arrest, so I brought 'em both in a few times. Donald Lee got fired every couple of months, but always got taken back on when Clinger needed another warm body on the line."

"Did they have any friends in this area? Relatives?"

Youngman snorted. "They didn't have any family, either of them. Couldn't find anybody to notify, nobody to bury them. As for friends, well, they weren't exactly part of the social life here. Anybody went to visit that shack of theirs, he was likely to get a face full of buckshot. You could say they kept to themselves."

"Crazy or just antisocial?"

"Personally, I thought they were both crazy, a mean kind of crazy like rabid dogs. Clinger said Donald Lee thought the factory was haunted. He kept talking about the machinery being taken over by vengeful spirits. Every time there was an accident out there, which was pretty often, Donald Lee said it was the spirits that made the machines hurt the operators. Sometimes I wondered if maybe he helped the spirits along a little bit."

"And the woman?"

"Cathy Lee," he said, looking thoughtfully out over his lawn. "I would describe her as evil. A crazy, evil woman."

Schultz picked up on the description as evil. It wasn't something Youngman would say casually.

"In a manner of speaking, you could say that Cathy Lee worked at Clinger's too," Youngman continued. "She'd head on out there every payday and swing her ass in front of the men coming out of the gate with cash in their pockets and hardons in their pants. She'd do 'em right in front of the plant, in a pickup truck with a camper top. Sometimes there'd be a line." He shook his head, remembering. "Can't imagine why anyone would pay money to be with that broad. I busted her a couple of times, but I stopped after Clinger put in a word for her. Seems he thought she was important for plant morale—probably getting a percentage of her price. Anyway, I didn't think it was important enough to pursue it. It wasn't like she was getting her arm twisted."

"Sounds as though they weren't missed after they were killed."

"Nope. Not that we celebrated, or anything. I mean, it was an awful thing. Done with such hate . . ."

"I understand they had a son."

"Yes. Paul, his name was. He was about ten years old when they first moved here, sixteen when his parents were murdered. Sometimes I wondered how they stopped fighting each other long enough to conceive a child. Or maybe they fought during that, too."

"What was your take on him?"

"The boy seemed bright enough but had some kind of learning disability. He could read and speak, but he couldn't write worth a darn."

Schultz thought of ketchup letters on a white kitchen wall. *YUR RONG.*

"Kept to himself a lot. He didn't have any friends at school, never invited anyone to his house. Would you?" Youngman continued without waiting for an answer. "There was some minor trouble, broken windows, smashed mailboxes, once a complaint about a neighbor's dog gone missing. Paul would come to school with bruises, sometimes cuts. It was obvious the way he was treated at home. He dropped out of school to get a job a couple of weeks before the murders. I guess the family needed money. Donald Lee was probably out of work, and Cathy Sue wouldn't give him any of her earnings to buy booze."

"What did he look like? Any family photos?"

"As far as I know, Paul destroyed the contents of the house before he left town. Had a bonfire out back. So there wouldn't be any photos. He wasn't a big kid. If he'd gotten his full height by then, he'd be only five-seven, five-eight tops. He was gangly, thin and all arms and legs. Brown hair. Shoulder length, although that's easy to change."

Youngman closed his eyes, pulling back a mental image. "Brown eyes, I think. Maybe gray. I don't remember the color so much as the intensity. Weird eyes, flat one minute and fiery the next. Thin, angular face, narrow upper lip, full lower. Good teeth, which was surprising since I doubt that dental hygiene was a priority at the Macmillan house. No scars or tattoos, that kind of thing. He wouldn't stand out in a crowd. Come to think of it, there might just be a photo in the high school year book. The school library keeps back copies."

"Where was he on the day of the murders?"

"You certainly don't beat around the bush, Detective. He was working at Specialty Orchard, right next to my place, picking apples. Quickest thing he could get, I suppose. The crew boss, Phil Trent, swore Paul didn't leave the field, but Phil was sometimes drunk on the job. He might have spent the whole morning sleeping one off under a tree."

"So the boy didn't have a reliable alibi for the time of the murders?"

"Nope. Maybe on paper he did, because of Phil's statement. But not in the real world."

Schultz sat expectantly, waiting for more. Youngman seemed reluctant to go on. Schultz thought he knew why, and he summoned what tact he was capable of exercising.

"But you didn't consider the boy a suspect," Schultz said. It wasn't said as a challenge.

"Wrong. I did. In fact, he was my chief suspect." Youngman sighed. "Detective, do you have any children?"

"Yes. I have a son."

"Then maybe you can understand what I'm about to say. Our own boy died in Viet Nam. We have two wonderful daughters, so we count ourselves blessed. But the loss of a child hits you in ways you can't even imagine until you go through it. It left me with a desire to help other kids get a good start in life. I organized a community center here to give the teenagers something to do besides drink beer and neck. I started a local chapter of Big Brothers/Big Sisters, and recruited folks to sign up. A few times I saw a kid headed down on the wrong side of the law, and I worked with 'em to turn the situation around. Sometimes I just scared the shit out of them, which was what they needed. I had some successes." He paused and twirled the ice in his glass, which was empty.

"Go on," Schultz said, as he reached over and poured the last of the lemonade into Youngman's glass.

"I had a pretty good idea what kind of home life that boy had. I figured he just snapped one day and couldn't take it anymore. Killed 'em both and tried to make it look like some bum broke in to rob the place and got surprised in the act. There was even money missing from Cathy Sue's hiding place, an old lard bucket in the kitchen. I couldn't really prove that he did it, but I couldn't prove that he didn't, either."

"What did you do?" Schultz gently prodded. His own excitement was barely contained.

"I understood how that boy could have come to hate his parents. I felt sorry for him. Now that they were out of his life, I thought he could straighten himself out. He didn't have any reason to kill anybody else, just them, the ones who made his life a living hell. A one-time deal, you might say. Plus I wasn't positive he actually did it. There wasn't a scrap of physical evidence, or even circumstantial. His prints were all over the house, but the boy lived there. If I'd been able to prove it in court, I would have hauled his ass into jail. I might have looked the other way when Cathy Sue spread her legs for money, but murder's different."

Schultz nodded. He understood that a cop has to look at the big picture, couldn't get bogged down in the little infractions that floated around any group of people like a bad odor. Especially a cop who lived in a small, fairly closed community. He thought about the case he could make. If a DNA analysis of Paul Macmillan's blood indicated a match with the blood under Sheila's fingernails, he could almost guarantee a conviction for at least one of the murders.

"Anyway," Youngman said, "I told him to move on out of the county. He took it well, said he had somebody he could go live with. I doubted it because our office hadn't turned up any relatives of the Macmillans. But I let it go."

"Any idea where he did end up?"

"No." Youngman fiddled with his glass, hesitating. The dog was asleep under the tree. Bees buzzed past, intent on honey business. There were probably hives kept near the orchard. Schultz let the silence stretch out.

"I have to ask you, Detective," Youngman said at last. "Do you really think Paul is the one who murdered your three victims in St. Louis? That after all these years, he snapped again?"

Schultz considered his answer carefully. Obviously it hadn't occurred to Youngman that Paul Macmillan could have killed frequently since leaving Fallsburg. He knew nothing about the more than two dozen probable victims in the intervening years, and Schultz wasn't about to tell him. He might find out eventually, if he followed the news. But not now. Not on this porch, sitting here in wicker chairs with flowery cushions, with the bees droning and Marge three years dead and a heart attack two years ago.

"It's possible. But it's probably a wild goose chase on my part," Schultz said. "After all, there's not that much similarity except the missing heads."

"Dear Lord, I hope you're right." Youngman turned toward him, eyes moist, voice a little out of control. "I'd hate to think I was responsible for letting loose a . . . a monster."

Schultz excused himself, saying that he wanted to get started on the drive back to St. Louis. He thanked Youngman for talking with him, bantered a little about the peach crop this year, and drove away, Oscar escorting him to the edge of the Youngman property.

He found a gas station with a pay phone and called Deputy Rita. She gave him directions to the old Macmillan homestead, after asking around the office and finding a clerk who knew the place. He also asked if he could get into the high school library, and explained why. She told him where it was located and said that she would call ahead for him.

He decided to go to the school first. He introduced himself to the principal, showed his ID, and was shown to the library. It only took a couple of minutes to unearth the year books from 1974 to 1976, the years Paul might have attended. The librarian told him that the class pictures pretty much contained everybody in the class except kids who were sick that day, but the individual pictures had to be paid for and only about half of the students (or their parents) coughed up the money.

He sat at a long table on a chair that was too small for his rear end, thumbing through the year books. The one for 1974 was a flop. Paul was probably too young. The freshman class picture for 1975 listed Paul Macmillan among the sixty or so students. Schultz eagerly counted over from the left. When he got to where Paul was supposed to be, all that showed was a glimpse of brown hair. It looked as though he ducked at the exact moment the photographer took the picture. Schultz wondered if the boy had bruises on his face that day, and didn't want them to be recorded. Disappointed, Schultz went through the rest of the book. There was no individual photo, which was understandable. Mom and Pop Macmillan would rather buy a bottle of booze than pay for their son's picture in his school year book. The 1976 book didn't list Paul at all. Apparently he was sick the day the pictures were taken. Or at least not caught off guard.

Schultz thanked the librarian and the principal. He could tell that they were curious, but he didn't offer to relieve their curiosity.

He drove the few miles out of town to the place where Paul spent six years of his young life. The directions took him from a blacktop road to a gravel county road and finally to a dirt feeder road that had a few houses on it. There were four mail boxes on a dilapidated wooden stand at the corner. The mailman didn't make it down the dirt road, and Schultz could see why. It was rutted, and in one place it crossed a rocky creek bottom with about six inches of water flowing over it. He didn't mind pushing the Pacer over the gravel and dirt. If it got a few more dings in it, that would just add to its already ample character.

The house was still standing, although it was more of a shack than a real house. It was cobbled together from wood scraps, odd-sized windows, and black tar paper on the roof. The front door was missing.

Schultz got out of the car and walked up the short driveway. The property was overgrown with weeds, but it looked as though that was its normal condition even when occupied. He stepped inside the front door, which brought him into the living room. The floor was bare mismatched planks, and there were holes in the ceiling. Birds had taken up residence in the rafters, and there were piles of bird droppings under the nests.

In the kitchen he ran his finger along the filthy, scarred countertop, trying to imagine what Paul Macmillan's childhood was like. He looked into the bedroom, where the bodies had been found. It had the same plank flooring, and there were dark stains in the wood along one wall, especially in the grooves between the boards. It could have been something else, though. Animals clearly had free access.

When Schultz walked back to his car, he was certain that Paul Macmillan was responsible for three deaths in St. Louis and at least two dozen elsewhere.

Now all he had to do was find him. And prove it.

CHAPTER

21

Merlin here. What's the buzz, Keypunch?

I'm trying to sort out some things that happened. Can we talk?

Wait just a minute . . . there. I've got my cyber-shrink hat on. Go.

You know I'm working on a murder investigation. It's been made clear to me here that I'm an outsider. I don't have cop mystique, or whatever it is that glues these people together.

You mean you don't get asked out for a drink with the boys?

That's part of it, certainly, but there's more to it than what equipment you've got under your trousers. There's a woman on my team, Anita, and I get the same feeling from her. It's us and them, and I'm definitely in the them crowd.

Aren't you used to that as a psychologist?

It's not the same. With a patient, I have to be able to empathize and still maintain some distance, for a lot of reasons. Here, I'm the one being held at arm's length.

Oho. Sauce for the goose. Think of it this way: you have your skills and they have theirs. Put them together, and whammo! The whole is greater than the sum of the parts.

I want to make a real contribution.

You have. You will. Now stop whining.

PJ told Merlin what had happened since their last online

conversation: Vanitzky's murder, the videotape with the off-screen humming, the red letters on her kitchen wall, Sheila coming to her, Schultz dropping the ball, Sheila's death.

I'm sorry to hear this news, Keypunch. It sounds like you and Sheila could have become good friends.

Yes.

No tears. You'll short out your keyboard. What about Schultz?

He's punishing himself, and he's good at it. He doesn't need any help from me.

Thomas?

Better.

How about that contact from Wash U.? Anything come of it?

Now there's a bright spot. Mike lent me the hardware I wanted, although I haven't had time to integrate it yet. He's very nice. A real hunk, too. You might have warned me he was bald. When we had lunch, I dropped some pizza and he wanted to wipe my chest with a napkin.

Sounds promising. Next time, let him.

Dirty old man.

Want some candy, little girl? How about a sucker?

Pervert. How unattached is Mike?

Got the hots, eh? No significant others, as far as I know. His divorce was finalized almost two years ago. Very, very messy. You'll have to get the gory details from him, if and when he's ready. You should be good at that.

Damn it, I don't want him to think of me as his psychologist!

Next time you see him, take off all your clothes and dance on the table. That will minimize, but probably not eliminate, the possibility of him thinking of you as his psychologist.

Thanks for the advice. Bye.

Wait! You haven't gotten your list:

1. On being an outsider: live with it.
2. On losing an almost-friend: live with it.

3. On Schultz messing up: live with it, or don't. But know which one.

4. On pursuing Mike: lust can be good.

5. On getting older (oh, that wasn't in our discussion?): live with it.

6. The word for the day, and a versatile word it is: lust.

Sleep well.

CHAPTER

22

All of a sudden it was Friday morning, Thomas's last day of school. PJ had spent the last hour on the phone in her bedroom, talking with Schultz, catching up on everything he had learned from his trip to Tennessee. The phone had rung just as she was stepping out of the tub. She was mildly peeved that he hadn't invited her along, as her psychology training might have been of some use in dredging up impressions of Paul Macmillan. She wasn't sure he was on the right track in pursuing the boy from Fallsburg, but she couldn't discount anything in which he had so much faith. She had a lot to think about, to try to integrate her own thoughts and feelings about the case with all the information he had dumped on her in the last hour.

PJ sat across from Thomas, watching him shovel cereal into his mouth while reading at the table. He must have been at an exciting part of his book, because his hand and mouth were on automatic, and his eyes were fastened to the page. She hated to interrupt.

"This is your last day, isn't it?" she said.

"Huh?" The rhythm was disrupted, and milk dribbled out of the corner of his mouth. She wanted to take a napkin and wipe it, but he was far too old for that. When had that happened? When had her little boy turned into this quasi-teenager?

"Last week we said we'd talk again about what to do when school's over."

"Aw, Mom, can't I just stay home? I'm twelve years old, you know. I'm not a baby."

"Ordinarily I would say yes. But after the break-in we had, I'm just not comfortable with you being alone in this house all day."

"I'm not alone. I have Megabite." As if waiting for her cue, the cat jumped up on the table. She approached Thomas for her customary stroking, then sniffed at his face. She delicately licked at the milk on his chin. "Look, Mom, she's kissing me."

"She's just after the milk, slop-face. And don't start with me about not being alone. Megabite doesn't count. I could call your dad today, and you could fly out over the weekend."

"I don't want to go stay with Dad." His face took on a determined look.

"Why not? It would just be for the summer, maybe just a month or so. I'm sure he would be happy to see you."

"I don't think so. He and Carla like privacy. They don't like having a kid around."

What, they're doing it on the kitchen table? "You could go out a lot, visit some of your old friends in Denver."

"I just don't want to go. I don't like being around Dad anymore."

Uh oh. "Can you tell me why not?"

"I guess I'm mad at him. What did he need Carla for, anyway? He had us. We were a family. Besides, he said some really nasty stuff about you. He blamed you a lot, and tried to make me think bad things about you. I know now that wasn't right."

PJ tried to hold back her anger. She and Steven had agreed early on that neither would disparage the other to Thomas. She had held up her end of the bargain, sometimes having to bite her tongue. She was disappointed to learn that Steven had not made the effort. She reached across the table and took both of Thomas's hands in her own.

"I'm sorry you got involved in that way," she said. "He's still your father. He's going through a difficult time, like the rest of us. I'm not trying to excuse what he did or said, but I know he still loves you."

"Mom, I don't want to see him now."

Searching her son's face, she knew that he was telling the truth. It saddened her, but she hoped that he would be willing to resume his relationship with his father sometime in the future. It wouldn't be wise to press it on him now.

"All right," she said. "But we need some other alternatives. I wasn't kidding when I said I don't like the idea of you here by yourself. Let's both work on it."

"I will, Mom. Actually, I've got an idea," he said, "but I have to check some things out first."

The HMD Mike had given PJ wasn't the sleek commercial type. It didn't have smooth black plastic and lightning decals down the sides. It looked more like something you would drain pasta in, and it was heavy and uncomfortable to wear. The balance was off, so that it listed to one side. After repeated use, the wearer's neck muscles began to ache from constantly correcting.

All morning, PJ had been working on isolated bits of the playback, in order to get the headset meshed with her software. When she first tried it, the virtual world that was placed in front of her eyes by the dual displays on the headset was flat and unconvincing, the motion jerky, the perspectives not right, and the response from the data gloves was practically nonexistent. Her software routines that handled the input from the gloves had only been tested a couple of times before, and that was three years ago with different hardware. But she found that her routines were basically sound, and simply needed tweaking. Small changes led to big improvements. Finally she was ready for a full run-through. She chose Burton's apartment and immersed herself in the recreation of his murder. She used manual mode, so that she, rather than the computer, was directing the action.

After a while, PJ took the headset off. Her heart was thumping in her chest, and her lungs ached as though something had sucked all the air from them. She stood up and circled her desk a couple of times, reorienting herself, pulling her familiar office around her like a blanket.

She hadn't been able to get very far into the simulation. Even though she knew that she was actually facing a wall of her office, her mind told her she was walking up the steps to Burton's apartment. Her hands, which she held in front of her body, carried a box of long-stem roses. She could look "down" and see the box. It was too real. When she swung her arm toward Burton's head, her hand tightly clutching a short length of pipe, and saw him crumple at her feet, she didn't want to continue.

She wondered if she should go back to the simpler screen simulations, without the headset and gloves that put her into the scene. What was to be gained by playing the part of the killer? Would it help the investigation, or was it a sick voyeurism, a desire on her part to vicariously murder someone?

Ridiculous. Get a grip, woman. This is a tool, nothing more, she told herself. She was about to put the headset back on when there was a knock at the door.

"It's open," she said. She couldn't deny her relief when she put the headset on the desk.

Schultz came in, dropped into a folding chair which barely survived the experience, and looked curiously at the hardware on her desk. Then his gaze shifted to the gloves she was still wearing, with their webbed network of wires and sensing terminals.

Letting him wonder about it, she asked what he wanted.

He cleared his throat. "The medical examiner says there was a blow to Armor's head, apparently not hard enough to be the cause of death. Left some very odd impressions in the skin, little spike points in a pattern of two rows. She has no idea what the weapon might have been. Didn't take kindly to my suggestion that Armor was whacked in the head with a golf shoe."

"I can understand that."

"My next suggestion was a meat tenderizer, one of those kitchen tools you use to pound a tough cut into something edible. Julia swears by them. Or used to, at any rate. Now she just swears."

"Have you spoken to her?"

"Yeah. She's living with her sister in Chicago. Didn't even ask about Rick the last time I talked with her. I can't figure it, Doc. I thought she left because I wouldn't get Rick off the hook. Now I think that's just part of it, and a small part at that. It seems she was about ready to give Rick the boot herself. Maybe she was just waiting for some excuse to get out of the marriage."

PJ didn't know how much she should involve herself in Schultz's private life. He seemed to want to talk about it, so she played her part. "Have there been problems before this?"

He folded his arms over his ample belly and began to talk.

"When we were first married, we acted like silly kids. We were in love, very romantic. Holding hands, kissing in public, six phone calls a day, that kind of thing. Hard to picture, isn't it?" Schultz didn't wait for an answer. "After Rick was born, we grew up a lot. We still loved each other, but it was a quieter kind of love. I was working long hours, didn't spend a lot of time with her and the kid. But I made up for it when I could. Lots of fathers are like that, aren't they?"

PJ nodded, not wanting to interrupt the flow, but she was thinking about how different her own father was from the kind of person Schultz was describing.

"Julia and I drifted apart. She had her friends, I had

mine. Mine were all cops. I hadn't realized how far apart we were until that time my partner got killed. I needed all the support I could get, but I couldn't even talk to her about it. From then on, we've just been two people living in the same house. She fixes the meals, I take out the trash."

PJ felt a hollowness inside herself. She knew firsthand how it felt when intimacy died. In his case, it had been a gradual process, hardly noticeable over the years, until that moment when his heart twanged and he realized it was all gone. It was like a garden slowly overtaken with weeds until the fine straight rows of flowers and vegetables were no longer visible. No longer harvestable either; they had been choked out. For her, the process had been telescoped into a few days, maybe a few hours within those terrible days.

"But we got along OK. Not a lot of fights. Like a couple of well-adjusted roommates, we knew what not to say to each other. It wasn't so bad. At least there was some companionship, somebody sitting across the table at breakfast. Then I had to go and stir things up about Rick."

"If it hadn't been that, it would have been something else," PJ said. "Once the slide begins, it's hard to crawl back up."

Schultz shook himself in his chair. "How'd we get on this, anyway? Christ, I sound like a sad drunk."

"I think it started with a meat tenderizer," PJ said.

"Oh, yeah. Mind telling me what that stuff is on your desk?"

"That," she said, pointing, "is a personal dilemma, Detective. Maybe you can help me out."

"Shoot."

"When I gave you that first demonstration of the crime scene simulation, I mentioned that there were two ways virtual reality could work. You can watch from the outside, or put yourself right in the action. This gadget," she said, picking up the headset, "puts you in the world. The gloves I'm wearing allow you to manipulate objects in that world."

"So what's the dilemma? Did you rip these off from a video arcade? 'Officer, I've never stolen anything before, I just don't know what came over me?' "

PJ laughed. It felt good to laugh, so she did it again. "These aren't in your run-of-the-mill arcade, although they probably will be in a few years. No, the problem is worse than that. I've created a monster."

"This is getting interesting. Go on."

"My simulation turned out to be so real looking, it scared me."

"Not for the squeamish, huh?"

PJ nodded. "Plus there's a question that just occurred to me this morning. If I can act out what the killer does, doesn't that make me, on some level, just like the killer?"

"Shit, no. Re-enactment is part of every detective's method, or it should be. I act out a crime on paper, in my head, and at the original scene. Sometimes I get an obliging fellow cop to play the victim. Anita and I have already been out to Armor's place, and we'll probably go back. I had her sit in the chair the Armor woman was in, but she would have bopped me one if I'd tried to tie her to it."

"And it doesn't give you the creeps?"

"No. It's my job."

PJ felt that there was more to it than that. It had to do with what she had sensed before about Schultz, that he connected to the killer in some way. As a psychologist, she had heard terrible things from her patients. She had experienced a whole range of vicarious emotions: fear and hatred and lust. But she was detached. She never opened herself to fully experiencing what her patients did. She knew that Schultz was willing to do that, willing to set up that vulnerability in himself, to risk understanding on a visceral basis. Again, that connection.

"So would you like to try it?" PJ asked.

"Said the spider to the fly. Why not?"

CHAPTER

23

Schultz cleared his mind. He wanted to give PJ's creation his full attention. After three murders, he was willing to look at just about anything.

At her direction, he pulled on the gloves. They felt like steel mesh, although they didn't seem to limit the movement of his fingers. He made sure the office door was closed before putting on the headset. He didn't want anyone else to see him wearing the contraption.

"I'm going to run a little demo before we get into the crime scene. Have you ever been skiing, Detective?"

"Do I look like the type to risk my neck going down a hill on a couple of match sticks?"

"Well, this should be quite an experience, then. It works better if you're standing up. There you go. The demo's automatic, so you don't have to do anything with the gloves. Just watch."

Abruptly an image formed in front of Schultz's eyes. It was all-encompassing; the headset blocked input from outside, both visual and auditory, and replaced it with a computer-generated world. The first thing that registered was whiteness; then it resolved itself into a snowy scene, a pine forest. Straight ahead was a narrow path through the trees. For a few seconds everything was frozen in place, like a 3D still picture. Given that time to study the scene, he could tell that it wasn't real: a tree had jagged edges, a mound of snow was too circular, the colors were a little too true, not the blended shades of the natural world. Everything had a diamond-like sharpness, a clarity that didn't exist in reality or in the human mind.

In front of him on the path was a rear view of a person in ski clothing. There was a moment of disorientation as the scene was set in motion. The skier in front moved arms and legs rhythmically. Trees approached, grew even with Schultz, and passed by, falling beyond the range of his peripheral vision. He became aware of a swishing sound, the sound of skis moving over snow in a quiet forest. He turned his head to the left to see what happened to the trees as they passed behind him. The scene changed smoothly with his head motion, and he could see trees behind him.

Then he looked down, and got a terrific shock. He saw the front of his body, clothed in a winter outfit, arms pumping, feet encased in ski boots, gliding along in a double track in the snow laid down by the skier ahead. His body sense, his muscles, told him that he was not moving.

His eyes and ears told him otherwise.

Looking ahead, he saw the skier in front of him vanish over a rise. Soon he reached the same rise, topped it, and found himself looking down a long hill. In the distance, the other skier was moving fast, crouched, poles tucked under his arms, easily swooping around widely spaced trees. Now Schultz felt his muscles tense, his legs brace themselves. He didn't want to go down that hill. But he moved relentlessly forward, picking up speed. When the first tree approached, he flung his arms out to prevent the crash that seemed certain. Instead, he swung smoothly around the tree, and headed for another. By the time he got to the bottom of the slope his heart was racing. He was barely aware of the headset being lifted off.

"What did you think?"

The glare of the snow was gone. He was standing in PJ's office, just outside the bright cone of light from her desk lamp. "That was amazing," he said.

"Draws you in, doesn't it? That was a promotional program from a company that's developing exercise equipment linked with VR scenery. You get on your cross-country ski machine in your basement, pop on the headset, and poof, you're on a scenic trail. This one is considerably slicker than my simulations. They've got some big money interested. Mine aren't quite as convincing, but unfortunately my imagination filled in what was lacking."

"Amazing," Schultz said.

"I noticed you turning your head. They have good peripheral flow, better than mine, and an excellent sense of virtual presence. You really feel like you're in that pine forest, don't you? I understand they're looking into adding a pine smell and a fan to blow air over your face like the wind. The production version will respond to your motion on the exercise equipment. If you move your legs faster, you speed up on the trail."

"I was more concerned about stopping than speeding up."

"You did look a little . . . anxious. Trust me, you never left the office. Are you ready to try being a killer?"

"Ready as I'll ever be."

"Let me explain how to use the gloves first. If you look down, you'll see a simulation of your own hands, minus the gloves. If you want to pick something up, just do what comes naturally. If you want to move around, first look in the direction you want to go, then tap your left palm with the fingers of your right hand, like this." She demonstrated a clapping motion. "You'll move forward into the scene one step for each tap. Unfortunately, there's no such thing as moving backward yet. You have to turn completely around, facing where you came from, and move forward. There's another method in the works, a kind of treadmill on which you stand and actually move your feet in the direction you want to move in the virtual world. But that's really cutting-edge, and I consider myself lucky to get these gloves."

Schultz nodded, and she helped him put the headset back on. The dual miniature monitors showed only a pleasant blue null screen. He heard some clicks as PJ started up the crime scene simulation, and then the image formed.

He was at the bottom of the stairs that led to Burton's apartment from the rear alley. Looking down, he saw the front of his body—a Genman body that didn't have his bulk—and his arms and hands. Floating in front of his hands was the box of roses. He reached out and picked it up with both hands. For a moment he thought how ludicrous he must look to PJ, pawing thin air. Then he let himself become immersed. Looking up at the stairs, he wondered how he was supposed to tap his right fingers to his left palm if he was holding the box of roses. PJ's directions hadn't been clear. So he just did it—tapped one time while looking up the staircase. The scene changed slightly; he had climbed the first step. Looking down, he saw his hands still grasping the box. He climbed the rest of the stairs and rang the doorbell.

It didn't take him long to get the hang of moving around in the world the computer spread out in front of him. He was aware that PJ's simulation was not as good as the commercial one with the skiers, but it was certainly convincing. He acted out the rest of the scene as he had done several times in his mind. It was eerie and deeply disturbing to see everything from the killer's viewpoint, but he did not have the same qualms about it that PJ seemed to have. Schultz was accustomed to putting himself in a criminal's place, trying to fathom the actions of those on the edge of humanity. He was fascinated in spite of his distrust of computers.

At one point during the simulation he went over to the ornate mirror that was right inside Burton's door. It topped a small table, the kind that would be used for keys or the mail. When he stood in front of the mirror, he saw a startling reflection: Genman's face, smeared with blood, features stilled into a primitive mask. He wondered if the killer had glimpsed himself like this, as a heart-stopping vision of savagery, the bounds of civilized behavior loosened and then cast off.

When he finally removed the headset, he discovered that he wasn't in the same position in the room. He had moved several feet, to the limit of the cables connecting him to PJ's desktop computer, and was facing a different direction. At some point during the simulation, he must have actually been moving rather than just looking and tapping. When he turned around, he saw that PJ had fallen asleep at her desk, head down on her folded arms. Glancing at the Mickey Mouse clock on her desk, he was startled to see than an hour had elapsed. He put the headset and gloves on her desk. As he was tiptoeing out, she woke up.

"Got the case solved now?" she said. She stretched her arms above her head and arched her back. "I should bring in a pillow. For my back, that is, not to sleep on."

"I have to admit there could be some potential in this."

"High praise from the Sultan of Skepticism." She rotated her neck, trying to stretch the tired muscles. "I added some information to the simulations based on finding out that the brain was missing from the recovered head. Would you like to go over it with me?"

She said the words in a straightforward manner, but Schultz heard the emotion underneath.

"Just a minute. Would you mind if I invited Dave and Anita to sit in on this? The truth is," he looked down at his hands on the desk, "I've been getting some flak over not involving them more in the computer stuff."

"From Anita?"

"From both of them. I told them about the original simulation, the one you showed me a few days into the investigation. I think they were jealous. They're just kids, after all."

"Kids? Dave is over thirty, isn't he? Go ahead, see if

they're available. I've been meaning to spend more time
with them anyway."

"I should warn you that they're a little intimidated by
you. Unlike myself, of course."

"Fetch, Detective."

Schultz was back a few minutes later with his two assistants. Dave had pushed a chair down the hall from his
own desk. Schultz and Anita settled in the two folding
chairs. Dave slouched in his chair, his six-foot frame draped
in it with the careless flexibility of the under-forty crowd.
Anita sat up straight, her pixie-like appearance delineated
by the light of PJ's desk lamp. They made an odd pair, but
worked well together. Each filled in the other's weak points,
plus Anita added that spark of independent thinking, so
that together they made a pretty good detective. Schultz
thought that he was probably being too critical. There had
been a time when he had eagerly hung on every word of
his superiors. He also thought, cynically, that maybe they
were just being careful not to outshine their boss.

PJ put the two newcomers at ease with small talk. He admired that; it was smoothly done. With so many people
jammed into PJ's tiny office, Schultz felt his personal space
getting cramped, shriveling up like his scrotum in a cold
shower. He liked to keep people not just at arm's reach, but
beyond. The small white fan was giving its all, but the tem-
perature began to rise almost as soon as he closed the door.
He wondered if PJ knew that her office, which she had
fixed up as nicely as possible, used to be a utility closet.

"Say, Doc, did you paint this place?" he said, gesturing
around the room.

"Thomas and I did it late one night," she said with obvious pride.

"Looks nice," said Dave. "You'd never know this used
to be a utility room."

Schultz winced, but the comment didn't seem to faze PJ.
He made a note to talk to Dave about tact, subtlety, chain
of command, and his lowly position therein.

He sat back and observed as PJ went through her spiel on virtual reality again, watching the reactions of those who were watching the computer screen during a simulation of the Armor murder.

"That's basically it," she said. "There's some additional equipment which gives you much more of a feeling of being inside the virtual world rather than just looking at it on the screen." She pointed at the headset and gloves, which had migrated to a narrow table shoved up against the wall. "Schultz and I have just gotten to that point today. You're welcome to try it out individually. Right now I'd like to go over a newly-added portion of the simulation you just saw."

She punched some keys and the screen showed the killer leaving Armor's apartment and loading the carrying case into the passenger seat of a car. Then the images faded entirely and were replaced by a mirror-image action: the killer unloaded the case and carried it inside a generic-looking house. In the kitchen, he removed the head, long hair trailing, soiled with blood. Genman put the head on a wooden cutting board and chipped at it with a hammer and chisel. Schultz again took inventory of the faces watching the screen. PJ and Anita were impassive. Dave looked a little green. The figure on the screen used a large spoon to scoop the brain out into a bowl. Dave now looked more than a little green.

"This is as far as we can go with the facts we have," PJ said. "The condition of the simulated head now matches the real one that was recovered. There are a lot of possibilities from here on, but of course they're all speculative. I'll run through a few, and then we can talk about them, plus any additional thoughts you have."

He hadn't seen this part. Schultz sat forward with interest as Genman went through three different scenarios.

In the first, Genman dumped the brain into a large jar, topped it off with liquid, and put it on a shelf containing other, similarly filled, jars.

In the second, he dissected it, studying the tissue carefully and comparing it to charts in textbooks.

In the third, he took a knife and fork and sliced off a piece, and then another, and another, eating them raw.

Schultz didn't bother to check Dave's face; he knew what he would see.

"Comments?" PJ said. She looked as composed as a professor lecturing a class of freshmen.

"I can't see this killer as the cerebral type," Anita said immediately. "No pun intended. I don't think he's hauling heads around to do anatomical studies of the brains. It's too clinical."

"Saving the brains as trophies in jars doesn't make any sense either," said Dave. "After all, you can't tell one victim from another if all you've got is jars of brains. Wouldn't they all look alike? How would he relive the specific experience for each victim?"

"Easy," said Schultz. "Photos. Tape one on the front of each jar."

There was silence for awhile as each mulled over the possibilities. Finally PJ spoke. "I really don't see how we can rule out any of these scenarios now, let alone ones we haven't seen on the computer. There's just not enough information. But I've got a hunch."

Schultz studied PJ. He saw the eagerness in her eyes, and thought back to that time in Millie's Diner when he had seen that contemplative look on her face. He listened attentively. Hunches could be very important in his line of work, and PJ had already proved the value of hers when she had been convinced that Sheila Armor was in danger. She cloaked her excitement in a lecturing tone of voice, but Schultz saw through it.

"I think the killer is consuming the brain," she said. "In many cultures, eating certain body parts of an animal is thought to confer an attribute of that animal. For example, it's a common belief in Pacific Rim countries that eating a tiger's penis or a rhino's horn increases virility. Since the time of Peking man, that principle has been applied to the human animal also. Consuming the brain is a ritual means by which the vitality, strength, or prowess of the person eaten might be obtained."

"So the creep's trying to take on the characteristics of his victims," Schultz said.

"Not all of the characteristics. Just their special skills, like dancing or painting. Perhaps he feels that his own existence is featureless, and he needs other peoples' abilities to add to the quality of his life."

"As though his life is black-and-white TV and he needs an injection of someone else's essence to liven up his life to the level of color TV," Anita said.

"Yes. Exactly. Someone else's essence . . . " PJ drifted off into her own thoughts.

"And it's addictive," said Dave. "Once he's experienced color TV, there's no going back."

CHAPTER

24

P J picked up Thomas from school and took him out to Giorgio's for an early pizza dinner. All during the meal, she kept picturing Mike Wolf across the table from her. Thomas gazed at her with questions in his eyes. He probably wondered why Mom was so mellow. They got home when it was still light, since the days were considerably longer now that full summer was practically on top of them.

"Mom, what's wrong with the flower bed?" Thomas said. They got out of the car and went over to look. The lilies of the valley were crushed, and the whole area looked as though a troop of dogs had scratched and scraped at the soil to bury a treasure trove of bones. A feeling of dread came over PJ, like the apprehension of a mouse hearing the wing beats of an owl, huddling, not knowing when or where death will come from.

"I don't know, sweetie, I just don't know," she said, trying to hide her emotions. "What a shame. Maybe a stray dog got in the yard."

Then she noticed the letters spray-painted across the back of the house. "STOP KUMPUTR" was on one side of the door in letters two feet high. On the other side of the door was "FUKIN BICH". She took in the shock and it spread in cold waves from the center of her body to her arms and legs. The back of her throat burned, and she swallowed and struggled to keep her stomach from heaving. She turned abruptly, hoping that Thomas hadn't seen the writing yet, but he had. He seemed to shrink in on himself for a moment, then he straightened, and spoke with the courage of the person he would become.

"Looks like the killer owes you a dollar, Mom. He used a word from the A list."

It took some time to sink in. When PJ finally reacted, she laughed nervously and pulled her son to her in a tight hug, shutting out the horrors of the world.

"A dollar and a quarter. Don't forget about the B list word," she said.

He let himself be hugged, resting his head on her shoulder, then pulled away. "Let's go call Schultz. Can I dial the cell phone?"

"Sure. I guess we're getting to be old hands at this."

She wasn't sure whether she was comforting him or herself. PJ was glad that she had gotten the portable cellular phone, as Schultz had suggested. She always left it in the car because it seemed to her that she would only need it if the refuge of her home or office was denied to her. Besides, that way the phone would be available for Thomas to use, too, which wouldn't be the case if she carried it around with her. He had a key to the car along with his house key. While Thomas dialed, she pulled the car around the front of the house and parked on the street. No need to shove their noses in the disfigurement of their home.

Schultz and a patrol car that he had summoned arrived at about the same time. He waved to PJ and disappeared with the officers around the back of the house. Schultz came back to PJ's car to get her house key. He said it didn't look like anyone had been in the house but he wanted to make sure. She let him fuss. It was probably therapeutic for him. After he left, she was startled when the cell phone rang for the first time since she had gotten it. She moved to answer it, but Thomas was quicker. He grabbed the phone before her fingers could curl around it.

"Doctor Gray's number." Thomas had learned phone etiquette early. PJ used to get a lot of business calls at home. He listened for a moment.

"Yeah, it works. I'm in the car," he said.

Apparently the call was for him. PJ was mystified.

"Cool!" Thomas said. "See ya."

She could see that he was excited, and she pushed a smile onto her face, trying not to think of why they were sitting out in the car at the curb. "So what gives?"

"That was Winston. Remember I said this morning that I had something in the works for this summer?"

PJ nodded.

"I'm going to stay at Winston's house. His dad just said yes."

PJ's eyes flew open wide. "You might have asked me first, Thomas. I barely know Winston, and I haven't even met his father."

"His dad's OK, just kind of sad. His mom has been away at a drug treatment center for awhile. She's living in a place called a halfway house now, and they think she'll get to come home in a few months. But for the time being, it'll be just us men. Plus Megabite. They both like cats a lot."

"I don't know what to say. This is so sudden. I suppose I could give Mister . . . what's Winston's last name, anyway?"

"Lakeland. His dad's name is William."

"I could give Mister Lakeland a call, and we could talk about it."

"Don't say no, Mom. It'll be neat! Besides," he said, "after what just happened, you're going to get really anxious to get me out of here."

Clearly her son was enthusiastic, and this was the most positive emotion he'd shown in quite some time. She didn't know whether to be angry with him for making these arrangements or proud of his independence. "OK, son, I'll really try to make it happen. But I have to talk to Winston's dad myself."

"There's something else."

"What? You're joining the Peace Corps and moving to Africa?"

"No, not quite. Not for a few more years, anyway. There's this summer course where you learn about computers, almost like a summer camp. It's very intensive, real advanced stuff. I'm dying to go, Mom, and Winston is too."

"It sounds interesting. Where can I get some more information on it?"

"Right here," he said, pulling open his backpack. After a brief search, he extracted a brochure that had been thoroughly handled and repeatedly scrutinized.

"It's at Washington University, hmm . . . " she said while glancing at the brochure. "Oh, Thomas, this course is for high schoolers."

"I've talked to the instructor, and she says Winston and I can attend. We meet the prerequisites."

All of a sudden Thomas sounded so grown up. Instructor. Summer course at college. Prerequisites.

"Well, you've certainly given me a lot to think about," she said.

"Think fast, Mom. The course starts Monday, and we're already registered."

"Already . . ."

"Winston's dad can drop us off there in the morning on his way to work. The class is over at three, so we'd have to wait at Olin Library for a couple of hours before he could pick us up, but we don't mind. There is one complication, though."

"Just one?"

"Winston's dad doesn't have a lot of money. We told him Winston got a scholarship." Thomas looked sheepish. "There aren't any scholarships available."

PJ sighed. Money was tight, and Thomas certainly knew

it. She had not tried to conceal their financial situation from him. She hadn't had insurance when she first moved into the rental house, although she did now. Her desktop personal computer was a total loss, and she hadn't replaced it yet. It looked like she wouldn't be shopping for a new one in the near future.

"I'll make it up. I'll get a job mowing lawns after the class is over."

"You certainly will. Starting with ours."

"Does that mean yes?"

She looked at her son's eager face. "Yes . . ."

"All right, Mom!"

"After I talk to Mister Lakeland and meet him in person. If everything works out, I don't see why you couldn't pack a few things and get over there tonight." *So I can paint over the letters tomorrow by myself,* she thought. Her son was practically bursting. There was something else.

"Don't tell me . . . " she said.

"Yup. I'm already packed."

PJ and Schultz sat in the kitchen of her home. She had already spoken to William Lakeland—Bill—on the phone, and he had invited her over at eight that evening. He seemed very pleased that Winston was going to have company, and proudly declined PJ's offer to pay room and board for Thomas, although he mentioned that Winston wouldn't have been able to attend the summer class without the scholarship. PJ saw no reason to burst his bubble about that, but she made a note to herself to talk to Thomas about white lies.

"Can you do me a favor?" she asked Schultz. "Could you check Bill Lakeland's background, make sure he isn't a convicted child molester or something?"

"Sure. And if he is, I'll go over there and crack him in the balls and get your son out of there. His friend, too."

"I'm sure you would, Detective. Your protective nature is one of the things that make you so lovable."

"That so? Didn't work on Julia. Seriously, Doc," he said, "I'd feel better if you'd get out of here, too."

"Where would I go where the killer wouldn't find me? A hotel?" She shivered as she thought of what had happened to Ilya Vanitzky in his hotel room.

"Out of town?"

PJ shook her head.

"I didn't think so, but it was worth a try."

"I'm scared, but I'm not going to be run off. I do feel a lot better that Thomas will be out of this. Whatever's going to happen, that is." Their eyes met, and she saw something reflected back at her in Schultz's eyes: his assessment of her courage. Or stupidity. "Coffee?" PJ had started a pot of coffee, and the smell filled the kitchen. She poured cups for herself and Schultz.

"I guess there's no question now that this," Schultz jerked his head toward the rear of the house, "is related to the killings. Dave and Anita are going to interview your neighbors, see if anybody saw the guy."

"The thing we have to figure out is this: where is he getting his information? And why has he got it in for me?"

"That's two things. Either somebody's leaking information about your involvement, or the murderer is a member of the Department." Schultz slurped his hot coffee noisily. "He must have some reason to think that you, specifically you, are getting too close."

"Do you routinely tell others about the details of this investigation? Who else knows what CHIP is doing?"

"That's the problem, Doc. This has been played close to the chest, but that still means a lot of people are involved. I talk to you, to Wall, to Anita and Dave. They swear they haven't talked about the investigation to their families, but pillow talk just slips out sometimes. Plus of course there are the officers who were first on the scenes and the evidence techs. Did I mention the medical examiner's office?"

"No," she said with a sigh. "The first time this happened, you said you would poke around, see if anybody in the Department seemed unstable."

"You mean besides the undercover guys?" He laughed at his own joke. PJ didn't even crack a smile. "I did ask around, even talked to Internal Affairs. Tried to find out if anybody's strung out, somebody's partner's acting weird, things like that. I came up with zip."

"Now that I think about it," PJ said, "wouldn't it be almost impossible for the murderer to be a member of the Department? There are written tests to pass, aren't there? Our man can't express himself well enough in writing to pass tests."

"Actually, he would probably do well at multiple-choice tests. According to Sheriff Youngman, he could read well enough."

"But surely somewhere along the line he would have run into questions he had to answer with a few sentences."

"What if he's not an officer? Case in point—you. You're a civilian employee. Did you take any tests to get on board?"

"No, but I filled out an application and submitted a résumé."

"Résumé services will do that for you. All our creep needed was fifty bucks. There's a lot of jobs where all you need is a clean police record. It's not like there's that many applicants for a job cleaning toilets."

"If he was cleaning toilets, how did he get access to information about the investigation?"

"I don't know. Maybe he divines it from sheets of toilet paper, like reading tea leaves. All I know is there's a leak someplace." Schultz stopped for a minute and fumbled in his pocket. He started to remove a pill bottle, then slipped it back and asked PJ if he could use the bathroom.

She was getting a little tired of his coyness. "If you need to take something for your arthritis," she said, "go right ahead. It's nothing to be ashamed of."

She could see emotions play over his face, and then he seemed to reach a decision. He took out the bottle and dumped three pills in his palm. They seemed lost in his large hand. He tossed them back with a swallow of coffee.

"Today's been one of the bad days," he said. "Left knee feels like it's about to freeze up altogether. Then every now and again a sharp pain goes through it, like somebody stuck a torch on it."

"What are you taking?"

"Ibuprofen. Sometimes aspirin."

"There are better medications than that. You haven't seen a doctor?"

"Nope. I have to pass a physical to stay on active duty, and if I went to the Department physician with this, he'd have me back at a desk. Or retired. This way, as long as he doesn't take X-rays, he won't ground me. And he won't take X-rays unless somebody snitches on me." He glared at PJ.

"What about a private doctor? As long as you paid for the visit yourself, you could even use a phony name. They don't take your fingerprints, you know."

"No."

"Why not?"

Schultz looked uncomfortable. "I just don't like going to the doctor, haven't since I was a child."

"Haven't liked it or haven't gone?"

"Both. Except for the mandatory Department physicals. And then I keep my mouth shut."

"The big, brave detective is scared to go to the doctor?"

"So you know one of my secrets. It certainly isn't the worst one."

"You're not being logical. If you went to a private doctor and got some effective medication, you could do a better job of concealing your arthritis on the job."

Schultz looked doubtful. "I hadn't thought of it that way."

"Well, now you have, and I'm going to nag you mercilessly until you go. I'm a champion nagger, too."

"That's a fact. Suppose I did. What doctor could I go to?"

"How should I know?" PJ said. "I'm new in town. Call a referral service, or let your fingers do the walking."

Thomas came bounding down the steps, with Megabite tucked under one arm, carrying a red cylindrical duffel bag stuffed so tightly it looked obscene. Both PJ and Schultz laughed when they saw it. Ordinarily Thomas would have picked up on it, but he was too focused on his adventure.

"What?" Thomas said. "What's funny? My hair messed up or something?"

"It's nothing," PJ said. "Let's get out to the car."

Schultz levered himself to his feet, feeling his left knee pop but ignoring it.

"You will think about our discussion, won't you, Detective?" PJ asked.

"Yeah, sure. By the way, what are the other things?"

"Other things?"

"The other things that make me lovable," Schultz said as he sauntered out.

PJ managed to keep herself in good spirits while visiting Bill Lakeland and dropping off Thomas. But when she returned home, she went through an emotional crash. No longer needing to hide her feelings from Thomas, she let herself fall apart, sobbing at the kitchen table. She was frightened, more frightened than she wanted to admit to Schultz or Thomas.

The killer had been to her home again.

She had dealt with sociopaths before, but they had been confined to hospitals or prisons. This one had freedom of movement, and had demonstrated that he had cunning and strength as well. He knew where she lived and that she was pursuing him. He lacked the inhibitions that society and his own conscience should normally impose. Where others might get some emotional relief by imagining killing a rotten boss, a rude salesclerk, or an infuriating teenager, this man might act. Nothing held him back except the demands of his own sociopathic behavior, which set the pattern for his killing.

As far as she knew, the only thing protecting her from a gruesome death was the fact that she had no artistic talent. She sent silent thanks to her mother, who had not insisted that she continue with her piano lessons when she was nine years old.

She remembered her speculation that this killer could break out of the pattern of his past murders, and that made her feel even worse.

For a time she was lost to fear, unable to break its grip on her mind and body. Then she could feel it receding, almost like watching a train disappear into the distance.

She wondered why she was pursuing him. It was like running toward a tornado; surely he was as dispassionate in his destruction as a funnel cloud. Why didn't she run away, run at right angles to the tornado and get the hell out?

The answer hit her like a fist in her belly, strong enough to shake not only her body but her deepest conceptions about herself. She wanted to stop him, to put a stop to the evil that walked around disguised as a person, to personally see to it that he didn't kill again. She didn't have much opportunity to get to know Sheila Armor, but she had talked with the woman, laughed with her, admired her, and seen a flash of the same kind of vulnerability that she herself possessed. Now that life, and all the promise that it held, was ended. His other victims she knew only through photos and bloodstains, but she felt their deaths too, as dark blows to her soul. She wondered how many blows Schultz's soul had taken, and whether hers would be as resilient.

Two years ago she would never have believed that she

would become deeply involved in police work. Now it seemed like there was nothing else that would be worthwhile for her. She had found a purpose, and her career before St. Louis seemed shallow to her now. Consumer studies? How could she have spent her time like that?

She splashed her face with water to wash away the salty tracks. It was nearly ten PM, and she didn't feel like doing any work at home. She opened a box that hadn't been unpacked yet, pulled out the first video tape on top of the stack inside, and popped it into the TV/VCR combo she had bought in the relatively flush days before she was paying for college courses for two boys. She watched three hours of Star Trek episodes before climbing the stairs and falling into bed in her shorts and T-shirt.

CHAPTER
25

When PJ woke up Saturday morning, she stayed in bed for a long time, reviewing the three murders and wondering how they would come up with the killer's identity. Schultz still seemed confident, almost serene. Ever since his trip to Tennessee, he felt that he was on the trail of a specific person, Paul Macmillan, and all he had to do was locate him. Where did his certainty come from? Did he have anything he wasn't telling her? At least he was finally willing to admit that the break-in and the outside destruction at her home were associated with the murders.

She showered and dressed in clean clothes. It was so time-consuming to go to a coin-operated laundry that she was starting to think of a clean outfit as a luxury. She was going to have to get a washer and dryer soon, but for now PJ put thoughts of money firmly from her head. There was a place and time to worry about that, and it wasn't here and now.

It was sunny outside, already at least eighty degrees at eight in the morning, and humid. As she ate her breakfast of crumb coffee cake and grapefruit, she felt the emptiness of the house settle on her like a bank of fog. She couldn't hear Thomas thumping around upstairs or Megabite crunching her dry cat food over in the corner of the kitchen, and she missed those reminders of life.

When the phone rang, she was brushing the grapefruit

juice splatters off her T-shirt with a damp dishcloth.

"Penny? It's Mike." For some reason, Mike wanted to call her Penny rather than PJ, but she didn't mind. She wondered what was on his mind at eight on a Saturday morning, but she was willing to let him take his time getting around to it. They chatted for nearly ten minutes about the weather and the input routines for the data gloves. Then he paused. She thought he was about to break off the conversation, so she beat him to it.

"Well, I'm sure you have a busy day planned, so I'll let you get to it," she said.

"Wait, I . . ."

"Yes?"

"I was wondering if you'd like to . . . that is . . ."

"Spit it out, Mike. It couldn't be all that bad."

"Have dinner with me. Here. Tonight."

Her heart jumped. She had been hoping he would make some move like this. She had been planning to call him when the case was completed, if he hadn't taken the plunge first. She had been thinking about him all week. She wanted . . . What? A lover? A friend? A husband? A father for Thomas?

"I'd love to," she said warmly. "I could use some company that doesn't have a keyboard."

"I'm actually a pretty good cook," he said eagerly. "Is there anything I should avoid? Allergies or something?"

It was an unusual question. PJ wondered if he or his ex-wife had an allergy problem. She suddenly realized that she didn't know if he had any kids. If he did, were they living with him?

"No, I guess I've got a strong stomach. Comes from all those Hostess Cup Cakes I eat. It's a well-kept medical secret—that creamy stuff inside boosts immunity."

He laughed. "I guess that was kind of an odd question. My daughter is allergic to peanuts. Not just mildly allergic, either. She could die from eating a handful of peanuts or even a peanut butter cookie. I've gotten in the habit of asking people before I cook for them."

So he did have children. "I can understand that. How old is she?"

"Patty's eleven, going on sixteen. My other daughter, Carolyn, is eighteen. She'll be starting college this fall."

"Do you see them often?" PJ couldn't think of a diplomatic way of asking if they lived with him.

"The girls are here every other weekend and all summer. Patty's got a sleepover tonight, and Carolyn's going out on a date. Most Saturday nights I'm on my own. But that's OK. I like to see them out having fun. Say, if you want to bring Thomas tonight, feel free."

"He's staying with a friend tonight," she said. She didn't feel like explaining that Thomas had moved out entirely. They settled on six PM, and she got his address. She was surprised to find that he didn't live in the city, but in a west county suburb, Chesterfield.

Looking out the window at the ruined flower bed, PJ's plans for the day fell into place. First she phoned Thomas at Winston's home to let him know she'd be gone that evening. He pressed her on where she was going, and she had to admit that she was having dinner at a friend's house, and that the friend was male. This led to hoots and laughter on the other end as Thomas shared some apparently crude joke with Winston.

PJ went out into the sunshine, got in her car, and drove to a hardware store. It was a small one, the full-service kind where you admit that you didn't have the slightest idea what you needed to repair the thingamajig. She left with a whole trunk full of supplies: topsoil, peat moss, a tray of annual flowers, a shovel and trowel, gardening gloves, a can of some chemical stuff called Graffiti Out, six gallons of white exterior paint, and a hefty paint brush, the kind that really means business.

She worked on the flower bed first, because the flowers she had bought looked as though they couldn't wait to get into the ground and under the sun. She dug in the topsoil and peat moss and set the flowers in the carefully prepared bed. When it was time to water them, she discovered that she had forgotten a watering can or hose, so she filled a kitchen pot over and over at the outdoor faucet and poured the water through a colander. It wasn't exactly a gentle sprinkling effect, but at least she didn't swamp the little plants.

She applied the Graffiti Out with an old bath towel. It was supposed to be left on for an hour, so she went inside, drank a soda, and worked on her PowerBook for awhile. When the time was up, she went outside and scrubbed the area with wet towels. It felt wonderful to be physically active, to be taking control, to be eradicating the stain the killer had left on her home. More and more she was thinking of the rental house as her home. She wondered if she could scrape up the down payment to buy it, maybe in a few months.

Painting was a perfect activity to free her mind. As she hoisted the heavy brush and spread the bright white paint, she pulled her thoughts together about the case. She felt that somewhere in all the scattered bits of information she had, there was something crucial she just wasn't seeing. It was as though everything was there, but she just couldn't get it in focus. It reminded her of those computer-generated flat images which, when you stared at them in just the right way, suddenly popped into a 3D view. You had to look beyond the image, not directly at it. She felt that if she could just see beyond the surface of the facts she had, a solution would spring out at her.

After PJ had finished painting over the large area where the letters had been, she stepped back to admire her work. She noticed that the newly-painted portion made the older section look drab. She might as well do the entire back side of the house. There were over four gallons of paint left. She wondered why she had bought so much paint. Apparently she had been subconsciously planning to do the whole side. During the rest of the summer, she could work her way around the whole house. The windows, though, would have to be scraped and done with trim paint. That would have to wait. She could borrow a ladder from Mrs. Brodsky next door after lunch.

Lunch. Her stomach rumbled. She had been working hard and had not had anything but a soda since breakfast. She decided to treat herself to lunch at Millie's. She hopped in her VW, thinking of an old-fashioned chocolate milkshake in a tall V-shaped glass with a spoon for the thick parts and a straw to suck up the melted ice cream at the bottom—just the way Millie served one.

Schultz slept in Saturday morning. Casey, the luscious blonde who worked in Vehicles, had graced him with another visit last night. She was turning out to be one of his more durable fantasies, in more ways than one. When he finally woke up, he urgently needed to get to the bathroom. He lurched to his feet. There was pain in his knees, sharper than usual, and he couldn't seem to get them moving. He shuffled along stiff-legged, but he wasn't making good enough time. The urge to urinate was too strong and the bathroom was too far away. He headed for the wastebasket that stood next to his dresser and relieved himself there. When he was done, he slowly made his way to the bathroom carrying the wastebasket, emptied it into the toilet, and rinsed it in the sink.

He was deeply embarrassed, even though he was all alone. What if this happened at work? He'd be put out to pasture for sure. Thinking of what PJ had said about consulting a private doctor, he went back to the bed, sat down heavily, and pulled the Yellow Pages out of the night stand drawer. He selected a private orthopedic clinic as a starting point. If that wasn't right, they could refer him to one from there. He used his own name when he called, but he planned to pay for the treatment himself rather than submit a claim under the Department insurance program. As he had hoped, there was an opening due to a cancellation, and they were able to see him at eleven-thirty that morning. By the time he showered and shaved, his legs were starting to limber up.

He breakfasted on instant coffee and a stale Danish he had bought a couple of days ago. The empty house seemed oppressive to him, and he was not looking forward to today's agenda: the doctor's office followed by a visit to his son. Schultz had posted bail for Rick, and the boy was living in the apartment he had shared with a roommate whom Schultz considered to be a bad influence. The day he drove his son home from his bail hearing, Schultz had unceremoniously kicked the roommate out.

Other than posting bail, he had decided not to help Rick avoid jail time. The charges against his son were serious, and in Schultz's mind, deserving of punishment. If it had been something like auto theft, he might have been inclined to exert pressure to get the charges dropped or reduced. But selling drugs to kids—potentially ruining young lives—was not something he wanted to brush under the rug. Since this was a first offense, if things took their normal course, Rick would serve maybe six months in jail and two or three years on probation. Schultz intended to be there for his son when he got out of prison, to give him a place to live, make sure he got a job, and simply be a presence in his life. Schultz had hopes his son could turn things around for himself with the proper environment, and that environment included a caring, involved father.

Schultz's biggest fear was that Rick would contract HIV from forced sex during his jail stay. Rick was a big, strong man, with the same powerful build that Schultz had at that age, so he would not be an easy target for exploitation. Schultz planned to share with him everything he knew about ways to avoid the most onerous possibilities during incarceration: rape and beatings. He would also use his network of contacts to ensure that the guards kept an eye on things and alerted him early if trouble was brewing. It was the best that he could do, and he didn't think it made up for years of looking the other way when Rick's difficulties first surfaced.

This afternoon he was going to visit Rick and let him know that Pop was not going to try to keep him out of jail. He fully expected an emotional, maybe even violent, reaction from the young man when it became clear to him that he was going to have to face the consequences of what he had done. Then Schultz could begin the difficult task of rebuilding his relationship with his son, and there was always the chance that he wouldn't succeed.

After breakfast, Schultz decided to use the slack time before his doctor appointment by going in to work. He would rather occupy his mind with the circumstances of brutal killings than dwell on the prospect of what he faced with his son. As he sat at his kitchen table, draining the last drops from his coffee cup, he thought he felt Julia's hand resting gently on his shoulder. Not the Julia of today, but the Julia of thirty years ago, when there was a kind of electricity, an innocent magic, in her touch. He tilted his head to brush his cheek against her hand, as he had done so many times, but the sense of her presence was gone. He realized that it had been gone for years.

He put his coffee cup and plate in the sink and left.

PJ slurped noisily on her straw, drawing up the last of the chocolate shake. Briefly she considered ordering another one, then decided that would be a bad idea. She had to get up on that ladder when she got back to the house, and she didn't want to be overly full when she started her afternoon of work.

Millie wandered over and sat down on a stool behind the counter across from PJ.

"I don't suppose you'd consider delivering one of these

shakes to my house at about four o'clock, would you?" PJ said.

Millie laughed, "Well, Dearie, I just might consider it. Lunch was slow today. By four, this place is gonna be dead." She reached under the counter and pulled out a coffee cup for herself. Glancing over at the commercial coffee maker at the end of the counter, she saw that both the regular and decaf pots were empty. That was the "quick fill" service area, and apparently it had been depleted during lunch. Face pinched in annoyance, she pushed herself off the stool and went into the kitchen where there was another coffee maker. PJ heard her voice drift out from the pass-through between the serving area and the kitchen.

"Cut that out, I tell you. Whaddya think this is, the ball park? If I hear the "Star-Spangled Banner" outta you one more time, I'm gonna go nuts. For Christ's sake, give it a rest!"

Millie came out with a steaming cup of coffee and sat back down on the stool, her chest heaving with an exaggerated sigh.

"I swear, that cook's starting to get to me. It's like a little kid saying 'You can't make me' in that taunting kind of voice. The first fifty times you hear it, you shrug it off. Then on the fifty-first, you haul off and slug 'em. I'm afraid I'm gonna deck that guy some day, poor kid."

PJ chuckled. Millie was a strong woman with a lot of street smarts. There was little doubt she could do what she said. "I know how you feel. I used to have a patient who . . . wait a minute, did you say the 'Star-Spangled Banner'?"

"Yeah. Sometimes I think he doesn't even realize he's doing it."

PJ closed her eyes. Memories were sliding into place like continental drift in reverse: all the land masses were fitting back together to form Pangaea.

"Millie," she said, leaning toward the woman and speaking in a low, flat voice, "I'm going to ask you for some information. I would appreciate it if you'd just go along with me and not ask any questions. It might be very important, or it might be nothing."

"Sure, Dearie. Ask away." Millie's voice matched hers, low and conspiratorial.

"I'd like to know the name and address of your cook, the one who's working now."

"That's it? I thought it was going to be something hard. You just wait right here, and I'll go get his paper." She bustled off, leaving PJ fiddling with her straw and trying not to get a glimpse of the man in the kitchen.

"Here it is," she said, laying a coffee-stained form down on the counter in front of PJ. "Everybody who works here fills out one of these, so's I can pay social security and workman's comp. I do everything by the book here. If I don't, my accountant, Eddie, screams at me with language I wouldn't repeat."

"Thanks." PJ pulled a notebook from her purse and copied down the man's name, Peter M. Hampton, and his address.

"Do you know what kind of car he drives? And when does his shift end?"

"He's got a red pickup, not new but real nice and shiny. Probably waxes it every week. Got those vanity plates, something like BADBOY . . . no, it's BADDOG. I asked him about it once. He said it didn't mean anything, just something easy to remember. He gets off at two today." Millie's eyes revealed her curiosity, but she had agreed not to ask any questions, and now it was a matter of honor to stick to that.

PJ put a five dollar bill on the counter for her lunch and tip. "Where's the phone?"

"Over by the ladies' room." She leaned over and laid a hand on PJ's arm as PJ rose from her seat at the counter. "Whatever you're up to, Dearie, you be careful, OK? I don't want anything to happen to my best tipper."

PJ nodded and headed over to the phone. She dug some

coins out of her purse and called Schultz at home. She got an answering machine, and left a rambling message.

"Leo, this is PJ. Something exciting just . . . I'm at Millie's, and I've got an idea. You just listen, and don't laugh, all right? You remember that video tape with the murderer humming the 'Star-Spangled Banner'? Millie says her cook hums that very song all the time. Remember we talked about the killer wanting to take on the characteristics of his victims? We heard classical music coming from the kitchen, that's Burton, the pianist. Then Millie said the guy broke some dishes dancing around the kitchen. That's Vanitzky. Remember that awful painting of a baseball stadium? That's Sheila Armor. Sheila said that the man following her was wearing a baseball cap. That waitress, Kelly, who gave you an eyeful of boobs, said the cook was watching her like a hungry dog looking at a steak. A hungry *dog*. Here's the best part . . ."

PJ got cut off by the answering machine, which apparently had a time limit for each message. She dialed back and continued.

"This is part two of my message. The best part is that Millie says he's got a red truck with license plates that spell BADDOG. This couldn't all be coincidence, Leo. I think he's the man. His name is Peter M. Hampton, and he lives at 8420 Long Drive in St. Ann. I'm not sure where that is, but I've got a map in the car. Millie says he works until two o'clock, so I'm going to drive out there and cruise by his house. If the red truck's not there, I might get out and poke around a little. I'll let you know what happens."

PJ hung up and, with her last thirty-five cents, called Schultz's office number. No answer there, either, so she left a brief message on his voice mail telling him to check his machine at home. Disappointed that she couldn't get him right away, she wondered if in the future they should each carry pagers. She considered contacting Dave or Anita, then decided not to. If this was a wild goose chase, at least she would only look foolish in front of Schultz.

She left the diner. On impulse, she walked down the short alley that led to the parking spaces around the back for the employees.

The truck was there, and the sight of it was disturbing. It was red and arrogant and threatening, like the engorged penis of a rapist. Shuddering, she wondered if she should just go home and let Schultz check out this man. Then she remembered what he had said to her earlier: that she hadn't paid her dues. If she could get a concrete lead on this cook, maybe that would be a down payment. She shook herself mentally, plumping up her nerve as though she were fluffing a pillow, and headed for her old VW.

"I need to have you on your hands and knees up on the table," the X-ray technician said.

Schultz, feeling a draft under his loose gown, scowled at her. Just the thought of resting his weight on his knees on a metal table sent little shivers of anticipated pain through him. "If I could do that, young lady, I wouldn't need these X-rays in the first place. Can't I just stand up for this?"

"I'm afraid not," said the tech, who had last qualified as a young lady two decades ago. "We have to get a shot of your knees in a bent position, from the side." She was sympathetic but possessed enough determination for a half-dozen marathon runners. "There is an alternative, though. You can lay flat on your stomach, bend your knees, and raise your feet up in the air. I can put a couple of pillows under your calves and get enough of an angle that way."

Schultz pictured himself in the position she described, and it was clear to him that there was a problem with his gown, which was open in the back. "Just a minute," he said. He went back into the small changing booth and took another gown from the top of the stack. He put it on over the other gown, but backwards, so that it was open in the front. Back-to-back gowns at least ensured that his posterior would not be offered for appraisal like a couple of hams in a cooking contest. "OK," he told the tech, "do your worst."

"Oh, no, Mr. Schultz," she said with an enigmatic smile, "I'm sure you wouldn't want that."

PJ drove slowly past the house. This was a neighborhood of boxy two-bedroom frame homes, built thirty or forty years ago. Most of them had two layers of shingles on the roof, aluminum storm windows, and single driveways with no garages on the narrow lots. PJ knew just by looking at them that the upscale houses here had air conditioning and finished basements with a third bedroom and a rec room with a bar, perhaps even a second bathroom.

The street dead-ended a few blocks past Hampton's house at a church with a school attached. For the second time, PJ pulled into the church parking lot and swung the car around. This time, she pulled up to the curb a couple of houses down and across the street, killed the engine, and studied the house.

It was humble even for this neighborhood. A concrete porch with a green fiberglass roof sheltered the front door. White paint was peeling from the wood trim, and the chimney was ragged on top, missing a few bricks. There was no sign that anyone was at home. The red truck was not parked in the narrow, shrub-lined driveway. The owner was at work, frying hamburgers or mopping the floor when the flow of customers diminished.

She pictured Peter Hampton fixing her lunch, sticking the little toothpick flag into her BLT on whole wheat. She thought about him using the butcher knives in the diner, quartering chickens or slicing onions, and on his hands the blood of her friend Sheila and who knows how many others.

"Innocent until proven guilty," she said aloud in the car.

She was already trying and sentencing this man, and he might not be the right one. Perhaps he hadn't held Sheila's head in position by her long reddish-blond hair, hadn't stroked her exposed throat with sharp steel.

PJ noticed that most of the houses on the street had large, rolling trash cans at the ends of their driveways. It was obviously trash collection day. The rolling cans were identical and probably furnished by the city, St. Ann, or at least rented to the residents. They were the type that hooked onto the trash truck and could be raised overhead and dumped automatically. Hampton didn't have one, or if he did, he had chosen not to put out the trash today.

She sat with her hand on the door handle for several long minutes until she made up her mind. Peter Hampton, if he was the killer, had been to her house twice. It was about time she visited his.

PJ got out of her car and walked toward the house. Glancing around nervously, she went down the driveway. There, behind some bushes which hid the area from the street, were a couple of old-fashioned battered metal trash cans. Evidently Hampton didn't go in for the rolling kind. PJ knew that she couldn't be seen easily from the street, but there was a house only a few feet away, and a curtained window looked out over the area where the trash was. She stared at the window. The curtains were pulled tight and there was no movement to suggest that someone was peeking out.

She was about to do something that would probably get her in trouble with Schultz, and for which she had no good excuse if she were caught in the act.

She was going to root through Hampton's trash.

She put out her hand and rested it on the lid of the nearest trash can. What if there was something terrible inside, bloody clothes or bags of brains tossed aside to be secretly disposed of later? Is that why Hampton hadn't put his trash at the curb?

Glancing again at the window of the house next door,

she lifted the lid. The can was only half full. She leaned over to investigate and caught a glimpse of something hemispherical and pale, and almost dropped the lid in her anxiety, clanging it against the rim of the can. Taking a better look, she saw that it wasn't a brain after all, just discarded cantaloupe halves, their sections neatly excised and the shells squeezed for the pulpy juice. In fact, the can contained only fruit and vegetable waste, no household trash or meat scraps. Banana peels, limp lettuce leaves, orange rinds, apple cores—there was a pungent smell of rotting produce, made worse by the heat of the day trapped inside the metal container. Even more terrible than the smell were the maggots. Like moist fattened grains of rice, they were moving on top of the produce waste and even, to PJ's disgust, on the inside surface of the trash can lid she was holding. Evidently the can served as a compost bin. Looking out into the backyard, PJ spotted a small garden plot and a mound of leaves and old grass clippings near the fence, kept in place by a short circular structure made of chicken wire.

Maybe her murder suspect was simply an organic gardener.

She couldn't bring herself to dip her arms into the muck, squirming as it was, and stir it to see what was underneath, and there was nothing handy to use, no stick or shovel. She replaced the lid, feeling rather foolish, and opened the next can. Inside she found the discarded things that might be in anyone's trash: empty cardboard tubes from toilet paper and paper towels; junk mail, unopened; wadded up tissues; a cereal box; Styrofoam trays used to package meat from the grocery store; receipts; soup cans; newspapers. She noted that Hampton did not bother to recycle anything except organic matter. She dug in gingerly, regretting that she didn't have any gloves with her and thinking that Schultz probably had gloves with him at all times, probably had them taped to his chest or something. She removed a few items and set them in the lid, which she had put on the ground next to the can. She was disappointed. It looked as though all she was going to get from this expedition was an urgent need for a shower.

Something small and shiny caught her eye. As she groped for it, it eluded her fingers and slipped further down into the can. Reluctantly, she upended the can onto the driveway, figuring that either the neighbors would call the police or the red truck would pull into the driveway, trapping her. She hurriedly sorted through the pile, putting the items back into the trash can. After a couple of minutes, she saw the shiny object which had attracted her. It was a small plastic tube, about two and a half inches long and as narrow as a pencil. There was a red plastic cap on one end. Inside was a small white object, generally cylindrical in shape, barely a half-inch long. It had dull red stains on it.

It took her a while before she was able to identify the object inside the tube: it was the stub of a styptic pencil, used to stop the bleeding from cuts or scrapes from a razor. Her ex-husband Steven had kept one in his side of the medicine cabinet. Years ago, when PJ had nicked her ankle while shaving her legs, she had grabbed Steven's styptic pencil. Unpleasantly surprised by the chemical sting when she touched it to the bleeding area, she had pulled it away from the cut and put it back in the cabinet. She held a tissue to her ankle until the bleeding stopped. She had never used the styptic pencil again. As she recalled, that "pencil" was a white cylinder, pointed on top like a crayon. The one she held in her hand now was just a nub; the rest must have been used, broken off, and discarded earlier.

She held the tube up and peered at the red stains. Blood had soaked into the white material: the killer's blood that would match the blood earned by Sheila's fingernails and Megabite's claws.

She put it carefully into the pocket of her shorts and stuffed the rest of the trash back in the can, making sure that the lids were placed lightly on top, as they were before. She looked at her watch. It was five after two, time for her to leave. The cook should be on his way home.

When she turned in the styptic pencil to the lab, she was given a rough time. It wasn't a formally recorded piece of evidence and the weekend crew didn't want to be accused of doing private work for somebody. It took all of her persuasive skills, plus liberal dropping of Schultz's name, to arrange for a simple blood typing. After accepting the sample, the supervisor groused about PJ storing it in a sealed container without properly air-drying it first; the blood might have rotted. Also, the container itself might have fingerprints on it; had she used gloves? PJ asked her to do the best she could, and then left, her enthusiasm for the find waning. There was still time to do some more painting before heading to Mike's house for dinner.

On her borrowed ladder, she worked steadily, rhythmically applying the paint. She put her thoughts about the case, including today's potential bombshell, on hold while she explored her feelings about Mike.

Was she falling for him? They had spoken on the phone numerous times but met only twice: once for lunch when she picked up the VR equipment, and the other time when he brought a journal article to her office. He could have faxed it, but he had come in person and lingered, finally being evicted from his folding chair when PJ had to go to a meeting with Lieutenant Wall.

She slapped away at the paint, her body responding to every sensation of wind and sun as if they were loving hands on her skin. By the time she had showered and dressed, she felt as though her body was made up of vibrating strings.

Schultz banged on the door for the third time. "Open up, son, it's me," he said loudly. Finally he heard the snick of the safety bolt, and the door opened to the width of a security chain. Rick, bleary-eyed, peered through the opening.

"Oh, it's you, Pop. Come on in."

The apartment smelled of stale beer and staler pizza. There was clutter everywhere, from old newspapers and magazines to empty beer cans. An old TV was playing but the sound was turned off. Schultz shook his head in disgust. He came into the living room, looked around for a place to sit, and ended up shoving a pile of dirty laundry off the couch and onto the floor to make room.

"Didn't I tell you to get this place cleaned up?"

"Some of this stuff belongs to Frank. He'll come back for it sometime, so I've got to leave it here." Frank was the roommate that Schultz had kicked out.

"Put it out in the hall. Christ, you could at least take the trash out."

"Yeah. Well, I've been busy."

Schultz didn't respond to the provocation. He was here to deal with something more important than sanitation. "So how's the job going?"

"OK, I guess. I don't see what good it's doing me, though. The pay is really crappy."

Rick's trial was two months away. In the meantime, released on bond, he was working as a dishwasher in a downtown restaurant, on the evening shift, from six until midnight. Schultz had insisted that he get a job to pay his own way as a condition of bailing him out. Rick had decided that he would rather be a dishwasher and live in his own apartment than accept the hospitality of the state of Missouri until the trial date. Now that Rick's mother was out of the picture, he didn't have a lot of choices. She had been forking over a substantial part of Schultz's take-home pay so that her little darling didn't have to get a job. That had left him with enough leisure time to get himself in trouble. Since she had split, apparently the little darling was going to have to fend for himself.

"Of course it's crappy. The good it's doing is getting you to show some responsibility for yourself."

Rick clearly didn't have a good opinion of that novel concept, but at least he kept it to himself.

"Want a beer?" Rick said. "How's Mom? Have you talked to her lately?"

"I'll take a soda, if you've got anything that isn't diet. Your mom is living with your aunt Claire in Chicago. She doesn't have a whole lot to say to me. Or to you, either. It looks like your cash cow has dried up."

"I guess you two aren't going to get back together."

"Nope."

"Mom doesn't want to talk to me?"

"Nope again. Actually, you were the one thing we managed to talk about on the phone. She said that she had made plenty of mistakes with you in the past, covering for you, sticking up for you, and accepting your excuses. She thought she was doing the right thing by you, but you repaid all of her tolerance and support by getting in serious trouble with the law. She said it was my turn to see what I could do with you."

Rick took this complacently, as if he expected it. That led Schultz to think he must have known that Julia would eventually realize that she was doing more harm than good with her approach. Perhaps there had already been the rumblings of trouble between them.

Rick opened the refrigerator and took out a bottle of beer for himself. "Cream soda's all I have. Frank used to drink that stuff."

"Now you see why I kicked him out. I'll pass."

"What's new on my case?"

Here it comes. "Nothing."

The tension in the room moved up a notch, to somewhere just below open warfare.

"Did you talk to that guy Ricardo? Maybe he didn't see what he thought he saw?"

"Ricardo's a good officer. He saw you peddling dope, and that's exactly what you were doing."

Rick smiled ingratiatingly. "You know it and I know it and Ricardo knows it, but the judge, he doesn't have to know it, right?"

"Wrong. You're getting sent up for this, son." The muscles in Schultz's shoulders tensed. Rick was twenty-five years old, fast and strong. His chest and arms would frighten away all but the most determined mugger. He had a narrow waist and a flat abdomen, and he liked to show it off by wearing cutoff T-shirts that bared his belly. His hair was brown and thick as Schultz's had been up until about the age of thirty, when his hair had thinned drastically and turned mostly gray—a double whammy, all in the space of a single year. Rick had the same brown eyes, too, so that looking into his eyes was like looking into a mirror for Schultz, except for the difference wrought by years of experience with the sadness and madness of the world.

Schultz wasn't sure he could take him, not with his legs like this. He studied his son's face, saw disbelief.

"You're kidding, right? You don't mean I'd actually go to jail?"

"That's exactly what I mean. You'll do a few months, maybe six." Schultz kept his voice level and calm. Rick was starting to raise his, as anger spread over his face like a summer thunderstorm over a Kansas prairie.

"My dad's a cop, and I'm going to jail," he said, sarcasm twisting his mouth. "You don't even care enough about me to fix this, to keep me out of prison. You bastard!"

Rick swung his arm, and Schultz started to rise from the couch. Too slow. Too slow. The beer bottle that Rick had been holding went flying by Schultz's face and crashed into the wall behind him. His face livid, Rick aimed his fist at Schultz's midsection just as Schultz got to his feet. Schultz took the punch, yielded to it, absorbed it, felt himself double over as pain shot through his gut. He braced his legs and came up fast, flexed his right arm, then punched it forward so that the heel of his hand connected squarely under Rick's chin. Rick's head snapped back and he struggled for balance. Schultz drew a deep breath and moved in close, grabbing Rick's arm and twisting it forcefully behind his back. From years of experience, he knew exactly how much pressure to apply to keep the pain going without popping the shoulder joint. He leaned close, his lips a couple of inches from Rick's ear.

"You listen to me, you little shit," he said in a cold whisper, "Papa's not going to fix things for you anymore, and Mama's not going to kiss it and make it better. It's over. You break the law, you pay. When you get out, I'll still be here and I'll make sure you behave like Joe Citizen." He pushed Rick's elbow a little higher, eliciting a groan. "I'm gonna ride you. I'll sit on your ass for as long as it takes. You may not know it now, but that's what caring about you means."

He shoved Rick away from him, hard, and the young man fell to the floor. "Damn, that felt good," Schultz said. "I should have done that ten years ago."

"You bastard!" Rick spat out. "You bastard."

"Well, son, at least your stay in jail will do wonders for your vocabulary." Schultz turned and left, slamming the door behind him before Rick could see the tears building in the corners of his eyes.

CHAPTER

26

Pauley Mac drove home from the diner, stopping once at a grocery store for some fresh green beans. He wondered where the poor limp things were grown. He wouldn't have real fresh green beans from his garden until the end of July.

At home, he opened a piece of newspaper on his kitchen table and prepared the green beans, snapping off one end, pulling the string down the length of the bean like a little zipper, and then snapping off the other end with the string attached. He removed the strings from all the beans first, then methodically went back and broke them into one inch pieces. It had been one of the first chores he did for Ma, and he was good at it, patient and precise. When he finished, he gathered up the corners of the newspaper and carried it out to the compost can. There Pauley Mac, with his eye for detail, noticed something unusual.

There were some maggots outside the can, on the ground. Most of them were already dried up from exposure to the afternoon sun, but some were still wiggling. He wondered how that could be. Maggots didn't leave their dark, wet, food-rich surroundings easily. They were not the type of creatures to make pilgrimages. Shrugging, he lifted the lid and inspected the maggots crawling on the under surface. Experimentally he shook the lid gently. The maggots clung on securely. He tapped the lid against the side of the can, and some fell onto the ground. Dog smeared them into the pavement with his shoe.

So someone had opened his compost can. Why? Today was trash day in the neighborhood. There were empty rolling trash cans at the curbs of most nearby houses. Maybe the trash collector had walked down his driveway and opened the can, had seen that it wasn't regular trash, and had replaced the lid. Doubtful. He couldn't imagine a trash collector going out of his way, actually walking down a driveway, to get at the cans. In the South, maybe, but not in the St. Louis area.

Puzzled, he dumped the contents of the newspaper into the can, put the lid on tightly this time, and started back inside. Abruptly he returned and yanked the lid from the other can. The inside looked ordinary to him, but something was off about it. The trash was sort of fluffy, not settled the way it should be. He distinctly remembered pressing down with the bottom of the wastebasket the last time he took out the kitchen trash. What could anyone be after in his trash? It's not like there were any heads in there or anything.

Pauley Mac boiled his green beans and ate a huge bowl of them with about a half a stick of butter melted on top. He sat at his table, shoveling in the beans in large forkfuls and thinking about his trash cans. He let his thoughts drift, let other voices have their say, and nearly gagged when something occurred to him.

He had seen Millie and the bitch talking, leaning together like two stalks of corn in a shock, their voices too low to overhear. Then there was the way Millie looked at him after the bitch left. Something was up. He knew with certainty that the bitch had been here, to his house. She had looked in his trash cans, looked at his private things, even if they were cast-offs.

Play time, slay time, ditch the bitch, chop off her head, good and dead.

He had to get rid of her, and soon, no matter how risky

it was. He took his bowl to the sink and scrubbed it over
and over, listening to an internal chorus of suggestions of
what to do with Doctor Penelope Fucking Gray. Underneath the babble, he felt a quiet presence, a strength, and
he knew it was the Armor woman, damn her to hell and
back.

CHAPTER

27

PJ admired the back yard of the house. The flower bed looked cheerful, and in a few weeks the transplanted marigold, phlox, and vinca plants would be covered with blooms. There was still a section of the rear of the house that needed painting. Because of her trip to Hampton's house, she hadn't had time to finish the rear wall. The ladder and paint supplies were neatly stowed, waiting for her next effort. Now that the letters painted by the killer were gone, she could get Thomas to help her with the rest of the work. She hadn't wanted to involve him in the cleanup.

She got in her car, checked the map for the third or fourth time, then pulled out of the driveway. There was a stop she needed to make before hopping on Highway 40 to West County. She went to a neighborhood drug store, the kind that was supposedly driven out of business years ago but still thrived in South St. Louis. Mrs. Bell was working the counter today; Mr. Bell waved at her from the stock room. Mrs. Bell greeted her by name and didn't blink an eye when she checked out her purchase, a package of condoms. PJ wondered what other secrets the Bells kept and whether they went home at night and traded gossip about the neighborhood residents: who's buying hemorrhoid cream, denture powder, men's hair coloring, pads for incontinence. Now PJ's sexual exploits were fair game, but only between the two of them. The Bells knew they would lose customers if they blabbed.

The fact that she was wearing a dress, and a dressy black one at that, surely had not escaped the Bells' notice. PJ had three evening dresses, but two of them wouldn't accommodate the extra twenty pounds she carried around since the divorce. She thought back over her coffee cake breakfast, the bacon and milkshake she had eaten for lunch, and shook her head in resignation. She was eating to fill an emotional need, and she knew that sometime she would have to stop it and get back to exercising. It wasn't her appearance which worried her but her health. She knew Merlin would say that she should live with it. But she did want to make a change, just not right this minute. She wasn't ready to give up the comfort that food provided and let it go back to being just nourishment.

The dress had thin straps and a silk sheath with a loose layer of chiffon over it. The sheath draped loosely from the bust line, just skimming her hips. Her chestnut hair fell in large waves to her shoulders and felt like an herbal-scented cloud around her face. When she had checked the mirror before leaving, she thought that the gray mixed into her hair was not very noticeable—not tonight. Her day's work outdoors had left her face with pleasant rosy accents. Underneath the dress she was wearing black panties and no bra or slip. Her breasts had not yet given in to gravity, and were the best feature of an otherwise unremarkable body. She took one hand off the wheel and rewarded each of her nipples with a few slow circles of her fingertips.

It might turn out to be an interesting evening.

When Mike opened the door, she could see the surprise on his face as he took in the way she was dressed.

They worked side-by-side in the kitchen, preparing dinner. She washed and tossed the salad, he layered the lasagna, stacking noodles, sauce, spinach, and ricotta and parmesan cheeses. As she tore the lettuce with her hands, she studied him surreptitiously. His strikingly bald head shone under the track lights over the kitchen counter. He was dressed more casually then she, wearing gray cotton slacks, the easy-fitting kind with pleats in the front, and a white cotton short sleeve shirt. There was that softness around his middle that she had noticed before, but who was she to complain?

When the lasagna was in the oven, they relaxed with a glass of red wine. Mike sat at one end of the couch and she took the other. Kicking off her shoes, she sat sideways, stretching her legs out on the couch toward him. They talked lightly of things from their past, drawing upon their common experiences with computers to draw them together in other ways.

Mike had prepared a beautiful table, with a white linen tablecloth, candles, and flowers in a small crystal vase at each place setting. The meal came off perfectly, with the scents of freshly-baked rolls and garlic and basil serving as an appetizer.

PJ guiltily realized she hadn't thought about the murders in hours. She wondered what the results of the blood test would show. Thinking about it now, surrounded by good food and wine and excellent company, it seemed unreal to her that she had actually gone to Hampton's house, had seen the maggots, and stood exposed in his driveway going through his trash. She had been in a different level of awareness then, with danger whispering in her ears and throbbing in her blood—not something she ordinarily experienced in front of her computer. She thought of Schultz, and wondered how he could contain all those moments in his own life. He was actually a far larger person than he seemed, like a kitten whose long, frightening shadow at sunset revealed the true nature of the wild feline inside.

They piled the dishes in the sink and Mike said he would clean up just a bit and leave the rest for later. He suggested she go into the living room and relax, he would join her shortly.

That sounded good to her. She liked a man who knew his way around the kitchen.

On the couch, she leaned back and closed her eyes, fantasizing, letting a fantasy play out as though it were projected on the insides of her closed eyelids:

They sat side by side, thighs touching. He reached up to stroke her cheek. His gentle fingers felt as though they were leaving glowing tracks on her skin.

"Penny . . ." Mike said. His voice seemed to come from that place deep inside where both love and desire dwelled in a man's body. She turned her face up to him, and he pressed his lips against hers gently, then covered her eyes, her cheeks, her chin with soft kisses. "Penny, I . . ."

"Sshhh," she said, placing her finger across his lips. "It's all right, I want you too." She kissed him fiercely, and felt his passion igniting under her questing hands and tongue. He tentatively reached for her breasts, moving his hand lightly over the black chiffon. His touch released the cravings that had been building in her all day, and her body was flooded with longing, her skin felt as though it were radiating sparks. Murmuring his name, she pulled away from his embrace and rose to her feet in front of him. She grasped the hem of her dress and lifted it up and over her head, and stood before him in her black panties.

He reached for her, putting his hands on her waist, and pulled her closer to him as he sat. Then he leaned forward and rested his forehead lovingly and gratefully against her bare stomach.

The phone rang, yanking PJ rudely out of her sensuous cocoon. Mike answered it in the kitchen. She couldn't make out what was said, but the conversation was short. He came into the living room wiping his hands on a dish towel. She could tell by the look on his face that something was up. She sat up straight.

"Anything wrong?" she asked. His face was serious.

"That was my daughter Carolyn on the phone. I need to go pick her up. We've got this contract."

"Contract?"

"If she ever gets into something she doesn't like, at a party or on a date or anywhere, I'll come and get her immediately, no questions asked. And we won't discuss it until the next day."

"That sounds like a wonderful way to handle things. Gives her a safety net and keeps communication open, too."

"She's only called one other time, and that one was pretty bad . . . " He was already heading for the kitchen again, evidently to go out the door to the garage and leave in his car. Then he turned and came back to PJ, who was standing in the living room. "I'm sorry about this. You're welcome to come along if you want."

Finally galvanized into action, PJ collected her purse. "No, no, you go ahead. I've never even met Carolyn. I'm sure she wouldn't want anyone but her father there. Thanks for a wonderful dinner, though."

He hesitated again, and then patted her arm in a way that struck her as brotherly. "I've really enjoyed your company, Penny. I haven't been much in the mood for socializing since the divorce, but you're different."

PJ took a deep breath. What was he going to say? What did she want him to say?

"People say that men and women can't really be friends," he said, "but I think that's wrong. I think we'll be great friends. After all, I grew up with four sisters. If any man can relate to a woman as a friend, it's got to be me."

So that was how it was going to be. A ripple of disappointment went through her, even though she wasn't certain she wanted anything else at this time either. "You'd better be going. Your daughter's waiting."

As she pulled out of his driveway, she berated herself for the way she had approached the evening. She, a professional woman, a psychologist for heaven's sake, had been fantasizing about sex with a man who simply wanted to have a friend over for dinner. Thank goodness she hadn't done anything brazen, like jump him on the couch. She looked down at her dress. Why hadn't she at least worn sensible clothing and a bra? And there were condoms in her purse.

As she drove, she mentally backed herself into a corner and forced the truth out of herself. Her confidence had been badly damaged when her ex-husband had rejected her and hopped into bed with another woman. Her new work with CHIP had begun the process of building up her professional confidence. In fact, it had pushed her to a new awareness of what she wanted to do with her life. But her sexual identity was still hurting. She had been trying to prove to herself that she was still a desirable woman.

Apparently the jury was still out on that one.

She tried to be cynical about it, even tried to see the humor in the situation, but it didn't work.

The red light on her answering machine was blinking when she got home. She changed out of her dress and into her customary T-shirt and shorts before she played the message.

"This is Georgia, at the lab. That blood you brought in looks like a probable match with the samples from the cat's claws and Armor's fingernails. Where'd you get it, anyway? Illegal search, no doubt. The fingerprint guys said the outside of the tube was pretty smeared, they could only get some partials from it and most of them were yours. Next time you go after evidence, do it right, OK?"

The news about the styptic pencil both frightened and exhilarated her. Her hunch had been right. She had no idea what to do next. After all, it was Schultz's job to handle things from here—he's the one who had to break the door down, or whatever it is he actually did, and make the arrest, not her. Also, she was reasonably sure that the blood match wasn't enough. A warrant was needed to search Hampton's trash legally, and it should have been done by an actual police officer, not a civilian employee. A defense lawyer could argue that she had compromised the evidence by not handling it properly, or that she had planted it there in the first place, since the trash can was so accessible.

She called Schultz. He still wasn't home. She left a message explaining what she had done and giving the results of the test, adding that they should get together in the morning and figure out a plan. Then she sat down at the kitchen table with her PowerBook and a package of Oreos. She unplugged the phone cord from the phone and plugged it into the modem receptacle on the back of the computer, then dialed up America Online. As she skipped mindlessly from movie reviews to shopping areas to chat rooms on the online service, she twisted Oreos apart methodically, licked the cream, then popped the two chocolatey halves into her mouth.

Schultz went straight from his son's apartment to a discount pharmacy. He wanted to see how much the prescription for his arthritis would cost. The pharmacist told him that the first medication that Doctor Mirrings wanted him to try, Voltaren, would be about sixty-five bucks a month. Not as bad as he had thought, but still not easy on the wallet, especially for a man facing a possible divorce settlement. Child support wasn't exactly an issue, but he was worried about a division of assets and alimony. His had been an old-fashioned marriage; Julia hadn't had an outside job in more than thirty years.

In his car he had a bag of vendor's samples which the doctor had given him, enough to last about two weeks. There were a number of medications available for osteoarthritis, and the doctor said that it would be a kind of trial-and-error to determine which worked best for him. If he hadn't gotten significant relief using the samples after a couple of weeks, he was supposed to phone the office to try another medication. If he was bouncing around like a spring lamb, he would just fill the prescription he had been given for a six month supply of pills.

After that, he would need to go back every six months for a blood test to make sure his liver function hadn't been compromised before he could get a refill. During his lengthy visit at the clinic, he had also been instructed in some special leg exercises using a stretchy tube that could only be described as a rubber band from the Jolly Green Giant's desk. As a parting piece of advice, Doctor Mirrings told him to lose thirty or forty pounds to take some of the stress off his knees.

Sure. Piece of cake.

Schultz was famished. He stopped for a couple of chili dogs, a huge plate of fries, and a regular Coke. On the drive home he was belching onions but feeling pretty good about himself. He had gone to the doctor and he had confronted his son. He thought he had earned a gold star for the day, two of them, actually. It was a two star day.

It was still light, just barely, when he got home around seven-fifteen. Pulling into his driveway, he noticed that the lawn had a ragged appearance and the grass was at least five inches long. He thought of running the lawn mower around the front yard, but the fullness in his stomach argued against it.

Schultz lived on Lafayette Avenue, a broad street that funneled traffic in and out of downtown during the rush hours. Fifteen years ago, the neighborhood had been in decay, one of the deteriorated pockets that ringed the downtown area. Then the architecture of the century-old three-story homes caught the fancy of yuppies who moved in, first a few pioneers who were willing to risk the crime-ridden area, then more and more until the drug houses were squeezed out and families began to buy in. These days children played on the sidewalks and parents walked over to Lafayette Park a couple of blocks away pushing strollers and carrying bags of stale bread to feed the ducks. Julia had visited some homes on an interior decorating tour and taken a liking to them. When a friend of a friend was suddenly transferred out of state, he and Julia bought the man's partially-rehabbed home for a reasonable price and lived for months with dust and noise as Julia directed the completion of the work. In spite of the disruption in their domestic environment, it had been a relatively pleasant time for them as a couple, and it had been good to see Julia so interested in something.

Schultz had always groused that he was going to sell the place because of the stairs. The ground floor had a living room, dining room, kitchen, and powder room, plus a formal parlor that Schultz hardly ever set foot in. The second floor had three bedrooms and two baths, and there was a third floor that was set up as an apartment, with a bedroom, kitchen, and bath. There was no separate entrance to the apartment, unless the fire escape that zigzagged down the brick exterior on the driveway side of the house counted as an entrance. Schultz kept the third floor closed off so he wouldn't have to cool or heat it unnecessarily. There were high ceilings throughout, ten or eleven feet at least, and an oak staircase that had been refinished. The basement was spacious but low-ceilinged, barely six feet. The house had been a funeral home at some time in its distant past, and there were mysterious bins and divided rooms in the basement and a detached garage out back with an extra large door.

It always seemed to Schultz that if he was on the ground floor, he needed something from the bedroom upstairs, and that if he was upstairs, he needed something from the kitchen. Now that Julia was gone from the house, it seemed ridiculously large and empty. He would be better off with a small ranch home. He told himself that every time he pulled into the driveway, and this time was no exception, but no "For Sale" sign had cropped up on his lawn yet.

Inside, he saw the answering machine light flashing, but he used the bathroom and got himself a soda from the refrigerator before playing the messages. As he reached for the playback button, the phone rang and he picked it up on the first ring.

"Schultz."

"This is Georgia, in the lab. How are you, you old fart?"

"Living up to that title at the moment, Georgia Peach. What's new?"

"Did you know that Doctor Gray brought in a blood sample this afternoon?"

Schultz sat down in a kitchen chair, stretching the phone cord, all the levity hissing out of him like air from a balloon. "No, I didn't. Fill me in."

Georgia told him about the bloody styptic pencil, the smeared fingerprints, the probable match with the samples from the cat's claws and Armor's fingernails.

"She say exactly where she got this?"

"Said it was from a trash can at a suspect's house. I figured there was more to it than that. Maybe she broke in."

"I'll check with her on it. Thanks for letting me know."

"You won't find her at home. I just called there and left a message with the results."

After getting off the phone with Georgia, Schultz switched on the lamp next to the phone. Night had come in earnest, and the small lamp cast a friendly little cone of light in the gloomy kitchen. He punched the playback button and listened to PJ's two-part message with growing excitement. His chest and throat felt constricted and his breathing was quick and shallow.

The truth slammed into him. If he hadn't been sitting, he would have staggered backward. He knew that the cook was the killer, knew it, felt the golden thread thrust itself out purposefully from his own heart and mind, seeking its termination, finding, clasping, taking root in the cook's aura as surely as if it had been Jack's beanstalk and the cook was a fertile patch of ground.

It was clear now how the killer had obtained information about the case, enough information to go after PJ. Schultz himself was the leak, blabbing away in the diner as though the world was innocent. He closed his eyes, fervently hoping that he had done no harm by it, that there was time to . . . to what? Save the maiden from the dragon?

He shook himself and started thinking, planning what to do next, feeling the onions bubbling up on him but ignoring them. Evidence retrieved from an outdoor trash can certainly wasn't enough for an arrest. Anyone could have disposed of the styptic pencil in the cook's trash can just by lifting the lid. He needed more, something that would stand up in court.

He tried to reach PJ at her home number, then her car phone, then her office. No luck. Suddenly he thought that she might have gone back to Hampton's house for some irrational reason that would make sense only to a shrink. He phoned Dave, told him to get over to PJ's house and if she was there, tell her to stay put. He got hold of Anita, told her to meet him a couple of blocks from Hampton's house. Then he went to a kitchen drawer and removed a set of lock picks he hadn't used in years.

Too much time with your ass planted in a chair these past years, he thought. *Wonder if the knack is still there.*

Things were moving, coming together now. Schultz had a feeling it could turn out to be a three star day.

The knock on PJ's front door startled her. It was Schultz's knock, one quick rap, pause, three more. Thinking that he wanted to discuss the case, she took a moment to clear away the remains of the package of cookies from the table, sweeping the crumbs into her palm and emptying them into the trash can in the cabinet under the kitchen sink. She went to the door and opened it, surprised to find Dave Cassidy standing there instead of Schultz. Slightly flustered, she invited him in, wondering if all cops used that special knock or just Schultz's team.

"No, thanks, Doctor Gray. Schultz just told me to check in with you."

"You mean check up on me, don't you?"

Dave smiled. "Well, you know how the old guy is. He got the message about the blood match. Said to tell you good work, and he wants to talk to you some more about it in the morning."

"He actually said good work?"

"Now that you mention it, no. But he did seem excited."

"Schultz? Excited?"

"In a manner of speaking. Also, it would be a good idea if you stayed low until we get a handle on this and figure some way to arrest the perp. He obviously knows where you live. Not that we think there's any immediate danger."

"He doesn't know I've paid him a visit," PJ said, "so most likely he thinks I've been scared off by his last threat."

Dave nodded and turned to go. "Goodnight. See you tomorrow, probably."

She watched him pull away from the curb, then closed the door and returned to the online chat she had been following on her computer.

Schultz had only been waiting a couple of minutes when Anita pulled up behind him. He was parked on Long Drive about three houses down from Hampton's. It was almost fully dark now, right around eight-thirty. Anita doused her headlights and waited. She had seen the activity on the porch next door to the target house.

A boy, sixteen or seventeen years old, rang the bell. Moments later, the porch light came on and the door was opened by a middle-aged man wearing an undershirt and a beer belly. Behind him hovered a girl, obviously the reason for the boy's presence. The man clapped a ponderous hand on the boy's shoulder, partly a gesture of friendship and partly a threat. They spoke for a couple of minutes, the kid getting some variation of the "get her home on time and intact" lecture. The girl kissed her father lightly on the cheek and left arm-in-arm with her boyfriend. The door closed and the flickering blue light of television escaped through a small gap in the curtains on the front window. The boy and girl exchanged a passionate kiss in the car before driving away.

The street was quiet. Schultz got out of his car and walked back to Anita's. She rolled down the window to talk to him.

"I think the house is empty," Schultz said. "I'm going to do a little exploring around back. If the creep shows, blow your horn and get out of here." Anita nodded. He doubted that she would actually leave. In fact, inspecting the set of her face, he knew she wouldn't.

He patted his gun, which he was carrying in a shoulder holster underneath a light jacket. The night was beginning to cool off, but it was still too warm and humid for a jacket. He felt damp under the arms, and figured it wasn't going to get any better inside Hampton's house.

He pulled on his favorite gloves, a pair of supple deerskin ones which he had used for years, the fingertips worn thin enough for sensitive work but not thin enough to leave prints right through the material. Flexing his fingers, he walked toward Hampton's house. He strolled casually past it as though he was out for an evening walk. At the corner, he turned and came back. This time, satisfied that no one was home, he went around the back, past the trash cans that PJ had raided earlier in the day.

The rear door was old and loose-fitting in its frame. The lock was a joke. He probably could have gotten in by putting his shoulder to the door and pushing, but he dignified the job by picking the lock anyway. Opening the door, he slipped quickly inside and pulled it shut behind him.

That thread, the almost psychic link between himself and the killer, was twanging like a guitar string at a Joan Baez concert. The sensation was a physical one, too, as his heart thudded and his hands clenched in the darkened room.

This was ground zero, and he knew it.

He was in the kitchen. The heat was oppressive. There were no windows open, and the air smelled of stew and garlic bread. There was a night light plugged in above the counter, casting a pale glow, not reaching to the edges of the room. He waited while his eyes adjusted to the level of light, listening for sounds of occupancy in the house. The refrigerator emitted a low hum as the compressor kicked on. There was a faucet dripping, not in the kitchen, so it must be in the bathroom. No footsteps, no bed creaking.

No one humming.

Removing a small flashlight from his pocket, he flicked it on and shone the light across the floor. He was looking for any unusual spills, intentional or otherwise, which would leave a record of his passing. Once, years ago, on a similar intrusion, he had left clear footprints in flour that had been sprinkled across the floor just for the purpose of determining if someone had searched the place. The incident had never been traced to him, but the idea went into his bag of tricks, which bulged like Santa's sack from years of such accumulations.

There was nothing on the floor but a few dust bunnies and some sticky-looking splatters next to the sink. Schultz moved quickly across the kitchen and into the hall. The kitchen would be the last place he searched. The pattern he used was to go through all the rooms rapidly and lightly, then work his way back to the point of entrance more slowly. That way, if he had to make a fast exit, at least he had given the entire place a quick once-over.

There were two bedrooms, a bath, a living room, and an eat-in kitchen. He ducked into the basement, but there wasn't anything obvious there, so he didn't waste time with

it. In all his years of police work, he had never found anything important hidden in the basement of a house, not
even a body buried under the floor. People tended to keep
things that were important to them nearby, in the living
areas of the house.

The guest bedroom was not furnished as a bedroom. Instead, it was a storage room with a jumble of boxes,
stacked almost to the ceiling. It apparently served as a
pantry, too, because there were canned goods, rolls of
paper towels, packages of uncooked pasta, a bin of pota-
toes with pale green sprouts curling out, seeking the comfort of dark, moist earth but finding only stale air. The
bathroom yielded nothing; the toilet tank held only water
and a used-up dispenser of blue disinfectant. The living
room couch surrendered unpopped kernels of popcorn.

In the main bedroom, Schultz slid his hand under the
pillow and discovered an envelope. It was brown and unmarked on the outside. Turning it over, he saw that the envelope fastened with bendover metal tabs, and it had been
opened and closed so many times that one of the little tabs
had broken off. His hands tingled as he handled the envelope, squeezed it, felt a thick stack of something inside. He
carefully bent back the remaining tab and slid the contents
out onto the bed. The flashlight picked out photos so startling and gruesome that Schultz felt his gorge rising as the
pain and terror depicted sank in on him. There weren't
enough photos, not for thirty or so victims. There was
probably another stash elsewhere in the house. With shaking hands, he replaced the instant pictures, closed the tab
on the envelope which thankfully did not break, and slid
the package back under the pillow.

In the kitchen, Schultz pulled open drawers, looking for
a cleaver and the knives the killer had used to carve the skin
of his victims. Nothing. Eager to get out now, he scanned
the countertops with the flashlight. He found a well-used
wooden carving board, scarred and gouged, with dark
stains that had soaked into the wood like red wine into a

linen tablecloth. Rare roasts? Or something more horrible, something his mind veered from considering.

He came to the refrigerator, and paused with his fingers on the handle, reluctant to open it, almost certain what he would see inside. Taking a deep breath, he opened the door. The light inside was bright enough to blind him momentarily, then he took in the milk, carton of eggs, and other innocent items. The cool air that drifted out and pooled at his feet felt refreshing. He closed the door, and the kitchen was plunged back into near darkness as though the light had been sucked back inside the refrigerator. He waited a moment until his eyes adjusted to the minimal glow of the night light, then pulled open the separate freezer door. There, held in the beam of his flashlight, nestled one on either side of the Pecan Swirl ice cream, he found two severed heads.

Their eyes were open, ice-glazed, and they seemed to plead for the dignity of the grave.

Schultz closed his eyes and then closed the freezer, but the image stayed with him all the way back out to his car. He told Anita, talking low and hurriedly, what he had discovered. As they had discussed earlier, she would now request a search warrant for the murder weapon, citing a "usually reliable informant" who had seen suspicious activity in Hampton's kitchen. It was tenuous, and Judge Harworthy would probably know that Schultz himself was the informant, but the judge owed Schultz a favor. Schultz knew Harworthy played bridge every Saturday night, and would sign the warrant between hands; he made sure Anita knew the address. Then he hunkered down in his Pacer to wait for the warrant and for Dave, who would be bringing the Evidence Technician Unit. When they arrived he would re-enter the house, legally this time, and "discover" the heads and the photos.

CHAPTER

28

Pauley Mac wanted to park his pickup in an alley a block away and walk to the bitch's house, just as he had done a couple of times before. But this time, he had to be closer. He was going to need the case, and he didn't want to carry it from a block away—too conspicuous on the street. He approached the house slowly, cut his headlights, turned boldly into her driveway, and pulled around the back of the house. He turned off the engine, rolled down his window, and sat listening and watching. The kitchen light was on, so she was almost certainly home. No outside lights came on, no doors opened, no face appeared at the window.

He was unobserved.

He pulled on his gloves, reached up and moved the switch for the interior light so that it wouldn't come on when he opened the door, and slipped out of the truck.

He was heading for the back door when he heard the sound of a car engine close by. He moved around to the driveway, prepared to make a break for it on foot if someone should pull in, trapping his truck. Edging a little further, he could see into the front yard. A car was parked on the street in front of the bitch's house, and a man got out of it and went up to the front door. Unseen in the shadows of the trees and irregular shapes of bushes, Pauley Mac ducked down and listened. He heard a distinctive knock, one rap, pause, three more. A minute later, the door opened and he heard the bitch's voice, but couldn't make out any of the words she or the man said. They talked softly, face-to-face, and the wind carried the sounds away from him.

One thing was obvious: he wasn't a door-to-door salesman. He had to be from the police, and his presence here was a clear threat to Pauley Mac. Should he leave, abandon his plans, try again some other time?

No, no. Get the bitch, scratch the itch, tonight, tonight is right.

Dog continued his tirade in wordless images that stimulated Pauley Mac. Other voices chimed in like disembodied sports announcers, calling the play by play: Ma and Pa; Arleen, that librarian he had invited into the inner circle who had the cruel, cruel center, like biting into a piece of chocolate, expecting caramel or mint or butter cream and getting a mouthful of dry leaves that turned to acid; Dick, the mechanic, the one guest who was himself a killer, had smashed his victim with a wrench and lapped the sweet, rich, warm blood; others who were jealous of the living . . .

By the time Pauley Mac focused on the task at hand, the man had gone back to his car. In another minute, all was quiet again. He slid his gloved hand inside his pants pocket, hefting the weight of the pewter toad that rode there. He could feel the metallic coolness of it against his leg through the thin lining of his pocket. He ran his fingers over the spiky projections on its back, then pressed his palm over them until his skin hurt through the glove.

Letting go of the heavy chunk of pewter, he checked the knife at his waist. He wore a four-inch serrated blade in a quick-release sheath attached to his belt and positioned so that he could punch the button with his right forefinger and have the handle eject up into his palm for a sure grip. He didn't wear the knife often; hadn't, in fact, since he moved to St. Louis. But this was a special case. He hadn't had time to stalk and plan like he usually did, so he brought along some extra insurance. The knife was good in quick, tight circumstances where he needed to bring his arm up into an unprotected belly rather than swing it in an overhead arc.

Pauley Mac checked the street: no cars moving, no one out walking the dog or jogging. He decided on the front door rather than the back because she had already opened the front door to the police officer. She would probably think he had forgotten something and come back. So he went to the front door, moving like the shadow of something evil flying overhead.

One quick rap, pause, three more.

Excitement rising, Pauley Mac disciplined himself— and Dog—by making himself count off the seconds until the door opened. Thirty, forty, forty-five. His senses were heightened. Standing in the darkness, he could hear the soft footfalls of a neighbor's cat out hunting, feel the breeze that rustled its whiskers, smell the faint scent of mouse here, rabbit there, see the tiny movements under dry grass where juicy mouthfuls squirmed. There, the sound of the bolt slipping back, pulling free of the door jamb, a sucking sound, like a miniature cock pulling out of a slippery cunt. The imagery turned on Pauley Mac sexually, and he held his breath as the door swung open and light spilled out, clasped him with bright hands and drew him forward.

PJ heard the knock at the front door. Someplace inside her it registered that the sound was a little off; the force of the knocks and the rhythm were not quite the same as last time. But she rose from the table, thinking that at least she would have a chance to ask when the team was getting together tomorrow.

She turned the safety bolt and opened the door. When it was just a few inches open, she felt pressure on the other side of the door. It was steady and strong. Intimidating. Fear bolted through her, weakening her legs and sending deep, silent shivers down her spine.

"Dave?" she said softly, knowing that it wasn't Dave.

Pauley Mac moved quickly to put his foot in the wedge of light, before she could see his face.

As the opening widened, he put his left hand on the door and shoved inward. Still she had not seen him, at least not fully, but surely she sensed that something was wrong, for there was resistance to his push on the door. He turned sideways and slipped into the opening, his right hand gripping the pewter toad in his pocket.

Inside, he saw her, her hand still on the doorknob. She was pushing against the door, a reaction to his initial shove, and without his counterbalancing pressure on the other side of the door, it moved freely, slapping back into place against the frame. She had slammed the door with him inside.

PJ began to push back on the door, but the open space widened in spite of her efforts, and someone slipped inside, like a slice of the blackness of the night outside suddenly intruding into her kitchen. She was still pushing on the door, and with no resistance, it slammed shut. She turned to face the intruder, already knowing in her mind and in her quivering gut what she would see.

It was the cook from Millie's Diner, a man she knew to be without conscience, a murderer who killed whenever the urge took him. She searched his face, looking for a sign of humanity there, something decent under the brutal mask. She looked into his eyes and saw chaos, a tumultuous churning of needs, and knew with certainty that this man intended to suck the life from her like a spider savored a moth, discarding the husk when the vitality was spent.

Blind terror gripped her, and for a moment she saw his face not as a solitary man's face at all, but a multitude of faces, all the people he had murdered, writhing beneath the skin of his skull.

His eyes held her, pinned her to the wall as surely as if they were sharpened wooden stakes, and she knew she was going to die.

Abruptly her eyes refused to focus on his face. She looked past him, at a picture on the door of the refrigerator, held by a magnet shaped like a butterfly. It was Thomas, asleep on the couch in their new home, this home, with Megabite curled on his stomach. He had fallen asleep reading, with the book toppled against his face and one hand draped across the cat. It was a picture of everything she would be missing, everything this man was going to take from her.

A little flame of defiance burst into being inside her, and she fanned it into a bright blaze with her anger and the knowledge that she had too much to live for to give up easily. She turned her face and met his eyes, waiting for his next move.

He relished the succession of emotions on her face, the surprise, the flash of recognition, and then the terror in her eyes when she read her own death on his face. Each of his victims had eventually worn the same look, but for most of them it came late in the process, late enough to be diluted by physical pain and resignation. Nevertheless, he treasured all those moments, perhaps a couple of seconds for each person, sixty seconds total in his life. One minute of living on a plane of excitement most people never reached in their lives. One minute to give meaning to the thousands of other minutes that didn't measure up to his expectations, the empty minutes during which he was lacking something, was never good enough, never could be good enough because of a bone-deep failing.

As he committed the moment to memory, he raised his arm, intending to swing downward with the carved toad. His eyes locked in contact with hers so as not to miss anything, any intense emotion that danced and flickered across her face like flames forever out of reach. He suddenly realized that he no longer saw fear. Rather, he saw defiance.

His arm was already moving downward, and it felt like it wasn't part of him, just a length of wood weighted at one end, pivoting. She threw up her arm and blocked his, the impact traveling along her arm, down through her body, and through her firmly planted feet into the floor. She reeled with it but didn't go down. The carved toad flew from his hand and bounced off the kitchen wall, gouging a chunk of drywall, then settled on the floor, facing toward him, mocking him.

Suddenly the knife was in his hand. He wasn't aware of pushing the release button and feeling the knife slide into his palm, but there it was. Dog growled, and Pauley Mac opened his mouth to let the sound pass out between his lips. The bitch held his eyes with hers, not looking down at the knife the way most people would. She backed up against the wall. He tried to think, to plan what to do next, but Dog wanted to get loose, was tearing at his insides to get loose.

Go ahead, Pauley Mac thought, *but save something for me.*

She saw his expression change, saw him pull something from his pocket and raise his arm. As if she were moving through a bubble of thick air that resisted her every move, she struggled to raise her own arm in defense. Impossibly slow, she couldn't make it, suddenly she did have her arm in the right place to block the downward arc of his arm. The force of his blow shook her and she felt as if her bones would break, but she stayed on her feet.

She caught the glint of a knife in his hand, saw it snaking out at her.

Dog lunged forward, slashing with the knife. Again she threw up her arm to protect herself. He felt the knife connect with the flesh of her forearm, slide through, glance off bone. The bitch must have felt the cut, felt the searing heat of it, because she froze in place, her arm raised and dripping with hot blood. He came in low with his other fist, felt her blood splash onto his arm, coppery-smelling drops like hot wax, and landed his blow in her stomach. He saw the grimace on her face before she doubled over. Pulling his left arm back before it could be trapped, he swung his right hand, the one holding the knife, high in the air and brought the edge of his tightly curled fist down on the back of her head. She crumpled at his feet.

She swung her arm wildly and felt the knife biting deep into her forearm. It felt as though a hot poker had been pressed against her arm, opening a gash and burning down through layers of skin and flesh. Blood welled from the wound, and she was mesmerized by it. She didn't see the next blow coming, only felt it, as his fist connected with her stomach like an explosion in her mid-section. Doubled over, she felt an impact on the back of her skull, and as blackness curled around her, she sadly let go of her hope of survival.

Dog stood panting over the fallen woman as images whirled in his mind, wordless sequences of cornering, biting, the shallow speeding heartbeat of his prey racing against the thudding of his own heart, taking hold of the warm body, feeling the blood pulse beneath the skin.

Lost in the sensations, Dog stood until his breathing slowed and Pauley Mac put the knife back in the sheath and checked the woman sprawled on the floor.

Not dead. Good.

CHAPTER

29

Schultz sat in his car, watching moths circling the gaslight on the lawn next door to Hampton's house. Something nagged at him, tugged at his thoughts, concerning what he had found at the house.

Or not found at the house.

Schultz sat up straight. The carrying case was missing. If the computer simulations were correct, there should be a large case with feet on the bottom that matched the measurements of the indentations in the carpet. Schultz closed his eyes and carefully walked through the house again, mentally this time, peering into each room. He saw no case, unless it was inside one of the boxes he hadn't had time to search, or in the basement.

There were several possibilities. The simulations could be wrong; maybe no such case existed. The killer might store the case elsewhere, such as in a rented garage or self-storage bin. He might have disposed of the case, weighted it down and dumped it in the Mississippi.

Or the case could be missing because it was in use.

That prospect propelled him into action. He called dispatch and requested an APB on one Peter M. Hampton, Caucasian male, thirty-five years old, five feet seven inches, one hundred forty pounds, brown hair, brown eyes, driving a late model red pickup, Missouri license plate BADDOG, suspect wanted for questioning in multiple murders. He felt a powerful urge to get moving, so he didn't wait for Dave and Anita. They could handle this scene by themselves.

Move. Go.

He drove off, hoping that his hunch was wrong.

PJ opened her eyes and the world began to spin. She closed them, and gradually the spinning stopped, but the pain in her arm and the back of her head didn't go away. She couldn't move her arms and legs, so she floated for a minute or two, just a torso with a terrible headache. She heard a door close, then heard humming nearby, close behind her. The "Star-Spangled Banner." A stab of fear unsettled her stomach, and she fought to keep from throwing up.

After the nausea passed, she took inventory of her body. Her arms and legs were tied, and she was sitting on something hard. Her T-shirt and bra were gone, but she was still wearing her shorts. Her breasts ached as though they had been mauled. The thought of him pulling off her clothes and squeezing her breasts while she was unconscious was hard to take, and she tasted the bile in her throat again. Her right arm hurt, but the terrible freshness of the agony was gone, replaced by a throbbing pain. Her arm was tightly bound in some kind of cloth. She could feel wetness seeping slowly into the cloth, and knew it was her blood. The back of her head felt as though someone had cracked open a coconut on it. She opened her eyes again, just slits this time, and was gratified to see that the world stayed in one place.

Humming. She knew where she was and what was happening to her. But she was still alive. She closed her eyes and thought of Thomas sleeping with Megabite curled on his stomach; of light glinting off Mike's bald head as he bent to put the lasagna pan in the oven; of Schultz dashing to her rescue when she was startled in Burton's apartment, his belly preceding him through the door and quivering after the rest of him stopped moving; of standing side by side with him sponging the ketchup letters from her kitchen wall; of Thomas and Winston looking at dinosaurs on the computer, Megabite lazily pawing at the moving forms on the screen.

Suddenly there was cold water splashed in her face, and she gasped with the shock of it and shook her head. The shaking made her woozy, as if she was at sea during a hurricane, rising and falling as huge waves traveled beneath her boat.

"Awake, I see," said a soft voice near her ear. "Good. All the best ones stayed awake."

A figure came into her field of vision. It was the cook, but with a subtle change: he was the one in control now, the one with the power, not just a man flipping burgers or pushing a mop.

She was in the kitchen, tied up, straddling a chair.

"My name's Pauley Mac," he said, extending his right hand as if to shake hers in greeting. "Oops," he said, pulling back his hand, "I guess you're not quite up to that at the moment." He used his left hand to clasp his own right hand, and pumped up and down enthusiastically. "Hello," he said in a feminine voice that parodied her own, "I'm Doctor Penelope Fucking Gray. Glad to meet you.

"Now that we've met, I'd like to ask you a few questions before we get down to business," Pauley Mac said in his own low-pitched, flat voice. As he spoke, he unpacked items from a large black case onto the kitchen table, deliberately within PJ's view. Plastic bags, which he removed from the case, turned over thoughtfully in his hands a couple of times, and then replaced. A cloth-wrapped set of sharp tools, whittling knives and picks for fine work. A plastic-wrapped bundle of fresh clothing. Finally, and most horrifyingly, a machete with a scarred handle and a foot-long blade that glinted and flashed sinuously under the light as though it were moving under its own power. His gloved hands lingered over the cutting tools and then traced the length of the cleaver affectionately, as PJ would pet a cat from nose to tail-tip.

PJ's mind worked furiously. She sensed that while he was willing to talk, he wouldn't pick up that machete. If she could keep him talking, she could stay alive longer. And suddenly every minute was precious. "Call me PJ," she said, finding her voice and marveling that it was far steadier than she felt.

"Is that what your man friend calls you, your Detective Leo Schultz? Is that what he calls you when he's sticking it to you, when you're begging him to fuck you so hard you'll split open, when you have your legs wrapped around his ass? Does he call you PJ then?"

Fear took over PJ's thought processes again, and for a moment she couldn't speak. She had to think, had to get a handle on how to talk to this man. This murderer.

"He's just a friend of mine, a co-worker, actually. We just work together. He calls me Doc."

"Doc, huh? I kind of like that. Doc. I think I'll call you Doc, too. You don't mind, do you?"

"Of course not," she said. "You can call me anything you like." He hummed some more as he rubbed his whittling knives on a polishing cloth. Her arm throbbed, and she felt a warm drop run down her arm. The cloth tied around the wound must be saturated.

"What I want to know, Doc, is how you knew about the murders. I mean, the little things, the case and the plastic bags and all."

She almost opened her mouth about the computer, then thought that he wouldn't want to hear that. He wouldn't want to know that his moves could be analyzed. Predicted.

"I've always been good at making up stories," she said, working to keep the strain from her voice. "Even when I was a little girl. I could start with a bare story, just a sentence or two, and add all the details like I was seeing them, but it would only be in my mind."

"You saying you made all those things up?"

PJ gulped. "Yes."

There was a pause, then a strange noise. Pauley Mac was out of her sight at the moment, and she couldn't see his face, so at first she didn't relate the sounds she was hearing to laughter. When she did realize that he was laughing, relief flooded through her. She had said the right things, at least so far.

"So you fooled everybody, did you?" he said. "They think you're some kind of slick-as-snot Sherlock Holmes, and all along you were just keeping your ass out of the fire making things up. That's a good one."

"Don't tell anybody, OK?" Her attempt at rapport fell flat. He went back to humming, and she worried about his next move. Suddenly he thrust his face into hers.

"Question number two: how did you know it was me?"

She could feel his breath on her face. It was hard to concentrate, but she had to say something. He expected an answer. Her professional instincts warned her away from the first thing that sprang to mind, which was his humming, the same humming as she had heard on the video tape. Then she thought of a way to test her theory that he was trying to acquire the skills of his victims.

"It . . . it was your painting, the one I saw at Millie's. It's very good. As good as Sheila Armor's work."

His face softened a little. "At least you can recognize true talent when you see it."

"The way you do?"

"Yeah, I see the things that other people can do, and I figure I can do them just as well."

"So you take classes?" PJ knew she was pushing it.

His benign expression melted away. "Cut the crap, Doc. We both know what I do." He turned away from her. "I'm not a cannibal. You hear that, bitch? Cannibals are scum. What I do has nothing to do with being a cannibal."

"I believe you. I never really thought that you were. I was just going along, you know, trying to keep my job."

"Just so you know that." He made an animal sound, a

growl deep in his throat. It was the most chilling thing PJ had ever heard. "Now Dog might just do something like that," he said, "if nobody was watching him."

She wondered what he was doing behind her back. Her head hurt so badly she wished she could slip back into unconsciousness, but she knew she couldn't do that. If she did, she wouldn't wake up again. She licked her lips and decided to try a different approach.

"Tell me, are you interested in their personalities too, or do you just collect skills?" She tried to summon some professional detachment. "You're really unique. I'd like to understand you a little better."

"Don't give me any of that shrink bullshit, bitch, or I'll cut your head off one little slice at a time. I know about shrink talk. You just want to hear about the voices. They all do."

She felt a hot pain, like a finger of fire tracing across the skin of her back, high on her right shoulder. Sickened and immobilized by the sudden pain, she realized that Pauley Mac was beginning to carve on her skin. Another streak of pain. Gasping, she fought back the blackness at the edge of her sight.

"What about your carvings, then," she said desperately. "Tell me about the dog pictures. They're done so well. You have real talent."

Pauley Mac paused in his work. PJ took several deep breaths, hoping he would answer, hoping he would talk to her.

"Do you really think so?" he said. "None of my other guests have really appreciated them."

PJ struggled to keep her voice under control as blood ran down her back and into the waistband of her shorts. She had to keep him talking. "I've never seen anything like them. Why did you choose a dog?"

"It's kind of a self-portrait." Another stroke. She tried to close off the pain, lock it in a little compartment in her brain. "I wasn't planning to do a full job on you, Doc, but

I just might change my mind. You're fun to talk to. Mostly I get moaning, that sort of thing. You're not part of this cycle, you know. You don't by any chance play a musical instrument? Dance? Paint?"

PJ shook her head no, and regretted it as the room spun.

"No? Too bad. But then I'm done with this cycle anyway. Time to move on to something else." He leaned forward over her back, and put his lips next to her ear. "I've already picked a new theme. You'll be the first to know. It's Childhood Innocence. Sad to say, you don't qualify there, either."

PJ tried to pull her thoughts together. There was something there, if she could just grasp it. *Voices. Guests. Self-portrait.*

"This is a waste of time," Pauley Mac said, suddenly irritable. His voice sounded odd. It was as if someone else were in the room and had just spoken for the first time. "Let's get on with it. You don't have to finish the carving. She's not part of the cycle. She won't be a guest."

PJ realized that he was speaking to someone else, discussing her fate with someone whose voice she couldn't hear.

Voices.

An idea burst upon her. It was far-fetched, but she had to try something. He had put down the carving tool and was about to pick up the machete.

"Sheila! I want to talk to Sheila," she said, the words pouring out. "She's one of your guests. I know she's there. Sheila, I'm talking to you. Only you. Remember when we met in my office? We were friends, Sheila. We liked each other from the start."

Pauley Mac hadn't said anything, but his face showed . . . surprise? He hadn't been aware that PJ and Sheila knew each other.

"I need your help now. Help me, Sheila," she said pleadingly. She didn't have to fake the desperation.

"Help me. Stop this man from killing me. Make him stop."

Pauley Mac put his hands over his ears and pressed tightly. He wanted to shut out the bitch's voice. He had to think, and her words were keeping him from thinking clearly.

She had perceived, or guessed, the true nature of his mind. He had partaken of the Armor woman's brain, as he had so many others, to get the special talent she had, to claim it as his own. But there were strings attached; it was a package deal. When he got the skill, he also preserved a bit of her, the essence of her, in his mind. It wasn't voluntary. He never would have chosen such a thing, to have his days and nights played out with internal commentary. Not just Armor, but all of them: the voices of his guests were with him all the time. Dog, with his no-nonsense animal conviction and predilection for brute force, dominated all of the guests and kept them in line.

He stood motionless, as his thoughts bounced from one corner of his mind to another. Not for the first time, he wondered if he was simply insane. Were the voices all just splinters of himself? Were they part of some grand psychosis that had gripped him since childhood, that had been born in that bed with Ma and Pa or in the closet where he was often locked for punishment, arms and legs tied, mouth gagged to stop the screams that welled up from inside, left for hours with only thirst, hunger, fear, and his own urine and feces for companionship?

Maybe nothing was real except the trail of corpses he had left behind.

No. No, the skills were real. He could play the piano. He could.

And dance, and paint. And play basketball, run like the wind, ski as though he had come out of his mother's womb with miniature skis on his tiny wrinkled feet.

He could.

So the voices were real, too, just a little unexpected side-effect of his method.

"Sheila, stop him. I know you can do it."

He heard her even though he was trying to block his ears. "Shut up, bitch!" he shouted. "Shut up! I know what you're trying to do, and it won't work."

Sheila Armor had been a strong-willed woman. He had known that, had felt it in her struggle, had seen the final defiance in her eyes when he lifted her head for the killing stroke. The remnant of her that he preserved in his mind was strong, too. He had felt her presence more than once. He had not been aware that Sheila and the bitch were friends, and now that fact grew in importance, magnified by the bitch's pleas.

Pauley Mac struggled to figure out what their friendship meant to him. No outsider had ever tried to talk to a guest before.

Dog was having none of it. Concepts like friendship meant nothing to him. The guests were simply *his,* to be tolerated or tormented. He reached for the machete, his hot thoughts channeled toward killing, thinking of the weight of it in his hand, the swoosh sound as it descended, the arc of blood.

Something fluttered inside Pauley Mac. Like a newborn antelope struggling to rise and run within minutes of its birth, something pushed itself up on shaky legs and took a tentative step.

The remnant of Armor's indomitable personality that Pauley Mac believed he harbored within himself, believed with all his heart and with decades of conviction behind it, was asserting itself. Pauley Mac screamed for Dog to re-store order, but Dog was lost in bloodlust and couldn't be yanked from it fast enough.

Armor's voice, raspy but recognizable, forced its way out of Pauley Mac's mouth.

"I want to stop him," he said, gasping, trying to choke

back the words. "I *will* stop him. Dog doesn't scare me. I'll kick his ass so hard it'll come out his mouth."

A cacophony of other voices burst into his mind, urging him one way and the other. Dog turned away from his images of death, reluctantly, to do battle and set things right. But a mutiny had taken hold, spearheaded by Armor, with its ranks swelled by the other guests who had abhorred the killing.

Dog trembled, indecisive for the first time in his life. Pauley Mac froze, his hand on the machete, immobilized by the struggle within.

On his way to PJ's house, Schultz had an increasing sense of urgency. He ran a few red lights and coasted through a couple of stop signs. He thought about how he had messed up the night Sheila Armor was killed, how the scale on which his personal accountability was weighed canted sharply down on the side of failure.

Again he was in the situation where he would blame himself, regardless of what anyone else said, if something happened to PJ.

While he was contemplating baring his ass in front of the X-ray technician, PJ was on the killer's home territory rooting through trash.

While he was twisting his son's arm, a lab technician was making the connection between the blood samples from the cat's claws, Armor's fingernails, and the styptic pencil.

While he munched on nacho chips outside Sheila Armor's apartment, her headless body waited to be discovered inside.

While he looked away, his son became a drug pusher.

While he buried himself in his work, his wife fell out of love with him.

While he smugly took the back entrance to the place where he and his partner were going to make a "routine" bust, his partner was blasted away at the front door.

He didn't want to add another entry to the list of self-recriminations: while he was busy being dense about the implications of the missing case, PJ lost her head.

By the time he reached her house, he was sweating. The Pacer had no air conditioning, but the window was down and the flow-through ventilation had created a strong current of air that stirred the few long hairs left on the top of his head as he drove.

Judging by the front of the house, no one was home. The front windows were dark, upstairs and down. He pulled into the driveway, killing his headlights so that they wouldn't shine into the windows and across the back yard. When he rounded the corner into the yard, he spotted the Dodge pickup. The color was red, but it appeared nearly black in the dim light that leaked from the kitchen windows. The license plate was in the shadows, but Schultz knew that if he swept his flashlight across the plate it would read BADDOG.

Restraining his urge to jump out of the car and dash into the house, he used his car phone to call for backup. Then he quietly got out of the car, grateful for a change that the Pacer's overhead light was burned out, and eased his gun from his holster. He approached the truck from the rear, and peered into the bed. Nothing but a few bits of trash and some cans.

He moved slowly up the passenger's side toward the window, aware that the pickup's large side view mirror could be showing his every move to the occupant.

No one in the cab, either. He wondered if he was being observed from the bushes, but he didn't have that feeling like ants creeping up his back that he got when he was being watched.

The house, then.

He reached the back door. The glass of the door was covered with curtains, but there was a one-inch gap where the two panels met in the middle. He leaned close.

What he saw stopped his breath and very nearly his

heart. Hampton—Macmillan—stood frozen like a statue, one hand gripping a wicked-looking machete that gleamed under the kitchen lights. In front of him, PJ, tied to a chair and naked from the waist up, body rigid with tension, blood-streaked back, eyes tightly closed. The hair on his arms rose as Schultz watched a rivulet of blood slide down her back and drip onto the floor.

Hampton's face had a puzzled look, as though he had lost track of what he was doing, or was undecided whether to swing the machete.

Indecision wasn't a problem for Schultz. He raised his gun, aimed carefully, and squeezed the trigger, firing through the pane. The first shot shattered the glass and hit Hampton low, near the hip, spinning him so that for a split second he faced Schultz. The second shot took him in the chest, bursting his heart. The machete clattered to the floor noisily, but Hampton dropped as quietly as a snowflake.

"Police," Schultz whispered. "Freeze."

Pauley Mac raised the machete but couldn't seem to muster the conviction to swing it. His muscles didn't want to obey, preferring to wait until the internal argument was settled before following the orders of the victor. Dog was snarling and snapping, trying to grab the taunting voices and shake them into obedience.

He felt something slam into his hip, and hot pain bolted out through his flesh from the point of impact. The force of it spun him, slowly, it seemed to him. Everything was moving slowly, except the pain, and that ricocheted and reinforced itself as it sped along his nerves. The back door came into view. Shards of glass were still falling, slowly falling, bright splinters that danced in his vision before settling gracefully to the floor. The light from the kitchen fell on the face and body that filled the opening in the door where the glass used to be. Jagged edges of glass framed the face, but Pauley Mac could only make out the eyes—eyes that had dealt death before and were black with it now.

Pauley Mac felt pain blossom in his chest. His muscles spasmed and the machete slid from his grip. The voices grew still in his mind, hushed as though holding their collective breath. Splinters. Splinters of glass, splinters of himself.

Then he was lying on the floor with a fluttery feeling on his chest, as though a huge moth were flapping gently against him. The pain was fading, must have happened a long time ago . . .

A triumphant voice erupted in his mind, and he was just aware enough to know who it was. That damned Armor woman.

Got you, you prick, she said.

CHAPTER

30

PJ got restless in the hospital on the second day, so Thomas brought in her laptop computer and the two of them played computer games for hours. She was at a disadvantage because her right arm was bound tightly where the knife wound was, so she had to play left-handed. Schultz came by with a cheerful house plant in an atrocious china dinosaur planter, a couple of magazines, and best of all, meatball sandwiches, chips, and Cokes for everyone.

After a small parade of other visitors left, including Mike Wolf, who held her hand and patted wisps of hair back into place; and Schultz, who took Thomas back to his friend Winston's house, PJ was finally alone with her thoughts. A feeling had been growing in the back of her mind, and it coalesced into a decision. She would not have a skin graft to cover the crude slicing on her back. Pauley Mac hadn't actually stripped away any of her skin by the time she called on Sheila, so the wounds would close and heal, with substantial scarring. It wouldn't be right for her to be unscathed by the experience she had just been through, while Sheila and the other victims lost everything.

She also sensed a change in herself. She had become strongly motivated in her new career of criminal investigation via computer, but now there was a depth to it that hadn't been there before. She knew that she carried the same pain and caring for those lost ones, the innocent victims, that she had seen clearly in Schultz's face and that came through so clearly in his gruff voice, once you knew what to listen for.

She had been marked with the arrogant strokes of a sociopath's knife, and her life would never be the same.

In a way, Sheila's concern and friendship had reached out to PJ after Sheila's own death, making Pauley Mac hesitate long enough for Schultz to arrive.

As a psychologist, she knew that the turmoil inside Pauley Mac's brain is what actually saved her.

As a woman, she would prefer to attribute it to the last act of a caring friend.

Read on for an exciting preview of Shirley Kennett's new novel, FIRE CRACKER—coming in July from Kensington Books!

CHAPTER

1

Will Carpenter sat up in bed. He knew he was screaming more from the shape of his mouth than from hearing the sound. Then he heard it: that high, childish wail that wavered between terror and anger, issued from some place inside him that never made itself known in the daylight.

He was drenched with sweat, and more than sweat. His bladder had emptied, and his palms were slick with blood. His clenched fists had forced his fingernails into the fleshy mounds just below his thumbs.

Will sat up and swung his legs over the edge of the bed. He rubbed his hands together until the heat of the friction dried the blood, then ran his hands up and down his arms, peeling away the shreds of the nightmare that clung to him like leeches. His wet underwear, the only clothing he wore, was clammy against his skin. He stood, steadying himself by leaning the side of one leg against the bed, and stripped it off. Then he pulled the sheets and mattress pad from the bed and jammed them into the small stacked washer/dryer that stood in a corner of his kitchen. He fretted over the fact that he should have dumped the laundry detergent into the tub first and briefly considered pulling the cold mass of bedding out to do so. Then he wrinkled his nose, not at the smell, but at the thought of touching the cold material. It was amazing how hot urine came out but how fast it cooled off. Opening the detergent box, he saw that he had misplaced the scoop. Again. Sighing, he dumped some of the bluish powder on top, closed the lid, and started the water running.

Hot wash, warm rinse.

Mom Elly would be proud of her only stepson, sorting the whites like a pro.

Naked, Will wandered over to the sink and scrubbed his hands. Then he pulled out a coffee mug that looked less used than the others, and ran water into it. He put the mug into the microwave to make some instant coffee. The apartment smelled like grilled cheese sandwiches, which he had fixed for dinner. He had noticed before that his place must have poor air circulation, because the smell of one meal lingered until it was overlaid by the next. While waiting for the bing of the microwave, he lifted the oversized terry cloth robe from the hook on the back of the bathroom door and wrapped himself in it. It felt good against his skin, but scratchy because he had run out of fabric softener.

Belting the robe about his thin waist, he simultaneously donned his professional demeanor, leaving behind the messy ineptitude, the misplaced laundry scoops, and the gangly body that had never outgrown teenage awkwardness. He was ready to flex his fingers and astonish the world.

Will "Cracker" Carpenter had gotten his start years ago in highway robbery—the Information Highway, that is. He earned more than most mid-level drug dealers by compiling confidential profiles for a price.

Cracker took his mug of instant coffee to the spare bedroom of his two-bedroom ground floor apartment in University City, a suburb of St. Louis that housed a lot of Washington University students and staff. Some of the profs lived there too. Cracker drove by their stolid two or three storied, ivy-covered homes on his way to the grocery store or deli. His own place was considerably humbler: a remodeled brick cube with one apartment up and one down. The upstairs apartment had an exterior stairway and entrance. The tenant was a quiet, serious Asian graduate student, a woman whom he hardly ever saw.

Cracker's apartment had none of the charming features of other homes in the area, such as leaded glass windows, fireplaces, architectural details like columns and arches in the interiors, and fine wood trim. These things were generally prized even in those homes given over to student housing. His building had been gutted by a contractor who sold everything to a salvage warehouse and reshaped the house into two functional apartments, breaking the home's spirit as well as its grand curved staircase.

Cracker owned the building now, and he liked it the way it was.

The bedroom he entered was illuminated only by the portion of moonlight that escaped the grasp of the tree limbs outside the window, but it pulsed with electronic life. Yellow-green and red dots glowed, the power indicators and status lights of computer equipment floating in the darkness like lightning bugs. The glassy stares of half a dozen monitors reflected the pinpoints, tossing them back and forth across the room. Cracker never used screen saver programs that would brighten his monitors with playful spirals or kittens cavorting on the screen. It seemed undignified. He preferred to let the screens go black when they were idle.

Soft whirring noises from cooling fans and spinning platters inside hard drives seemed louder now, in the middle of the night, than during the daytime. A clock atop a black metal bookcase read 3:12 in three-inch red numbers that reflected in the smooth surface, distorted and foreshortened there as though they were shining up through water. In one corner, one of the several modems in the room was in a programmed search mode, trolling through a promising list of phone numbers Cracker had recently purchased. Red, green, and yellow lights flashed as it silently dialed one number after another, marking those which not only responded with a modem on the other end, but which required a password or other security measure to complete the connection. Over the next few days, Cracker would check out the new hits to see if there were any worth adding to his toolbox.

He stood for a moment, thinking that the same lights bouncing among the monitors in the room were also bouncing from the smooth, moist surface of his eyes.

If someone was watching, he thought, *I would seem like another piece of equipment: eyes like tiny monitors, lungs for a cooling fan, brain for logic and memory, a digestive system for a power supply.*

It was a pleasant thought, and it dispelled the last of the nightmare jitters. He walked into the room, automatically steering himself around the rolling chairs, and switched on the desk lamp. The lamp was an industrial model, with a head holding two eighteen-inch fluorescent bulbs on the end of an extension arm that flexed in three places. The whole thing was weighted down with a circular black base that could probably have held a patio umbrella in a stiff wind. The starter buzzed loudly when Cracker pressed and held the yellow rocker switch. He released it when both bulbs glowed, and the buzz diminished to a hum just at the edge of his awareness.

There were folding tables set up along three of the walls, and every inch of their mismatched surface space was occupied by keyboards, mice, monitors, external hard drives, printers, speakers, CD-ROM drives, a scanner, and cables and cords tangled like electronic spaghetti. The battered metal desk in the center of the room held, in addition to the formidable lamp, the few business necessities that Cracker committed to paper.

To visitors, were any to be allowed into this room, it would look like techno-chaos. To the young man who earned his nickname by breaking into supposedly secure computer systems, it was comfortingly familiar.

Cracker sat in an armless chair and rolled up to one of the computers. He dialed in to Wood Memorial Hospital and put in a request for callback. The hospital's computer security system intercepted his call and quickly disconnected him. He waited while the system checked the phone number, name, and password on file, and called him back. When the password he entered a second time was verified, he was in.

He immediately exited the front end processor that presented user-friendly menus and got into the underlying operating system. Ordinarily, that was off-limits to dial-in users, but Cracker wasn't the typical dial-in user. Once there, he checked the volume of transactions going on and the number of terminals in use, and decided that his own activity wouldn't look conspicuous. At least, the risk was small, and he was awake and drinking coffee, smelling grilled cheese and thinking about fixing a couple more, and sitting in his clean white bathrobe, ready to work.

Going back to the user menus, he checked the census for nursing station 3-PT. Room 3PT-3302, one of the eight private rooms on the nursing station, still held the object of his interest: Rowena Clark, a seventy-nine year old woman with emphysema and congestive heart failure. Cracker had been following Rowena's case since admission. She was on a respirator, and her condition was deteriorating. He had snooped into enough cases similar to hers to know that she would probably be dead soon.

He knew from the nursing notes that Rowena was domineering and unpleasant with her visitors, but she was compliant, almost sweet, with the "angels" who took care of her in the hospital. She wouldn't question a confident Resp tech who told her that she was getting better and assured her that it was time to cut back on the oxygen and the positive pressure that was helping her to exhale. Rowena would be told that she would have to start doing some of the work of breathing on her own. She probably wouldn't press the nurse call button afterward, not wanting to be a nuisance as she lay gasping in her private room, struggling with damaged lungs and weakened heart to get enough oxygen to her brain. She would try to reach for the call button at the end, but by then her vision would be going black, just like the resting monitors in the room with Cracker.

Her reach would fall short.

Rowena would die in just a little over eight hours, he estimated, not knowing who had murdered her or why, perhaps not even realizing that she had been murdered.

He dropped back to the operating system level and activated the special program he had devised called the Time Bomb. It would cycle patiently in the computer's background processing, sampling conditions periodically, like a snake using its tongue to sense its surroundings. When the preset time arrived, the program would come to life, creating a Respiratory Therapy order and then walking through Rowena's online record like a malevolent cyberghost, altering lab results, vitals, and observations so that her overall picture would be consistent with the order to wean her from the respirator. If her file did not present a consistent view, the Respiratory Therapy tech would question the order. In fact, there was still a possibility that the tech, upon actually seeing Rowena, would decide to delay and consult with the physician. The tech might even check the manual hard copy file that was kept at the nursing station. Or someone could check on Rowena in person and discover her condition before she had time to die. There wasn't much he could do about that; some factors were out of his control. Although he could make computers dance to the tune in his head, he couldn't always do the same with people.

In a few hours, if everything went well and Rowena Clark breathed her last, the Time Bomb would remove all traces of its work, including itself. It would put her online file back in order so that it matched the manual medical record, with one exception. Cracker wanted to leave the computerized Respiratory Therapy order intact, hanging inexplicably at the end of Rowena Clark's file like a maple leaf found growing among the needles of a pine tree.

He sat back in his chair and relished the moment. After years of planning, he was finally doing it. Striking back at Mom Elly. Not killing her the way she had killed Dad, the wet agony of it sharp in his mind, but striking out indirectly, and in his own fashion.

Having made his transition smoothly from hacker-for-hire to murderer, Cracker signed off and quickly slipped into dreamless sleep on a blanket thrown over his bare mattress.

WILLIAM H. LOVEJOY
YOUR TICKET TO A WORLD OF POLITICAL
INTRIGUE AND NONSTOP THRILLS. . . .

CHINA DOME   (0-7860-0111-9, $5.99/$6.99)

DELTA BLUE   (0-8217-3540-3, $4.50/$5.50)

RED RAIN   (0-7860-0230-1, $5.99/$6.99)

ULTRA DEEP   (0-8217-3694-9, $4.50/$5.50)

WHITE NIGHT   (0-8217-4587-5, $4.50/$5.50)

POLITICAL ESPIONAGE AND HEART-STOPPING HORROR. . . . NOVELS BY NOEL HYND